the
turning
pointe

the
turning
pointe

Vanessa L. Torres

Alfred A. Knopf

New York

THIS IS A BORZOI BOOK PUBLISHED BY ALFRED A. KNOPF

Text copyright © 2022 by Vanessa L. Torres
Jacket art copyright © 2022 by Jonathan Bartlett

Visit us on the Web! GetUnderlined.com

Educators and librarians, for a variety of teaching tools,
visit us at RHTeachersLibrarians.com

Library of Congress Cataloging-in-Publication Data is available upon request.
ISBN 978-0-593-42613-5 (trade) — ISBN 978-0-593-42614-2 (lib. bdg.) —
ISBN 978-0-593-42615-9 (ebook)

The text of this book is set in 11.75-point Adobe Garamond Pro.

Printed in the United States of America
February 2022
10 9 8 7 6 5 4 3 2 1

First Edition

This book is dedicated to my parents,

for always giving me the freedom to be . . .

Star in Studio 6A

Charcoal. No, sulfur—the familiar stench of my arm hair singeing. I correct my posture. One more second and I'll leave class with an ugly blister, my punishment for having droopy arms and being late—again. My father, Master Geno, pockets his lighter and moves on. I let my elbow drop again, while the Master's threat terrifies the rest of the swans into perfectly lifted ballerina form. None of the dancers have actually witnessed him burning anyone for real. I'm the only girl with enough balls to test that rumor, even though I like my skin the way it is, the chestnut Mexican in me unscarred by Geno's infamous red cigarette lighter.

"Rosa, croisé devant," he barks, stomping his steel-toed cowboy boot way too close to my straying pointe shoe. "Late to class *and* poor position. Unacceptable."

Again, I adjust myself, though I know my way is better. Effacé devant would present the dancer. Like, *"Hello! You're about to see something totally rad."*

I swear Geno's pointy ears twitch, cold ashy eyes piercing through my skull as if he hears my thoughts. I switch it up, and he chills.

The setting sun floods my space and I unravel, losing myself in its midsummer intensity. This ancient ballet studio with its cracked mirrors and peeling paint doesn't exist. It's no longer 1983. Gone are the black-and-white photos that line the brittle plaster walls. Dancers past, my mother among them—and my older sister—freeze-framed in moments of graceful elegance. I'm far away from here, adrift in a time when my arms could do whatever they damn well pleased. The piano adagio morphs into a funky keyboard that pulsates my fingertips. My head rolls a full circle as if my long curls are down.

I bourrée out of the sunbeam. The funk disappears and I'm back in the present, just in time to see the side-eye Geno's giving my midsection.

"Suck it in, Rosa darling. I shudder to think how big your lunch was." He messes with the collar of his leather motorcycle jacket, then smooths his feathered gray hair.

I do as he demands because he's a junk-food bloodhound and a sniff away from sussing out the Pudding Pop I'd scarfed earlier. I can smell the chalky chocolate on my upper lip.

Introducing my stomach to my backbone, I roll up to a relevé en pointe, groaning through the shooting pain in my toes. I'd skipped padding them with lamb's wool. The inside of my shoe is warm and slippery with blood, and I'm pretty sure my big toenail has finally deserted me. Another pair of stained ballerina-pink tights. Geno will be proud.

I'm not even in the company yet, but well aware my skills have become the best in my level. This is according to the whispers in the dressing room and my best friend, Kat, whose

2

sweaty reflection is sticking out its tongue at me—the Master's daughter, the girl who needs a sunbeam to remember a second of her life before her first pair of pointe shoes.

He nods at my fluid arabesque, and for a quick feathery scale on the piano, it's as if we're the only ones in the studio. It doesn't last. But his rare show of approval pushes me to point my toes until my arches cramp. He leaves my mirror space to torment another sorry swan, and I contort my pissed-off foot into an ugly sickle—so unlike the principal I'm supposed to become.

Principals are the elite, the company's top dancers, Geno reminds me to exhaustion. Every. Single. Day. On the outside, I have all the pieces. Paris Opera Ballet feet, flexible back, complete one-eighty turnout, and strong tireless extensions. Stuff my genetics get all the credit for. If only I had the heart. I was born with one. I know this because I feel it speeding up as Geno circles back around to me. But only a tiny part of it belongs to ballet. The rest . . . well, this is the reason I'm here. Because she can't be. The Dominguez-principal legacy rests in my God-given high arches now.

"Save the purple eye shadow for your school dances. It's garish and distracting." Geno flips his hand in my face and I wobble, rolling off pointe. His boots clack over to Miss Stick-up-her-tutu Stacy. He stands behind her, cupping her face. "Ladies, if you're going to wear makeup to class, this is the proper way to do it." He glances at me and I'm sorry I hadn't rainbowed the shit out of my eyes like Cyndi Lauper.

Stacy bats her baby-pink eyelids. But everyone knows I

am the baby, the lone sixteen-year-old in a class flitting with eighteen-and-then-somes. I glance around the stuffy studio at the dancers I see more than my own family—the girl with the perfect ballet body, but horrible turnout. The intense scowly chick next to her, the one whose parents let her drop out of high school after she got one callback for the TV show *Fame*. And the twins no one can tell apart. They even sweat the same, I swear.

Geno homes in on Kat, and I want to dive in front of her, take the bullet. She flicks her eyes at me, crossing them. He pokes a sharp finger beneath her chin, adjusting her head, like, a millimeter.

He's on a roll today. No one escapes Geno's wrath. He's a tough, Harley-riding genius choreographer with his tight ass shrink-wrapped in torn Levi's. He smells like smoke and gasoline and looks like a piece of bacon with eyes. And he's brutal with a capital *B*. All those years of perfect pirouettes beaten into him and now he's finally found a reason to pass the slap. Maybe this is why he's so unforgiving. But I swear right here and now, banish me to hades if I ever become like him when I get old—feared, prancing around in shredded jeans, abusing starving stomachs and looking like some kind of ancient David Lee Roth.

He smacks my stomach and I pooch it out more. MDC worships him because he's the best. And the best are toughest on each other. He spins around on his heels like he's going to leave me alone, then snaps back, jabbing my middle with a sharp finger.

I let out a defiant grunt and pull in my center like I should've the first time.

Stretching my arm overhead, I arch back into a deep cambré derrière. If only I had Superman's laser-beam eyes, I'd zap through the ceiling and flee to the studio above. Because while I'm sweating through another of Geno's impossible adagio combinations, a private dance class is happening, the kind with the rhythm that lives in my soul. I've tried, and failed, to crash it—four times this week, a decision that'll cost me fifty extra jumps at the end of the hour, maybe even a closed-door lecture from Geno.

Totally worth it. Because for one perfect evanescent moment, mid-sashay, the dancer in studio 6A noticed me when I'd peeked inside—my weepy brown eyes fusing with his smoldering dark irises. And Jesus-Christ-on-a-stick my withered heart surged to life, proving resurrection doesn't only happen on Easter. Of course, an enormous bodyguard wasted no time shutting me out. But the man behind the giant will remember me, Rosa Dominguez in the rose-colored leotard. And no one, not even dream-killer Master Geno, can smother the scent of lavender lingering in my nose.

Sweat trickles down the deep ravine between my shoulder blades, my face flushing hot like the flame from Geno's lighter. I turn a perfectly lifted promenade, but inside my head I'm releasing my center to gyrate my hips. My daydreaming dulls the ache in my feet and I risk a glance at the cracked ceiling, every hair wound in my godforsaken bun desperate to escape and show floor six what I can do when freed of these pointe shoes.

Born legacy isn't the only reason I torture myself at the Minnesota Dance Company. Master Geno isn't the only genius parading around in high-heeled boots.

Studio 6A—Prince, the Purple One, is in the house.

Pizza and Teacups,
Hamstrings, Sweat and Slam

The entire class is a collection of sickly wheezes, some doubling over before the end of our final combination. Geno is especially brutal, demanding it again and again until I'm freaked Kat might hurl on my back. She's every shade of cadaver pale as she leaps across the floor in my wake.

I finish my last grand jeté in the corner, soaking wet and sucking in the sour hot air. Prince's lovely lavender is gone, smothered by the musty varnish off-gassing from the hardwood, earthy rosin, and sweat—smells that have taken up residence in my nose hairs since the womb. Legend is, when Mom was pregnant with me, she danced full-out until her water broke on this very floor.

Gross.

"Nice work, ladies," Geno praises, with a heavy clap.

The pianist wipes her brow and collects her music. The studio is without air-conditioning in the middle of a soupy Minneapolis July, something I suspect Geno has everything to do with. More sweat equals leaner dancers.

Baby-Pink Stacy is all in, already pulling on her plastic pants to suffocate more ounces from her sleek body.

Kat hip-checks my side, pointing out the giant wet bloom on the butt of our accompanist's khakis. "Would it kill her to play some Fleetwood Mac, or anything remotely cool by someone non-dead?" She lets loose her blond Stevie Nicks hair. "Come on. Pizza?"

The sun makes a last-ditch effort before giving in to the night. I gaze out the floor-to-ceiling windows. Back in the eighteen-hundred-whatevers, MDC used to be a Masonic temple. The same ornate Roman-like architecture on its exterior frames the windows inside. I run my finger along a dusty line of columned trim, watching the naked bulbs race around the XXX theater marquee below.

Summer intensive programs suck. We dance more hours than we sleep. It's Sunday and I've been here since ten a.m. Another day has happened without me while I pray for flawless piqué turns in the church of classical ballet. It's not like I don't know every single piece of the company's repertoire already. But Geno insists on my participation. And yeah, I'm even worse at defying him than I am at avoiding the sixth floor.

"Let's go, chica." Kat pulls the last of her bobby pins from her hair and then starts on mine.

I wave her off. "Can't. Punishment jumps."

For the rest of the students, one second late means watching the entire class from the corner with the dance bags. But Geno's no dummy. He knows forcing me to skip class is the opposite of penance for me.

"Besides," I say, "no chance of sucking in my gut if I've got Slice of New York stewing in it." I shove my bobby pins back in. My legs are quivering, but I'll choke out more jumps. I always do.

"Like a pancake, even after pepperoni," Kat says, brushing her fingers across her flat stomach.

How she manages to stay so skinny and eat whatever falls on her plate is a mystery I wish she'd bottle and sell to me. Just thinking about melted mozzarella softens my abs.

Geno eyes my grumbling midsection and I hug myself.

"Ladies, I have an announcement." He doesn't have to wait for silence. When the Master speaks, dancers shut up. "As you are aware, the apprenticeship auditions are in six days, Saturday."

I groan and reach for the ceiling, pretending to stretch. Another audition where I'm expected to kick ass. I'm too tired to even—

"And I'm sure all of you know," he continues, "our very own Prince has been rehearsing upstairs."

Umm, okay. He has my attention.

Some girls giggle, probably reminiscing hard about the dirty thoughts Prince plants in their virgin brains every night. My dreams since discovering his song "Let's Pretend We're Married" belong in the XXX.

Geno claps the studio into silence again. "The announcement is this: Prince has offered to do a benefit concert for MDC. He and our director, Joyce, are good friends."

My head snaps to Kat. Her mouth hangs open so wide her forbidden gum rolls off her tongue and onto the floor.

Prince. Friends with our director? Only a brainless mosquito could space how much I totally live for the man. Geno keeping such a juicy detail from me is so deliberate and nasty, I see purple first—and then red.

"In two weeks." He holds up two fingers as if we need clarification. "He will perform at the First Avenue night club."

I squeal. And Geno doesn't give me a flicker of a glance, which makes me shuffle uneasily in my pointes.

Mother Mary, please let me have this. I rub my cross necklace, the only piece of jewelry Geno allows me in class. I'll wear the tarnished thing until it rots off my neck.

He lights up a cigarette, making us pine for the rest. Because there's more—lurking behind the tiniest tug of a grin. "A few select dancers, company and otherwise, in addition to those awarded an apprenticeship . . ." He takes a long drag, the paper sizzling off his Marlboro. "Those individuals will be performing a piece onstage—with Prince."

I claw at Kat's arm. My body doesn't know what to do first—puke, or jump up and down like everyone else. One second. That's all it takes to change everything. I know that better than anyone.

The rest of the girls swarm each other, Stacy the glowing nucleus.

"I'll be like a . . . a Korean *Friday Night Videos* vixen," she brags, as if she'll rule the stage, smoothing back her glossy dark hair.

I guess we all feel entitled to our hometown royalty, like a birthright. But where was Stacy and her gaggle of posers when I snuck upstairs? Not that I don't want Prince all to myself. I've totally earned it. None of these suburban mall rats have a speck of inner city in them. Me—born and raised in Minneapolis, just like Prince Rogers Nelson.

Geno stops our freak-out with a commanding boot stomp. "Attention, ladies!"

Everyone shuts it. Kat and I cling to each other in prep for another bitchin' announcement.

"Back to business. Dance bags down. You've all got jumps to do."

"What?" the class blurts in panicked unison. Only half drop their bags, hoping he's joking, I'm sure.

But Geno doesn't know how to joke.

"Rosa was late. And when a dancer is late, there are jumps."

My damp skin ices over and I shiver in the ninety-degree room. I despise him. And hate myself even more because all I do is stare at the floor while twenty pairs of ballerina dagger-eyes shred my perfect, throbbing feet. I stop myself from pleading, or whining—the kiss of death. Things are bad enough for me at MDC. But this is a new low for Geno, dangling Prince in front of everyone and then punishing them for my mistake.

I find Kat's hand and press my thumb into her palm—*I'm sorry.*

It's okay, she presses back, her posture stretching skyward like a sturdy elm tree. She's been my pillar of steel through Geno's tyranny since I joined her level one year ago. Nothing fazes the girl.

"But *we* weren't late!" Stacy dares to point out.

Stacy makes her living being a total hag to me, but I come to her rescue for the sake of the whole, before Geno tacks on fifty more changements. Really, there isn't anyone in class who doesn't have enough gas to do more jumps. It's the principle of it all. Geno is master of a lot of things, and making an example is one of them.

"Master . . . *Dad*, let everyone go." My words come out squeaky like a defenseless mouse—another kiss of death. "I'll do twice as many, okay?"

He makes us sweat the last of our saltwater while he paces and ponders my lame offer. I give Kat the tiniest blink that says *We're screwed*. She scrunches her lips as she piles her hair back into a bun. The other girls don't know Geno like we do. He's already made up his mind, and it isn't good. I'd called him Dad in front of everyone, and that is as unacceptable as my eye shadow.

"Here's an idea." He traipses to the grand piano, cowboy boots rapping like a ticking bomb. He picks up the teacup our pianist left behind. "If Rosa can balance this cup on the tip of her pointe for ten seconds, in a développé à la second, of course, then everyone may leave. And . . . I'll provide pizza at the end of next class."

The daggers morph into gloomy gazes of defeat. Even the promise of free greasy calories isn't enough to buy me a fan club. Kat, however, remains as bright-eyed as ever, the sole person in the studio with total confidence in my ability. The girl loves an impossible challenge.

I gape at Geno, who's dangling the delicate piece of china from his pinky.

"And if Rosa fails, then it's one hundred jumps."

The united gasp practically fogs the windows.

"At the end of *every* Sunday night class for a month," Geno adds, burying the knife deeper into my curdling stomach.

The remainder of the dance bags fall with a thump, along with a sizable cardboard box in the doorway, colorful sprays of flowers sprinkling the floor.

"Sorry," a boy apologizes from the threshold. He's doing a terrible job of gathering the fake petals strewn around his feet, because he's staring at me like I'm about to turn inside out.

This is all I need. Some random boy watching me nail my humiliation coffin shut. He presses his glossy lips together, and for a flicker of a second I let myself notice his dark muscular legs in shorty-shorts—his double-hoop gold earrings twinkling in the sliver of sun. He has the nerve to jut his chin at my untucked pointe ribbons, as if my shitty appearance matters a rip to me now. Still, I can't stop myself from stuffing them back where they belong.

He nods approvingly, picks up the box—and doesn't leave.

Geno snaps his fingers three times and breezes past Flower Boy.

I straighten up, fumbling for my scattered focus. Because backing down isn't an option—ever—for the daughter of a master.

The aftermath of the Prince announcement gives me a hit of energy. I puff out my chest like Geno hates and march to the barre. I place myself where I never do, dead center along the longest wall—Mom's spot, and my sister's too. I rest my hand on the warm, smooth wood, careful not to grip too tightly.

"Does pepperoni sound good to everyone?" I take fifth position.

"Yes!" Kat cheers, letting down her hair again. "You got this, Rosa!"

The rest stay silent, huddling by the door in their wet, sticky pink leotards like a blob of Pepto Bismol.

Geno strolls toward me, every step siphoning my confidence. By the time we're face to face, my mouth is so dry my upper lip is stuck to my teeth. I stretch my spine to its limits, meeting his bitter glare with an inferno in my own. We're the same height, tall compared to the rest of our family, which isn't saying much. His worn Laredos give him a few inches, but he may as well be Jason in a hockey mask.

"I didn't say you could use the barre." His mouth is moving, breath reeking of sour, burnt coffee and cigarettes. But I'm not sure I hear him right.

Kat claps. "No biggie, Rosa. You still got this." Her cheers have lost some spunk. I've heard him quite correctly.

I take my time getting to the center, willing the floor to open up and swallow me whole. A new scent, baby powder maybe, coaxes my gaze toward the door. Flower Boy is still there, clutching his box of silk and plastic. He nods at me, and I snap my head back to my reflection, wishing I'd set myself in front of the "skinny mirror." Instead, I'm in the seam, my right side elevated a few inches higher than my left.

Taking fifth position again, I stare longingly at the distant barre because it's suddenly all I see.

Geno holds up the cup between us. "Let me know when you're ready."

Snot slimes over my upper lip, my nose running because I refuse to let the rage swelling behind my eyeballs push out a cry in front of everyone. "Never been more," I say, and lace up my rib cage—shoulders back—pelvis neutral.

I try to tune out Kat's ecstatic energy, but she's like a hundred-pound ball of live wires sparking in my periphery. The others stick to their silent freak-out and I figure I'd better watch my dance bag from now on, unless I want the crotches of my leotards cut out again. The last time I pissed everyone off, my leos paid the price. I had to borrow one of Kat's extra-small talls until my order came in—and we are not even close to the same size.

There's no pianist now. Just a whole lot of wailing sirens outside. Part of me wants to bolt and disappear forever into the nighttime riffraff. But then I remember who's dancing above, and I glance at Kat. Her reassuring eyes calm my trembling—everything.

Geno gives me some room, taking his hard stare with him to my diagonal.

I prepare with a sweeping port de bras, my arm graceful and fluid like Mom's in the photo behind him.

Breathe in . . . breathe out . . . The air tastes like salt and iron. I've bitten my lip, but there's nothing to do about it now. I peel my foot from the floor, the right one, of course. My left has always been the stronger standing leg. My arm mirrors my leg's flowing movement, plunging down then rising slowly, my toes tracing the inside of my leg . . . calf . . . knee, until there's nowhere to go but up and away to prove myself worthy of Geno's time once again.

Engaging my hamstring, I extend my leg, paying special attention to squaring my hips. Which is ridiculous as hell, because stressing about form when I'm about to teeter a piece of china on my pointe is wasted stupidity. But then I hit the sweet spot, that perfect fusion of balance and strength. It's so seamless that for a second, holding a teacup over my head with my foot doesn't feel like work at all. Everything disappears. It's just me and my body. I'm aware of every muscle, every twinge of pain, and exactly where my hand is all at once. I am in ultimate control. A total rush.

Sweat drips from the tiny curls at the back of my neck. I close my eyes and lift my leg higher, imagining I pierce through the floor of studio 6A and escape. I conjure up Prince's bedroom voice teasing, "All the critics love U in New York." If I can do this, I'm capable of anything—like dancing at First Avenue.

Geno moves in. Concentration thrums the inside of my skull, the mechanical beat of "All the Critics" pulsating between my ears.

I sense the slight weight of the cup on my toes, but I see nothing because my foot is suspended in the heavens.

My muscles suck to my bones.

I don't dare breathe.

And I'm pretty sure no one else does either.

My standing leg screams for relief, my knee locked so tightly I fear I might hyperextend it. The cup wobbles on my toe box and I wish I'd had enough sense to use some rosin to help it stick. I feel Mom's soft eyes on me, hear my sister whisper, *Pull up, girl.*

And Geno. I'm barely aware of his countdown, especially when my foot rolls and I almost lose my balance. Then Kat lets out a tiny squeal and I know I've done it.

I empty my lungs and drop my leg, briny perspiration mixed with Aqua Net stinging my eyes. The cup shatters at my feet.

"Yeah!" Kat shouts. "You are totally bad, Rosa!"

No one else cheers. They're already fleeing for the dressing room. Flower Boy is gone too, a lone lavender petal skimming the scuffed floor as dancers funnel out.

Chest heaving, I glare at Geno. He doesn't return my hard look—rather, a smile creases his sallow cheeks. But his hint of pride inspires nothing this time. I don't even care that Kat's losing her shit while doing a victory dance in the corner. I am ever more beneath Geno's thumb, his grin putting me on notice. I'll be subjected to more pointless tests if I don't behave.

"May I go now, Master Geno?" I ask, wiping my mouth and distracting purple eyelids.

"I don't play favorites, Rosa."

I nod at the floor.

"If I catch you upstairs again . . ."

Then what? You'll kick me out? A few minutes ago, I was so ready for him to finish that sentence. Prince changes everything.

"The apprenticeship auditions." The click of Geno's BIC snaps me to attention. He lights up. "I expect success."

"And you will have it," I say, on total autopilot.

"Principal dancers don't come from failure. And they sure as hell don't thrive amidst distractions."

I want to say, *Dad, I can't do this anymore. I don't want to be a principal anything.* "Yes, Master Geno" comes out instead.

He blows a column of pale smoke over my shoulder. "You will come to class on time, with your respect in hand, understand?"

"Yes." I'll agree to anything if it means freedom from his coal-dust eyes.

"The Prince concert. There is one caveat."

Kat stops pretending she's not listening.

"You must be eighteen to perform. That which, you are not."

My scream never has a chance. It's trapped inside, choking on one more reason to hate him. I lose sight of everything but how bad my feet hurt. Pain—the only thing I've ever truly mastered.

"First Avenue's rules. Not mine," he adds.

Bullshit!

Kat tugs on my arm. "Come on."

Liar!

But again I say nothing, because if I open my mouth I'll barf. I do a weird half-curtsy thing as if he's done me a fucking favor, and I don't wait one more second to bolt. Not even when I catch a glimpse of guilt clouding his steely eyes.

My dance bag—gone. As predicted, a trip to Teener's for new leotards is in my near future.

"Rosa darling," Geno calls, a sprinkle of regret within the rasp.

A funky bass seeps through the ceiling.

"Rosa . . ."

I shove the door off its wooden stop and slam it behind me.

Baby, I'm . . . Indiana Jones

I speed-walk down the stifling hall toward the stairwell, telling myself it's sweat, not tears, burning my cheeks. Chopin and Stravinsky fade in and out as I pass one windowed door after another. The first studio is scattered with beginning-level "littles" in their navy-blue leotards. I slow up to watch Madame Rebecca line them up by height. The giggle gaggle pays no attention to the Madame while she arranges them like dolls on a shelf. Things were so much simpler when I wore navy.

I pick up my pace again, Kat skittering along beside me like a drooling, bouncy puppy. "Jesus. You are the shit, Rosa. No way around it. I would've punched him."

"If you hadn't yanked me out of there, I would have."

A trail of petals leads to the costume room, the faint aroma of baby powder mingling with my own body odor.

"You delivered," Kat says, all proud. "Geno was speechless for, like, ten seconds. Totally worth the ticket."

I scuff my feet along the gray industrial carpet. "Yeah, I'm a one-woman circus, all right. And what about that boy, the one gawking in the doorway while I made a total ass of myself? As if Stacy and her corps wasn't enough?"

I don't know why Flower Boy is lurking in my brain. Never seen him before and doubt I'll ever see him again.

Kat plucks a petal from the carpet, handing it to me. "He was probably just delivering stuff for costumes."

I sniff the crimpy purple fabric, expecting it to smell like baby powder. It doesn't, and I'm disappointed.

Kat touches my shoulder. "The concert—"

"I don't want to talk about it." I can't. I shoulder through the heavy door to the stairs, my trembling arms too weak to push.

"Ugh, stairs?" Kat whines. "Come on, the elevator's right there." She points behind me. "It's only two floors down to the dressing room. I'll even hold your hand, you big baby."

"What if I'd dropped the cup, Kat?" I wring my clammy hands. "What then?"

She shrugs, and it's in rare moments like these that I fear the only friend I have doesn't know me at all.

"Why do you think he didn't tell me about the stupid eighteen-and-over thing before I did his ridiculous teacup test?" I ask.

Kat scrunches her face like she's already apologizing for being clueless.

"Because he didn't want any distractions, that's why. Geno just dumped on me, and I curtsied. *Rosa the Shit* doesn't exist in that studio."

"So, maybe we'll find that Rosa inside the elevator?" Kat presses her hand against the stairwell door.

My stomach cartwheels, but not because I'm considering

riding the metal-box-of-nightmares down. Only sixteen steps up and I'll be on the sixth floor.

I make it up two when Kat grabs my arm. "You're torturing yourself. Is the man up there really worth it?"

"You really have to ask?"

Kat blushes. "Yeah, you're right. But what kind of best friend would I be if I let you sabotage yourself twice in one day?" She pulls me to her step.

I plop onto the cold metal, undo my ribbons, and peel off my shoes. "Prince is taking a dance class right over our heads, breathing the same air, sweating on the very floor where I learned how to spot my first chaînés. You seriously expect me to ignore that?"

Kat shrugs again. "Maybe a little. Long enough to get through the day without extra jumps."

Now she's just being ridiculous. We both know that's an impossibility. I squeeze some feeling back into my toes. "I'm doomed. Curse the day we watched him on *Saturday Night Live*."

Late-night TV, two years ago, Kat's bedroom and a bowl of popcorn. The night we discovered a man named Prince. I'd never seen anyone like him. He performed "Partyup." A hot fox in a trench coat and bikini bottoms. His bare legs wrapped in black thigh-high stockings and fringed boots—a confusing combination of femininity with a perfectly trimmed mustache.

And the way he moved . . . My world shifted.

"Hellooo." Kat waves her hand in my face.

I snap back to my house of pain and push my pulpy feet

through the slits I'd cut in the soles of my tights, revealing exactly what I wanted—meat-grinder toes.

"*Uff da!* You've got the torture thing down, that's for sure." She holds out a tube of antibiotic ointment. I swear her dance bag is a bottomless dime store.

I don't take the tube. She's right. I'm aces at the torture thing.

"I can see it now." Kat bats her eyes. "Prince finally lets you into studio 6A. And you impress him with your bloody stage-three infection."

I snatch the ointment.

"Just remember me when you're famous," she says with satisfaction.

My toes are hot beneath my greasy fingers as I smear on the antibiotic. "First Ave is off-limits to me, remember?"

"Ooooh! Maybe Prince will cast you in the movie he's rehearsing for."

Kat's blinded by an impossible dream, but I smile anyway because I love it when she gushes. Even though she's two years older, we're kids again, like it was before my body decided to outgrow my training bra.

My feet and turnout may be perfect, but I also possess something most ballet dancers fear—the C-cup curse. I enter the studio, and the rest of my body is just an entourage for my breasts. I pretend it doesn't bother me. But it does. Leotards and tights leave nothing to the imagination. No hiding imperfections here. Some days I'm so tired of the A-cups' snark I'm tempted to call on the Johansens. There's got to be some perk of having a best friend with two plastic surgeons for parents. I'm pretty sure Geno's been saving for my breast reduction since I hit puberty.

I pluck my detached big toenail from the tacky blood at the bottom of my shoe and look around for a place to flick it. "Maybe Prince is into girls with disgusting feet?"

"Give it." Kat holds out her hand like a mom waiting for chewed gum.

I drop the black nail into her palm and make a face when she balls it up in a used tissue. "You're going to make a great doctor someday. Nothing grosses you out."

"And I'll be able to stuff my face with whatever I want, whenever I want."

"*Pfft.* You already do that."

"And it shows," Stacy says, suddenly invading our privacy from below. I should've smelled her Dippity-do coming.

Kat crowds Stacy on her step. "Not everyone obsesses about their body the way you do."

"Well, they should. Unless they want to pas de deux with the scrims in the back." Stacy wrinkles her nose at my naked toe.

She's made a quick change from her pointe shoes to a pair of jazz Mary Janes. She looks as though she skimmed a stack of *Cosmo* mags and piled on every trend over her leo. Michael Jackson meets *Flashdance* and everything in between her single glittery glove and terry sweatband.

And good God, her hair. It's still in a bun, but her bangs are ratted and sprayed like a stairway to heaven. And Stacy never rats anything, other than narking on me when I try to get away with wearing a real bra underneath my leotard.

Kat leans closer. "What's that on your face?"

"A beauty mark." Stacy pats the black spot above her upper lip that suddenly appeared since class.

"It's not working," Kat scoffs.

Stacy scrunches her mouth, gaze on her feet. She wipes away the mark, leaving a long black streak across her face.

I feel kinda bad, until I peer up the stairwell, suspicious of where she's sneaking off to in her neon leg warmers and cut-up sweatshirt.

"Where are you going?" I ask.

She bounces up a few stairs, pouting her shiny lips like Madonna. "Class. And you're not invited."

I jump to my feet, Kat quick to hold me back. Stacy has to be messing with me. No way is uptight Miss Balanchine worming her way into studio 6A with Prince. The most shimmying Stacy has ever done is getting into her pink tights. Even so, my face calls me out, flushing hot with envy. Yes, Stacy's dancing lacks heart, but her technique is perfect. And don't remind me how gorgeous she is, with her sleek black hair and legs that leap into the next stratosphere. She could do an interpretive squid dance in clodhoppers and people would still leave mesmerized.

She's on the next floor before I think of anything to slam her about, the dagger in my heart twisting as she hums the melody to Prince's "1999."

I collapse onto the steps again. Of course, her voice sounds like Snow White's.

"I know what you're thinking, and she's bluffing," Kat reassures. "The girl's totally slinking off to raid her secret stash of Ding Dongs . . . *mmmm, Ding Dongs.*" She pats me on top of the head like a good dog. "I wonder how long it'll take her to find your disgusting toenail in her dance bag?"

"You didn't!"

We snicker like when we were mice together during our first year in *The Nutcracker.*

Kat's flushed face shifts to all business. "And I'm not worried about Stacy, or your dad. Because I've got a foolproof plan to get you front and center of Prince."

I bury my head in my knees. I have no capacity left to believe such a thing is possible.

"But this plan requires no more hesitation from you. No more guilt trips about disappointing your family. You've got to be all in."

My tights stink of musty rosin and BO, the only reason I straighten up. "Meaning I could get kicked out . . . lose the apprenticeship. That is not an option, and you know it."

"That is your father talking. Not you." She pops in another piece of Fruit Stripe gum, pacing like a coach giving an epic pep talk at the end of some sporty movie. "Come on, girl. Let's crack some rules. *My way.* Forget sneaking around upstairs."

I shake my head. "I don't know."

She blows a tiny bubble, then sucks it back in. "You're a

brilliant ballet dancer, Rosa. But everyone here knows you're just going through the motions."

"Everybody?"

"Every. Body. This is an opportunity of a lifetime—to dance for Prince. I mean, Sally Ride just went to space. You think she didn't have a thousand people telling her she couldn't?"

"Dancing for Prince is a little different than being the first woman in space."

"Not really. Because you were made for those moves upstairs."

I point and flex my toes. No. I was born for ballet. That's what everyone tells me, at least. I have satin and tulle running through my veins whether I like it or not. Still, Kat has cracked open a door with her offer. And the light on the other side is brighter than anything I've seen in a long time.

Kat leans closer. "Tell me you're in for the ride of your life, Rosa."

And there's the Kat I love, my double-dog-dare partner in crime. I color outside the lines well enough on my own. But with Kat bumping my elbow now and then, we're fucking unstoppable—and she knows it.

I gaze upward, thinking about where Stacy went.

"Well?" Kat pokes my sticky arm.

My heart kicks against my ribs as if powering through one of Geno's petit allégro sequences. I'll never have perfect skin like Kat. Or legs for days like Stacy. But my best friend is offering me a chance to be seen. The way I am in my deepest fantasies—onstage, illuminated by a purple follow spot, a funky four-count rhythm and soulful voice sweeping me into another dimension. I'm more than Geno's trained pony in pointes . . . aren't I?

"I'm in." My head spins like I'm seconds from blasting away in a rocket.

"That's my girl! We'll go all Indiana Jones on this place, snatch that hot-pants-wearing holy grail." Kat's blue eyes bug, her long lashes and rosy cheeks suddenly inches from my dry lips and stinky dehydrated breath. She has a thing for Harrison Ford and her face has gone full-on puffer fish.

I lean away. "If your plan doesn't involve satin pointes and flouncy tulle, I think Geno may have a thing or two to say about it. This can't get out, to anyone."

"I don't care what you wear. But maybe we should stop at Teener's before class tomorrow. Indiana Jones would never go on a quest in a crotchless leotard."

"I hope your plan doesn't include a whip, 'cause I'm not sure I can pull that off without taking out an eye."

She snickers. "I think Stacy would look good with an eye patch."

"God, she would. Can we hate her for that too?"

"Of course, Mamacita-Rosarita."

I groan, the unmistakable Minneapolis sound reverberating through the steel stairwell. I've agreed to Kat's plan. But the real leap won't happen until I run this insanity by the person who matters most. She is the reason I peel my butt from the steps—the one and only reason I go home anymore.

Home

Down two flights, and I find my dance bag in the boys' dressing room behind a hairy toilet. There are two things left intact: a roll of cloth tape with the words *tit tape* scrawled across it and, thank God, my Walkman. The vultures even crushed my stale package of saltine crackers, wrapping the crumbs inside my mutilated leotards.

My street clothes are gone—the biggest bummer, my bedazzled Doc Martens—the ones I'd painstakingly glued purple rhinestones on. I bought them with my own money, the very last time I received birthday cash from Abuela, two years ago. It was the year she died and the most I'd ever spent on a pair of shoes that weren't pointes. Abuela wouldn't allow me to use the money for anything ballet-related, so I went for the Docs. And now they're both gone.

I check the trash for my shoes. Finding nothing but used batts of stinky lamb's wool, I bum some shorts from one of the boys and throw them on over my leotard and tights. The lost and found provides a pair of scuffed red heels and holey leg warmers, and aside from my bun, I fit right in on Minneapolis's seedy Block E, a small section of Hennepin Avenue surrounding MDC that's responsible for a chunk of the city's total crime.

A new shopping mall called City Center went up down the street, a giant mauve monstrosity with preppy stores like Esprit and The Limited. All stuff I can't afford and wouldn't wear anyway, but totally Kat's style and price point. I've heard there's a food court with an Orange Julius and a Sbarro's pizza that'll probably put Slice of New York out of business.

Kat and I exchange scowls as we pass the Center, its skyways protruding like an urban octopus. I'm pretty sure her mom shops for her there, but I appreciate my best friend's show of solidarity. Still, there's a heaviness in the pit of my stomach, like everything's about to change. The Center is the beginning of the end of an era. Minneapolis is systematically leveling Block E to make way for the boring people—people who wouldn't dare dye their hair blue or shave their heads—flushing away the boys who wear hot pink and makeup, and the working girls in holey fishnets and thigh-high boots.

"I'll never go in there, you know?" Kat says. "Total boycott."

I smile at her. "Total boycott," I say back, hooking my arm through hers.

The heels are killing me, classic "crying shoes," as Kat calls them. My eyes water from the pain, and I'm pretty sure the pumps are a half size too small, but I find the tiniest bright side as I click down Hennepin Avenue. Kat and I are forever a united front. And even without my Docs, for however long it lasts, Block E's shady energy is a part of me.

"I'm going to miss our bus rides this fall," I say as two punkers in matchy-matchy faded black jeans, sweaty bald heads, and Corrosion of Conformity leather jackets board the number nineteen ahead of us.

"I'm not disappearing. Just going to school," she says with a twinge of irritation.

Her snap catches me off guard for a sec. But I let it blow over as we flash our passes, saying hi to George, the driver. We plop down somewhere in the middle.

Kat always takes the bus with me, though she has a cool yellow Camaro collecting dust in her driveway. It even has a cassette player. I christened the car "Blondie," although the backseat has seen zero rapture, if you know what I mean.

"So, you gonna suck it up and drive to school?" I poke her side.

She doesn't answer.

I focus on the strobes shooting from the open door of the arcade, rather than on how much life will suck without Kat in the studio every day. She's promised she'll still take class, but I know that will be a challenge, balancing her time between dancing and premed stuff at the University of Minnesota. She talks big about becoming a rich plastic surgeon like her parents, but I think she secretly wants to move somewhere off the map and mend wounds for chickens—someplace she'll never need an expensive *Knight Rider* car.

Me? I don't even think about school. And no one at Roosevelt High wastes a second of thought on me either. MDC has tutors for those of us in the upper levels who are still in high school, which means I'm barely a presence at my actual school. When I do make an appearance, I'm this weird dancer girl who shows up out of nowhere in a Prince T-shirt, jeweled Doc Martens, and a purple ruffled skirt. Geno's so clueless, razzing me about my eye shadow and school dances. Normal high school things like prom will never happen for me.

"We could take Blondie out again. Practice?" I say.

Kat shakes her head, her blushy color draining. "Some people have no business driving. Are you forgetting I careened into a billboard?"

"It was a cardboard YARD SALE sign. And there was no careening. We were going ten miles an hour."

"Give it up." Kat exchanges her stale gum for a fresh piece. "Only somebody dying will get me behind the wheel again."

"Coward. A yellow car suits you."

Kat flicks my bun and I flip her hair across her face. The bus pulls over a few blocks down Hennepin. We're so busy messing around, it takes me a second to recognize that it's Flower Boy dropping change into the collector. I elbow Kat.

"Oww!" she squeals. "What?" Kat follows my gaze toward the front. "Ohhh. He's the . . ."

"The boy with the flowers."

"He's cute," she gushes as he asks for a transfer and grabs some standing space a few rows ahead.

Hell yeah, he's fine—in shorts that spare nothing for the imagination and a super-tight tank top. All I can do is stare. The rest of my brain is stuck on how big a fool I must've looked, sweating like a pig with a teacup perched on top of my foot. It's like someone's yanking on my ankles because I'm sinking in my seat.

The boy sways with the movement of the bus as we race down the Ave. I scooch up a little, watching his Doc Martens skim across the floor as we turn. He doesn't even use the bar to steady himself.

My lips part, letting me exhale.

Kat nudges me. "You gonna talk to him, or just drool all over yourself?"

Is she high?

"No way," I whisper. What kind of ballet dancer has time for . . . *that?*

Besides, my nonexistent chance is already working his way to the front. He pauses at the top of the steps as the bus slows. And then . . . he totally busts me gawking.

Cool.

My core tenses as my cheeks catch fire. Fuck if I don't sink into the abyss, and I'm not looking away either, so it's this thing, like in the movies, where it's suddenly just the two of us on the nineteen. He flashes me the peace sign as we jolt to a stop. And then the fox clears all three steps with a leap to the curb.

Holy Mother of Hail Marys, my heart's leaping too. No shame, I plaster my face to the window as Flower Boy bounds across the street to another bus shelter.

Kat pretends to brush something from my shoulder. "Smooth, my cowardly friend. I think you bored a hole through his sexy parts with your laser-beam eyes."

33

"Shut up." I pull out my Walkman, my skin all goose-bumpy. I hand her a spongy earphone and pinch the other between my ear and her shoulder, leaning in.

"After that display," she says, "I think you need some track four."

She's fucking hilarious. Eject. Flip. Close, and I fast-forward the tape three clicks: Play. Prince. "Private Joy."

We sing along, and I know Kat's totally off tune, especially when the crab-ass woman across the way tells her to step off Prince unless she can hit the G-spot notes like he can.

Damn. Not helping ease Flower Boy from my mind. The woman gets it, though. There's no one like Prince. You'd have to live under a pretty big rock in Minneapolis to be unaware of him. He's kinda everywhere, his influence on the music scene putting Minnesota on the map for more than just hockey, ice fishing, and Land O'Lakes butter. And now he's on our block, in our building, getting ready to film a movie. And I'm totally shut out. I sink deeper into Kat's side.

Too soon, the brakes hiss and Kat gives back her half of the phones.

"See you in the a.m.," she says, and scoots out.

"Wait," I call after her. "What about Indiana Jones? The plan?"

She blows me a kiss at the door, the guy in the front side-seat loving every second of Kat in her tight Guess jeans and crop top—an outfit her parents would never approve of.

"Patience," she says. "When it's time, you'll know."

Patience? When it comes to Prince, the word doesn't exist.

I wave and she leaps off the steps like Flower Boy, then prances down Minnehaha Parkway, where the houses are ten times the size of mine and have more than one story.

Kat disappearing around the corner always brings out the anxious in me, as if my best friend is part of a life I don't really have. I wear costumes all the time, pretending to be someone else. But no matter who I am onstage—one night a delicate flower, the next a glittering snowflake—the number nineteen always delivers me home to reality. And *real* is less than a mile away.

The stop before mine, and my stomach tightens like always. Six more blocks and I'll be home. A boy on his battered Huffy races the bus, towing another kid on red-white-and-blue roller skates. Playing cards clipped to the spokes tick a perfect flamenco rhythm as the boys speed past and jump the curb.

We leave them at a row of ramblers lined with squared-off bushes. I pull the cord and the bus jolts me forward as I stand. George waves and the back doors open before we completely stop.

"Thanks!" I shout to the man who's driven me around more hours than anyone else.

I exit onto the sunburnt grass of the boulevard and stare at my house, the switchback wheelchair ramp still needing a second coat of paint. I'm sorry that I feel like turning around, knowing I can run across the street and catch George on his way back downtown and ride the loop until the end of his shift at midnight. I sleep better on the nineteen than at home, and George never minds. I wonder if he's heard what happened, right here, on this very street.

The sunset transforms our faded yellow siding into a brilliant orange. The whole house is closed tight, except for the screen door. I can't wait to see her, and dread it all the same, the war inside my heart every time I step off the bus.

Hot, damp wind slaps stray curls against my cheek. I stop at the bottom of the ramp. George makes his U-turn, slowing up like always before he passes. I swipe away my hair, and wave him on.

The sounds of Mom clanking around in the kitchen, water running and fans humming, float through the screen as I navigate the ramp. Clutching my empty bag, I go inside.

The door smacks the peeling trim behind me and I flinch.

"Shhh," Mom hisses.

"Sorry." I set my bag on the table. "Is she sleeping?"

Mom nods without looking up and continues flushing a piece of plastic tubing with saline.

"I can do that. Why don't you sit?"

Her dry, cracked hands work faster, the thin strap of her tank top falling off one shoulder. "I'm almost done. Eat something. There's Tater Tot hot dish in the fridge." She doesn't seem to notice my lost-and-found heels and shorts, but blending into the dingy orange-and-brown wallpaper has become my usual.

"Did she have another seizure?" I slide her strap up onto her tensed shoulder.

"It's on the second shelf," she says, and I know our conversation is done.

I want to tell her about Prince, cry about my missing Docs, spill about the horrible teacup test while she pulls me into her arms to hug it all away—be *that* family. Then I notice Mom's wrinkled shirt. It's saturated with sweat, the front splattered with something brownish. Another seizure. They're becoming more frequent. My shoulders scrunch up like hers and I stick with keeping my mouth shut.

I turn up the oscillating fan in the corner, point it at her, then try to pry open the window over the sink. Three AA sobriety coins balance on the sill—one month, three months, and six—Geno's proof of staying sober since January. Besides that, maybe a couple of T-shirts are the only remnants of him in this house. My parents aren't legally separated, just apart because Mom booted him. He's only been in the house three times since, to drop off his AA medallions, like they're proof he's trying or something. But Geno always splits when stuff gets real. Everyone under this roof knows that. Mom used to call him about every seizure. Now I think they only talk about money things. Geno leaves a check in the mailbox and scurries back to his couch and a bottomless pot of coffee in his office at MDC, where he's lived for the last half of a year.

The window won't budge. I move the coins aside to try again.

"Don't," Mom says with a bite.

I slide them back to their circle of dust and go to the fridge, sandwiching myself between the door and the wire shelving. The fridge stinks like whatever's rotting in the bottom drawer, but the cool air feels like paradise in an avocado-green second-hand appliance.

"Shut that, Rosa. Electricity isn't free."

I pull out the hot dish, give myself a healthy scoop, and eat it cold. The hum of the fan drowns out the metrical artificial breaths from down the hall but does nothing to buffer the stench of sour food and rubbing alcohol. I take one more bite of ground beef and peas before throwing the rest away.

Mom shifts from one shapely leg to the other, proving the body stores memories just like the brain. She hasn't danced since before the accident, but her balled calves hint at the principal she once was. Now the only balancing she does is with time—between sterilizing, wiping, suctioning, and pretending I'd been the daughter hit by that truck.

"Don't bother her," she says as I open the freezer.

"I won't." I pull out a full-sized pillow stuffed next to the peas and tuck the frozen thing under my arm.

I leave Mom to her scrubbing and move my dance bag to our worn plaid couch, the same one Abuela slept on when she could no longer get down the stairs to her bedroom. My parents never embraced any one style, just hodgepodged the hell out of the house. A tacky velvet bullfighting painting is the only thing we own that screams *Mexicans live here!* And I'm pretty sure Abuela bought it from some white people's garage sale around the corner. I named the bull Paco, which makes Mom's mouth twitch with a tiny smile. And she hasn't taken him down yet. So yeah, Paco's been worth every penny.

I tap his steamy-looking nose as I pass, wishing he had a friend or two on the walls. But my parents aren't exactly brimming with Mexican pride. Other than barking Spanish to each other on the phone when they don't want me to know what they're talking about, my parents have turned their backs on everything south of the border. Like they're ashamed or something.

The small amount of Spanish I do know is thanks to Abuela. And we had to speak it on the sly, the two of us sneaking off to the basement to get our verbs on in this "English only" house. She'd pretend to do her sewing work, and I'd repeat after her. When her fingers stopped cooperating, she quit doing alterations for people who could afford to pay her more but didn't. After that, we tried to find the time and place. But it was tough in such a small space, and always ended in a fight with Geno.

"How are these girls supposed to know where they are going, if they don't know where they came from?" she'd say. But she really didn't mean it. Not totally.

Geno came over when he was, like, fifteen—this much she shared. And there were three of them in Mexico, and only two when they reached Texas. The rest is static. Geno refuses to talk about what happened to his father. Abuela too. She wouldn't even crack on her deathbed, and I'm a terrible granddaughter for trying to drag the truth out of her. Anyway, our secret lessons ended then too. Geno can chill. My Spanish still sucks.

I pad down the hall of our two-bedroom rambler toward Mom's cave.

Mom was born here. And her family is from money, the kind of family that must distort priorities, because they've been in this house only once, the same amount of times I've laid eyes on them.

I was ten, and I remember two things about that day: one, an older version of Mom in an expensive-looking lime-green polyester jumpsuit, fingering my tight curls and scolding me for not straightening them; the other, a mustached dude in a boring blue suit. He handed Mom an envelope, then marched right past Geno, Glo, and me, and back into his shiny black car. That's it. My Corredor grandparents. They may as well be dead like Abuela, because I know in my gut they're never coming back.

I snag my heel on a hole in the shocking-orange shag carpet. Geno may be a celebrated choreographer, but no way will he beg for more money for things like new carpet, because according to the U.S. government, he's also something called a resident alien. I think it makes him sound like he's from the movie *E.T.* But there are no glowing hearts in this house.

Geno says he's lucky to get paid the money he does. His photo on his card looks like a mug shot, but I think it means he can live here—work here. For now. It doesn't give him permission to empty a whiskey bottle and pass out behind the bar like he's done. Another trip to jail for fighting, or driving under the influence, and the lawyer guy who helped Geno get his card says there's not a lot he can do to keep him from being deported back to Mexico. I'm not going to lie. This terrifies me. With Mom not working . . . well . . .

I touch the closed door in front of me, a laminated sign tacked to the wood warning FLAMMABLE/OXYGEN IN USE.

I back away and into Mom's dim bedroom, the staging area. Every spare space is crammed with boxes and bags of expensive medical equipment—disposable bed pads, medications, rolls of gauze, more rolls of tape. A lot of this stuff, all of which is totally off-limits to me, is donated by our church. Mom doesn't trust me anymore. She never lets me help with anything. My shoulders weigh heavy on my collarbones as I shuffle to her dresser.

I slide open the third drawer. It's stuffed with her old tights and leos, chiffon skirts, and a pair of ratty leg warmers. There's not a single dusty-rose leotard in the drawer. I don't know why I expected there would be. Mom always wore black, like the rest of the professionals.

Before her bedroom became a supply closet, she was a mother, the kind who held my hand, and made rainbow Jell-O pops in the dead of winter just because I asked. But first and foremost, she was Analisa Corredor Ramos, principal dancer at MDC. I draw a skirt to my face, the material light enough to be a whisper. She hasn't danced in over a year, but a faint trace of the rosewater lotion she doesn't wear anymore lingers. I'm ten years old again, damp-faced and spellbound, hovering between the heavy velvet wings of a hot stage.

No one escaped tearless after four acts of Mom's tragically romantic Odette in *Swan Lake*. And all she walked away with was a huge bouquet of long-stemmed roses the night of her last performance, like it was her funeral. She barely made it through the last act, her career-ending ankle injury holding on for one last bow. Mom threw the flowers straight into the trash when we got home. Just like she did with the envelope my grandfather gave her.

I've never told her, but I fished that envelope from the trash. It was a check made out to her for twenty-five thousand dollars, the numbers written across the piece of official-looking paper in fancy cursive. Even at ten, I knew that check had everything to do with leaving Geno behind. The money went back into the garbage. And I've confessed Father Thomas's ears bloody about my confusing regret.

The mini fridge next to Mom's bed is open. I put back the skirt and then close the fridge, feeling the plastic bag sitting on top. Almost room temperature. My sister will be up for her evening snack soon, a beige liquid Mom infuses through her feeding tube—every single day, without fail, at seven, noon, six, and nine.

I trip over a box, my sister's roller skates tumbling out. Dirt clings to the hot-pink wheels she painted black, as if just yesterday she was turning fast circles in the driveway. Our lives changed in an instant. But the house and everything in it is taking its own sweet time.

The breathing machine across the hall squeals, then releases a mechanical sigh. She's already awake. I put back the skates, shoving them into a dark corner. Clutching the frozen pillow, I peer into the kitchen. Mom's moving on to a pile of dishes.

Grandpa's check wasn't the only thing I fished from the trash. I pulled out a blossom from Mom's bouquet too. Unlike the check, I saved the flower, pressing it between the pages in my *M* encyclopedia. It's flat, brittle, and brown now. But I'm glad I kept it. Because if I gently peel back the petals, I can still see a seam of bright crimson.

I tiptoe across the shag carpet and let myself into my sister Gloria's room, closing the door with a soft click.

Little Red Machine

Gloria blinks when she sees me. It's an excited blink, not the sluggish kind like when the pain in her head gets too bad. She must be over being pissed at me. I'd taken off with her MTV T-shirt this morning. And hell if I'm telling her it's gone for good, like my Docs.

"Good evening, Princess Glo." Her bedroom is dusky, curtains closed, wheelchair jammed in the corner, purposely hidden like her urine catheter and stomach tube.

Glo zeroes in on my heels.

"Yeah. Long story. But I kind of like them. You?"

She flutters her eyelids like Blair, her favorite character from *The Facts of Life.*

"Then it's settled. They're yours." I hold up the cold pillow. "But first . . ." I slide my hand behind her sweaty, matted head and exchange pillows.

Glo's brow scrunches.

"I know. It does smell like frozen peas. But it's, like, a hundred degrees out there today." I kick off the shoes and uncover Glo's feet. The bottoms of her socks are caked with grayish fur from our tomcat, Mork.

"You've been up and around today." I pluck a few fur balls from her toes. "That's good, right?"

She nods *no*.

My world is divided. Before the accident. And after the accident. And after that horrible day, Glo's nod really means *no*.

I take in the metal-band posters tacked to her walls, pausing at the one with David Lee Roth in red tights, kicking his leg to his ear. She used to have more dance posters than hard-rock hair. But since the accident, the dance stuff is covered with pictures of AC/DC and all the others she demands I buy her from a head shop called Sun's on Block E.

"You need the newest Def Leppard, sister. It's called *Pyromania*. Mom'll kill me, but I'll pick up the tape."

Glo's arms bounce like they do when she slides up the volume on the boom box next to her bed. I cling to these defiant moments like they're my last. Because Mom hating Glo's loud music means some things haven't changed at all.

The painting she's been working on is propped against the wall, her brush-mitts crusted with shades of cornmeal yellow like the sunnies we used to catch with Abuela. Another before—a glassy northern lake, and a salty grandma calling us *Mexican'ts* because of our terrible Spanish.

I miss Abuela's slams. I wish I sensed her haunting the house like she said she would, but I don't. It's like when she'd cover all the mirrors during a thunderstorm. I can't picture the details of her anymore. I can't remember her laugh. Not exactly anyway, and that was the absolute best part about her. Glo's laugh too. It's boxed up with the rest of her stuff in Mom's bedroom.

I touch the canvas, thick vertical strokes running off the edges. She's had a good day. If they were horizontal, or worse, muddy blotches—look out, world, Glo's on fire.

"Okay . . ." The ventilator interrupts her raspy whisper. "Fine," she adds during a long exhale.

I pull back. "Still wet . . . Got it."

Glo may be used to forcing words through the tube in her neck, but I'll forever catch myself holding my breath during the long pauses in our conversations. When the ugly box is tethered to her, she can only make sounds while breathing out. Probably the reason for the anxious glare I'm getting from her now. She wants me to disconnect her.

And I want to, so badly. But Mom needs to be more than a room away for me to try anything that nuts without permission.

I wriggle my hand into one of her mitts, the entire setup an invention of Mom's. Glo has trouble holding traditional brushes, her fingers in perpetual flexion. So Mom raided the winter closet, cut out the knuckles of our gloves, and sewed in pads my sister could dip into saucers of paint.

The result—masterpieces. Sometimes on the floor too, when she really gets into it. This drives Mom mad-crazy. But Glo doesn't care, and I love this new thing about her. Because before there was a hospital bed in here, Glo kept her side of the room all annoyingly perfect and mine was the only tornado aftermath.

"I'm still waiting for my lesson," I say, peeling off the mitt to hang it on a drying hook, another of Mom's ideas.

Mom and Glo—warriors.

I smooth down the edges of the red heart stickers decorating the machine Glo can't sleep without. The doctors say her brain will forget to tell her lungs to breathe when she's in a deep sleep, just like it no longer remembers how to make a smile or swallow very well. The machine is a new thing. Or I guess I should say, getting to take one home is new. Glo is in some kind of medical study, like a guinea pig. But it means we get the ventilator for free, and a cranky nurse comes once a week. I don't know what goes on in Glo's room during these visits. I'm never allowed in. I've convinced myself I'm okay with being shut out. Because the little red machine is here, and that translates to my sister being home instead of *in* a home. The only thing that matters.

Gulping down the sharp lump in my throat, I pull off Glo's furry socks. Her feet are dry and flaky, toenails a sickly purple. The white-coat experts say my sister is partially paralyzed. She's unable to walk on her own, but on a good day Mom gets her upright to take a couple of shuffling steps. I can't tell if these days excite Glo or make her sad. I'm not sure I want to know.

I wriggle her cold, flaccid feet into the red pumps. Her legs are swollen from the knees down, but her feet are still smaller than mine—always the delicate one. I've watched Mom perform in *Swan Lake* so many times I know the choreography as if the part were mine. But Glo is the daughter meant for elegant roles like Mom's Odette. She should be the one going for the apprenticeship. Our similar facial features may trick people into thinking we're twins, but the likeness ends there. My broad shoulders and husky thighs aren't fooling anyone.

"There. Cinderella would be jealous." I massage her shins like I've seen Mom do, hoping she's forgotten how beautiful her en pointe bourrées used to be. Just as I pray to God she has no memory of why our matching beds are gone and a single hospital bed stands in their place.

"Okay . . . Fine," Glo says, the only words she's been able to say for a year and a half. It's like the accident erased the rest. Or maybe everything is still there, her head pinging with one-sided conversations. I'll never know. Glo can paint forms and shapes, but as she would've said, "My bitch of a brain blocks out the rest." That's what I envision coming from her snarky mouth, anyway.

Mom made up a chart with simple pictures, each image meaning something. She calls it a communication board. It's this thing that stands up on Glo's tray table, and she points at it with her knuckles, columns of images with headings like "I Am," and "I Want." Today, the chart is on the floor. Glo knocks it away when she doesn't want to use it. I don't know, maybe I kind of understand. There's not nearly enough sass on that boring board for Glo. And like she's doing right now, she's pretty good at hitting me with a nasty glare when she wants to use her words. Even if there are only two inside her now.

I glance at the pile of soiled clothing in the corner. She'd vomited, probably during the seizure. And I'm a horrible sister because I'm relieved I missed it.

There is nothing but helplessness in the room when my sis-

48

ter seizes. When Geno lived here, he would bolt, leaving Mom to hold Glo's twitching, contorted body on its side. Then we'd wait it out, listen to our beautiful Gloria grunt and tick until the angry part of her brain found peace. Kat tells me Mom holds Glo this way so she won't suck anything back into her lungs. Mom used to cry the whole time. Now she just stares off into space. And I stand in the corner, the cinder blocks of terror tied to my feet keeping me from doing anything to help either one of them—Glo isn't the only one partially paralyzed since the accident.

I pick up her dirty clothes, inhaling through my mouth so I won't smell her fermented lunch. I am no Kat Johansen. Never have been. It's a wonder I can look at my own pulpy feet.

Throwing Glo's clothes into the laundry bin, I pause in front of the fan, my roiling gut chilling my skin. I take in the fresh air until my queasiness passes. I'll die first, rather than have Glo think I'm a total wimp.

"Okay . . . Fine . . ."

I straighten up and drag over a chair, wishing I wasn't so scared of Glo's medical equipment. Then I'd remove the ventilator like a big girl. Glo only uses it to sleep anyway. But the noisy machine outdoes Mom in the intimidation department. So many buttons and hoses, beeps and evil hisses.

Before the accident, Glo and I shared secrets. We feathered each other's hair and traded *Charlie's Angels* cards. Our four-poster beds are long gone. The *Angels* cards are in the trash, and Glo's hair is cropped short for ease of care. But I lost my sister's MTV shirt today, and she's defiantly sporting my coveted *1999* concert tee. What else is there to do but spill some dirt?

"I snuck up to studio 6A again."

Glo's rashy cheeks crease, the smile her doctors say isn't possible.

"Totally," I say. "*So* much trouble. I'll spare you the details."

Her eyes dance like her body used to, but her arms flail with confused purpose. She wants the details. The ventilator chimes, then goes back to its whooshy sighs. I freeze, listening for Mom's rushed pitter-patter. When the clink of dishes goes on uninterrupted, I glare at the flashing box, daring it to make another sound.

Before I chuck the thing out the window, I rest my head in Glo's lap. Her pale legs twitch like they do sometimes, the heels of the red shoes Dorothy-clicking. The slight weight of her arms sinks into my back like elegant protective wings. My sister—always the strong one. I melt into her legs, wanting to be this way for her too. Instead, my body curls into itself beneath her touch.

She nudges my shoulder.

"All right, all right." I sit up. "He saw me today—looked right at me, Glo," I whisper as if Geno's eavesdropping. "And to answer your next question, no, I didn't get in. His body-guard, Big Chick, caught me again."

Glo's eyes sharpen.

"I know. I will." I bend closer. "There's going to be a ben-efit concert. *Prince* and MDC dancers. Geno says I'm not old enough to perform, but Kat's coming up with some Indiana Jones double-dog-dare plan. And you know what that means."

My sister's gaze widens. Kat once dared Glo to show up to class with her pointes painted rainbow colors. Glo barely made it to the barre before Geno booted her from the studio. She cried the entire hour in the dressing room. I thought she was so lame, bawling over missing one stupid class like it was the end of the world. But now I think she cried because Geno failed to notice her pointes were a work of fucking art—because those shoes looked like she'd chaînéd through the sun itself to get to MDC.

"Okay . . . ," Glo rasps.

I leave my thoughts in the before, and take ahold of the after—Glo's cold, contorted fingers.

"I can't believe he's here, Glo. *Prince—at MDC.*" I clutch her hand tighter. "He's rehearsing for a movie. And when he dances . . ." I'm totally lost for a second. "It's like watching Fosse's *Cabaret,* a ballet, and a rock concert all at once. It's everything I've ever dreamed of being a part of, rolled into one. And the choreography," I gush. "I could create moves like that, you know?"

Glo's arm bounces over mine. The girl knows me, not to mention she's just as hot for a guy in tight pants as I am.

"And then there's Geno."

Glo deflates.

"He expects me to pirouette the other direction."

My sister pushes her fists into my palms.

"I don't know . . . he's so pissed at me." I peek at Glo's turned-in feet. "I should just focus on the apprenticeship thing and forget I ever heard Prince sing 'I Wanna Be Your Lover.'"

Glo wriggles free of me and pinches the pleated hose connected to her trach between her knuckles. This angers the machine, scattering its rhythm. Her face reddens as she erupts into a silent coughing fit.

I grab her hands again. "Settle, Glo. Wait for Mom."

She squeezes my fingers, and hard too.

"*Ow*, Gloria."

Her bloodshot eyes narrow, reminding me she is two years older. I glance at the communication board on the floor, but I don't need it to know what she wants. She's glowering at the purple plastic thingy on her nightstand, the valve that will allow her to speak her two words without pauses. If only I had the balls to do this for her.

"Just . . . wait a second. I'll get Mom." I untangle our fingers.

The ventilator hisses. I steady her hands again, my eyes rummaging for the machine's Shut Up button, but everything's a blur of flashing livid-red digital numbers. I know I should call for Mom, but Glo wants out now—and I'm not supposed to be in here in the first place.

My heart races, utter panic erasing anything that makes sense. Glo thrashes and I let her go because my head is screaming, "What if something pops out? Her stomach tube, urine catheter, or her number-two collection bag?" Mom would lock me out of Glo's room forever.

"Quit it," I utter through clenched teeth. "You'll get us both in trouble."

But Glo's the big sister and she isn't about to listen to me. She punches herself in the face.

"Glo! *Stop.*"

Blood gushes from her nose.

I yank the blanket up to her face. "Oh Jesus . . ."

She's really pissed off the ventilator now. Air rushes from the cockeyed hose dangling from the hole in her neck. My hands are shaking like crazy. I can barely hold on to anything, so I do the most horrible thing and smash the blanket against her nose harder.

Glo snaps her face away, mouthing, "Okay . . . Fine."

My fingers cramp into a total spasm as I scramble to reconnect the tubing. If she would just stop moving! My head lightens into a spin and I barely notice when Mom shoves me out of the way.

"Rosa Dominguez, what in the world?"

I fall onto my butt and roll over onto my hands and knees.

"Get out!" Mom shouts over the frantic ventilator.

"I'm sorry, Mom."

"I said, get out!" She detaches the hose, then presses something that silences the traitorous machine.

My feet are beneath me and I'm standing, although I don't remember how. Glo gives me two slow blinks. She's saying *I'm sorry.*

Mom plucks a handful of tissues from the bedside box and pinches Glo's nose the way I should have.

I shrink away like a fucking coward, the tears I want to keep to myself acid-cold against my fiery cheeks. I'm the one who's sorry—every hour of every day.

The red heels sail from Glo's room as I stumble out. Mom slams the door and the hallway shrinks to a dark pinhole. I clutch the shoes and press my sweaty forehead against the wall, sucking in ragged gulps.

I'm sorry you can't share your secrets.

I'm sorry you can't feed yourself, or breathe fresh air.

I'm sorry you'll never pirouette again, or glissade across the floor like a northern loon taking flight.

I'm sorry you were hit by that truck, Gloria—so sorry I am the reason.

Sew Blue

Mosquitoes I don't bother to swat usher me into the twilight, swarming the back of my sweaty neck. I hadn't bothered to change either. Glo's blood speckles the rose fabric of my leotard like black stars against a blushing July sky. After Mom kicked me out of the room, I'd jammed some stuff in my bag and split. Cried the entire time too, which is so babyish.

My sister never cries, though she has every right in the world. She's lost so many abilities, but making tears isn't one of them. Even so, I've only seen her lose it twice. Before the accident—her rainbow pointes. And after, the time she had a headache that must have felt like an earthquake in her brain.

"Dude, you look trashed." Kat gasps at the sight of me hunched on her front porch—flushed and clammy—with gnats freckling my face. "Did you ride your bike here?"

I nod. "Can't find my bus pass."

My best friend doesn't ask what I'm doing on her doorstep with my ten-speed. She knows. When the crushing happens, I escape to her house. Sometimes my chest throbs so badly, the fist I imagine strangling my heart becomes more real than anything else.

I wipe my eyes, smearing black eyeliner on my fingers before tangling them in my ratty hair. I really do look the Block E part—kind of like the beat-up prostitute Kat and I saw stumbling around Slice of New York last week. Kat had offered her hand, even tried to give her a tissue and some money. I think the girl would've accepted it all if it weren't for her pimp lurking in the corner like a drooling hyena. Kat could hardly choke down her pizza that day.

Now she's taking *my* hand, looking at my blood-spattered leotard with pity-party eyes. I can practically see her heart bleeding. My stomach sinks another level. I've become tragic, like the girl at SNY.

"Come on," she says. "I'm making popcorn."

The pain behind my ribs pulsates like my aching feet. I smash my fist against my chest, which is not helping like it usually does. I can't even spew how shocked I am that Kat is *cooking* and the house is still standing.

I push harder as she leads me through the sunken living room, to the chef's kitchen that could swallow my entire rambler. I take my first real breath since leaving Glo's room. The central air feels like winter in heaven and the entire spotless house smells like flowery cleaning solution. Nothing to trip over in Kat's house. My muscles melt over my bones, and with the magic touch of Kat Nightingale, I feel like I'm going to be okay—at least for tonight.

I take a seat on a stool and watch Kat shake the Jiffy Pop over the flame, the only food I've ever seen her make. "Are your parents here?" I ask.

"What do you think?" she says, and I realize how dumb my question is, because they never are.

I think her parents tolerate me well enough. It's hard to tell, when I've spoken fewer words to them than, say, to Baby-Pink Stacy. From what I've seen, Bob and Betty Johansen run their lives like they wear their clothes—super-tailored clean lines from the muddy-mushroom section of the color wheel, and shoes you can see your reflection in. But her mom lets me stay over whenever I want and rarely asks me any questions, which is cool. Her dad I've only seen a handful of times at performances, and once when Kat broke her arm while skateboarding behind my bike. A tired look and a mumble were all I got before he loaded her into their BMW.

"Operation Indiana Jones is really coming together." Kat hikes up the top of her strapless terry romper, shouting over the frantic popping. "I just have a few more details to work out—"

"Forget it. I don't want to do it anymore." I hardly believe I say it out loud, but after today it's the truth.

"What?" Kat spins around on her bare feet like a jewelry-box ballerina, her tanned skin shining from the baby oil she uses. "Of course you want to do it. It's all you've talked about for weeks. You've gone stealth to the sixth floor, like, how many times?"

"I can't get kicked out of MDC. I'm committed to the apprenticeship and Glo. End of story." Letting go of my Prince obsession steals my air like death. He lives inside my head twenty-four seven. His *1999* album is the only reason I get out of bed some days. And the way my heart goes all warm

57

and fluttery when his "Little Red Corvette" video plays on MTV, well, this is the only proof that I'm not a corpse inside. But I've made up my mind. I rest my cheek against the cool countertop.

Kat snaps her fingers in my face. "Glo would tell you to blow off the apprenticeship because the road to principal was never yours to begin with."

"But she can't tell me that. And you know why." I chase away the memory of my sister leaping across the studio, her toned legs in a sharp aerial split.

My leaps have become just as good. But it wasn't always this way. Before the accident, I think Geno expected I'd be in the corps the rest of my dance life—maybe a demi-soloist if I was lucky, and that was good enough for him. I certainly didn't put the effort into ballet that Glo did. My heart was made for whip-ass head rolls with my hair down.

My face presses heavily into the icy granite. "Things have changed. The road to *Swan Lake* is mine now."

"Oh, honey, stop. You don't owe your family anything. And honestly, I don't know why you have to audition for the apprenticeship anyway. What Geno says, goes at MDC."

I lift my head. "The popcorn is burning."

Kat yanks the foil pan from the burner and fumbles for the correct dial. "And dancing is dancing. Why should he care whether it's ballet or not? We do contemporary pieces all the time."

I jut my chin at the dial on the left and she gets it. "But in pointes," I say. "And for MDC, under his direction. Don't you know, *classical ballet is the foundation of all dance.*" I make my voice all raspy like Geno's, scrunching my brow the way he does during his tiresome lectures. "And Geno doesn't have the pull he used to. Not after he lost his place on the board, remember? After all the drinking, when Director Joyce got sick of covering for him?" I rub my cross necklace with my thumb.

Kat fans away the gray smoke streaming from a split in the foil. "I remember."

God, I wish she didn't. Especially the time we had to peel him from the pavement behind his favorite bar, Moby Dick's—at nine a.m., with pigeon shit and stale whiskey pasted in his hair. We got to him just in time, before the cops did their morning sweep for the leftover drunks.

I rake my fingernails across my itchy legs. "Can I use your shower? And washing machine?" I'm ready to ditch my scratchy tights—not talk. But Kat drags confessions out of me better than Father Thomas. She pushes the burnt popcorn toward me and waits.

I sigh and cross myself. "Glo had a bloody nose . . . and another seizure earlier." The last few words stick in my throat like the dry saltine crackers I claim to live on.

"I see." Kat opens the fridge and hands me a pop. Nothing's rotting in the Johansens' bright white refrigerator—no liquid-nutrition bags sitting on top. The shelves are organized and stacked with Tupperware, premade meals Kat's parents leave for her. Well, not her parents exactly, but their "helper," as they call her. Her name is Martina Hernandez Barerra. We go to the same church. I've seen the paper-clipped dollar bills the Johansens leave for her, a Post-it note on top with her name spelled wrong. They pay her under the table and way below minimum wage. And I'd be lying if I said the air doesn't change when I run into her here—like we're both embarrassed or something.

Just when I think I'll blubber all over again, Kat's soft gaze holds me together. She'll make an awesome doctor one day, no doubt about it. Kat's one of those people—inherently brilliant. I'd hate her if she wasn't so awesome.

I slide off the stool. "I should've taken that first-aid class with you last month. I'm totally useless."

"So, blood, snot, and lung cookies aren't your thing. Your sister needs more than a medical caretaker. Let your mom do that stuff. What you give Glo is just as important."

I shuffle toward Kat's room. "Then how come I always make things worse?"

"Well, you do stink. Glo's probably happy to be rid of you." She tosses the popcorn in the trash and grabs an open box of Smurf-Berry Crunch cereal instead, herding me down the hall. "And since you're here and so committed to the apprenticeship, we have some shoes to abuse. If we do it now, we won't be rushed tomorrow before partnering class."

Partnering class. I'm not in the mood to watch a gaggle of girls fight over Straight Jeffery and the skinny mirror.

Kat turns on the shower and leaves, humming the theme to Indiana Jones.

I stay in the shower long enough to wrinkle like a raisin and smell like a bottle of Prell. I even shave my pits. After wrapping myself in a thick towel, I take my time getting to Kat's room because the tight plush carpet feels like thousands of tiny pillows beneath my sore feet.

Prince's "International Lover" undulates down the hall from her room. Kat isn't about to give up on Plan Indy. I follow the music, finding Dr. K sitting on her floor, legs spread in a perfect center split. Like always, MTV is on the TV, the sound turned off.

I love that "our thing" is to watch all the videos to Prince music. And right now, Prince singing about flying an orgasmic airplane while Sting mouths the words to "Every Breath You Take" is kinda working for me.

I stay at the threshold, watching Kat line up our tools like surgical instruments—box cutters, pliers, scissors, needle, thread—and suddenly I'm sinking again. There's a pile of grad cards on her dresser. Half of her stuff is neatly packed in boxes for the dorm, the same handwriting labeling the cardboard as on the Tupperware in the fridge.

"Packing already, huh?" I ask.

"I can pack myself," she says with a snap. "I don't know why my mom insists Martina do it."

I do. I've seen Kat's idea of folding, and it's more like a ball-up-and-stuff deal. Still, when I look at Martina's handwriting, something shifts beneath my skin. Kat could do a lot of things herself, but I never really see her push the issue. Like, she just lets it happen without any protest.

I shove aside a U of M maroon-and-gold throw pillow and drop my bag onto her bed. Dr. Betty had Kat's room "tastefully redecorated" in Gopher colors the second she received her acceptance letter.

Kat pours Smurf-Berry Crunch into her mouth, straight from the box. She already feels a jeté away from trading me in for a bunch of doc-in-training friends. She's been super busy lately, gone to places I have nothing to do with because she never talks about it. Maybe she thinks I won't understand. I know her mother's more than ready for her to stop messing around with me and get serious about rearranging people's faces. Then Kat will be buried. I've had eyes on her premed schedule for U of M's first term—brutal.

"You smell better," she says without looking up.

I sniff my shoulder. My hair is full-on damp poodle. I don't get the whole perm thing. I'm totally screwed if straight hair becomes the rage. I grab a scrunchie from Kat's dressing table and wind it around my frizzfest without bothering to comb it out.

"It's always so mellow here," I say, because it is. My house is a continuous reel of background noise. Stuff I don't really notice anymore—until I do. And then it's like all I hear is Glo's ventilator. Which is why I didn't make a fuss when Mom moved my bedroom to the basement.

"Mellow?" Kat says. "More like deserted. My dad's in the OR with a full caseload of nose and boob jobs, and Mom's covering rounds at the hospital for two other plastic surgeons again. What kind of life is that?"

Kat never speaks negatively about going into the "family business." The possibility of her giving it all up to dance floods my heart with selfish warmth, even though I know I'm being totally unrealistic.

I drop my towel, never self-conscious around her. There's no racing to get back into clothes at light speed like I do in the dressing room at MDC.

"If you want endless racket, come live at my house." I slip into a pair of sweats. "Unless you see a busy ER in your future." My *Fame* T-shirt goes on last.

She shrugs. "Shoes?"

I pull my last new pair of pointe shoes from my duffel. She holds out the pliers. I take them and sit in a center split too.

We never wear pointes without three-quartering them. Kat, especially, needs a more flexible sole. Her arches aren't high, and getting over her toe box is difficult in a stiff shoe. Me? I have big boobs and a healthy ass, not at all the George Balanchine body type like Kat or Stacy. But from the knee down, I possess exactly what every ballet dancer would kill for—high arches, super-strong ankles, and flexible feet.

"I don't know why you do this when you inherited your dad's flawless feet," she says. "I could drive a truck under his arches."

"You? Drive?"

She waves a pink ribbon in my face. But Kat's right. I don't need to cut anything out of my shoe to get a pretty line. I just like the ritual and hanging out with her. Besides, mutilating my shoes feels satisfying—like lighting them on fire would.

I set down the pliers. "Does everyone at MDC really think

I'm just going through the motions?" I ask her this because ever since she said it, I can't stop thinking about it.

"Well, aren't you?"

Turning my left shoe inside out at the heel, I peel back the fabric layer from the inner sole. "I guess. Just . . . do people think I'm in the top level because of who my parents are? I don't know how to feel about that if they do." I drop the shoe in my lap. "Sometimes . . . I wish I wasn't so good at pointe work, you know? How much easier would everything be if I had Hobbit feet or something? It's really hard to fake bad ballet when every molecule in my body knows the opposite. Believe me, I've tried. That weird?"

Kat stops peeling. "Rosa, you've worked hard to get where you are. Do you act like you don't care sometimes? Yes. But somewhere along the way, in the middle of everything that's happened to you and your family, you became a seriously awesome ballet dancer. Who cares what lame-o's like Stacy say? There's always going to be jealousy for the best in class. And you are it. Own it. Do whatever you want with it. Feel however you want about it. But let it be your choice. Not Geno's or anyone else's."

Sounds cool, but it comes with unbreakable rules. The first being no shoulder rolls or swaying hips.

I watch Sting fade to black on the TV, and Duran Duran get "hungry like the wolf," which isn't meshing with Prince at all. I want to turn it off, but I'm too lazy to get up and cross the room.

"You don't know what it's like," I say. "Your parents are solid and sober. You never have to worry about anything."

"Just because I live in a big house doesn't mean everything's cool beans all the time."

"Like, what's not cool here?" I glance around her swanky bedroom. The flowery wallpaper, the perfectly placed hanging plants, the expensive bedding—it all belongs in a magazine.

Kat glances at the boxes. "Never mind. Everything's fine." She goes back to peeling.

I cross my legs. I would be all kinds of fine in this house. "If Geno starts drinking again"—my chest tightens—"if he gets arrested again . . . We need him. I hate that we do, but it's true. Glo's care. The house. All that stuff costs money. I mean, we get some help from the government. I've seen the checks. But I'm telling you right now, I could make more working the counter at SNY. Ten times as much on the other side of it with the rest of the working girls."

I'm joking, but Kat doesn't find this funny. She keeps messing with her shoe while I draw a deep circle in her spongy carpet with my finger.

"Sometimes we get food boxes from church." My face heats up when I admit this. I've never told Kat about all the packets of Hamburger Helper, mac and cheese, and powdered milk. I'm not sure why I'm saying anything now, but it's wigging me out. I drop my chin to my shoulder. "We need Geno's paycheck, that's all."

Kat spins her gold charm necklace around to her back. I'm pretty certain I've made her feel guilty about everything she has. I'm torn between the urge to apologize and the need to make her understand. So my shoe gets my attention instead. I go to work on separating the inner shank. This takes some effort, and usually I love this part because of the skinning sound of the protesting glue. Tonight, not so much. This is my last pair and, like always, I'll wear them way longer than most dancers would. These are my second pair this summer, and as much as I've been dancing, they'll "die" within a month. There's not a lot of dancing hours between fresh out of the box and total marshmallow. And these will have to last into the fall season. My feet already hate me anyway. But it means there's more money for Glo's stuff, or at least to put something on the table besides Tater Tot hot dish.

"Pliers," Kat says, and things shift to normal again.

"Pliers." I pry off the nail underneath the inner sole, then hand over the tool.

I bend back the portion of the shank I plan to remove and grab the box cutter, rolling up the blade. There's no need to mark the spot. I've tricked out my shoes a thousand times since I was eleven.

"International Lover" is at its climax, Prince's erotic flight announcement beckoning me to cling to my dream of sharing a stage with him. Slicing through the shank, I let my mind wander.

The fantasy is always the same, with a few variations in clothing. Tonight, I'm wearing a purple tiered minidress, cinched at the waist with a thick silver metallic belt—ditch the shoulder pads. The stage is perfectly illuminated, hazy hues of violets and blues. And then there's Prince, unable to look away as I sweep my leg to my ear like I'm Debbie *fucking* Allen in *Fame*.

"She smiles." Kat hacks away at her shoe. "And blushes."

"*So* not blushing." I finish my cuts, then thread a needle. Making two stitches, I tack down the remaining inner material over the hollowed heel. "It's not like I have any clue what he's singing about anyway. Virgin central here." Which Kat is not—twice over.

She pinks up, probably revisiting her fling under the docks at Detroit Lakes last summer. "See, you need Prince. At least, until you experience the real thing. Like, maybe with that hot fox on the bus today."

I squeeze my shoe. "Oh, I'm so sure!"

Kat grins, squaring her bare shoulders. "Throw it. It'll work out your . . . frustrations."

My arms go numb.

"I'm sorry. I wasn't thinking." She crosses her legs as Prince is replaced by static.

"No. It just brought me back for a second."

"You sure?"

"Yeah . . ." But I can't look at anything but the green carpet.

I flip over my pointe and score the leather sole with the cutter. "You should've seen her today. She punched herself in the face. Glo got a bloody nose because I couldn't help her." I slice my shoe, almost all the way through.

Kat snatches the cutter from me and gestures for my pointe—my destroyed Freed, the maker's mark of a crown stamped on the sole, the same maker I've worn since the beginning.

Glo used to wear Freed castles.

67

"You think I could come over this week?" Kat asks. "See Glo? It's been a while."

It has. I have to sneak Kat in, usually when Mom falls asleep on the couch. She's weird about visitors. Even Kat, who Glo was friends with before I was.

"Yeah," I say. "She'd like that."

The record player clicks and the needle lifts.

I still have to darn the toe box for added grip, and sew on ribbons and elastic—and then do it all over again to the other. I stare at my hamburger feet, wishing they'd bleed more, maybe give up another toenail. If Glo's feet suffer, then mine will too. I'll skip the lamb's wool again tomorrow.

Kat pierces her shoe with the needle, drawing the thread through the satin again and again—*pop, swish . . . pop, swish.*

Lulled by her cadenced stitching, my body gives in. "I'm tired. I'll finish up tomorrow."

I crawl into my side of Kat's fancy canopy bed and bury myself under a cloud of covers. The sheets are softer than satin and smell like Mom's rosewater lotion.

"I'll finish these up for you."

For a sec, I'm so close to dreamland I imagine Kat is Mom.

I open my stinging eyes, too exhausted to thank her as she gets up to turn over the record. The 33 spins and the arm lowers. I drift off, my head awhirl with this new uneasiness around Kat, Glo's nose job, and Prince in 6A. The rhythm taps my temples, like a hypnotizing metronome, as the needle rides the grooves around "Lady Cab Driver."

Nikki

Kat and I hop off the bus on Hennepin, ready to pas-de-deux the crap out of Straight Jeffery and battle Stacy for the skinny mirror. I slept like a day-old cadaver and probably look like one. I've recycled my recycled outfit from the day before—leg warmers, teal satin shorts rolled over at my waist, with leo and tights underneath.

Glo's blood seems determined to come to class with me, two cycles in the washing machine having no effect. I hug myself.

"I'm starving," Kat whines, eyes fixed on Slice of New York. We're totally cool now, all the weirdness from yesterday gone the moment we rolled out of bed.

I wave her away. "Meet me at Teener's, you junkie."

"I made you a mixtape." She moves my headphones from around my neck to my ears.

"Really? When did you have time?" I lean in to hug her, but she's already darting across the street for her pepperoni hit—the only innocent fix that ever happens at SNY.

The place is full of prostitutes and pimps, but it really does have the best pizza, not to mention a wealth of sex-ed opportunities. Thanks to a wild-eyed oily dude wearing a trench coat and nothing else, I saw my first real penis at SNY. Total creep central, but I couldn't tear my eyes away from the shadows between his legs. He took up space in the hazy corner, leaning back in his chair so he could open his knees just enough to give Kat and me a peek at the goods. *So* wrinkly and sickly pink, it reminded me of how my feet look after an all-day rehearsal. No. Thank. You.

I press Play on my Walkman, hooked to my waist. Of course, Prince.

It's a lazy Monday, but no one bothered to tell Hennepin Ave this. I bump elbows with a group of college-looking guys who must be heading to Augie's. Word is, if you get to the club before noon, it's only ten bucks for a steak and a lap dance.

I cross, ignoring the red light like everyone else, except I'm strutting to "Let's Pretend We're Married." My legs take on a life of their own, rotating my body into a spin, and then I'm all fast feet like Prince, on and off the curb.

Happy hour must be happening down the block, Harleys lining the curb in front of Moby Dick's. I kick an empty carton of cigarettes from the gutter and slide over the hood of a parked car, sticking the landing on the sidewalk.

As always, the gritty tavern's front door is propped open, a relentless allure despite Geno's promise to slaughter me three times over if I step one precious foot inside his stomping grounds. He's said as much, his eyes shifting the way they do into scorching black rocks of coal. But I'm forever dying to see what's inside. I want to know what's a bigger deal to him than my perfect turnout.

Hot dust and little pieces of wadded paper skim across my tights and I slow to a sultry saunter, because that's what you do in satin shorts on Hennepin. I'm missing my rhinestone Docs like mad, but my feet are thanking me for my broken-in Keds with no shoelaces.

Teener's is where I'm supposed to be, to buy another piece of pigskin-colored spandex. But ballet class is a whole blissful hour away. I can breathe, Geno's grasp a little weaker outside the walls of MDC's nineteenth-century brownstone.

I pull off my headphones, passing a bus shelter with a poster of two marijuana joints forming an *X,* the words JUST SAY NO at the bottom. First Lady Nancy Reagan's going to have to put a little more effort into her no-drugs campaign for a place like Block E. The thick black middle finger scrawled across the glass is the third bird I've seen this week.

The greasy aroma wafting from McDonald's tortures my stomach, which has nothing in it but stale popcorn and black coffee. I lean against the sticky wall and let my imagination eat a Big Mac and fries, my gaze stalking the doorway of Moby's. I'm sure I look like I'm trolling for work, holding up the McDonald's wall with my lazy back. Some dude cruising the block in a flashy Caddy whistles. The maroon boat slow-rolls past.

Gag. Never, ever, dirtball. I wave him off, pass up Moby's, and don't stop until I reach Teener's.

It's a Minnesota summer outside and a steamy jungle inside Teener's Theatrical. For once, the place is quiet. I wipe my forehead and bushwhack through an overstock of fabric bolts. Past the tassels, wigs, masks, and fake teeth, the best theater store in the city always looks as though a glitter bomb just detonated. The place smells like the giant Barbie Doll makeup head I used to have. It's a ménage à trois of circus hoarder, vaudeville performer, and drag queen. Teener's is perfection.

My arms and legs gleam with sparkles by the time I reach the naked mannequin sporting her rooster head. The leotard section. *Ugh.* I push aside all the cool colors I'm not allowed to wear: purple, red, every shade of blue. I stop at the pink section. Wearing dusty rose at MDC is supposed to feel like some sort of top-level badge of honor. For me, it's the same tint as my barf after Kat and I experimented with the sloe gin from her dad's liquor stash.

I need one with good stretch, otherwise it's cleavage-central for me. Which means I'll buy a large and take in the sides. Bras are forbidden, as A-cup Stacy never fails to point out. Those of us who need a little extra support get around it by using surgical tape or, occasionally, some old tights. Cut off the legs, then make a hole in the crotch big enough for your head to slip through. Arms go where the legs used to be and ¡ahí está! Insta boob-masher.

I rifle through the rack, finding no size large. *Sigh.*

Craning my neck, I peek over a stack of top hats. The long front counter is littered with random face paints, stacks of feathered masks, and rolls of ribbons. No Oz.

"Ozias," I call.

An electric guitar riff blasts from the speakers, practically popping me out of my heels. Then, the drums.

Oz? Jamming to Van Halen?

He won't hear any complaints from me. I step out from behind the hats.

Tap shoes. Someone's tap-dancing to Van Halen's "I'm the One." I snake around a stand of gorilla suits and then the other way, navigating through a gauntlet of barrels filled with glitter. Fast feet shuffle and slap the tiled floor, challenging the bebop guitar.

A head bounces behind the bolts of chiffon—and it isn't Oz's. I sneak around the fabric, staying low.

Flower Boy. He spins a tight set of chaîné turns on the tips of his patent leather taps, sweat spraying from his Jheri-curled mullet. He slams into the wall, pushes himself off with a flamboyant shove, and then twirls toward my hiding place.

David Lee Roth is belting out, "Come on baby, show your love." But I shrink back.

Glo. Would. Die.

He springs into a run, sliding past me and snatching a cane and top hat on the way. Shorts hiked up, he moonwalks like Michael Jackson and then stops, grasps his hat, and tucks into a tight backflip. It's a kick-ass tap combo from there. Such a rush, from the top of my bun all the way down to my mangy toes.

Who is he? Flower Boy sure has the legs of a trained dancer, lean and muscled. His deep-russet-brown skin glistens as if he's coated it with nonstick cooking spray. He's smiling, a cute crinkle of concentration pinching between his brows. And the way he moves—like he doesn't give a damn about who's watching. And I'm having no problem staring at his pelvis as he pauses to gyrate.

I'm clutching my chest like an old lady in church pearls. Maybe it's the Van Halen. Maybe it's the glimmering hotness gyrating for my eyes only. Or maybe it's simply that Geno would never approve, but I want to throw down my dance bag and join in, though I haven't worn tap shoes since kindergarten.

I completely forget where I am and lean into a rickety over-stuffed shelf. The entirety of it crashes to the ground, leaving me surrounded by a moat of red plastic clown shoes.

The boy whirls around, meeting my guilty stare just as David Lee Roth starts the second chorus. He throws his cane aside and grabs my hand before I can ditch the place and my total embarrassment.

I'm suddenly against him, my breath where my feet used to be. He whips me into a spinout and my dance bag flies, taking my Walkman with it. Before I can recover, I'm whipping back around again. I slam into his chest and by the holy grace of God, it's the most ungraceful thing I've ever done and the best all at once.

His heart hammers like a snare drum against my palm, the faint scent of lavender masking my vision in purple.

Jesus, I'm touching his chest.

I swallow my gasp. He leads me to his side and begins tapping.

Flower Boy takes it easy at first, his dazzling eyes urging

74

me to imitate his steps. Jumping backward, he spanks his heels on the floor, then heel-toes to the rhythm. I giggle and shake my head like a total goody-goody, when really my body is on fire in places I never knew existed. He does the combo again, my head clearing enough to notice our sweaty hands are still connected.

"Come on!" His gaze sharpens like Kat's when she double-dog-dares me.

I let everything go, his hand, my hang-up about how much my boobs will bounce.

Roth jumps into his "Bop bada, shoobe doo wah."

I follow the boy as best I can. He adds a time step, the one combination I remember from my limited tap days. My heel slips. He catches me before I land on my butt, and I'm aware of nothing but his tight grip around my waist.

My feet must be in the clouds because I can't feel them anymore. But when I look down, there they are, failing miserably at mimicking his patent leathers. I have no clue what I'm doing. It's been forever since I wasn't the best in the room. But I don't care. My heart never beats like this at MDC. I'm dancing with a boy, and it isn't ballet—daring to do it right out in the open.

Too soon, Van Halen ends and we both double over, our faces dripping onto the scuffed floor. The sudden silence kills the mood, trapping me under the unforgiving glare of the fluorescent lights. I straighten up, rolling the waist of my shorts.

"Umm, I need to order a leotard," I pant. "Dusty rose . . .

size large." My face catches fire again when Flower Boy's eyes drop to my chest. "Uh, where's Oz?" I cross my arms.

"You're a decent tapper, for a bunhead."

I stiffen and stick my nose in the air like a proper bunhead. "Van Halen brings out the best in me."

"And she knows Van Halen." He smiles, and all the glitter in Teener's has competition.

Rivulets of perspiration trickle in my cleavage, which he's still checking out. I stroll to my dance bag. Sensing his gaze on my ass, I bend over, totally okay with how many Hail Marys Father Thomas will assign. And Geno. Grounded for one thousand eternities. That's what'll happen if he finds out I risked breaking an ankle flirt-tapping.

"This bun doesn't siphon brain cells," I say. "I like all kinds of music." I pick up my Walkman, which must be bombproof. Not a scratch on it. "And I only wear my hair like this because it's required. For ballet, I mean." God, I sound like such a snot.

He wipes his sweaty upper lip, gazing past my shoulder. Yup. He's over me. "Ballet, huh? Like yesterday?" He yanks on the neck of his T-shirt.

"Did you enjoy the circus?"

He holds my stare as I wind the cord for my headphones and dump them in my bag.

My gaze follows his graceful hands. "Do you do ballet too?"

"Nah, I—I don't have time for that." He flicks a stray rhinestone across the counter. "Oz is gone for the day," he says, fanning his face. "But I can write down what you want and pass it on."

I'm about to protest, and then he peels off his wet shirt.

Holy Mother Mary, Jesus, Joseph, and everyone else in church—Flower Boy is a work of art. I turn my back way too fast, trying like hell to forget the glint of his nipple ring.

By the way he chuckles, he finds this amusing. "Sorry. Dancers usually aren't so modest."

"What? No. I just have something in my eye." I pick at my twitching eyelid.

Where is Kat? I want to leave and die. But I need my stupid leo ordered. By the time I've stopped messing with my face, he's moved behind the counter and somewhat covered up with a red satin kimono.

"You work here?" I worm my way to the front.

"I'm crashing on the cot in the back, doing deliveries, and taking orders. So, yeah, I guess I am."

A cop car races past, fully lit with sirens blaring. This steals his gaze. He's far away, somewhere that compels him to rub the gloss from his lips with the back of his hand.

"Like the flowers yesterday?" I say, bringing him back around.

"Uh, yeah. Oz is getting a jump on all things *Nutcracker*," he answers. "And Mama Flower's tutu needs a revamp. Size large, you said?" He's looking at me again, eyes swirling like the cognac Geno used to drink, and I'm lost too.

He taps his pen. "The leotard? Or did you come here to spy on me?"

"Yes. I mean, yes to the large," I clarify, hunching my shoulders. "And . . ." I point to the mess I made. "I'll take a pair of those clown shoes." Look at me, being all flirty. Kat would be proud.

He grins and it's impossible not to smile back. Like me, he's wearing purple eye shadow, and a thin streak of black eyeliner on his bottom lid—and he has an accent.

"¿Cómo te llamas?" I find the nerve to ask, noticing the name "Nikki" drawn in sweeping cursive on the back of his hand.

Flower Boy's curious stare sends my heart into a gallop. It feels so strange speaking Spanish outside the house. It's been forever since I looked at the flash cards Abuela made me. I'm sure my accent sounds totally diluted.

"Nikki," he answers, but doesn't ask mine.

I try not to care, or notice Nikki's smooth chest peeking from his kimono, but there's, like, seriously an embroidered dragon pointing its tongue right at his nipple ring.

"Okay, Nikki." I rub the Prince button pinned to the strap of my bag. "Uh . . . can you just make sure Oz gets the order—dusty rose. I need that leotard like yesterday. I have apprenticeship auditions this Saturday."

He fiddles with his hoop earring, fingernails painted with red glitter. "You're wearing one. Looks dusty enough to me."

I can't tell if he's trying to be cute or annoying. "I take class six days a week. This'll be pretty gamy by Saturday. Write it down and give it to Ozias when he gets back. Por favor."

Nikki purses his lips and scribbles something on a piece of crumpled paper. "Well, nobody likes a gamy 'tard."

"Like I said—"

"I got it. Apprentice-whatever on Friday. Don't pop your hairpins over it." He seems satisfied with himself, grinning and all.

"Apprenticeship auditions. On *Saturday.* They only choose four dancers, two male and two female, and those four usually move on to a paid position with the company. So, you see, it's important." I say it with such conviction I freak myself out. Saturday *is* important, and the finality of where it could lead is real for the first time. If I'm chosen, I'm one step closer to being locked in as a professional ballet dancer. Teener's suddenly feels ten degrees hotter and a whole lot smaller.

Nikki's sweet lavender is gone and all I smell is myself. It's not good. "Umm, you can just charge it to Eugenio Dominguez."

He stops writing. "Whose account?"

"My father. Geno Dominguez. You were there. The tyrant with the teacup?"

By the way Nikki remains frozen, I know I've screwed up somehow.

"Great. You know Geno." I clutch my bag. "Just . . . don't mention what we did?"

"Nervous much? It's not like we did the nasty. We just tapped." Nikki's staring at me as if my eyes are more than a pair of brown irises and two ordinary pupils.

"You're gonna tell him, aren't you?"

"Relax. I don't know your pops. Your secret's safe with me." He smooths out the paper, folds it, and then tucks it into the kimono's pocket.

I hike up my bag. If Nikki's full of crap, I'll find out soon enough. "I'll be back in a couple of days, then."

"I'll have your clown shoes bagged and ready." Nikki clips a twinkling rhinestone barrette above his ear. It'll take me all day to get over how cute it looks.

"Is there a number I should call? To check on my order, I mean."

Holy hell, did I just ask Nikki for his number?

He looks at me like he's wondering the same. Then, with the faintest smile, he beckons me closer with a red glittery fingernail.

My heart won't settle. I shake my head. "You know what? Never mind. Teener's is in the phone book, so . . ." But I'm already leaning over the counter, sweating bullets like I'm tapping again.

Nikki's warm fingers graze my shoulder and I can't do anything but breathe the air between us. He picks up a purple marker, pressing the tip against my collarbone. Now I can't breathe at all, because he's drawing something on my skin.

I back away and look down. It's a teardrop. No, a flowery paisley.

"You're right," he says, capping the marker. "Teener's is in the phone book."

I turn to leave and then spin back again. "Umm, thanks for the dance."

My head is all tangled up in how I'm supposed to feel. Nikki doesn't have time for ballet, and I certainly don't have time to wonder what just happened between me and this kimono-wearing foxy boy in matching makeup. Still, I want to see him again, as much as I need to know what kind of eyeliner pencil he uses.

Nikki presents his hand like I should kiss it. "It was my pleasure . . . ?"

"Rosa," I say, leaving his flared fingers hanging as I scurry away with my tongue tied.

If I'm entertaining Nikki, I don't dare look back to confirm.

"Mucho gusto, Rosa Dominguez," he catcalls after me like a pack of hyenas.

My cheeks flame. Kat breezes in, and I shove her right back out. I'm not prepared to explain something I can't. But she misses nothing, craning her neck over the top of my head.

"Oooh! Flower Boy works here?" she gushes.

"Umm, his name is Nikki. He's crashing on the cot in the back." I avoid her probing eyes as we make our way to MDC.

"You're all red and sweaty." She stops me. "And what's that by your neck? Did darling Nikki bring you to the back and show you around his *cot*?"

I punch her arm. "God, no . . . but, he dances."

"Ballet?"

"No. Tapper." I skim my fingers over the paisley.

No doubt, Nikki is a killer dancer. Only instead of pink tights and Tchaikovsky, he's down with frayed jean shorts, Van Halen, and sparkly eye shadow.

My insides tumble as Kat and I negotiate the crowded sidewalk. I replay the tap dance—the part where I moved the way I wanted. The part where I got a purple tattoo, and for three minutes of "I'm the One," MDC ceased to exist and there was only Nikki.

I Could Never
Take the Place . . .

Mirrors don't lie, the floor-to-ceilings in studio 5B reflecting the ugly truth. I smash down my frizzy hair, then rub away my smudged mascara. I'm horrified I danced with Nikki looking like a total hag. Then again, what do I know? Maybe he's into the *Night of the Living Dead* look. My heart surges when I think about his fingers wrapped around mine. I've never danced with a boy. Not like a regular girl at prom or something. My partners have all been in the studio or onstage, and assigned to me by Geno. How freak-show depressing.

My calves are tight from tapping. I fold over, nose to thighs, seeing nothing but Nikki's glistening dark skin stretched over an intricate map of hard muscles.

"Five minutes, dancers!" Geno barks as he marks out a combination in the corner.

I roll up. I haven't seen him since he banished me from the Prince concert. The floor has been swept clean of any evidence of the shattered teacup. And Geno appears to have moved on with a clear conscience, whispering through positions under his breath like nothing's happened.

He's wearing the same clothes as yesterday, which stirs up

the uneasy in my stomach. I scan him for other signs—besides day-old clothes, a reddened nose, the giveaways that he's been drinking again. Seeing none, I roll my shoulders a few times to relax.

Geno brushes his foot across the floor, toes pointed like a deadly missile. I want to look away, pretend I'm not charmed by his grace when everything else about him has such a sharp bite. It's impossible to believe he was once a young dancer with dreams like me—except during these moments, when his weathered arms float through the hot, thick air like ethereal wings.

He catches me staring. "Four minutes!"

I jump, and wipe my forehead for the hundredth time, already wasted from the humidity. The boys from our level, and the company men farmed out for partnering, guzzle water and mess around. Straight Jeffery thrusts his arms and rolls his hips, making fun of the moves from the new John Travolta film, *Staying Alive.* Kat thought the movie was totally terrible. But I fucking loved it. The clunky dance scenes left so much to work with. I look away before I do something like sashay over and fix the hell out of the choreography. I find my corner along with the rest of the girls and get to the serious business of putting on my pointes.

Men have it so damn easy.

Kat punches me in the arm, and I snap out of the stink eye I'm giving the opposite sex. "They have to do all the lifting, and I ate a gigantic lunch." She flashes a clownish grin. "How about this? I'll partner with Eddy. Now that's paybacks."

It is. Eddy's an elf compared to Kat. She sits and opens her bag. Tape, ointment, foot powder, Band-Aids, lamb's wool, extra socks and tights—Kat's prepared for the ballet apocalypse. She tapes her toes individually and then surrounds them with pillows of lamb's wool. Then she cuts off the toe sections from a pair of thin socks, and those go over the wool. Lastly, she stretches the feet of her tights back on top.

I open my bag, a few cracker crumbs sprinkling the bottom and that's about it. My pointes go on—barefoot.

"Give." Kat yanks my right foot toward her. "I saw that blister." She's already undoing my ribbons.

"Leave it," I say, but my pointe is off and she is coming at me with a cotton ball of alcohol and a needle.

"Just . . . hold still."

I do as she says because there's no use arguing. And in a sick way, I know she lives for this shit.

She wipes down the needle and my fluid-filled blister with the alcohol. It only stings a little, and not at all when she pops the thing. She gently taps down the deflated skin on top of my big toe, then stretches a piece of dry bandage over it before covering it with tape.

"Thanks. But you didn't have to." I get back into my shoe.

She pulls me from the floor, her pity eyes back. "Yeah, I did."

I alternate smashing the heel of one foot into the toe box of the other. "Thanks for finishing my ribbons," I say. "They're perfect. Unlike this annoying piece of tissue paper." I adjust the wrap skirt we're required to wear for partnering.

Geno prances to the center, zeroing in on my Nikki tattoo. Or maybe it's my spattered leotard, or chiffon skirt bunching in all the wrong places. Kat ties hers, then swivels the waist of mine until it's right. She descends upon Eddy, and I retreat to the rosin box to coat the bottoms of my shoes.

Geno snaps his fingers and points at the floor in front of him. "Rosa. Ven acá."

Shit. He's breaking out the Spanish. I do the opposite of what he commands and plant myself where I am, covering Nikki's paisley tattoo with my hand.

Maybe he smells the tap dancing on me? Or worse, Mom called him about Glo's bloody nose.

My head takes on heat as if I'm onstage beneath a searing follow spot. Stretching my leg over the barre, I prepare for another ridiculous challenge as punishment. I mean, what more can he possibly do—

"Rosa, ¡ahora! Al frente y al centro." Geno's words are sharp and thunderous—the fire fueling the looming fight.

My foot hits the floor with a thunk. I've heard normal families speaking Spanish to each other at the bus stop. Talking about regular stuff like what's for dinner, all out in the open in front of God and everyone. But we aren't those people. Mom must've told him.

My abs tense when he jabs his finger at me. "You and Jeffery. Center. Everyone else, find someone to love and trust for an hour."

Jeffery and I have neither between us. But by the screwy

look he's giving my upper torso, I trust his hands won't have a problem loving all over me for the next sixty minutes.

Jeffery saunters to my side. I mean, he does look like he could be in the movies. I'm thinking *The Outsiders*. Classic Matt Dillon greaser look, complete with dimpled cheeks. But when I look at Jeffery, all I feel is how much I wish Nikki's glittery hands were the ones touching my waist.

Stacy struts past with Angelo, her second choice. Like Jeffery, he's a total fox with a hot bod, although a lot less annoying. And he's in the company. A real paid dancer since last year. But you'd have to be dead to miss Stacy's crush on Jeffery. Which is why I don't squirm away when he suction-cups his hand on the small of my back. She turns all shades of green, which gives me radical satisfaction.

Geno's clap calls us to attention. "Today we'll begin with a few simple lifts. Arabesque press, into a fish. You've all done it a thousand times. Should be easy . . ." He glances at the Kat-Eddy pairing. "For most of you."

Eddy squirms like he has to pee.

"I will demonstrate exactly what I'd like to see." Geno comes to me, and I catch myself shrinking away in the mirror.

He holds out his hand, eyeing my tights rolled up around my calves. No doubt I'll hear about that later.

"Rosa"—he flutters his fingers, his voice soft and calm— "ven acá por favor."

I think I clutch Jeffery's arm. I'm not sure because everything's a blur. There must be something in the air besides misty sweat. Geno is asking me to partner with him, and with a *por favor*?

My stomach twists with tiny tornadoes, but the rest of me won't move. The last time Geno and I held hands he was calling me things like his flor pequeña. Doesn't he know? His little flower wilted a long time ago.

The entire class hushes. Even Kat's silent for once. Stacy crosses her arms, tapping her elbow against one of the twins, who's gawking at me like everyone else.

My focus is a mess, but it's clear I have to do something.

Tension trickles off my shoulders when I look at Geno waiting so patiently. How quickly I forget I'm supposed to be mad at him.

I leave Jeffery's side and place my hand in Geno's. We've evened out since I was a kid, his palm far from swallowing mine like it used to. My pointes tap softly across the wood floor as he leads me downstage like a cherished pas-de-deux partner, past a photo of Mom and the rest of the pictures—a gallery of Geno's eye for perfection. All of the shots are his, from when he used to do photography on the side. Until he hocked his camera to pay for more pointes for me. Glo's arabesque silhouette in the corner was the last photo he took with his fancy Nikon.

I face the front, not caring which mirror space is mine because the couple reflected is totally surreal. My mind insists this is just another version of the teacup test. But there's no red lighter, no ridicule or slap to my bloated stomach. Geno's touch doesn't feel at all like punishment. I freeze in the sun-beam.

He nods, his intense stare demanding I focus. Jesus, he looks just like Glo.

I nod back, calming my shakes.

"The dancer will start with an arabesque, finding her balance." His fingertips keep me steady and I go for it—piqué to arabesque, lifting my leg behind me. I hold the arabesque as if my everything depends on it. His eyes soften, catching my gaze in the mirror.

Maybe he's totally lost it and thinks I'm Glo? And then he says, "Muy bien, Rosa."

Sweat drips from my temples. *Muy bien, Rosa,* I say to myself.

"Gentlemen, it's important to use your legs when you lift. Ladies, hold your centers with power in your backs."

Geno lets me go, and I stay in my arabesque. He steps behind me, one hand at my waist, the other beneath my inner thigh. He prepares with a plié, and I'm airborne, suspended over his head, my arms extended toward the sixth floor. For once, reaching for the sky isn't about Prince. I . . . I can't breathe.

"Ladies, stay strong," he says. "Keep your position. Don't overextend. Rosa is pushing her leg down against my hand as I lift. The couple should meet each other with equal strength."

Geno's strength doesn't falter, not one quiver beneath my weight as he walks in a diagonal. I dare to believe he'll never let me fall. Everyone else in the room fades, little pops of pink among the boys' black and white. It's just the two of us in the mirror. The studio isn't haunted by Mom's impossible grace, or Glo's lost legacy.

Sunlight shines through the tall windows, casting an aura behind us that warms my back. I'm five again, his flor pequeña, tossed into the air and spared the ground at the very last possible moment.

"Deep breath, Rosa," he says, bringing me back to the silent studio.

I drop from his arms, only for a second, but my heart surges from the roller-coaster ride. He catches me, swaying my arched body into a graceful fish dive, my nose inches from the scuffed floor. My father—my anchor.

He swings me onto my arabesque again.

I think I manage to turn out of it and finish pretty. I'm not totally sure, because part of me is still flying.

"Just like that." Geno pats my back. "Do it just like that, Gloria."

I'm an instant ghost, pale all the way to my fingertips. Geno leaves me scattered and dumbstruck at Jeffery's side, without a second, or even a first, look. I shrink into myself as if it'll make me disappear.

Kat leans in my direction as if she wants to hug me. I wave her off.

"Let's go." Geno claps out an eight-count and everyone scrambles for placement.

I don't move until Jeffery pokes my side. I piqué to my

arabesque again, somehow sticking it even better than before. Jeffery's hands snake around my middle and inner thigh, and up I go. I barely think about what I'm doing, eyes tracking Geno like a raptor.

I hit the lift perfectly. But no one, not my handsy partner and certainly not Geno, pays any attention. Eddy's too busy crumpling beneath Kat's elegant giraffeness.

Her reflection winks at me as I plunge into a fish dive.

Geno's back, stomping to my side. "Energy all the way to the end, Rosa. Your hand looks like a dead fish."

I splay my fingers. Christ help me, I want to do the lift with Geno again. Jeffery releases me and I wrap my arms around my waist, the hug I refused from Kat. I'm ashamed to admit I want to feel it again—my father's heart filled with warmth. And Gloria, reflected in his eyes.

Willing and Unable

The rest of partnering class is as hazy as my head, a confusing combination of Nikki's chest in a kimono and flying with Geno. And Prince is back on the brain, taunting me with a deep thundering bass coming from above.

"You can thank Rosa for your lunch," Geno says at the end of the hour. "Pizza is in the break room, as promised."

Thank me? For almost costing them a million extra jumps? Doubtful.

Dancers file out, the twins flashing me the jealous shark-eye. Kat says everyone thinks I'm just going through the motions, but competition never takes a day off at MDC and I struggle to keep my head high from the exhaustion of it. Geno using me to demonstrate the lift obviously hit a nerve. He called me Gloria, the Dominguez everyone loved.

"Tomorrow, ladies in here. Gentlemen across the hall." Geno breezes from the studio. Places to be, people to see, and none of it includes me.

And yeah, I'm stoked to avoid another of his lectures about focus. Or my favorite, fifteen extra minutes of meticulous one-on-one corrections en pointe while Kat draws penises in the rosin box. Geno left without reminding me how he came to this country, worked his way to the top, and now I'm throwing it all away because of my dead-fish hands. I'm . . . cool.

I collapse onto the closest window seat, pulling my legs in tight.

Jeffery smiles at me, his peachy skin and dark feathery hair dewy from our hard work. Half of the sweat on me is his.

"Thanks for the memories, girl." He plops next to me and holds up the Polaroid camera he's never without, snapping a photo of the two of us.

Stacy seizes her pointes, using them to smack his shoulder. "God, you perv. Get off her."

I elbow Jeffery away and untie my ribbons. "Wow, coming to my rescue, Stace?"

"Rosa doesn't need rescuing," Jeffery says. "She's tough enough on her own." He waves the photo a bunch of times, then hands it to me. "See?"

I stop undoing and snatch the picture. Jeffery is no Geno, but I'll give him props for capturing the moment. I look like I need a week's worth of sleep.

He shoulders his bag, heading for the door. "You looked beautiful up there."

Stacy's face falls. I almost switch it up and say something halfway nice to her.

"With your dad, I mean," Jeffery adds.

My dad. Kat's the only one who refers to Geno as my dad. When Jeffery leaves it at that, I go back to unwrapping my ribbons. He's only turning on the charm to get into my tights.

Stacy shuffles out behind him.

Kat gulps her water, checking the neon watch she rarely wears. "Looks like you have a fan, Prima Rosa. He's cute."

I shrug. Naked lips, naked eyes—wrong guy.

Kat rolls her tights from her feet and slips into a pair of white Dr. Scholl's. "Okay, now that everyone's gone, who invaded your dad's body?"

I lean against the hot window. "Oh, it's still Geno in those boots."

"Umm, the Master only yelled at you once. Not one single *Rosa, quit snapping your head like this is a music video.* Or, I love this one: *You're off the rails, Rosa! Get back on those tracks!*"

She's right. Fish hands gone, and Geno left me alone. My stomach unsettles, sourness bubbling up the back of my throat. I squeeze the barre next to me. It feels different already, rough in places it shouldn't be. What if I'm not worth the effort anymore? What if after the Glo fog cleared, Geno decided to give up on me? It's what I've hoped for, isn't it? But what are we to each other if I'm no longer his muse?

I stare at my feet, still in pointes. The silence in the studio is my answer. I'm waiting for him to come back. How twisted is that?

"He called me Gloria."

Kat shuffles her feet. "Yeah . . . maybe he was just having a moment."

A moment. What does that even mean?

Kat looks at the clock, her watch, then stuffs my towel in

my bag. "Let's motor. All the good spots will be taken in the dressing room."

"Chill. Since when have we cared about that?" Kat knows I almost never change in the dressing room, so she's freaking me out. I come and go in my leo and tights. Way better than dealing with everyone staring at my huge breasts like I'm a pole dancer at Augie's.

She grabs my foot, giving me zero time to wallow or tell her my raw big toe is stuck to the inside. She rips off my shoe like a Band-Aid.

"Jesus! I've got the other, thank you very much."

Kat Nightingale appears to have left her bedside manner at home, because she's squawking on and on about pizza while she plucks bobby pins from my bun. "Those piranhas have probably devoured all the pepperoni already."

My hair unravels onto my shoulders, then spills down my back. I cringe when I pull on my Keds. My toes are twice as pulverized as yesterday. Mission accomplished.

Kat fluffs my damp curls until I swat her away. She goes to the door and does a little fidgety dance. "Oh my God, Rosa. You're a snail today."

"Geez! It's official. You're an addict." I gather up my pointes, sling my bag over my shoulder, and follow Kat's dust as she makes ridiculous time down the hall. "You just ate pizza before class," I holler after her.

Classes are over for the day, the fifth floor settling into hibernation as the last of the students pile inside the elevator.

Kat stops as the door dings. "We'll take the next one."

She checks her damned watch for the millionth time, and the doors close.

My feelers are standing at attention now. Something's up. And it has nothing to do with getting to the dressing room or pepperoni first.

I inch toward the stairs. "Uh, I'm not taking that . . . that evil piece of steel anywhere."

"Oh yes you are." The wooden soles of Kat's Dr. Scholl's scuff along the old, gross carpet as she slinks in my direction.

"Umm, *no,* I'm not."

The second elevator chimes.

"Right on time." She punches the Down button, then snatches my arm before I can run.

"Right on time for what?" My heart's going nuts. "Seriously, Kat!" I struggle to squirm free, but her bony fingers are like wicked crab claws around my wrist.

"*Relax.* You'll have company." Her eyes bug and then shift to a sultry bedroom flutter. "And it won't be me."

I squint. "What's wrong with your eyes?"

She has me in front of the elevator in one yank.

Like a total dork, I gape at the doors as they part.

Everything disappears, my crazy best friend, the dingy hallway, the bitter stench of my underarms—everything but the stunning person inside the elevator.

Plan Indiana Jones is a go.

Right.

Now.

Prince.

He is smack in front of me, leaning against the back of the elevator. A bouquet of sweet-and-sour sweat lingering with . . . something else.

The taste of cedar swirls inside my gaping mouth.

Kat gasps, her fingernails stabbing my shivering skin. She releases my arm, probably getting a head start on the run for her life, whereas the floor beneath my feet has morphed to superglue. I just stand there, alone, staring at Prince—and he at me. Me, a drooling statue wrapped in ratty tights, a catawampus skirt, and a blood-stained leotard.

I've only seen him from afar, and now he's so close—touching distance. I want to memorize every glossy hair on his head, and the tiny patch of curly ones between his pecs too. My stormy brain takes a snapshot. He's not much taller than me, if at all, but his presence consumes the entire space: lime-green pants with white buttons down the sides and diagonal at the fly. Heels. No shirt . . . again, *no shirt,* and a crucifix hanging mid glistening chest.

I grasp the cross around my neck and Prince nods. *Nods. At me.*

I can't . . . do . . . anything.

My lips are on fire, while my breath is frozen behind my ribs. Just three small steps and I'll be inside, face to face with the only man who's given me the good kind of dream.

"Going down, honey?" his bodyguard, Big Chick, grumbles. The huge scruffy guy in rainbow suspenders has kicked me off the sixth floor so many times. Now I'm being invited inside—a tiny elevator—with Prince.

Move, Rosa! Do something—say something! But all I can think about is breaking into a damn time step. My eyes start watering. *Oh God, don't cry. Don't. Cry.*

I become all twitchy, scrambling to cover the embarrassing Prince button pinned to my bag, forgetting there are, like, ten of them.

His dark eyes drop to my chest. And then . . .

A tinkle of warm pee trickles between my legs.

Mother of all that is holy in the universe, have I just peed in front of Prince?

I swing my bag around like a shield, catching my skirt and yanking the hem to my waist. One of my pointe shoes flies into the elevator, landing at Prince's feet.

Forget not breathing. I'm panting so hard I might swallow my tongue whole.

Big Chick grins.

Prince . . . does not. And he isn't staring at my chest anymore, though I quickly realize he never really was. Nikki's purple paisley. I'm such an idiot.

Chick pushes a button.

My abandoned shoe takes a cue from me and plays dead against the toes of Prince's white patent leather heels.

All I have to do is step inside and grab it. My right foot thinks about it, but my left foot and wet leotard want nothing to do with it.

"Maybe next time," Chick says.

The elevator dings again.

I open my mouth to say something that will definitely

sound stupid. And then Prince picks up my sweaty, scabby shoe and holds it out to me, his dewy dark curls falling into his eyes.

God curse me, I don't take it.

I do the only thing my dead brain will allow besides the time step. I make the sign of the cross as the doors move. For a split second of heaven, the Purple One's eyes pierce mine.

The doors seal together. My bag drops from my shoulder. My idol, a gigantic bearded bodyguard, and my satin Freed leave me starstruck in wet tights.

Groove Off

Kat's waiting on the corner when I slither outside like a dehydrated snake. She's sure changed in a hurry, totally looking like she's jetting off to play a round of golf. She's in a pair of khaki shorts and a white Izod polo, an outfit that screams *My mom shops for me at the City Center.*

"You okay?" She rushes me. "You look . . ." She eyes my ripped skirt, grasping her chest. "Did something bad happen?"

A rusty car honks as it rounds the corner. We both flip it off.

I can't feel my legs, my livid feet either. I adjust the dance sweater I tied around my waist, for once wishing I could skip talking to my best friend. "Nothing happened," I say.

Kat bounces on her tiptoes. "Plan Indy didn't pay off? *Man.* I stalked Prince's schedule for two weeks. Did you at least check out his killer pecs? I think I died for a second!"

I did. The pecs and the dying part.

But I don't answer, any excuse for my lameness smothered by catastrophic embarrassment and the bucket of wuss that's been dumped over me.

"Please say you didn't barf." Kat's trying not to smile, but I see the teasing in her eyes.

"*No.* I didn't puke." Never will I admit I'd peed instead. I lean into her. She smells like pepperoni. "I need pizza—extra large to drown in grease what pride I have left." My tights are already wet anyway.

She rubs her cheek like she does when she's nervous about an audition. "Can't. I, uh . . . promised my dad I'd meet him. I'm busing it to the hospital."

"To do what?"

"An early dinner thing."

"Where? You look like you're about to park cars at the country club." Now I'm being mean. But Kat's acting weird again.

"Harsh." She flips up her collar and smooths the braid down her back.

"I'm sorry. You look awesome. It's just . . . you're all jumpy. Is this a serious dinner?"

"Dr. Johansen's always serious. You know that. But, no. Just a regular old foodfest."

I collapse against a battered mailbox. "Okay. I'll go to SNY solo." I pick at a peeling sticker on the box, wishing Glo could come with me. She'd been a sausage-and-mushroom girl. She would've gotten in that elevator.

A police car pulls over and I back away from the mailbox like I'm doing something wrong. And then, all at once, I'm terrified Geno has.

The officer inside leans over the passenger seat. "Hey. You girls dance here?"

Kat peers inside the open window while I shrink behind her. All I can think about is where'd Geno rush off to.

"Yeah, we dance here," Kat says.

The officer scratches his blond hair. "Have you seen Stacy—Stacy McGee?" His brow does the worry crinkle.

Kat and I exchange looks and every pore in my skin takes a breath.

"Umm, not since class ended," I say, conjuring up all sorts of righteous reasons there's a cop on the hunt for Miss Perfect McGee.

The doors to MDC fly open and Stacy scuttles out. "*Dad.* I've been waiting around back, *like always.*"

Stacy's face is so red. She hurries to the car like we're not there, a weird hitch in her step. She's still in her plastic pants, which is strange too. Lately she's been changing into cute sundresses after class. Probably for Jeffery.

Kat crosses her arms. "Your dad is—"

"Not Asian like me," she blurts. "Yes. I know. I'm adopted."

"Wig out much?" I open the back door for her, glancing at the cagelike partition. "I'm pretty sure Kat was gonna say *a cop.*"

It's totally a ballet-school thing, not having a clue what anyone's life is like away from the studio—Kat and me being the exception. For the rest, when the music stops and the shoes come off, it's scatter city. Cars pull over, buses scoop us up, and we go back to whatever hours we have left outside the air we breathe at MDC.

Stacy smirks and closes the rear door. And it's a good thing too, before I dwell on Geno cuffed and stuffed into a worn backseat like Officer McGee's.

Stacy's face hints at the start of a good cry, and the twinge of sorry I feel for her comes out of nowhere.

"Hey. You okay?" I ask, though she's been nothing but a pile of garbage to me.

"Stop," she snaps.

"Stop what?"

"Stop pretending to be nice. I know you don't mean it."

"I don't?"

"No one does." She gets in the front seat and yanks the door shut.

Maybe Jeffery gave her the ol' brush-off.

"Did you see the list?" Stacy says, adjusting her side-pony. "It's posted outside the Master's office."

Kat shrugs.

"What list?" I ask. I can tell she's dying to spill.

"Congratulations, Kat. You're one of us. You know, for the benefit at First Ave?"

Kat gives me a quick glance, squishing her lips together.

Stacy leans out the window while her dad answers his radio. "So, I guess on the minuscule chance I don't get the apprenticeship, I'm still locked in to dance for Prince. Jeffery too. Oh, and there's another piece that night. Odette's solo. Can you guess who's been cast?"

I grip the edge of her door, which backs her off. "You're performing Odette's solo? *You?*"

Kat clutches my arm before I liquefy into a puddle on the crushed cigarette butts and flattened chewing gum lining the sidewalk. Stacy knows damn well Odette's role at MDC is synonymous with my mother. The company hasn't performed *Swan Lake* since she was their principal. I'll never be worthy of the part. But Stacy, horning in on my legacy? I can just imagine the technically perfect robotic swan she'll be.

Stacy stretches her birdlike neck. "The company wants to showcase our classical side with a student solo." Her gaze flicks to her dad, who's scribbling on a clipboard, and then to my warped outfit. "You think you're special because the Master used you to demonstrate the lift? Well, your turnout fails you after the first hour and your jumps are heavy. Something you might want to correct before the apprenticeship auditions. Only two girls. That's not great odds for an open audition. I mean, the next Natalia Marakova could show up."

I hunch my shoulders like I'm in the middle of a spring downpour. Stacy's face falls for a sec, like maybe she feels sorry, especially when Officer Dad shakes his finger, scolding her.

An ambulance races past. Kat steps off the curb to watch it run the red light down the block, the siren's echo trailing behind.

The police radio squelches and now we're all distracted. Something about a fight, and someone hurt at the Gay 90's, a club down the street that always has cop action.

Stacy flips a toggle on the dash that swirls the red-and-blue lights on top of the car. All she's missing is a badge. "Ladies."

She flicks her eyes toward me and then rolls up her window. The car peels away, its siren piercing the haze.

I plug my ears. This day is becoming a top-three worst.

Hyperventilation and I don't mix, always a prelude to the chest crushing. I double over, hands to knees, pretending to breathe through a straw like my doctor said to do. It never works.

Kat usually rubs my back, but she's standing in the parking lane, gawking at the Gay 90's commotion happening the next block down. There are, like, at least five cop cars there now, people in the streets yelling. It's a mess.

"The lights," she gushes. "The sirens. It's such a rush, huh? My heart is totally pounding."

"I don't think anyone's emergency is a rush," I huff.

She hops onto the sidewalk. "Sorry. That sounded awful, didn't it?" She rests her hand on my back. "Don't listen to Stacy. Your turnout never fails. And your father probably did the lift with you to push you to take this audition seriously. That's all. No one thought you were getting special treatment or anything."

Something in my gut snaps and I bolt upright. "So, it was all about the audition? Why can't it be that he wanted to dance with me?"

We both know that's an improbable reason. He was dancing with Glo. I don't even know why I'm jumping Kat's shit right now. But I can't stop myself. I'm so angry. About Stacy performing Odette, and Prince. But most of all, for letting myself believe that I'll ever be more to Geno than a replacement for Gloria. Christ, Stacy was right. Geno being nice . . . meant nothing.

Kat's pacing like she's winding up for something big.

"What?" I yell.

Her bag falls from her shoulder. "Geez, keep it down."

"Why? We're on fucking Hennepin Avenue!" I shout over the hustle and flow of the seedy street.

She presses her hands together. "I was only saying, you know Geno. And with the apprenticeship coming up—"

"*God*, the apprenticeship. I don't even want the damned apprenticeship," I snap.

"Then chill with a pill and tell your dad. Don't take it out on me. Where's the girl who sneaks up to 6A? Because that girl would've—"

"What—would've gotten in that elevator? This coming from someone who's afraid to drive her own car."

Kat rifles through her bag, producing her bus pass. "*Ugh.* I'm just—"

"Sick of it? Sick of *me*?" I'm totally spewing dumb shit now. I don't really believe any of it, but when I look at my best friend in her preppy beige outfit, she feels far away again. It's like all the anxiety I've had over her leaving for med school is suddenly bearing down on this grimy corner. "Say it. You're ready to ditch me and all my problems."

"Oh, Rosa, my only hope is that you do what you want— *whatever* that may be. Why are we even fighting about this?" She jabs her bus pass down the block toward Moby's. "You know your dad does what he wants. It's his choice to be an asshole. It's his choice to drink. You act like everyone is against you when, really, you sabotage yourself. All. The. Time. You did it with the elevator. And you're doing it now."

I ball my fists, my yarny hair fuzzing my periphery. "Am I?"

"And guess what, you're not the only one with problems."

"I know that!"

"Do you? So, you can ask Stacy if she's okay, but not me? What was that about?" Kat shouts back.

"You have problems? What part of having Martina cook and clean for you for pennies is throwing you off?"

Ah, shit. I went there. I stare at my Keds while Kat pushes a bottle cap around with her toe.

A crumpled Big Mac wrapper blows into the gutter and tumbles down the sewer grate. I sit on the sticky curb. We're both throwing words at each other, but Kat will never get it. How could she? Her future is wide open. The Johansens know nothing about things like eating government cheese, wearing bread bags on their feet under holey Moon Boots—cleaning up after drunk dads. For the first time in our friendship, I resent Kat for it. And it feels like the worst kind of terrible.

When I finally look at her, her face is all blotchy and on the verge of a cry. My vision blurs.

She hikes up her bag. "You, my friend, are being totally un-fair. And not listening to me at all." She backs away, her chin quivering. "And as much as I'd love to have a shouting match with you on *fucking Hennepin Avenue*, I have to go. When you're ready to stop doing whatever this is, maybe I'll call you."

"Are you going to dance in the benefit?" It just comes out. I'm being a major jerk. But a teensy part of me expects her to boycott dancing for Prince, because I can't participate.

"Well, are you?" I prod when she doesn't answer.

"Yeah. I guess I will . . . I want to, anyway."

"Don't," I say.

"Don't what?"

"Don't . . . don't call me later."

Kat's eyes spill over. My crap-bag attitude is new territory for us.

"If that's what you want." She scrapes her foot along the sidewalk, waiting for me to say something else—something nice.

When I don't . . .

"I'm late to meet my dad."

I grasp the mailbox. "Kat, wait."

She does pause, but she won't look at me.

"I'm . . . I'm sorry."

She stubs her toes against the box. "We all have major stuff, Rosa. Whether you believe it or not." She bolts across the street on the yellow and waits at the bus shelter.

Peeling myself from the curb, I cross the other way. Kat's bus slows to a stop. I almost follow her, then take easy street and let it go. Something's up with her. I've been feeling it for days. But I don't know how to be there for her, like she is for me. If her parkway life is shit, then I'm lost. I rub my elbow, wishing I understood. But that part of my brain is smothered by singed arm hair, cheap whiskey, and Tater Tot hot dish.

A grimy Greyhound bus rumbles past, dusting my face with hot exhaust. Pizza doesn't sound good anymore. I fan my tights with my skirt.

A squirrelly dealer eyes me from across the street and I let the sidewalk move beneath my feet. I'm not going anywhere in particular, which is why I fail to notice the amoeba of punk girls approaching. They swallow me up in their armpit stench and fishnets, a thrash pit of bony elbows and shoulders. I don't even push back when the one in the Ramones T-shirt shoves me—hard.

The tallest girl, in black-and-green witch tights, gives me the mother of all once-overs, her eyes coming to rest on my frizzy hair. "Nah," she says with a husky laugh, her shellacked mohawk quivering. "She's too bunk to bother."

The rest offer a foul review of my appearance, then follow the leader toward the 7th St. Entry, a smaller club inside the First Ave building, a line already forming for the Urban Guerrillas show.

Too bunk to bother . . . yeah.

I lean against the searing light pole, giving my heart a sec to settle. But there's barely a chance of that with all the sirens happening at the 90's. Now there are two ambulances and a news truck, which makes me wonder if Stacy's in the thick of it and hunkered down in her dad's cop car.

Blossoms of blood have seeped through the toes of my tennies. I kick them off and start walking, not caring how totally gross it is doing it barefoot on Hennepin. My hips ache, my knees hurt, and the bottoms of my soles are scorching from the hot pavement. But my thoughts won't lay off of the fight I just had with Kat.

"Trolling today?" A gruff voice interrupts my self-pity moment, and I clue in to the fact that I'm in front of Moby's. The bouncer gives my chest a lingering scan that makes me shudder, but I don't leave. Even when he fires up a cigarette and I jump from the flick of his lighter.

I peer through the doorway. Leering eyes stare back, like starving wolves in a dense forest. *Pac-Man* flashes and blips in the corner, Pink Floyd urging me to feel "Comfortably Numb."

"I'll buy you some fries to go with that shake, honey," shouts a biker wrapped in leather.

Original—but tempting. My appetite is back. Fries and a shake sounds like utopia.

The dingy wall behind the bar is decorated with off-the-wagon AA medallions. I scan the coins as if I'll know immediately if Geno's is among them. Word on the street is, if you hand over your medallion, the drinks are free at Moby's the rest of the night. And Geno's quivering hands suggest the temptation is endless. I'm sure Mom eyes those medallions on our windowsill as much as I do.

The bouncer offers his cig.

I look around, then take an amateur puff, blowing it off with my shivers. "When was the last time you saw him?" I ask.

He shrugs. "Girlie, if I kept track of every drunk—"

"When, Martin." He shouldn't be shocked I know his name. I stare down the guy who's made a career of tossing Geno out the back door.

"Been a while," he eventually says.

Coming from Martin, this could mean anything. A day. A week. But hopefully, at least six months.

Martin lights his own cigarette like I'm gonna hang with him. Geno will totally smell the smoke on me and I'll be balancing an entire place setting on my toes. But I draw in another long drag anyway because the burn deep in my lungs feels like, for once, I don't care what the hell anyone thinks.

The guy behind Martin is barely holding it together on a corner stool. He barks at the bartender for another, then teeters before toppling over and belly-flopping onto the hardwood—change, glasses, and a Twins baseball hat littering the ground.

A vinegary stench slaps me in the face, moist floorboards soaked with years of spilled drinks. My empty dance bag is suddenly so heavy.

I can't get rid of the cigarette fast enough, smashing it out in the coffee-can sandpit next to the door.

A slimy frown tugs on Martin's pockmarked cheeks.

A car honks and pulls over. I wave the john off.

It honks again, and this time Martin flips him off.

"Duty calls." He slides from his stool, glaring at the john with mealy bloodshot eyes before heading inside to scrape the drunk from the floor.

I wrap my arms around myself and pass beneath Moby's

sign, A WHALE OF A DRINK, heading nowhere until I'm in the grimy alleyway, staring at Geno's poop-brown Buick in the parking lot at the other end.

I don't think. If I do, I won't have the balls to fish around under the wheel well. Geno's drunk mind has lost his keys so many times, even when he's sober sometimes he keeps them with the car. Because really, who would steal this hunk of junk anyway?

I guess *I* would. As my hand brushes metal, I grab the keys and unlock the door.

G-Ma

There are cops everywhere, hauling ass down Hennepin Ave.
Or maybe it's always like this and I'm just paranoid because I'm
about to drive without a license. I mean, I have my permit . . .
expired permit, if we're talking technical.

I get in and fire up the Buick, my heart hammering like a
Van Halen drum solo. I've never stolen anything in my life.
Not even when Glo dared me to follow her lead and pocket
some strawberry Bonne Bell Lip Smackers at the dime store
when we were kids. So, I'm idling and thinking it through like
you do when you're a barefoot virgin criminal. If Geno sticks
to his usual Monday, I'm cool for another hour or so. And I
don't want to go home. Not after choking on my opportunity
to meet Prince—not after trashing my friendship with Kat.
Glo will be so disappointed in me.

The pleather steering wheel is searing from the hot sun. I
wrap my fingers around it, my hands firing up too. I'm in control. No bus driver, no begging Kat to take us for a ride—no
Geno. It's all me. The drums in my head are beating hard now,
the rest of me buzzing like I'm about to bust out a combo I've
made up in secret.

I shift to Drive.

The passenger door flies open and I scream, about tuck and roll out my side too.

Nikki tumbles in with a couple of shopping bags and slams the door. "Drive it like you stole it, bunhead."

Umm, I did. And why is Nikki in my car?

He looks over his shoulder, his face all sweaty and alert. "Go, girl!"

Raw toes clinging to the accelerator, I'm flooring it. And not sure why until something shatters against the trunk—a beer bottle, I think. A couple of guys chase the Buick, but they're no match for this boat because I jump the curb and run the red light like I'm in *The Blues Brothers.*

Nikki smacks the dash. "Yeasss, Rosa!"

"Are those guys chasing you?" My heart's thrashing as I take the first available turn. Not that I know where I'm headed at all. This girl hadn't thought through that part.

Nikki stuffs the bags at his feet, and I wonder if he went on a shopping spree without his wallet.

"Did you steal that stuff?" I tip my chin at the bags.

"Ah, I see. You go right to that."

"So, you're personally delivering my new leo, then?" I glance in my rearview and ease out my breath before I faint.

Nikki's checking himself like he's making sure he still has all his parts. "I didn't kipe anything." He rolls down his window.

"Then what?"

"Those dudes weren't down with my kickin' wardrobe, that's all."

"*That's all?* So, they chased you with a beer bottle?"

"Sometimes they chuck condiments too."

He wipes away a smudge of what looks like mustard from the hem of his satin shorts.

Jesus.

"God, Nikki. I'm so sor—"

"Don't," he utters, then pulls down the visor and messes with his hair in the mirror.

I think about putting my hand on his shoulder—*something.* But I don't, just like he asked.

"You remembered my name," I say.

"You made me write it down. Ro-sa Do-min-guez."

I grimace.

This day. Totally off the rails. I peer out the windshield, half expecting to see Paul Bunyan stomping down the street like Godzilla because I'm driving illegally, with tap-dancing Nikki riding shotgun looking like a hot Puerto Rican Olivia Newton John about to get physical in pink shorts, scrunchie rainbow leg warmers, and high-top Reeboks. Those bastards and their beer bottles can screw themselves.

I'm cruising the same block for the second time. So many one-ways and I'm not used to navigating the city in a car.

"Can I take you somewhere?" I ask.

He takes a sec to answer, then points straight ahead. "Hiawatha Avenue."

"Hiawatha Avenue it is." I settle in on the straightaway, leaving the skyline in my rearview.

No way can I keep myself from sneaking glances at Nikki.

His eyes are rainbowed, just like I love mine, his cheeks streaked with shimmery blush.

"Where were you coming from?" I ask.

He shifts around, then rubs some of his blush off with the shoulder of his tank top. "The 90's."

I straight-up look at him. "The 90's? The club? It was nuts down there just now. What happened?"

Nikki flicks his finger against the door handle. "Just another ordinary day."

"Serious?"

"Let's close it there. Cool?"

I nod and grip the wheel. "Cool," I say, though it's totally not.

The Buick has no air-conditioning, the car suddenly small and sweltering. Or maybe I feel this way because Nikki's sitting two feet away with sad eyes and smelling like a salty flower.

And . . . I'm all dumpy in my pee-pee tights. I pull my dance bag over my lap, leaving my bloody shoes all alone between Nikki and me.

I'm halfway down Hiawatha when Nikki points his finger out the window. "Uh . . . just drop me at the corner by the grain elevators up here."

"You're going to a grain elevator?"

"My g-ma lives across the tracks. It's easier to let me out here."

"Why? She lives on a street, right?"

He sinks into his seat when I drive the Buick through the bumpy crossing. I'm positive I'm leaving behind a few essential rusty bolts, but I keep going. I slow down when we're on the other side, a section of the city I've never seen before. The chewed-up street matches the peeling paint on the houses—rows of single-stories with tall, reedy brown grass. I roll past a dog food plant spewing out a stench so strong I taste the gamy meat.

I'm waiting for Nikki to tell me which house, but he's busy wiping off his lipstick and doing his best to get rid of his eye shadow too.

"The yellow one on the right," he says, gathering his bags, which, I now see, contain boxes of Pop-Tarts.

I pull over. This is . . . this is not that bad once you get past the dog food smell. It's obvious someone takes care of the house. Flowers line the pathway; the lawn is brown and spotty, but mowed.

"Cute house," I say.

Nikki pauses, looking at me like he's deciding if I'm lying or not. He shoots from the car to the only spot of sunshine on the block.

He opens the chain-link gate. "You coming?"

I pull on my shoes and scramble out of my seat, following him inside the gate.

The door opens before he knocks.

"Ahhh! Mi Nico." A tiny old woman in a flowery house-dress gathers Nikki into a huge hug.

"Hey, G." Nikki kisses her papery forehead and squeezes past. "This here is Rosa."

"Hi." I wave. Her clouded eyes squint as she shuffles close to my face.

"¡Qué belleza! Huh, Nico?"

Nikki doesn't answer, but I'm red-faced just the same.

"I got the Pop-Tarts you like," he calls from the kitchen. "The brown sugar ones."

"Those are my favorites too," I say, and that does it.

G-ma grins and hooks her arm round mine, like Abuela used to do. My legs go all mushy. G-ma even smells like Abuela, rose lotion mixed with Bengay. And she's wearing her hair the same too, short tight curls pinned back above her ears.

Her house is spotless, though it smells of cigarette smoke. There's an empty ashtray on a brass stand next to a comfy chair in the living room. The couch and ottoman are covered in what look like huge shower caps. And there's this green plastic runner thingy over the carpet in the hallway.

"Your flowers outside are beautiful," I say to her. I don't even try with the Spanish. "Did you plant all those?"

"No." She waves her hand at Nikki.

We go into the kitchen and she maneuvers to a chair with a deep divot in the vinyl on the seat. She lets me go and lowers herself to sit. Nikki is putting groceries away like he's being timed. I don't think we're staying.

When they start up in Spanish, I know I'm totally being talked about. Christ, I'm back at home with Geno and Mom. I try to pick out their meaning, a word here and there recognizable. But they're talking, like, so fast. And the way they sound, their accents and stuff, it's different than what I'm used to.

I smile like I'm enjoying myself when, really, I'm ready to leave.

"I'm gonna go," I interrupt. "You good, Nikki?"

He kisses G-ma on the forehead again. "I'm gone too. Can I catch a ride?"

"Oh . . . don't you want to stay?"

"He never does," G-ma pipes in.

She catches my surprise at hearing her perfect English. Now I'm totally bugged. They *were* talking about me.

"It was nice to meet you," I say, because that's what Abuela would have expected. But I glare at Nikki before I go outside.

Then I'm in the car, Nikki right after me.

"We weren't talking about you," he says.

Damn, he's good.

"Why would I think that?" I turn onto Hiawatha again.

Nikki smiles for the first time since he became my partner in crime. I can't not stare at him. *That face.*

"What?" He bats his long lashes, his eyes just as beautiful without all the eye shadow.

"Bad on you," I say. "Assuming I don't understand Spanish."

"Nothing to be ashamed of, girl. I'm guessing you didn't grow up speaking it. A lot of kids around here didn't."

"Another assumption." I turn on the wipers, squirting what's left of the washer fluid on the dusty windshield. I'm totally embarrassed he's right. A part of me is hollow and always will be. "So, Nico, is it?"

He becomes all shifty again. "Yeah."

I have no idea what time it is, but I've got to be cutting it close. "Well, Nico, I'm headed back. You?"

His hand slides across the seat, shoving my shoes aside. He turns his palm up.

Does he want me to take it? My upper lip is instantly sweaty. It's the elevator all over again.

I drive another block, the world suddenly quiet. I let go of the wheel, and rest my hand in his. His fingers wrap around mine and, Mother Mary, I'm Sally Ride shooting into space— the peaceful serene part, when the rocket's left the atmosphere and floating toward the shimmering stars.

Nikki's skin is soft and clammy, just like mine. I squeeze his hand and signal my lane change with my other.

He looks at me. "You don't have a driver's license, do you?"

And so I laugh. "What gave it away?"

"Your driving is perfection. Like you're in . . . What's that class y'all take?"

"Driver's ed?"

"Yeah, that."

"*Hmph.* If that was true, I'd keep my hands at ten and two."

Nikki lets me go, and I'm sorry I said anything.

"Then we'd better keep it real," he says. "Don't want to give the cops a reason."

"A reason for what?"

He adjusts his side mirror. "Drop me at Teener's?"

"Sure." I've got so many questions. I mean, I kinda get it, Nikki wiping away his makeup before we went inside G-ma's. But she's not totally blind. And they seemed so close.

Nikki's practically hugging the door handle now, his gaze in the side mirror searching the blocks for something I can't see.

I pull over in front of Teener's and he's out faster than he tumbled in.

He leans into the open window. "See ya around?"

"I'd like that."

Nikki smiles. He's got this aura ardiente, as Abuela would've said, like he's radiating fire.

His gaze drops to my collarbone. "You wear my ink well."

My hand goes to the purple paisley. I'd totally forgotten it was still there, and now it's burning a hole through my skin.

"Thanks for the dance . . . and the ride," Nikki says as he slaps the roof. Then he's gone.

I idle outside Teener's like he'll come back. After a few, I'm pushing the limits of stalking. So I drive back to Moby's, total instinct getting me there because my brain is still holding hands with a flower boy named Nico.

Maybe I park in the same spot? I'm not sure of anything until I catch a glimpse of cowboy boots behind me as I'm putting the keys back in the wheel well.

"Need a ride?" Geno says, the flick of his lighter making my shoulder go rigid.

Damned If I Don't

I grasp the keys, uncurl, and turn around.

Geno lights a cigarette.

"I missed my bus." I hold out the keys, hoping to God he's too clueless to see how bad my hands are shaking, or snag the fact that I've just pulled in. "I thought I'd wait it out here . . . for you." I never ask for rides. And he certainly never takes me anywhere anymore. He'll know something's up. I'm so toast.

Geno tucks a bag of White Castle under his arm and takes the keys, his lips scrunching at my dance sweater all tangled with my ripped chiffon skirt. He nods at the passenger side and I let out some air.

When I get in, the seat is still warm from Nikki. The car smells like him too, his briny floral scent making my heart flutter.

Geno speeds off the second I close my door. When he peels around the corner without a word, I might be in the clear. When he punches it on the green after a motorcycle rumbles up next to us, I'm sure of it. I'll bet he misses his cycle like mad. But like a lot of things gone, Geno's Harley got lost between a bottle of whiskey and a game of cards.

Being this close to him in such a small space feels all sorts of strange. For once, I'm glad he's smoking. Maybe he won't smell it—or Nikki's scent—on me.

I roll down my window.

He turns onto the parkway.

I kick off my shoes and prop my feet on the dash.

"Soak those when you get home," he orders, totally incapable of saying anything that's not a command.

Thanks a million for calling me Gloria in front of everyone is what I should say back.

Covering my toes with my hands happens instead.

The lingering aroma of dried pee and sweat wafts from the seams of my body, overpowering the leftover smoke and the glorious aroma of french fries escaping from the bag of food between us. He doesn't ask why my feet are black around the edges, which isn't a shock. As long as I can still dance.

"No Miss Katherine today?"

"She has a dinner thing with her dad."

I cross my arms, the wind chilling my skin. My fight with Kat rushes over me. Her life can't be shit, can it? Have I been so busy spewing about my stuff, I forgot to check in with my best friend? I glance at the greasy White Castle bag, then snatch the saturated paper sack before Geno protests. If Kat's having a foodfest with her father, then I'm having dinner with my dad too. I clutch the warm bag on my lap, feeling every kind of sorry I yelled at her.

We're taking the long way home, around the Chain of Lakes. The houses framing Lake of the Isles, Calhoun, and

Harriet are as big as Kat's. The look-but-don't-touch lawns are empty, the grass a cool kelly green like her plushy bedroom carpet. The lush blades call to my feet, and if it wasn't for the White Castle, I'd eject from the Buick and make it to her house by sundown to apologize for being such a turd.

We get to Lake Nokomis and Geno surprises me when he drives into the beach parking lot and turns the key. I wait for whatever comes next, every muscle wired because I know we're not here to watch the sunset. Maybe he's sussed out my joyride with Nikki? When the silence between us stretches, I open the sack of White Castle and find the fries and four sliders. I hand one to Geno and take one for myself. Not exactly a feast, but it'll do. A silent dinner and the beach with Geno. This is a day of firsts, for sure.

The sun has weight to it, sinking into the orange haze behind the trees. Parents round up beach blankets and snotty, sandy kids. The lifeguards are packing up too, the water cleared of the last few stragglers. Nothing has changed since Glo and I used to come here, the park with the metal animal-shaped swings, the freakishly steep slide I refused to do without her. Second to ballet, this was our summer home. Mom's too. Never Geno's. He was always too busy at the studio.

Geno's cig goes in the ashtray, then he unwraps his burger. I notice something missing from his finger—his wedding ring. I also notice how much his hands are shaking. Which is good, I guess. It means he's not drinking.

I take a bird-sized bite of a cold crinkled fry. "Why'd you

ask me to do the lift today?" So much has happened between then and now, I'm shocked I even care.

Geno picks at his bun, then takes a bite.

"Glo had another seizure yesterday," I blurt. "Second one this week." I don't know why I say anything about my sister. Maybe I just want *him* to care.

He finishes his burger, balls up the wrapper, and tosses it in the backseat. "You looked good today."

Grease from the burger runs down my fingers. "You should come and see her—*Glo.* She'd probably like that." Really, she wouldn't. My sister gave up on Geno a long time ago.

Geno messes with the steering wheel. "I've got a lot to do before Saturday."

Tell that to Mom. By Saturday she'll have sterilized more than a dozen syringes, set up just as many infusions, and made a mountain of Tater Tot hot dish.

I stuff my slider into my mouth, whole.

He lights another cigarette. "Your extension energy is better, but the last half of class you revert to bad habits."

My second burger goes in exactly like the first, Geno's disgust worth a near choking.

"So, Stacy's really doing Odette's solo at First Ave?" I mumble through the bread and meat.

He clears his throat. "You will partner with Jeffery for the auditions. I've already spoken with him."

He's pushing all my buttons, and I know why. He wants me pissed off. I'm a Dominguez, which translates to: competitive as hell. Nothing like a little jealousy to make me dance the shit out of the audition.

"You and Jeffery are a good match," he goes on. "He's strong, your heights are perfect together. He's done growing, and so are you . . . in most places." He eyes my full belly.

I chuck the empty bag over my shoulder and in an out-of-body moment, I pick up his cigarette, perched on the ashtray. I wait for him to slap it from my hand, yell at me in Spanish—anything. Instead, he lights up another one.

It's like one of Kat's double-dog dares. I bring the cigarette to my lips, hesitate, and then take a drag. My lungs immediately curse me for it, not to mention the White Castle is messing with my stomach in a major way.

"I've been smoking for, like, a year. Don't you care?" It's a complete lie. I've had one cigarette in my life, and that was today.

He flicks a crumb from the front of his fitted T-shirt, not an ounce of flab on his flat stomach. "Keeps the weight off. And, Rosa darling, you were always an eater."

He thinks tacking *darling* to my name softens his slam. It doesn't.

I wipe the ketchup from my lips. "Not everyone has the skinny gene, like Stacy."

"Exactly." He pushes his pack of Marlboros across the seat to me.

I'm not sure what to do. Plenty of dancers use smoking as a diet pill. But I've never liked the idea—not as much as I like food. And this feels like another teacup test to see what I'm made of. My mind plays ugly games, parading flashes of

Kat and her dad in matching polos, eating expensive food at a snobby restaurant and talking about normal things like dorm furniture. Meanwhile, in my universe, Geno hands over his cigarettes to keep me in the slim section.

I crush my cigarette and drape my head out the window, nausea coming at me fast. The burgers will probably come out the same way they went down, whole soggy squares of pressed meat. Sweat pools in the crevice between my shoulder blades. I grip the door handle.

"Watch your lazy elbows," Geno lectures.

Please, God, make him stop.

"And remember, strong arms. Pay attention to that on Saturday, Rosa darling."

I dig what toenails I have left into the dash. I'm ready. I'm going to make Kat proud and finally stand up to Geno, tell him I'm not going for the apprenticeship. I can't have First Avenue anyway. Prince has slipped through my hands. Kat's right. Geno's decisions are on him. I should own mine too.

I open my mouth and a tiny squeak comes out.

"The benefit," he says. "I'm willing to make a deal."

My feet slide from the dash as my head snaps in his direction. A deal? Geno doesn't compromise for anything.

"I may not be the director, or on the board anymore . . . but I still have some say. I'll convince Joyce to work around the underage thing."

"What?" I look right at him. I've stared at the floor during our conversations for so long, the creases in the corners of his eyes are deeper than I remember. "You—you would do that for me?"

"Yes."

I lift and hold my center as if preparing for barre. "What do I have to do?" I ask, because it's Geno. And this isn't a negotiation. It's a bribe.

"Saturday, the apprenticeship auditions. You arrive on time, in a *clean* leotard, hair in a proper bun, and no purple ink on your skin."

"And . . ."

"And, you do what I expect. You nail it. I know you can, because you did it today. This is your legacy. Your birthright. Do you have any idea how many dancers wish to be in your place?" He stamps out his cigarette, adding under his breath, "I'm sure your sister does."

My body goes rigid. I've totally underestimated Geno's craftiness. Dancing for Prince. I'll do anything, and he knows it. The Master played it perfectly, beginning with his lame attempt to make me feel special during the lift. Hell, maybe he even called me Gloria on purpose.

"The board will make the selections," he continues. "Along with myself and Joyce. You show up, ready for nothing less than excellence, and you may perform in the benefit."

I wring my icy hands. "And if I don't make it?"

"If you're not chosen . . . I don't know. Take class at Betty's basement ballet. Make a cute hobby out of it. Go back to high school full-time like a regular girl." He says *regular girl* like it's a disease.

I am Geno's daughter, and the Master's student, but neither has a clue who I really am. I would take classes in Betty's basement—if I had the money to pay for them and it meant I could move across the floor—my way.

A 'burb dad in plaid Bermudas is buying his kid a red-white-and-blue Bomb Pop from the food stand—my favorite. Geno wouldn't know that about me either.

"Do we have a deal?" he asks.

I look at the Marlboros, curling my battered toes against the dirty floor mats. He believed in me today. Before he called me Gloria, I swear I saw something different in his eyes. It was fleeting, but it was there. Maybe if he sees me dance for Prince, he'll finally get it—that I'm not her and never will be. I'll be free to do what I want, dance the way I want, like Kat said. We could move on. All of us, open the dingy curtains and let the light in.

I brush my fingers over the paisley. "Deal." It only takes a second to say it, but the moment holds all the power.

The Buick turns over after a protest. "Eight a.m. sharp," he says. "And no tolerance for lateness. Doors will be locked."

I glance at my lone pointe peeking from my bag. The other . . . got closer to Prince than I'll ever be if I screw up this chance. It kills me to ask. I don't want new shoes. I don't want Geno to spend money we don't have because I peed and then choked in front of my obsession.

"Can we stop at Grand Jeté on the way home? I need new pointes . . . for Saturday."

Geno nods. "Coffee and a small bowl of oatmeal the morning of. That's breakfast, okay?"

I take the cigarettes, drop them in my bag, and sink into the Buick's pokey springs.

Heart First

Geno dumps me off at the house, making up some fake excuse about why he has to go back to the studio. I navigate the wheelchair ramp and sneak inside.

The kitchen is cluttered with dishes and unopened mail. Strobes from the living room TV give off the only light. I tiptoe around the corner. Mom's crashed on the couch, her feet still in sneakers. I pull them off and cover her up with a quilt Abuela made.

I sit by her feet and watch her sleep. It's like a rare glimpse of a hummingbird with its wings still. We could have more help. I've heard the nurse say she has two more days available. But Mom always refuses. I fight the urge to curl up next to her. Even my hair feels exhausted. My head drops to her shoulder and she shifts around. I flinch and the blanket falls away. Her wedding ring. It's there, a plain gold band encircling her twiggy finger.

Her cross is around her neck too, the one identical to mine and Glo's—Abuela. She gave Mom hers when she married Geno, six months after they met at church, probably the only thing about them not tangled up in MDC. We used to go to Mass, before the accident, during Geno's sober times. I'm the only one who goes now, and never on Sundays. I like an empty church. There's no kneeling and standing, followed by more kneeling and the body-of-Christ stuff. I can think there, blow the stink off of me, as Abuela used to say.

I take a chance, carefully winding my fingers around Mom's. She used to be a hand-holder, her first three fingers between my thumb and pointer—our special way. I squeeze her gently, wishing we could be this way again. I'd even take once in a while, like when Geno's fury becomes too much. But I don't think she remembers how to be around me anymore.

She fidgets again and I draw my hand from hers.

She's folded a mountain of laundry, our faded beach towels on top of the stack. She washed my purple newsboy hat too, and did my shirts the way I like them, which is actually folded once and then rolled so they fit in my tiny dresser. I take my hat from the basket, stretching it over my bun.

On *60 Minutes,* some tired old guy in a tweed jacket is going on about President Reagan's "Star Wars" plan, and how the United States can intercept a nuclear missile from the Soviet Union. I'm already in the middle of my own cold war. Ground zero. And all I can think about is, *Soviets, please, don't nuke us before I get the chance to dance with Prince.*

I tuck Mom back in and balance the stack of towels in my arms, carrying them to the linen closet down the hall. Glo's door is open a crack. She's been folding too, a remnant of fabric Mom gave her to calm her nervous tics. By now, my sister's gnarled fingers can practically do origami with that piece of material.

I slink inside, careful not to wake her, then draw the worn square of blue patchwork from her hands, placing it on her nightstand next to a city of medication bottles. Her TV is on too, a different tweedy news dude reporting about the AIDS crisis, and how some people want to round up gay men and ship them off to conversion camps—turn them straight, and away from the "gay disease."

There is no limit to how much people suck.

The remote balances on Glo's leg. I turn off the TV and set the clicker aside. My feet are filthy, but I push her tray table away and slide under her covers anyway, spooning her marshmallowy body. The hospital bed whooshes, inflating more air into the mattress in response to my weight. I rest my head in the nook of her thin arm, the scent of rubbing alcohol and baby lotion mingling with my smoky hair.

The ventilator breathes with her, tiny drops of moisture dancing inside the clear tube. Her hand skims across the starchy sheet, hovering over mine before settling down.

She squeezes my fingers.

"Sweet sister, I just made a deal with the devil." I squeeze back, then lick my thumb and wipe away Nikki's purple paisley. It's like his touching me never happened.

Glo's fingers shuffle back and forth across my knuckles. I drape my leg over hers, the pressure relaxing her twitchy muscles.

"Apprenticeship auditions are Saturday."

"Okay . . . Fine . . . ?"

Why am I gambling with my future? This she asks me when I'm surrounded by hers. My feet can knock out a time-step tap combo after years of no practice. Glo's future is ensnared in whatever won't leave her brain alone. I glance around the room for evidence of another seizure. Seeing none, I shift closer, my chest burning so badly I'm thankful she can't sense everything going on beneath my skin.

I want to tell her about Nikki, but suddenly feel weird about it. And what happened in the studio today? That'll stay with me too. "Geno will bend the rules and allow me to dance at First Avenue," I say.

"Okay . . ." The ventilator spews against Glo's gasp.

"*If* I get the apprenticeship." I press my thumb into her palm, her skin callused from rubbing the guardrails that are now down.

". . . Fine." She bobs her head up and down, her body becoming restless again.

"I'd have to commit to the company—be just like Geno, I guess."

"Okay . . . o-o-okay," Glo stutters.

I push my knee into her flaccid quad, tiny spasms radiating from her leg and into mine until, eventually, she settles. I should know better. Comparing myself to Geno means I'll eventually leave and never come back.

She taps my back when I sit up. "Okay . . ."

I turn around but look at Glo's Led Zeppelin poster instead of her sleepy brown eyes, the ones just like mine. "This was supposed to be you," I say to Robert Plant instead of my sister. "It was always supposed to be you. You were the principal in the making. Not me. Your turnout never failed you the second half of class. Your jumps were never heavy. I wish I could fix it—fix everything."

I've never said such a thing aloud, so I welcome the shadows, because Glo doesn't need to see me cry.

I stop myself from saying a thousand sorrys, for fear of making her life seem—well, sorry. And it isn't, is it? I'm so desperate for Geno to see me as more than a prima ballerina in the making. But this makes me the world's biggest hypocrite of all, because when I walk into Glo's room, I see hoses and tubes first, and my sister second. Will it ever be the other way around?

The streaming moonbeam illuminates Glo's newest painting above the television—a layered galaxy of vivid brushstrokes. Is this really what the world looks like through her eyes?

She punches the button to raise the head of her bed a bit more. The easel next to her holds an earlier work. Her hand takes a sec to settle on the canvas. Then she pinches it between her fingers and slides it aside, revealing a different piece.

I prop up. "*Whoa.* That is . . . racy," as Abuela would've said. And Glo would be red-faced in front of Father Thomas if Mom found out about it.

Glo likes my reaction. She snaps her knuckles better than I can do with my fingers.

"Umm, yeah, it's *snap,* all right."

She laughs, a raspy naughty wheeze.

I've hidden a few paintings of Glo's from Mom. Stuff she'd probably find too . . . naked, because Mom's kind of a prude. She gets all nervous and jiggety about anything related to "private parts," as she calls them. Which means I can't play half of my Prince songs outside my Walkman. Glo and I were totally on our own for sex ed and period stuff. The most we got were a couple of xeroxed pages from a book some guy probably wrote, *"Any questions, see me"* scrawled in Mom's handwriting at the top. She left us each a copy on our beds. And hell if any questions were asked.

I think Glo's nudes are beautiful. And what I'm gawking at now is making *me* blush. Like all her work, it's abstract. But even the vacant sex part of my brain has an interpretation. A man and a woman—or is it? I can't tell. Bodies intertwined, a flowy weave of fleshy arms, legs, and secret places. My heart thumps faster—deeper. I feel exposed just looking at it.

"All that Prince talk got you going, huh?" I pick up the painting before she asks. This one will definitely need to disappear.

Glo stops me with a quivering arm.

"Really?" I ask.

"Okay . . ."

"Girl, you are Wonder Woman." I place the painting back, this time in front of the other, and snuggle in again.

I pick at a splotch of dried paint stuck to her old iron-on *Super Friends* shirt.

"I took Geno's car earlier. Like, drove it around and stuff."

Again, I don't tell her about Nikki, though my entire world rocks just thinking about him. I hug myself as if it'll settle my flutters.

Mom's feet shuffle across the shag carpet and I can tell Glo wants to freak out about my joyride, but she's chilling like me. I hold my breath, wishing I'd closed the door. Mom's long, thin shadow haunts the hallway as she passes the slivered opening. Glo squeezes my hand, her grip solid, present—real. My sister survived that January day, but Mom became a ghost. Her footsteps retreat back to the living room, and I relax.

Glo slaps my hand, bringing us back around to my confession.

"I don't know. The car was there and I needed to split."

She gives me a tiny shrug.

"Because . . . coming home meant I'd have to tell you what happened."

Glo's shoulders tense.

"I saw him," I whisper. *"Prince."*

Glo waves her arm like the lucky kitty at the Chinese restaurant she used to love.

"And I peed my tights." I peek up at Glo, my embarrassment worth her flicker of an impossible smile, which erases every reason I conjured to stay away. I'm giggling now. *"Stop.* Seriously, he was right there"—I point at the air above us, imagining Prince in his body-hugging lime-green pants—"and I froze."

She slaps my leg—*up-down, up-down.*

I hissy-cackle with her, probably way too loud to keep it from Mom. But then I quiet down. "My deal with Geno. I did the right thing, didn't I?"

Her eyes squint in the corners as she takes a deep inhale. It overrides the ventilator in a way I don't like. The machine hates it too, squeaking in disapproval. Glo's eyes bug, her fingers clawing the sheets.

She could punch herself again, is all that matters. I hold her arms down, which feels so wrong but I'm lost in my own panic. Then I remember something—Mom gently tapping Glo's chest to calm her.

"Shhh," I whisper against her cheek. "In and out, Glo. Just like I do, okay?"

Her hands struggle to spread out flat when I release them, and we exhale together.

"Breathe in." *Tap-tap-tap-tap-tap.* I pat the bony center of her chest with light fingers. "And out." *Tap-tap-tap-tap-tap.*

After a long and steady exhale, she comes back to me, her veiny lids heavy.

She takes my hand, squishing it against her body. "Okay . . . Fine." My sister's brain is injured, but her heart remains untouched. It thumps against my palm with the intensity of a conditioned principal dancer.

"Yeah. I feel it. Your heart."

Glo's all scrappy today, smacking my hand.

"Yes. I really feel it, Glo." I tense up. "You okay now?"

Before I can grab her communication board, she slips her

flexed thumb beneath my fingers and I understand. I let my-self go limp, waiting for her to show me the way. It takes some effort, but she manages to push my hand to my chest.

"*My* heart?"

"Okay . . ." Glo's arm falls to her side. I'm exhausting her.

"You want me to follow my heart."

"Fine . . ."

I rest my head on her pillow and stare at her one and only Prince poster. I have the same one in my room, the man himself in a pair of smokin' red pants and a purple iridescent trench. Soft gray clouds swirl around his legs, but in Glo's poster, there are splashes of silver glitter and pastel watercolor paint within the mist—a touch of Gloria.

She bedazzled Prince just a few months before the accident, purple and green rhinestones speckling his trench. And that's when it started, the two of us sneaking down to the unfinished side of our basement when Mom and Geno were gone. For the Dominguez girls, no dancing anywhere but MDC is a rule engraved in stone with the blood of virgins. Enter, the Vault.

With our old Donny and Marie record player in the musty corner, my Lava Lamp, and some old Christmas lights, the Vault became our secret club. Even Kat never knew about us shaking our booties to whatever made it from my brain to the concrete—street moves infused with funk, rock, and in-your-face intention, everything meant for Prince's stage. Man, I choreographed some righteous funky combos to Prince's "Up-town" in the Vault. I only wish Abuela could've stuck around long enough to see them.

My back sinks into the curve of Glo's bed.

Her next *okay* is through gritted teeth. I'm not answering and this is pissing her off.

My gaze traces the thin stroke of magenta in her painting. Round and round it spirals toward the center until disappearing into an infinity of warm light.

"Well . . ." I lift Glo's slack wrist, drawing a spiral in the air over our heads. "I could go for the apprenticeship and then quit—after I get what I want. Or maybe I won't have to quit. Maybe Geno will see what I'm really made of when I dance at First Ave . . . like we used to in the Vault, remember?" I utter the last part tightening my grip.

Reminding Glo of what used to be is something I never do. I rest my hand on her chest, wondering if hers hurts like mine.

Her entire body erupts in a happy shimmy and I go soft. She remembers the Vault, and she's stoked about my plan. She raises a fist toward her painting.

My chest warms. "Yeah. Extreme to the max, sis."

She pats my arm.

I've never considered it until now, but what if Glo never wanted to be a principal dancer? Maybe she fantasized a different future for herself, just like me? I thought I knew her better than anyone. But what if she used to imagine herself becoming a famous artist? What if she still does? There's nothing on her communication board about hopes and dreams.

I tuck Glo's fist in the curve of my neck, my heart racing at the thought of both of us going our own way. Glo feels it too, tapping my chest like I'd done for her. It really does work.

I melt into her touch. She smashes my hand against my heart again. She wants me to go for the apprenticeship—my chance with Prince.

My sister's approval—I never could make a move without it. She's the only person who totally gets me.

Glo's breathing transitions to slow and shallow.

I scrape at the magenta paint beneath her fingernails, straighten the covers over her arms, and then recline her bed. "Sweet dreams, sister."

Her brush-mitts are drying on their rack, the splattered wooden surface of her tray table a work of art on its own. Without even trying, I've completely forgotten we're surrounded by sterile medical equipment.

My brain pings in every direction. Me—dancing for Prince? I toss and turn, replaying his "Little Red Corvette" video in my mind until I almost roll onto the floor. Slipping from Glo's bed, I head for the shower. I need to wash myself of the old Rosa.

I'm no longer just going through the motions like everyone thinks. I have an Indiana Jones plan of my own. I've been running with a pack of coyotes for too long, as Abuela would say. Starting tomorrow, I'll be the girl who goes for it. I'll be the girl who follows what's left of her heart.

If I Was Your Boyfriend

It's a regular Tuesday morning, but I hop off the bus waving farewell to George like a dairy princess on a parade float. I'm minus the waterfall bangs and satin ruffled pageant gown, instead sporting a blood-stained leo and a jean mini. But today is still a celebration. For the first time in eons, I'm right where I want to be, headed for class at MDC. I'm not even bugged that I discovered my Walkman's batteries were dead after I left the house because, seriously, I was born with an internal beat. I sway to the funk inside my head, keeping perfect time with the pulsing Don't Walk sign.

I called Kat before leaving, wanting to tell her I've grown some cojones overnight. But she wasn't home, nor was she on the bus. She took off without me. And I swear it doesn't sting.

I'm crossing the street just as a cop car pulls around back of MDC. Stacy hops out. Of course she's two hours early. A panhandler using a phone booth as a bathroom claws at my shoulder as I pass. I drop the last of my change onto the metal shelf beneath the phone, then do a double take outside Shinders, a corner store that's basically a giant indoor newsstand.

I peer through the crusty window, a river of dried pee

cascading down the glass. It's Nikki, browsing in the porn section. My chest cartwheels, carrying the rest of me inside.

The Dead Kennedys replace the outside racket and I take a second to breathe, in a crouch—hiding from Nikki for reasons I can't explain.

I smash my forehead against a copy of this month's *Cosmo,* the model on the front wearing a rad one-piece Kat would rock ten times better.

"Yo! Crank that!" Nikki shouts.

The music amps up. I lean back, craning my neck around a rack of newspapers.

He leaves the XXX section and picks up a copy of *Drag* magazine, flipping through it.

Again, I'm a voyeur, because my eyes have no problem whatsoever watching Nikki shake his hips as he mouths every word of "Too Drunk to Fuck." I said I'd see him again—and I am, right?

He pulls at the neck of his tight mesh muscle shirt. His ass is wrapped in a cutoff jean skirt like mine. His toned legs kick the air in Doc Martens combats, and I miss mine all over again. I mean, who cares if he's into drag queens? Or *is* a drag queen. I can deal. I might be a total mess of an existence, but I'm not a nun.

I open my mouth to say something cool, then shrink into an overstuffed armchair that stinks like it was rescued from the dump. All I can think about is holding his hand again—maybe more.

I'm stewing between a wall of Brooke Shields's killer eyebrows and a rack of *Teen Beat* mags, Ralph Macchio's puppy eyes staring me down, when someone from the other side of the rack says, "Hey, bunhead."

I don't dare look. Maybe I'm not the only bunhead in Shinders?

"Am I missing out on something good in that chair?" he says.

Every crease in my body is damp, the backs of my knees cooled by the floor fans as I stand up. Then there's only Nikki—staring at me with Ralph and Brooke.

He once's me. "Girl, you've gotta be somebody's baby."

Whoa, his smile . . .

I snatch a magazine from a shelf.

"Shopping instead of stealing cars?" he teases.

"I didn't steal it. And I like Shinders's selection of"—I look at what I've grabbed—*"Ranger Rick."* I gulp, holding it up.

Nikki rubs his smooth chin. "Hmm. I'm down with that. Baby bobcats are cool."

He's so full of it, but I'm totally buying the magazine now. "And what about you? What're you into?"

I never expect Nikki to show me what's rolled up in his hand. But he passes it over, our fingers grazing during the handoff. I do a five-second inhale.

"Just a little light reading," he says as I unroll the magazine.

I study the drag queen on the cover—an elegant, muscular blonde in a white romantic tutu that curls over the mag's binding. But it's the shimmery eye shadow and perfect eyeliner that pop from the page. Only Glo could come close to this level of precision. Her performance face had been a work of art. I slap on rouge and powder like a kid raiding her mother's stash of Mary Kay. Even the funeral director did a better job on Abuela's face for her open casket.

I read the article title on the front. " 'Les Ballets Trockadero de Monte Carlo'?"

"Beautiful, right?" Nikki says, suddenly at my side and totally peering down the front of my leotard.

I swallow the hitch in my breath but do nothing to cover up. "Yeah, she is . . . or *he*? Which one is right?" Now I feel super dense. Why would I expect Nikki to answer?

He moves closer, his sweet breath smelling way better than my coffee halitosis. "*She,* when all dolled up. But not always. Everyone has their preference."

I find my balls again and look at him, studying how close we are in height—his frosty blue eye shadow and flawlessly lined lids. "And you? What do you prefer?"

Again, I never expect Nikki to answer. I've probably crossed a cavernous line of assumption and he'll throw the mag in my face. But every part of me wants to hold his hand again. I give him back his light reading material.

"Does it really matter?" he says. "We had fun dancing and driving, right?"

"Yesterday felt more like escaping," I say, and his lids close for a beat. "But yeah, more fun than I've had in . . ." *Almost two years.* I point at the mag. "She's wearing pointe shoes. I thought you didn't have time for ballet?"

He runs his hand along a pleat of magazines and I'm jealous of the leather bracelet wrapped around his wrist.

I squeeze the life out of the *Ranger Rick* because I have no idea what's happening to me. "I've gotta go," I blurt, then rush to the counter to pay for some smushed baby bobcats.

"Where to?" he asks, right on my heels.

Good question. New Rosa showed up two hours early for class like Stacy to prep and stretch. But Old Rosa is back. And she's sweating in weird places.

"Umm. Sun's," I utter off the top of my head.

I guess I'm going to Sun's.

Nikki's eyes light up. "Cool. I'm headed there too."

I scrunch my face.

"Seriously." He backs away, hands up in a surrender. "They've got the stuff I need." His shoulders do a sexy roll. I'm not even sure he's aware of it. And maybe I roll mine too, pulled in by Nikki's infectious energy. All I can think about is our Van Halen tap dance, and the wind in our faces as he held my hand. I welcome it like cool autumn air.

I open the door for him. "After you."

He strolls out. I catch a whiff of his baby-powder scent, and like John the Baptist without his head, mine is gone too.

We take our time getting to Sun's, the air so thick it's like we're dragging our bodies through pudding. We're surrounded by people, Nikki and me—a boy and a girl strolling in matching acid-washed jean miniskirts. It's a collision of glorious and strange, totally noticeable by the sultry stares we get from some, and by the way others walk around him like he's got a disease. I hate that being with Nikki feels taboo at all. Because as I tuck my *Ranger Rick* into my dance bag and check him out on the sly, the gush he gives my heart feels like I found the courage to get on the elevator with Prince.

I wait for Nikki to talk first, mostly because my balls are shriveling and I want to delay something brainless coming out of my mouth. A girl like me doesn't have time for boyfriends—*any* friends outside of MDC. And Jeffery is the only guy who talks to me there, his motives no secret. The rest of the boys, I suspect, are either terrified of Geno or gay—or both.

Today, Nikki doesn't seem afraid of anything.

When we pass a handful of businessmen in wrinkled suits, two prostitutes, and a roller-skating dude in pigtails and rainbow knee-highs without a word, I decide to go for it.

I tip my head the same way Stacy always does when she doe-eyes Jeffery, envisioning myself as a graceful swan. "How long have you worked at Teener's? Not long, because I would've seen you, for sure. I mean, I would've remembered you. Not that you stick out or anything. That's totally not what I mean. Uh, so, how do you know Oz? He's pretty cool, huh? Oh, and how's G-ma?"

Nikki grins.

Fear. Realized. No swans here.

A bus pulls over, the squealing brakes saving me from spewing more questions.

"A month," he says. "And, thank you. Blending is a bore. Corrosion of conformity, *right on.* Oz is a friend of my uncle's.

He's pretty tight. And G-ma's good. Again, cheers for the ride. That cover everything?"

Gawd. Why can't my mouth communicate as beautifully as my feet?

The accordion door in the back of the bus opens, an old lady in a ratty winter coat battling with a foldable shopping cart on the stairs.

"I gotcha." Nikki bounds over and yanks the cart out.

Note to heart: Please don't pop from my chest and sizzle on the sidewalk in front of this boy who just got a whole lot hotter.

The lady squints at me. "You got a real sweet one there, honey."

I nod, meeting Nikki's sweet dark eyes.

She fishes something from her pocket, squishing it into his hand. "Go buy your girl some ice cream."

His girl. I've never been anyone's girl.

Nikki straightens the crumpled dollar bill and tries to give it back.

The woman waves him away and rolls her empty cart down the street, her swollen ankles peeking from the hem of her coat.

"Well, my girl, chocolate or vanilla?" he asks.

I lick my lips, wanting to believe it's possible. A boyfriend—me.

"Strawberry," I say.

He's staring at my mouth now. "Strawberry. You're full of surprises, Rosa Dominguez. And fire. You have that spirit in you."

"My abuela would've said the same about you." The heat from his aura pulls me closer.

He glances at my splattered leo. "And I should've ordered your fiery ass two leotards. What's up with this one?"

What happened to my leotard will stay between Glo and me. Besides, I'm still hanging on the word *fiery*. And he's touching me, his pointer finger pressing against my quivering stomach. I've been lifted off my feet thousands of times. Countless random hands have been where Nikki's lingers, but none ever sent me flying—like millions of tiny wings fluttering within my fire.

I wipe the corners of my eyes, suddenly aware they've watered. I almost touch Nikki back, his mesh shirt doing a horrible job of hiding the shadowed valleys of his cut abs. But I am *totally* not that girl—not like Kat, a smooth talker with lemonade-colored hair and cool moves to match. A flash of Prince holding my shoe sends my gaze to the ground.

"Hey." Nikki pokes my hip. "Where'd you go?"

We lock eyes, and imaginary feathers skim every inch of my skin.

We haven't moved from the bus stop. In fact, nothing moves—the rust-bucket cars, the suits, the shaved heads, the pimps. I'm caught up in Nikki's spell, the entire Nikki—the one with a rolled-up *Drag* magazine sticking out of the back pocket of his jean mini.

"You're a regular crime scene today," he says.

"What?" I mutter, distracted by the turd-brown Buick rumbling past.

He points at my stained Keds.

I let the car go—not enough rust to be Geno's. "This." I pop up onto my toes. "Trashed feet. One of the awesome perks of pointe shoes."

We walk again. "But you love it, right?" he asks.

His hand brushes mine and I can hardly speak. "I guess. Sometimes. Because I have to."

"Why do it, then? Why do something if you're not feeling it?"

"No one loves anything one hundred percent of the time. There're ups and downs with everything, right?" I'm trying to convince myself more than Nikki, and he's way too sharp to miss it.

"Don't fear the downs, girl. They bring on the evolution. That's when everything comes together, because the love is there. You know it, Rosa. Even on the low, you feel it, right?"

He rolls his *R* when he speaks my name, which stars my eyes.

"Like you, with the tapping?" I ask. "The way you danced yesterday, it was like nothing else mattered but the music and your two feet." I spin my cross between my fingers.

Nikki's close to me again, his earrings glinting in the sun. "Universe, gone? Ah, girl, I don't need tap shoes for that." He waves his hand over a magazine rack outside Sun's. "I'll do just about anything if it takes me away from all the bad in the world."

I pay attention to the covers.

Time magazine warns of a Soviet nuclear threat.

Newsweek: two men embracing under the title "Gay America: Sex, Politics and the Impact of AIDS"—right next to another mag informing "You Can't Get AIDS from a Glass."

My shoulders burn beneath the searing sun. I feel like Nikki just poked a giant hole in my bubble. MDC lost two male dancers last year from AIDS, and another soloist in the company is very sick with the disease—the "gay disease," I've heard people call it, and not just on the news.

"So, do what you love, no matter what?" I say. "You really think it's that simple?"

"Honey, you can't tell me you tear up your feet dancing—what'd you say? *six classes a week*—and have no heart for it. Not possible. No one's that much of a masochist."

He goes inside Sun's, taking his powdery perfume with him.

I stay outside like I'm welded to the hot pavement. I'm not sure what *masochist* means, but it doesn't sound good. Greasy fingerprints on the glass door point at my chest.

Nikki peeks outside. "Hey, girlfriend. You coming?"

"What's a masochist?" I cross my arms.

"Someone who gets pleasure from their own pain."

My mangled toes pulse.

"Come on." He beckons. "I know where they keep the good stuff."

Damn this boy's eyes—all the way to hell and back. I leave the magazine rack behind and follow Nikki inside.

A Spin Around the Sun

Slice of New York's pepperoni kicks ass. Shinders is a trash-mag utopia. And for the best posters, Sun's is the mother ship, every inch plastered with famous pouty lips and smoldering eyes.

The funky rock of Morris Day and The Time is spinning on a player in the corner. I bob my head to the beat and wander to the Michael Jackson–Prince area. They hang on opposite walls, as if Sun's doesn't want Prince's dirty mind corrupting MJ's halo. I own every poster on both walls, but there's something about seeing them tacked up at all angles, diagonals, crossways, some curling at the edges. It gives the illusion of movement—dancing.

I walk on my tiptoes to a display and peer inside a colorful glass bong—blue swirls mingling with green, an ocean teeming with algae.

"I'll need ID for that," points out the green-haired girl behind the counter.

"Oh, I'm not buying." I step away from the bong, doubting that Sun's cards for anything.

The girl snaps her gum, eyeing my bun. "Didn't think so." She goes back to pushing tacks into a Vanity 6 poster.

"Damn." Nikki raises a brow, ogling the girl group posing in thigh-high stockings and garters, their cleavage spilling over lacy corsets. "Careful where you're putting those pins, Greenie."

Greenie shimmies her hips.

I do a stealthy self-check, wishing I'd changed into the sundress I stuffed in my bag. Then again, nothing in my closet can compete with Vanity 6's Frederick's of Hollywood wardrobe.

A framed copy of *Rolling Stone* magazine hangs behind the register: "Prince's Hot Rock." The same issue I have parked on my nightstand—Prince, in a white unbuttoned ruffled shirt and purple shimmery jacket. Vanity's fingers—which I imagine to be mine—inside the waistband of his purple jeans.

Nikki nods at Greenie and motions for me to follow.

I tear my eyes away from Prince and scramble for a way to tell him drugs aren't my thing, assuming that's what he meant by *the good stuff.* Nancy Reagan got through to one of us. Nikki may be willing to do whatever it takes to escape. But there's no crack for this girl.

We push through a swinging door leading to a basement stairwell. Halfway down, Michael Myers from *Halloween* hacks into my reason.

"Uh . . . where are we going?"

Nikki waits at the bottom in the dark. He tugs a metal chain, a bare bulb flashing on. "Come on. It's like twenty degrees cooler down here."

And like twenty times creepier.

"Seriously, I think I need a jacket." He rubs his arms.

The stagnant air above does nothing for my sweatfest. And I do love basements, my sublevel bedroom the best thing about going home—besides Glo.

"Okay. But if you have a butcher knife rolled up in that magazine, I must warn you, I know karate."

"Noted." He leaves the bottom of the rickety wooden staircase.

Another yellowish light comes on around the corner. When I get to Nikki, he's leaning against a washing machine, a shelf stacked with detergents above it.

"You have some laundry to do?" I ask.

"No. But you do."

"Huh?" He's called my bluff. I don't know shit about karate.

"Your leotard won't be in until Friday. And that mess of a thing doesn't follow dress code." He tosses me a pink button-up oxford and I clutch it against my chest, wondering why Nikki knows anything about MDC's dress code.

"You're right, it doesn't. Not according to Master Geno, anyway."

"Girl, not according to anyone. Now, strip for the spin cycle." He opens the washing machine lid.

How many girls—or boys—have "done their laundry" in this dewy cinder-block basement with Nikki? Do I really care?

He crosses his arms and faces the wall. Christ, he looks just as hot from the back.

My head goes straight to Prince in the elevator.

Fuck it. What the hell am I waiting for? Nikki's such a fox

and I'm so ready. This is it. I'm going to undress in front of a boy—someone other than a grumpy old stagehand in the wings during a quick change.

"You don't have to turn around." I say it super low, but fully aware Nikki heard me. He's facing me again.

I kick off my shoes, letting the oxford and my bag drop to the floor. I can't look him in the eye, but whatever. I'm pretty sure he isn't gazing into my eyes either. My hands are trembling like hell, but I manage to slide one leotard strap from my shoulder.

I hear Nikki sigh, because I'm totally holding my breath. I follow the first strap with the second, careful to keep my chest covered for the big reveal. My heart's pounding so hard it hurts. Footsteps creak across the floorboards above and goose bumps shower my naked arms. My makeshift dance bra didn't make it onto my body this morning. There's nothing between my apprehension and the beginnings of second base.

Nikki grabs a bottle from the shelf, his mischievous grin the best thing I've seen in forever. "I can wash it in place."

Annoying shyness overtakes me. I'm nothing close to the dancer on the cover of his magazine. And what if he touches me again? I've seen stuff in R-rated movies, caught glimpses of the working girls with their johns in the back alleys. But really, I have no idea what I'm doing, where to touch him back— none of it.

I could just smear myself all over his gorgeous, sparkly body?

Baby powder mixed with lavender fills the space as he steps

toward me. My fuzzy brain frantically skims through a Rolodex of Prince music, clamoring for some impromptu sex ed.

Face on fire, I clutch my leo, sweat sliming up my armpits. "Turn around," I blurt before the buzzing in my tights takes me to my knees.

Nikki hesitates. "A modest dancer. A rare breed."

"What's that supposed to mean?" I hike up my leotard to my chin. I'm suddenly eleven years old again, hiding my new breasts, which showed up way earlier than everyone else's.

He turns away and pulls the magazine from his pocket, flipping through it like I'm being ridiculous. "You've got nothing I haven't seen before, Rosa."

"All those boobs are fake, you know." I fish out my sundress and throw it over my head, pissed at myself for letting myself get all hot and bothered over someone I've known for two minutes.

"To the people in the magazine, they're real. That's what matters, right?"

Somehow, both of my arms end up in the same hole. I wriggle back out, and then in again.

Nikki peeks over his shoulder. "I sure hope you don't have a lot of quick changes."

"Shut up." I peel off my leo, then my tights, gathering them together in a tight ball.

He snatches my stuff before I protest. "*Hello.* Ain't nothing gonna get clean all balled up like that."

"I can do my own laundry. Just, give them." I swipe at my clothes, getting a handful of cool air and nothing else.

Nikki tosses *Drag* aside. He brings my clothes to a table next to the machines and dear God, spreads them out flat. There they are, dried pee outlines in the crotches of my dress-code leo and tights.

I scoop up my shoes, unable to see anything but the evidence of my weak bladder. "I . . . uh . . . You don't have to do that. I sweat a ton, and it's gross, so . . ." This is what a slow death must feel like.

Dance bag already over my shoulder, I'm ready to fly upstairs and never look back. "You know what? Forget trying to save them. Just trash them and I'll see you later." Like, never.

I'll wear a Hefty bag for the rest of the week, balance a thousand more teacups, do a million more jumps, if it means an end to watching Nikki examine my urine crop circles.

He pulls on a pair of rubber dishwashing gloves, then turns my leo inside out.

"Whaaaat are you doing?" I squeak.

"Your laundry. And like I said, nothing I haven't seen. Hand me that sponge, will ya?"

"Sponge?"

"Yeah. Green-and-yellow thing up there." He points to a dusty shelf. "It's used for cleaning."

I want to motor the hell out, but leaving Nikki with the impression that Rosa Dominguez is a dirty urchin *and* dumb—no way. The cracked concrete floor is cool against my hot soles as I tiptoe to a spidery corner and grab the sponge.

"Here." I hold it out, staying in my own space.

Nikki takes the sponge, wetting the corner with something

from a brown bottle that stinks like dissecting day in science class.

I cover my nose and mouth. "What is that?"

He dabs the blood spots. "Ammonia. The stuff reeks, but there's not much it won't kill."

He works on the rusty stains like a pro. "Toothbrush."

I go for the shelf again, remembering a bristly pink one there. "Toothbrush."

Nikki uses the brush to gently scrub a few stubborn places. I creep in closer, peering over his shoulder. He leans back, his curls grazing my cheek.

I spread my toes, the cold cement soothing like ice. "You've done this before?"

"The mob hires me to hide their evidence."

I tilt away.

Nikki flips my leo right side out and inspects it. Good as new. "Cold wash, and you're back in the biz."

"The mob? Seriously?" Another glance around the eerie basement and I almost have to believe him.

He tosses my stuff in the washer and adds detergent. "My mom taught me. She's a lavandera—you know, washes clothes for a living. . . ." His voice trails off, his arrogance fading with it.

"Wow. She must be really good. My stuff looks awesome." I want to hug him. He suddenly looks as if he needs one. But I chicken out and stay on my side of the machine. "Thank you."

He closes the lid, spins the dial to Cold, and punches Start.

I rotate my stiff right ankle, and then my left. "What now?"

Nikki hoists himself onto the dryer. "Now we wait."

Funk It

I drop my bag, expecting more conversation, but Nikki's nose goes back into the *Drag* magazine. I hop onto the washer and bang my heels against the machine. He doesn't look up.

"Les Ballets Trockadero," I say, reading the *Drag* cover aloud. "Are they real?"

"Of course."

"No, I mean, are they a legit dance company?"

"Have been since the seventies. I guess you could say they're a righteous mix of comedy and professional ballet."

"Comedy and ballet. Together?"

Nikki nods. "In this world we're livin' in, I'll take the smiles all day."

The dancer on the cover is wearing pointe shoes that must be at least size thirteen.

"And they're all men, dancing en pointe? Why would they want to do that?"

This gets his attention. "Why do you?"

I shrug like my answer is simple. But we'd have to spend the entire day in Sun's basement to cover my reasons.

Nikki totally checks out again.

"Where does your mother do laundry?" I ask.

"Not here," he says.

"So, where then?"

He drops the mag in his lap. "Miami."

"Is that where you're from?"

His cut biceps flex. "We moved from Puerto Rico when I was eleven."

My prying is either irritating Nikki or making him sad. But I have a thousand more questions. I'm dying to know everything about this hot tap dancer who's a whiz at washing out blood stains.

"What's your full name?" I ask.

"Nico Madera."

"That's it? Is Madera your father's name, or your mother's?"

He crumples the corner of his magazine.

"Your father's—" I say, my assumption hitting a nerve. Nikki frisbees the *Drag* mag across the room.

"My full name is Rosalia Lorena Dominguez Corredor. Is your whole family in Miami or Puerto Rico?"

He rocks back and forth, as if contemplating telling me to mind my own business.

"Mine's from Mexico," I say, like he'll care. But I'm trying to turn back the minutes. I already miss the way he looked at me when he said the word *strawberry*.

Nikki slides off the dryer. "I came here to live with my uncle for a while, on the Southside. Now I'm bummin' a cot at Teener's."

"Why?"

"My uncle's on the road a lot and had to sublet his apartment. Oz is a friend of his, so he lets me stay."

"No. I mean, why did you leave Miami?"

Nikki runs his fingers along the frayed edge of his skirt, all the spark in his brilliance gone. "My dad died of AIDS. Been about six months, I guess."

I grip the edge of the machine. "Jesus. I'm—I'm really sorry."

"He doesn't feel pain anymore, so there's nothing to be sorry about."

Nikki paces the basement, heel-toe, heel-toe, as if he's tapping. I wonder if he learned how to dance from his father, but now I'm afraid to ask more questions.

"My uncle's a musician," he says.

I go with it, relieved we're moving on. "What does he play?"

"He's a kick-ass bass player." Some of the light returns to the murk flooding his eyes.

"That's cool."

"Yeah. He always has been—taught me how to hammer out nickels to make quarters, stuff like that."

"Does that really work?"

He fishes a coin from his pocket and tosses it to me. "There's a peep show down the block. Only costs a quarter."

I turn over the flattened nickel in my hands. "Didn't you just watch one?" My cheeks fire up.

He picks up a broom and pounds on the ceiling, showering our heads with tiny dust bunnies.

I sneeze, like, ten times, and Prince's "Do Me, Baby" drifts through the floorboards.

My hips gyrate before I can stop them. Then the washer sloshes and I wish I could throw myself inside and emerge a different person—someone who has the guts to get inside a stupid elevator. I collapse over my legs.

"Don't stop now, honey." Nikki . . . is back.

"Ugh!"

"What? No love for The Man? Hard to believe with that button shrine on your bag."

I sit up, glancing at the *Dirty Mind* one. "Are you kidding? So much love it's paralyzing."

"Paralyzing, huh? That sounds serious."

"It's, like, when you hear a song for the first time, and—"

"—and it hits you, straight up in the heart," Nikki says, finishing my sentence.

"Exactly," I gush. "And the whole world fades—"

"—like a backdrop for the groove." He does it again, and I swear I'm falling in love right here on the washing machine.

Nikki's warmth has definitely returned. His soft hands are on my arms, his face so close to mine I'm mesmerized by the silvery glitter in his mascara.

"I—I saw Prince, yesterday at MDC," I say. "He was in the elevator. I dropped my shoe at his feet. Well, it more like, flung from my hand. Oh God! Why am I telling anyone this?" I claw at my face.

Nikki busts out laughing. "Most chicks throw panties, but I

guess footwear could work. Prince is really into shoes. . . . What'd his look like?" His cheeks stretch into his biggest smile yet.

"White patent leather heels," I gush. "At least four inches," I add, because it's obvious he needs to know.

Nikki lifts his foot, studying his chewed-up combat.

"And mine wasn't just any shoe either. It was a new pointe. Can you order me another pair along with my leo?" I pull in my legs, burying my face. Never, ever will I admit to Nikki he just washed away the rest of what happened. "Okay, my mortification is complete."

"Girl, don't sweat it. Prince has moved on. You're not even on the man's radar."

I pop up. "Thanks a lot."

Nikki bats his long lashes, the slosh and swish of the washer keeping perfect time with Prince above. I think for a second I'm about to be kissed. Okay. Hope. To. God.

He peeks over my shoulder. "On deck, the spin cycle."

I shift my buzzing pelvis around. "Thanks again, for helping me with my laundry. Hopefully my new leo will be here by Saturday. I need to be perfect, focus more than ever."

"So, focus." His dreamy gaze traces my mouth.

"I have to kill the apprenticeship auditions. If I don't, I won't be allowed to dance for . . ." Two dark eyes with golden specks devour my thoughts.

"Dance for what?" Nikki's plump lips ask.

"A benefit concert at First Avenue. The best will be dancing onstage with Prince. I have to get the apprenticeship, or kiss . . . kiss First Ave good-bye."

"So, what's your plan B?"

Nikki's spell shatters.

"Plan B? I don't need one. Because I'll get it."

"Wow. Humble much?"

"Hey! I've got moves."

"Oh yeah? Let's see." He gives me some room.

My stomach seizes. "Right here?"

"Come on, Strawberry Girl. Break it down." He spins a flawless triple, then pops up on his toes like MJ.

Shitbirds.

I watch Nikki's boots step in close again and I unfold my legs, dangling them. His hip nudges my leg and I swear on Abuela's grave, my knees part on their own. He slips his steamy body between my bare thighs, resting his hands on the machine.

Mother Mary, why didn't I shave my legs?

Any past confusion about Nikki disappears. In this drafty basement, I am definitely his type.

I'm not sure what to do, where to look, where in God's name to put my hands. Prince takes a cue and erupts into a chorus of sensual moans above.

I shiver as smooth lips brush my neck. "So, a bunhead wants to dance for Prince? Is that all?"

The spin cycle sweeps up the room. For a second I can't get air. "Yeah," I whisper against his warm cheek. "And I want to slay it, you know?"

"I can help with that."

"Humble much? Who said I needed hel—"

Nikki's mouth touches mine and everything goes soft. I'd melt right off the washer if it wasn't for his firm grip on my hips. My entire body lives up to Nikki's claim—every inch of me white-hot with fire. His hair smells like mint—no, eucalyptus. His lip gloss tastes like cherries. I lick my own salty mouth, sorry I didn't wear my root-beer-float balm to exchange. That's what people do when they kiss . . . right?

Holy buckets, I think I'm drooling.

I let out a nervous giggle and Nikki seizes the opportunity, slipping his tongue past my teeth. My hands find his twitching pecs and I finger the hoop piercing his nipple. We've become Glo's painting, arms and legs wrapped around each other like we'll never let go.

And then he breaks our kiss, the spin cycle at its climax and—holy shit on Good Friday—myself and Prince are not far behind.

"Wait." I grip his shirt. "I want . . ." I can't say what I want. My cross will sear right off my neck.

Nikki dabs the corner of my mouth and gives me a quick peck on the lips. "The Purple Funk Factory, Strawberry Girl. That's what you want."

Slice of New York

I sway back, Nikki catching me winded. My head whirls to a slow spin along with the Maytag. "The Purple Funk what?" I ask.

"Factory. And I'll keep the rest to myself until Friday."

"Friday? What happens Friday?"

"You. Me. And then we'll see." He lifts me from the washer like a pro, setting me down gently, the way Geno did after the fish dive.

I teeter, my legs in the clouds.

He scoops out my leo and tights, rolls the pair in a loose package, and hands them to me.

"These should air-dry, so I guess you'll have to go to class . . . wet."

I touch my pulsating lips and grin. "Uh-huh." The basement steadies. "I like Nico better. Just so you know."

He checks me out, which quakes everything below my waist. "Don't stress the audition. I'm sure you'll kill it."

"Oh, I'll kill it," I say, and then deflate a little. The thought of auditioning without Kat hits me hard. "Just would've been nice to have a friendly face there."

Nikki hesitates, then picks up his *Drag* magazine, cramming it in his back pocket. "I gotta fly." He pushes my straying hair behind my ear. "Friday, at nine—Teener's. I'll be the one with the friendly face and the new leotard. Can't do much about the shoes." He glances at my pointes poking from my bag. "We don't carry Freeds."

"Yeah, I know." I study him for a second. For a guy who doesn't have time for ballet, he sure knows a lot about the business. "So . . ."

"Thanks for keepin' it real." He squeezes my waist and I want to be against him again, the flimsy fabric of my dress too much between us.

Nikki does fly. Right up the stairs two at a time and out the door.

Did I just totally make out with a drag queen?

My lips are raw, the faint taste of cherry lingering on my tongue. Queen or not, I really don't care. Because I'm so into Nikki. And I've finally been kissed! And somewhat positive I was pretty good at the kissing-back part. I'm already dying to tell Kat everything, if she'll listen. If I haven't totally wrecked things between us.

I saunter to the empty center, brushing my feet across the concrete floor. So much room to move, like the unfinished side of my basement bedroom. My heart won't settle. And with the rumble of cars above, the shadows on the cinder blocks—I am about to be somewhere else. My eyes close, the beat in my head teasing my fingers and toes.

I'm buzzing like I'm about to burst. I snap my fingers,

strutting a full circle—catching a groove only I can hear. My leg does what it wants, an aggressive battement.

"Pow!" I shout, spin, roll on the ground. I pop to my feet and do it again. "Pow!"

I bust out another kick and then two sharp claps, followed by a triple spin on the balls of my feet. I'm covering the entire floor now, sashaying, clapping, and twirling on my knees. The world is a beautiful blur.

"Hey! What the fuck?" Greenie's shouting stops me mid-spin.

I give her two last claps and a sailing grand jeté. "It's all cool!"

She leaves the top of the stairs and I catch my breath, resting my hands on my hips until I see straight. When I'm good, I gather my stuff and wriggle my feet into my tennies. My sundress is totally crooked when I leave Sun's, but whatever.

Greenie gives me a sly wink.

I skitter out the door and into the urban oven, my gummy soles making a sticky sound as I cruise Hennepin. My knees are screaming from the spins, but I strut anyway because *hello*, I've been kissed by a fox named Nikki.

The Purple Funk Factory.

I have no idea what it means, but just saying the words aloud gets me amped. With Nikki, it could seriously be anything. I touch my neck where his lips were. His powdery scent clings to my skin and I sniff my shoulder, imagining his hand there.

The cloud of residual Nikki dissipates when I catch a

glimpse of the magazines on the curbside racks. They look different to me now, as if the headlines are a bolder shade of black: THE AMERICAN AIDS CRISIS. After Nikki, those words are attached to something real. I don't know why I blew it off before, even amidst the loss of some of our own MDC dancers. I feel shitty that even for a minute, at my worst, I wished Geno gone. And then, I come up on Moby's.

Down the block, a man in faded jeans and leather staggers from the bar.

I duck behind a parked car and close my eyes.

Please let it not be him. I look again. But it's no use praying to someone who's not listening. I'd know Geno's stumble anywhere.

He trips over his own feet, recovering like only a dancer can do, spinning out of it and aiming for MDC. I haven't seen him drunk since the winter, but the memories of what a bottle of bourbon does to him never leave me. They're imprinted in the cruddy windshield of our secondhand Buick. In the tin coffee cans filled with cigarette butts in our overgrown backyard. And in the deep fissures of utter disappointment on Mom's face.

I follow him, keeping my distance. His entire stance is different when he's smashed, perfect posture pickled and limp. My balled fists leave half-moon dents in my palms.

The Dominguez family can't go through this again—another round of drunken Geno. Mom will wither like a fuzzy dandelion, the storm scattering her in so many directions. I know in my gut this time she'll never be whole again. And Glo . . . I shouldn't have told Geno about Gloria's seizure.

I collapse against a telephone pole, staples from the tattered flyers piercing my arm.

Geno slams into a newspaper dispenser, flipping back around in my direction. I dodge behind a sandwich board outside SNY, my fingers landing in something squishy on the hot sidewalk. Jesus, he's supposed to teach the two o'clock. What a joke. I should go to him, make sure he lands somewhere other than jail. And then everything glazes over, anything that involves me helping him yet again.

So what if he gets arrested? Maybe Mom, Glo, and I would be okay. Geno is here in Minneapolis, but he left us a long time ago. And we've been . . . fine. Or has life sucked for so long I can't tell the difference anymore?

Geno pours himself inside MDC. He made it, but I can't move.

The door to SNY is propped open, smoke and steamy yeast wafting from the grunge inside. I stand up and follow the smells, my feet dragging like a pair of anvils.

I expect to find Kat downing an entire pie. When she's not, I get worried. I work my way to the counter, bumping elbows with a sleazy guy taking up space on purpose. Yanking my bag past him, I accidently swing it into a pair of bruised knees.

"Hey! Watch the goods, honey. I'm cruisin' in a few." The girl props her spindly legs on an empty chair.

My eyes flick to the newish blue-and-purple marks on her

upper arm. Maybe it's a good thing Kat's fragile heart isn't here.

"You keep your head down, Rosa," Bo says from behind the counter. He slides a slice of pepperoni on a paper plate. "People are squirrelly in here today. Must be a full moon." He pushes my pizza across the high counter, his black knuckles like prunes sprinkled with powdered sugar.

I dig around my bag for some bills and give him a five. "I think I'll need two today, Bo."

"*Hmph,*" he mutters, lips pinching a stubby cigarette. "That bad, huh?"

"Not the whole day." I sniff the Nikki on my shoulder again. "Just . . ." I flick my eyes toward MDC and Bo catches on. I've peeled a passed-out Geno from this very floor more than once.

He drops another slice next to the first, then tucks my five under the plate. "On the house."

"Oh, I couldn't."

"You can, if you go now before I change my mind."

"Thanks, Bo." I take my lunch and scope out a table in the back.

The fluorescents overhead flicker, but this isn't nearly as annoying as what the boom box is polluting the atmosphere with—an awful B side from some Luther Vandross wannabe. The radio is tethered to the dead radiator, so there goes chucking it to the curb. I've reached my limit of bad shit. Nikki's a distraction of paradise proportions. But his lips are gone and MDC's right across Hennepin, with Geno sleeping one off

170

inside. I find the beat and transform the horrible song inside my head to something worthy.

I peek at the Marlboros inside my bag, think about it, and . . . screw it. Once an eater, always an eater.

My first slice is gone before the afternoon shift change. When I start on my second, a quartet of nicked-up legs and gum-snapping mouths filters inside. The swing-shift workers vacate their parking spots, every one of them looking as if their scuffed-up skin hurts to high heaven. I wonder what sad situation landed them here. I'd do almost anything to avoid blowing a bunch of scumbags for money.

The a.m. ladies line up to pay off their pimp at a round table opposite mine. I glare at the slimeball in his stupid leopard-print coat. Yes, *leopard-print coat*—in the dead of summer.

He gnashes his teeth, giving me a greasy once-over. I put my head down like Bo warned, and bite into my slice.

"Kitty-Kat!" Bo shouts, followed by a chorus of meows from the rest of the kitchen crew. They have Hello Kitty heart-eyes for her. Kat doesn't need a drunk dad to score free pizza.

She scans the place and I wave to her like a drowning girl. She spots me, but is in no hurry to be my lifeguard. I practice my apology while she worms her way back.

The bruised swing-shift girl squeezes Kat's hand as she drifts past. It's only for a second, maybe just an accidental bump, but Kat's nod back is enough to make me feel uneasy about it.

I drag a chair so she's next to me, facing the door. Block E— Safety 101.

She sits, two slices too.

"On the house?" I ask.

Kat nods and digs in. "You're on the block early."

"Yeah. Came to get in a good warm-up." I touch my sore lips and grin.

Nothing registers with Kat. She doesn't even call out my bullshit about being here early for a warm-up. I'm totally bummed she doesn't appear to notice my transformation either, the one oozing *I just had Nikki's cherry-flavored tongue down my throat.*

She eats without looking at me, not perking up when Michael Jackson's "Beat It" comes on the radio.

I poke at a pool of grease in the middle of a curled pepperoni. "Do you know that girl?"

"What girl?"

"The one up front."

Kat stuffs her face some more. "No."

"Aren't you boiling?" I tug on her dance sweater.

She flinches away. "No. Freezing, actually."

Her glare is so icy I at least believe her about that.

I push away my plate, no longer wanting a second piece. "I'm sorry about yesterday. I was such a bitch."

Kat stares and chews, her face blank and extra pale.

"And, if there's something going on . . . something you want to talk about, I'm here. Okay?" I wave my hand in front of her.

"Okay." She goes back to nibbling on her crust.

I've really fucked up this time. She's not going to tell me shit. I go for my pack of cigarettes, tapping one out.

"What the hell are you doing with those?" she asks, suddenly present.

"Adding more tar to the atmosphere."

The guy at the next table clicks his lighter and I lean over to spark up.

"Yeah, and to your lungs." Kat's straight nose wrinkles as if I smell like a turd scratch-and-sniff sticker. "I get taking a drag here and there, but since when do you own cigarettes?"

I take a long inhale, then hack up a virgin lung. "Curbs the appetite."

"Since when have you cared about calories?"

"We're not all blessed with great metabolism like you," I say with more irritation than I intended. "I have to be perfect on Saturday. Ready for excellence. And then Geno will pay up."

"Pay up, how?"

"He'll let me dance at First Ave if I get the apprenticeship."

"And you believe him?"

"Yes." I sink into my chair. "I don't know."

Geno's offer. It never occurred to me that he'd be the one to back out. I glance across the street at MDC. Or maybe he'll be too lost in a bottle to follow through. I kick the chair next to me.

Kat balls up her napkin, tossing it onto her plate. "You're so much stronger than this, Rosa."

"Sorry to disappoint." I crush out my cigarette and scoot back. "He's drinking again. I told him about Glo's seizure and he's right back at Moby's."

Kat sighs. "Oh, geez. I had no idea." She wraps her sweater tighter. "But telling him about Glo was the right thing to do. The guy should know what's happening with his daughter."

I want to admit how confused I am about everything. I want to go back to this morning, to the five minutes I felt like badass Rosa. I want her to talk to me, about anything. As long as we're all good again. But I say nothing. And neither does she.

The morning girls have paid, doing their best to get comfortable around a table. By the way they nap amidst the mayhem of SNY, I doubt any of them have a real bed anywhere. Maybe we aren't that different after all. I've slept hundreds of hours on George's bus with nowhere to go.

Kat crosses her legs, her prairie skirt riding up.

"Oh my God!" I reach for her. "What happened?"

She flinches away, stretching her skirt over her black-and-blue knees.

"What the hell, Kat?"

"It's nothing."

"Nothing? That looks really bad."

"I'm fine."

Bo is right. It is squirrelly town in here. Kat hardly stays in her chair as she collects her stuff.

"Where are you going?"

"I need to warm up too. I'm stiff today." She drops her pizza.

"Leave it. Talk to me, Kat."

All I see is the prostitute at the front with identical bruises. And that girl did *not* get those marks from falling. My stomach turns inside out.

"Wait!" I grab her sleeve. Her sweater falls from her shoulder, another bruise on her upper arm.

"No. *You* leave it, okay?" Kat covers up again. "It's not what you think."

"Really? What is it, then?"

"I can't say just now. Not here." Her eyes dart to the pimp, who's squinting at our little scene.

"Why?" I'm racing inside. My best friend is not a prostitute, is she? She has everything. She certainly doesn't need the money.

Kat doesn't answer, already halfway to the exit.

"Kat!" I pick up our mess, throwing everything in the trash.

She slips outside. I worm my way around the girls until their boss blocks me with his jeweled pimp stick.

I glance at Bo.

"No trouble today, y'all," Bo says, hard eyes on both of us.

The cane lifts, and I'm sprinting. "She's long gone, sweetheart," the boss caws after me.

I pray to the heavens he's wrong. But Kat is a gazelle, and I am not a cheetah. My soles slap the asphalt as I skid outside.

Shine on Sister's Shadow

The heat draws the air from my lungs as I tear across the street. It's actually a relief when I pop inside MDC.

The main office is on the fourth floor, where all dancers have to check in before class. I take the stairs, even though I know Kat went the lazy way up. When I reach the fourth, MDC's lobby is deserted, with the exception of our secretary, Lou, and his perpetual sweeping.

"Did Kat check in yet?" I huff.

Lou doesn't bother looking up. He props his broom against the wall and strolls to the attendance book as if I'm putting him out. I probably am, but everyone and everything bothers Lou, especially interruptions of his compulsive cleaning frenzies, which happen twenty-four seven.

He flips through the attendance binder, one excruciating page at a time.

"You don't have to look," I say. "I'm just asking if you saw her. It would've been, like, a second ago."

Lou stops flipping and takes out a tin of lip balm from the pocket of his tight Jordache jeans. "I take attendance. I'm not paid to track the superfluous goings-on here. If your friend doesn't have a check by her name, then I don't know where she is. 'Kay?"

I sigh. "Does she have a check?"

Lou pretends to search for Kat's name on the list, even though he totally knows she's smack-dab in the middle. "Nope. No check."

The pepperoni I devoured is roiling in my stomach. "Well, I'm here, so I guess mark me in."

He purses his lips and puts a blue check next to my row of green *T*'s-for-tardy. "Rosa Dominguez is early. Must be my birthday."

"Sorry, I didn't get you anything," I snap.

"Master Geno was early too," he adds with a bit of seriousness.

I pause. "He made it to his office, then?"

Lou peers over his tortoiseshell glasses. "I helped him remember where it was. Then left him with a full pot of coffee and some Tylenol."

I squeeze my lips together.

He shoos me away as if I'm going to bawl all over his precious binder. He doesn't despise everyone at MDC, his dedication to Geno the only key to his guarded compassion. He knows the drill. They're in the same AA group and the struggle is real. I'm betting Lou's constant sweeping has something to do with that.

Coming up on Geno's office, I slow at his door. Abuela would march right in and smack him with her purse. All I want is to get as far from here as possible. If Geno and Kat are skipping out on class, why can't I? But . . . I'm here, and Geno's out. It'd be a waste to ignore the freedom, as Kat would say, which makes everything ache.

So, I'm up two flights in what has to be record speed for me. My head catches up as I maneuver down the hall. The door to studio 6A is wide open, which means Prince isn't here. My feet drag.

I reach the empty space, totally unashamed I'm considering smearing myself around the floor in some residual Prince sweat. For real, I almost do. Then I notice studio 6B's door is open too, long shadows casting across the hall from inside— the fluid arc of a port de bras.

"Again." A voice carries down the corridor. "This time with the music."

I leave Prince's sweaty ghost and sneak up, pausing alongside the door to take a peek.

MDC's company members are a full sweat into rehearsal. Sylvia's directing, our female version of Geno. They even smell the same—smoke and coffee with a dash of Old Spice deodorant. My knees give a little. This should be Geno's rehearsal. I can tell by the way the dancers are positioned—the Master's eye for putting the strongest downstage.

They take their places, and the synthesizer intro of Prince's "D.M.S.R." begins. My feet erupt from the ground. I take over the hall, marking the steps.

Studio 6B doubles as a performance space, and the company is turning it out for broke. Black velvet curtains are drawn across the alcoves at the long ends of the massive room.

The windows are even bigger here, sun streaming through the glass, dust and rosin lighting the place up like a powdery disco.

I sprint down the hall and slip into 6B's side door, which pops me into a dim alcove—and straight into Stacy.

"Ouch!" she spits.

"Gah!" I collect myself while she peeks through a narrow opening in the velvet. "Stacy McGee, are you poaching a company rehearsal?"

"I'm so sure. Isn't that why you're here?" She turns an attitude pirouette, in sync with the rest. "I'm getting a jump on the First Avenue choreography. The company's learning it first, and then those of us who are *chosen* will get our places."

My feet sink into the floor as I watch her. Her thick dark hair is down, swishing past her waist. She's wearing a nude-colored unitard, the exact one we all dread—well, I guess not all of us. Those of us in the upper levels are required to wear them the first week of class at the beginning of the season. Nothing reveals flaws like skintight beige cling wrap. Stacy's like a lone lithe willow branch, swaying in the breeze. I hate to admit, if I had a shape like Stacy's, I'd wear my nude unitard fucking everywhere.

She prepares again. I claim my spot and follow along.

This is definitely Geno's choreography—intricate and bordering on impossible, not a single count wasted. I love the challenge of it and how the combination pushes me to my limits. The foundation's totally classical ballet, but at the same time, the piece is so . . . me. I wouldn't change a thing.

Stacy's grand battement swishes past my ear, way too close.

179

I jump away, crossing my arms.

She shimmies past, her shoulders stiff like she's paddling a kayak.

"What're you thinking about?" I ask, careful to keep my voice down. Sylvia wouldn't think twice about booting us out.

She stops. "You really want to know?"

"I mean, when you're dancing. What's in your head?"

"I don't know . . . pulling up my center, smooth transitions, lifting from beneath my leg. Things you should be thinking about." She cringes as I walk toward her. "What are you doing?"

"Watching you do it again."

"Why?"

Good question. But she preps and does it again like I ask.

"Easy neck," I say as she dances. "It's okay to let your head follow the momentum. Shoulders soft. I can see you anticipating the turns."

Stacy's technique is her usual flawless, but as I talk her through it, she stiffens up more.

She falls out of her attitude pirouette. "I don't know what you mean," she whines. "I was over my center, totally balanced, before you decided to pick me apart."

"You're right. Perfection. But, don't you want to give . . . more?"

"More what?"

"*Emotion.* Don't just move through the steps."

This whole thing is probably a terrible idea. But I've failed royally at being there for Kat. And there's nothing I can do about Geno. It feels good helping someone, even if it's Stacy.

Sylvia cuts the music, lecturing the company about losing marks if they don't spot stage left.

I sweep my arms over my head and close my eyes. "Dancing . . . it's like crashing into the music until a story emerges from the wreckage. I swear, only Prince comes close— his fingers fluttering over the strings, or across the keys, light as feathers for a few bars and then sharp and angry the next as he burns up everything around him. His heat radiates off the stage, to the audience, you know?" I open my eyes. "Listen with your whole body when Sylvia presses Play again. And ask yourself, how does dancing make you feel?"

Stacy looks like she's on the verge of a breakdown. "It makes my feet hurt."

I do a grand battement of my own, arms slapping my thighs. "What do you hear? Like right now, what music's in your head?"

"There is no music. She hasn't pressed Play yet." She jams her fists into her hips. "And I don't have to feel anything to make it, you know?"

I wish I felt nothing. How much easier would everything be?

"That's my girl." The slur of Geno's voice spins me around.

I'm pretty sure Stacy's bolted, but then again, I can't see anything but Geno's sloppy silhouette between the curtains.

He stumbles from the shadows. "Gloria . . . you are here. How?" His tobacco-laced hands cup my face, and I'm frozen. His brain is totally gone, but his eyes are my father's. And he's looking at me like I'm principal-dancer-to-be Glo.

"You are radiant. And you've grown your hair back." His eyes well up. I push my chin against his grasp to look away.

I want to scream my name in his sweaty face, unload everything—I should. But he thinks I'm Glo. And man, how good it feels to have a real dad for even a second.

"Dad," I say, every inch of me quivering. "You should go and take a nap, okay?"

Sylvia can't see him like this. No one can. After he lost his place on the board, he promised Director Joyce he'd stay sober. I grasp his arms, my fingers digging into his leathery skin.

"A nap?" Geno loses his balance and I catch him before he falls. "But I've got rehearsal." He sways toward the curtain.

"Sylvia's got this." I yank it shut. "A nap, Dad. Because you're so tired, right?"

He squints at me, like he's not sure I'm Glo anymore. "Gloria?" His swirly gaze travels down my legs, to my feet.

I pop onto my toes, closer to Glo's height. "Yeah, it's me . . . Gloria." I swallow, a sharp stone clawing at my throat. "Come on. Let's get you back to your office."

Geno leans into my side, shuffling along. He stinks like he slept on the floor at Moby's, which scrunches my nose.

I manage to make it to the door and Stacy's there, holding it open.

Christ.

There goes the shitty neighborhood. By tonight everyone will know.

But she doesn't look at me, not even a tiny smirk. And when Geno stumbles in the hall, Stacy's with me. She catches his other arm and the two of us drag the Master back to his office.

The Vault

When I climb my basement stairs late the next morning, I'm sore as hell. Even with Stacy's help, dragging Geno down two flights and into his office took every muscle I had. He was totally passed out by the time we dumped him onto his couch. All of his Gloria hallucinations were done. I could've been Princess Diana and he wouldn't have known the difference. Stacy left before I could thank her. She jetted without a word. I hope to God she keeps it that way.

There's a plate of peanut butter toast and half of a banana perched on the top landing of my steps. This is a first, Mom leaving me breakfast. I mean, yeah, a plate on the floor kind of makes me feel like the family dog. But she woke up and thought of me, right down to cutting the banana in half because she knows I get a little gaggy after too much mushy texture.

I take the plate, set it on the kitchen table, and savor the visual. She even spread the peanut butter in tiny waves like in the commercials. The refrigerator hums in the corner. And the TV—it's not on. I'm alone in the house.

My head snaps to the corkboard by the back door. Mom

left a note. She's called a wheelchair van and has taken Glo to a doctor's appointment. Something about her feeding tube being infected, which happens sometimes. Restlessness tenses my shoulders. I don't like it when Glo leaves without saying good-bye.

I fold some clean kitchen towels, then eat the toast and banana, lost in a replay of yesterday.

Nikki and all the kissing.

Kat at SNY.

And yeah, dancing, letting myself totally go with Stacy in the alcoves of studio 6B.

I try to block out Geno. Tried all night and failed. I don't want to look, but here I go. I count them three times. One of his AA coins is gone from the windowsill. Did he think we wouldn't notice? My arms break out in goose bumps. The crushing starts, a slow burn within my core.

Then I'm doing it—picking up the phone to call Kat.

It's Wednesday and I've already missed first class. But I guess she has too, because she answers.

"Hey," I say, a quiver in my throat garbling my voice.

"Hey."

"Can you come over? I want to show you something."

There's this forever pause, and for a sec I think she's hung up.

Then, "Yeah, I guess. Be there in an hour," she says.

"Great. I'll be in the basement." I hang up. Don't even give her the chance to change her mind and blow me off.

I swipe Geno's remaining two coins into my hand, then

whip up a cold tuna casserole for Mom with crushed tortilla chips on top, like Abuela used to make. After cleaning up the kitchen and opening all the blinds, I spend the next half hour prepping the basement, which includes digging out my old Donny and Marie record player. It's this tacky suitcase thing with the brother-and-sister duo in red sequined getups on the cover. Lift the lid, and they're in blue. Christ, I used to think it was the baddest set, and now it's collecting dust under a stack of rag mags.

My side of the basement is a disaster, but it's mine. No one ever comes down here but me. Even the laundry room is on the main level, which keeps Mom away. There isn't a spot of wood-paneled wall or ceiling tile without something tacked to it. Prince's abs are literally everywhere. David Lee Roth's too, and a few worthy others.

I strip the Christmas lights from over my bed and hang them at the cave end of the basement—the Vault.

"Okay, what's up?" Kat asks, suddenly at the bottom of the stairs.

I about chuck my Lava Lamp at her.

"Jesus," I gasp. "You're like a zombie, sneaking up on me like that." And she looks like one too.

Kat's hair is down and a total mess at the ends, like she slept in a tornado—or didn't sleep at all. Her bruises are still there. I hadn't imagined them.

"Where'd you go after SNY?" I grip my lamp. "I looked for you."

"I didn't feel well," she says. "Maybe I'm done with pizza."

Calling her bullshit might make her dash again. So I leave it.

"You hungry?" I ask. "I made a tuna casserole."

Kat shakes her head. "Martina made me something. . . ." She trails off at the end and we're back to totally awkward.

I sit on the edge of my waterbed, the one that came with the house—the one Abuela died in. Toward the end, she had us help her from the couch to the basement. She said she wanted to ride the waves to heaven. And so she did. Glo and I crawled in and listened to her wheezy lungs take their last ragged breath. We stayed with Abuela until some stuffy funeral guy came and got her. And now the bed is mine—no weirdness at all sleeping here either.

"Glo's at the doctor," I say. "Feeding-tube infection."

Kat nods. "She'll be okay. Antibiotics, a good flush, and she's on the mend. The girl is—"

"Strong. Yeah, I know." I don't tell her about drunk Geno calling me Gloria again. The grapevine will get to her soon enough.

She touches her cheek, jamming her other hand into the front pocket of her jeans.

"Anything you want to talk about?" I say. *Like, how you're NOT a fucking prostitute?*

"Is that what this is?" she snaps. "Some kind of an intervention?"

I'm standing now. "Are you saying you need one?"

Kat turns around and hesitates. She points at the blinking

lights I've draped from the low ceiling by the furnace. "Are Donny and Marie having a disco moment?"

Mother Mary, she's as good at deflection as I am. Whatever happened to being each other's person when shit went south? I need it back. So I carry over my Lava Lamp and plug it in.

The corner glows deep purple. Gravity bears down on my shoulders. Glo hasn't been in the basement in a year and a half. She was the one who started the Vault—for us.

In the Vault there's no such thing as Geno's lighter, or smack talk about how much I ate for lunch. My breasts are not a sideshow. Things like bruised knees and drunk dads don't exist. There's not a dusty-rose leotard for miles. And yeah, it is totally possible to smile and dance at the same time.

I go to the center and turn a slow circle beneath the lights. "This is the Vault."

Kat joins me in the middle, flashes of green and red light twinkling her face. "And what happens in said vault?"

I step up in her space. "Funking magic."

Kat's eyes bug, and somewhere in the world there is hope for us.

"Glo and I used to sneak down here and groove our asses off." I sweep my foot across the floor, letting the weight of it carry my leg above ninety. "I'd choreograph and she'd have it down in, like, one run-through."

Kat nods with a tiny grin. "Sounds like Glo."

The memories slow me up as my brain presses Rewind.

"Come on, Rosa." Glo tugs me down the stairs, her nails painted black with permanent marker. She has a heart drawn on each knee too, encircled by her new fave thing, holey jeans that drive Mom nuts.

"Why in the basement?" I ask, because Glo's eyes are all twinkly and huge. The last time I saw her like this, she thought she saw Eddie Van Halen leaving a Tom Thumb convenience store. It was so not him.

She sits on a chair in the hall and changes into a pair of black character shoes I didn't know she owned. "We can dance here. Minus the tights." She fastens the buckle on one, then starts on the other.

I'm not sure I get it, because I'm watching my sister shift from the obedient hall monitor I've shared a room with my whole life to the fearless girl I've always wanted to be.

"Dance. Here? How?" I glance at the giant waterbed swallowing up the room, and what little Abuela had, packed in boxes.

Glo stands up and has my hair out of my bun in seconds. I'm sure she can see I'm about to cry. "Just put one foot in front of the other. Work your magic, Rosa." She winks at me. "I'll try and keep up."

She takes down her own hair, whipping her long waves around like a video vamp. "Buns are extinct here. And we can wear whatever we want. Isn't it awesome?"

She unzips her sweatshirt and plants herself in front of me, hands on hips and wearing another secret. A super-duper tight T-shirt with an iron-on patch on the front—a skull and crossbones and the words FUCKING ROCK—FUCKING ROLL—FOREVER—TILL DEATH DO US FUCKING PART.

Anything awesome is swallowed up by the shock wave that's tripping up my heart. I'm terrified enough to glance up the stairs for Mom and Geno.

Glo grasps my shoulders. I can smell her fresh Sharpie nails. "Breathe in . . . ," she says.

I do as she says.

"Breathe out . . ."

I let out a giant exhale, locking eyes with my sister's soft browns.

"He's got company class. He'll be gone for hours. Mom too. I promise." She brushes a few stray locks from my face. "Now . . . your hair is free. Follow its lead. Let's see what you've got."

Glo's hearted knees knock together. Geno was so pissed when he saw that black marker bleeding through her pink tights. It cost her one hundred extra jumps at the end of class. She knew it would. But she did it anyway.

She grips my waist and spins me around. Then moves the divider curtain aside.

Colorful lights glint an allegro beat. Our Lava Lamp undulates in the corner next to my Donny and Marie player. I almost forget I'm looking at our creepy furnace room.

Glo rests her chin on my shoulder. "Welcome to the Vault."

"I had no idea. Why didn't you tell me?" Kat says, pulling me back to the present.

I hug my arms. "We all have secrets. Even from our best friends."

This doesn't budge Kat.

"Your vault," she says. "So, you and Glo dancing on the sly, no ballet?"

"Well, I wouldn't say that. Ballet *is* the foundation of every kind of dance."

"Whoa!" we blurt in unison. I cover my mouth. Kat actually laughs.

Me, quoting Geno. What the hell?

"Ah, Kat. This was *my* choreography. *My* creations."

"Tell me." Kat waves her arms through the flickering lights.

"God. Where do I start? It was like my moves meant something, you know? Love, rage . . . grief." I glance at the waterbed, balling my fists like I'm readying for a punch. "I worked it out on the floor, whatever came at me. I hip-checked and rolled my shoulders. I felt right in my skin. And hell no, Glo and I weren't Master Geno's bunheads here."

I lean against the wall, my head churning with the memories. "It felt like . . . like I was finally fighting for the right to be who I wanted to be."

"The right to be who you want," Kat says. "Does that really exist?"

"Remember when MTV started?" I ask. "When we saw music videos for the first time?" I move the needle to the record—the sharp rap of Prince's "Lady Cab Driver" sputters through the tinny suitcase speakers.

"You said you'd never turn off the TV." Kat taps her foot. " 'Video Killed the Radio Star.' "

"Totally," I gush, rocking my hips to the beat. "With three minutes of art in motion." I'm immediately thinking about Glo's paintings, and how they do the same.

"You were desperate to dance in those vids," Kat says. "Like the Pat Benatar one, remember?"

I snicker. "Yeah . . . but I'd choreograph much tighter moves than endless eight-counts of shoulder shimmies."

She smiles and I think we're getting close to normal.

"So, where do you go from here?" Kat asks, her gaze back on the grayish concrete.

I blow out a sigh. "I've been training my whole life to fit into an impossible mold." My feet pace the cool, damp space. "Everywhere you go, you fit, Kat. To feel even a fraction of that, like when we jam in your room to Prince videos." *And the way I did, tapping with Nikki at Teener's the other day.* "Here with Glo, the floor got the real me. And maybe the First Ave stage will be that way too. That's where I go. What about you?"

She turns her back, rubbing her arms.

"You're so lucky," I say, desperate for her to see it. "You know exactly what you want, and your parents support it. Celebrate it, even. I want that too. A place where being me, just the way I am, is enough."

Kat's still facing the wall, her shoulders hunched like she's cold. "Be yourself . . . sounds like a Mister Rogers song."

"Umm, I think it is."

She spins around. "Rosa."

"Yeah?"

The front door above opens and the screen door smacks closed. Only one person besides me does that in this house—Geno.

I freeze as Kat grips my arm. Prince is about at the point where he's giving some woman a righteous orgasm. Kat reaches over and skids the needle off the record. We listen to Geno's boots creak around the living room. Sweat beads up my forehead. He clacks through the kitchen, stopping at the sink, and I'm sneaking up the stairs because Geno isn't here for the Tater Tot hot dish.

"Looking for something?" I ask, Kat on my heels at the top.

Geno starts like a squirrel. I'm the one busting him today.

"Rosa! Jesus Mother Mary." He rakes his fingers through his greasy feathered hair. "You're supposed to be in class, young lady."

I cross my arms. "So are you."

Stale and mostly sober, he's all darty-eyed, glancing around the kitchen for something to lie about. His jeans are somewhat clean, T-shirt . . . not so much. Pizza sauce and grease stain the front.

My gaze flicks to the empty windowsill, my fist around the AA medallions in my jean overalls pocket.

"If you're here to see Glo, she's at an appointment."

He nods, messing with the stack of clean towels I folded until they topple over. "I am aware."

That's it? So, his reason for being here is crystal. The coins.

Fishing them from my pocket, I hold them out. "You're looking for these, right? This is why you're here."

Kat inches up behind me, her breathing faster than mine, I swear.

Geno doesn't even try to act like I'm being ridiculous. He goes for the coins.

I snap my hand closed. "No."

His eyes shift from half-lidded and tired to solid-bore black holes. "Give them to me, Rosa."

"No way." I shake my head as he crosses the room.

Kat has a fistful of the back of my overalls, like she's prepared to toss me aside and take on Geno herself.

He shifts again, cocking his head, a crinkle between his brows. "Come on, Rosa . . . mi flor pequeña." He reaches for me, fluttering his fingers. "You know I love you, darling. Just hand them over."

My face is burning, but my hands are cold. Blood must be leaving my body through the giant hole in my heart. I love you. Sure, he says it now, after never.

"No," I utter, my throat like a desert. "You need to leave."

He doesn't like this, taking his Master Geno stance, stone eyes back in an instant. "Rosa, if you don't give me my coins, then . . ." Geno's one big fidget, legs quivering, hands tearing at his clothes like he doesn't know what to do with them.

"Then what?" I ask.

"Then consider our First Avenue deal off."

The room seizes; even the summer wind stops blowing through the screens.

Kat tightens her grasp on me as I stretch my hand out to Geno.

My heart protests, throbbing at my temples. I just want whatever this is to end, however it may. And then I glance at the note Mom left, and I'm thinking about no one but Glo. I yank my hand away just as Geno goes for it. But I'm not fast enough. He's got ahold of my wrist, prying open my fingers just enough to pinch a coin.

"Master Geno!" Kat shouts, holding my arm steady. "Stop!"

He does. He got what he wanted.

I rub my wrist, but I can't see anything clearly. I think Kat's checking out my arm.

Geno's ragged breathing is in my face. I wipe away my steaming-hot cry.

"I'm so sorry, darling," he mutters. "I'm . . ." He stumbles backward, hands smashed together like they're in a vise.

I turn away, erupting in shivers. When I look at him again, with his cheeks sucked to his teeth and his brow cinched together—I see regret. I know it so well my eyes burn. I step closer. Geno shrinks away, until the front door opens and closes with a smack.

Emerald and Blue

I couldn't stay in the house after giving up the coin to Geno, so Kat walks with me a few blocks and then to the bus stop down the way.

"Let me see that wrist again," she says after eons of silence.

I hold it out, no bruises—unlike her.

"Tell me that was all a bogus dream," I say.

"Well, it was bogus, all right."

"I caved." I plop onto the curb, the dried grass poking my backside.

Kat sits too. "You didn't cave. He ripped it from your hand."

"I let him."

"Only because he is freakishly strong for a tiny guy."

The last coin is in my pocket. I stop myself from wondering what Geno will hang over my head to get it.

Down a few blocks, the nineteen rounds the corner. Kat covers a greenish bruise on her arm.

"You gonna tell me what's the deal with you?" I ask.

She rocks back and forth. "After what just happened, we don't need to talk about me."

"Why not?"

She stares straight ahead. "Is that why you showed me the Vault, after all this time?"

"If I say yes, will you be pissed?"

Kat picks at the buckle on her Dr. Scholl's. "You've got guts, Rosa. The Vault, doing your own thing. And standing up to Geno like that."

"Umm, not really how I see it."

"We all see ourselves differently than those around us."

She gets up as the bus approaches, and I get a little panicky. I don't want her to leave.

I touch her arm. "I see my best friend, and I'd like her to stay and talk to me."

Kat shakes her head. "I don't fit everywhere like you think."

"Okay . . ."

"I'm not hooking, if that's what you're getting at."

"Then what?"

The nineteen comes up fast, hissing to a stop. The doors open.

Kat grabs the handrail. "Thank you for today. I know what I have to do now."

"What?" I hook my finger in the back pocket of her jeans.

"Just give me some time, Rosa. I'll let you know when I'm ready."

She climbs the steps and I back onto the boulevard.

Kat wants time. Why does it feel like I shouldn't give it to her?

When I get to my block, Mom and Glo are home. I know

this because our blinds are closed again like we're hiding something. It drives me nuts that Mom keeps the place like a cave. Glo needs the sun. She needs to smell real air—flowers on the wind, cut grass. But my sister never goes anywhere anymore that doesn't reek of rubbing alcohol and sterilized metal. Mom won't allow it. I think she's scared something will happen. So . . . there's just a whole lot of nothing.

Inside, the house is just as I left it—silent. No Geno. No coins. My tuna-and-noodle concoction is untouched on the counter. My feet take on weight as I go for the foil to cover the casserole.

"Mom," I call, getting no answer. "Mom!" I speed-walk to Glo's room, finding it empty.

I race back to the kitchen. Mom's note is still on the board. Shoving Glo's supplies aside, I drag over the answering machine. The red light isn't blinking. There's no message—the one that says Glo was taken to the hospital after another seizure.

Just as I'm about to bolt for the bus—

"Rosa?"

Relief hits me hard, and I hold myself up with the counter. "Mom?"

"Out here."

The back door is propped open, the ramp Mom built with her own two hands sprinkled with kernels of popcorn.

I follow the crumbs. My sister is up and outside, Mom next to her eating popcorn and drinking a Tab. Mork is curled up on Glo's lap, his nose sporting a fresh scratch mark. He's a scrappy Dominguez too.

Glo is painting, her easel cinched up close—paints to her left, plastic bag of liquid nutrition on an IV pole to her right, infusing through a brand-new tube. Mom and Glo are having a picnic together. And the ridiculous jealousy I feel makes me look away for a sec.

"Nice day to be out," I say, always nervous around Mom because I'm a pro at doing wrong things. Today's no exception. I pick up a piece of popcorn at my feet, blow on it, then pop it in my mouth.

Mom scowls.

See.

I hope to God Glo can't smell Geno on me.

Mom slathers some goopy sunscreen on my sister's face. "You have a short day? Was class canceled?"

"Ummm."

"Okay . . ." Glo beckons me over, saving my ass.

Her painting shimmers in the sun. "Wow. That is amazing, sister."

It really is. So many shades and textures of green in the background. I'm looking at spring clover, lime Kool-Aid, and our pea-soup bathroom wallpaper all at once.

She knocks her fist against her Walkman.

I unclip it from her waist, flip over the tape, and press Play.

Glo didn't lose her rhythm. She bounces her head to the beat, Def Leppard's "Rock of Ages."

Mom puts down her bowl of popcorn, disconnects Glo's empty nutrition bag, and scoots her communication board closer. "How was your father today?" This is something she never asks, so it trips me up. She's totally fishing. The empty window—Geno's coins.

I scratch Mork behind his ears. "Uh . . . he seems really busy." My eyes flick to Glo, and Mom gets it, though the way her hands are shaking, I really should show her that I still have Geno's remaining medallion. But then I'd have to admit I dropped the ball. And I can't go back there with her.

A flash of warmth washes over me, my whole body desperate for her to hug me, make me popcorn, and tell me everything's going to be all right. I take a step toward her, and she collapses into her chair as if she'll never get back up. I pluck another piece of straying popcorn from the grass and eat it.

The sunlight shines on Mom's legs, the road map of bluish veins on her thin ankles and pale feet aging her. It's the kind of wear and tear that comes not from too many birthdays, but rather from sleepless nights and popcorn diets—the only thing I ever see her eat anymore. She used to be a nineteenth-century Spanish portrait—long, thick, flowing hair, smooth fair skin, and angular features. She used to be a lot of things.

Glo rests her painting hand on Mork's back. "Okay. Fine."

I remove her headphones. "Beautiful." I wipe her sweaty ears. She shakes her head, letting me know not to fuss.

Mom gazes into the neighbor's yard, their two daughters playing on our hand-me-down swing set. I don't think she considers Glo's paintings art. Just something to fill the endless hours. If only she'd let me take her to a museum, the park, anywhere. Buses with wheelchair ramps go past galleries just as much as they stop in front of the doctor's office.

I cross my arms, warding off a sudden chill. "I made Abuela's tuna casserole. I can scoop you some if you'd like, Mom."

"I'm fine." She shrugs.

Eerie, how Glo and Mom are becoming one person.

"Okay. Fine," Glo says.

I look at her work in progress again. The sun has shifted, the details easier to see. Although abstract, the shape is clear now. It's a pointe shoe, exploding from the center of the canvas, pieces of dirty wrinkling satin at the edges. She's painted *that day*. My breath stays in my lungs.

Mom's eyes shift from Glo to me, her lids sagging like we're at a funeral.

"Okay. Fine. Okay. Fine," Glo chants. She reaches for my hand and I flinch. Mork springs to the ground, and she glares at her empty lap. I think I've hurt her feelings. For once, I can't tell. She reaches for her communication board, but I look away.

"I'm going inside to stretch." I leave Glo and shuffle up the ramp.

"Rosa," Mom calls after me.

When I turn around, she's up. I glance at the spindly hands that made me peanut butter toast this morning. "Yeah?"

Glo's gone back to her painting, her board on the ground. The wind picks up like our furnace kicking in.

Mom looks as though she wants to say something, or come to me, but the words are stuck and her feet won't move.

She sighs, "Thank you for the casserole. Go ahead and eat without me."

I guess that was it.

Inside, I don't eat. Though I know she's probably not home yet, I go straight for the phone to call Kat. My hands shake as I dial, which takes *for-ever* because we don't have the push-button kind like everyone else on the planet.

Kat's phone rings, like, ten times. I tug on the cord and then hang up.

I wipe down the counters again and stack the clean dishes. The dirty ones, I leave. I never do them right. Then I head to the basement.

The cooler air hits my ankles first, crawling up the rest of me like a damp fog as I slog down the stairs with my bag. I click on the lamp on top of my dresser, pick up my bag, and hang it over the corner of my mirror. It's not really full-length anymore. More like a tiny oval, framed with photos of Kat and me, stickers, and a collage of magazine cutouts of hair and makeup I'll never achieve.

My body sinks into my waterbed. I fish out Geno's coin, flipping it between my fingers. Abuela's rosary is draped over my old Holly Hobby doll on my nightstand. I take the beads down, balling them up in my hand like she used to when she needed to think. Dozens of sable Prince eyes tacked to my popcorn ceiling loom down on me. I roll to my side, pulling over me the purple-and-white quilt Abuela made.

The Vault is still flashing like Glo will clear the stairs and follow my lead any second. She remembers the Vault. If those days are still in her head, does she remember the accident?

We've never gone there. Is this why she painted a pointe shoe? We talk about so many things: Prince, art—how stupid that *Matthew Star* show was. But never that day.

Flipping onto my back, I stare into Prince's raven eyes as if they'll give me the answers.

What if Glo remembers everything?

I white-knuckle the rosary.

What if her memory of January 5 is sharp like the hardened February snow?

What if, all this time, her *Okay, fine* has really been a *Fuck you?*

Father's Keeper

Late afternoon. I emerge from my basement hole, shuffle through the kitchen, grab a package of Pop-Tarts, and leave the house with my hair in a high bun beneath my purple newsboy hat. I've done this exactly the same way so many times there should be a trench worn in the floor from my bedroom to the front door.

There was no peanut butter toast and banana waiting for me this morning, and I try not to read anything into it.

Usually I stop and say good-bye to Glo on my way to MDC. Today I'm clutching Geno's coin and lingering at the end of the hall, listening to Mom's tired voice encourage her to play fifteen minutes of Simon. The doctors say the electronic memory game is good for her brain. She's pretty okay at following the patterns—*red, red, blue, yellow, green, red, red.* Until the lights speed up. I don't think this has anything to do with her inability to remember the colors. Only that her fast-twitch muscles, the same ones that used to jump an entrechat six like beating wings, well, they aren't what they used to be.

Simon blips, followed by a repeat of the same tones. Mom

claps. Glo's brain stores more than we think. I don't know why I needed her painting to confirm it.

Kat's a no-show on the bus, so I get the headphones all to myself—killer electric funk and both seats in the middle. We blow by her stop, and even with Prince's falsetto teasing me the whole way to MDC that he wants to "do it all night," I'm thinking about Kat. Watching *Porky's* on the sly in her room is the only reason I have any clue what he means anyway. I can't even take off my leo in front of Nikki, which— Holy crapsicles, tomorrow is Friday. I'll be face to face with his shimmery lips again, when he takes me to the Purple Funk whatever-it-is. And I haven't had a sec to tell Kat about any of it. I sink deep into my seat, jamming my knees into the one in front of me.

My heart is a solid lump when I climb the stairs at MDC for another ballet class, followed by another en pointe. No matter how fermented Geno's brain is, I won't let him pull the rug out. I'm here to follow through on my promise to be ready for excellence come Saturday.

I left the house determined not to care about Geno. Curse me, because now that I'm here, I home in on his office like a lab rat in a maze.

My stomach wants to give back the Pop-Tarts I ate. I pause behind the exit to the fourth floor, rubbing my gold cross as if it'll help. The surprise part is the scariest. Not knowing where I'll find him—how I'll find him. I push through the door, then knock on Geno's.

A muffled grumble answers, and I exhale a puff of air.

I knock again. "Master Geno . . . Dad . . . it's Rosa." I try the door.

It opens. I slip inside, set the lock, and turn around. The dark, stuffy office stinks like a whiskey barrel full of burnt coffee. My eyes adjust to the lump across the room—Geno, sprawled on the couch that is really a love seat. His feet hang over the end, one scuffed boot on, one off.

Leave this office and never come back. This is what I want to do. Yeah, everything would still suck. But the suck part would be so much easier if I didn't give a shit. Who cares if Geno's unfit to teach another class because of my weak-ass grip strength?

Not. Me.

My Prince buttons clack together as I grip the strap on my bag. My hat is sweating up my head. I pull it off, stuffing it into the pocket of the jean short overalls I'm wearing over my tights and leo. And then of course I'm picking up the White Castle wrappers from the floor on my way to the edge of the couch. I stand at Geno's feet. It's nothing like watching a beautiful bird, more like spying on a sleeping dragon that could spew fire at any moment. He snores into a threadbare pillow.

I'm so pissed at him that I'm denting one of my Prince buttons with my thumb. He rolls faceup and I jump back as one of his legs plops to the floor. He mutters something I can't understand and then he's out again.

As I creep up close again, my anger flickers. With his matted old-man nursing-home hair, his cheeks sunken rather than chiseled, he's a pile of brittle bones wrapped in heavy cowhide.

205

I take my hat from my pocket and wave it in front of my sweaty face, the stagnant air suffocating.

Geno's leather jacket squeaks as he fidgets again, his car keys falling from his pocket. I switch on the fan in the corner and point it at him like I do for Mom.

The coffeemaker is ready to go.

Thanks, Lou.

I take out my water bottle and slam it down on the table next to a couple of Tylenol. "I'm just going to leave this here," I say super loud. "Don't choke on it."

He groans again.

I trip over something. I pick it up. A dusty frame—a photo of the four of us. Geno has his arm around Mom while Gloria scowls in her white First Communion dress. She really hated that lacy thing, the veil, the white patent leather shoes, all of it. She wanted to dye it black, which made Abuela do the sign of the cross, like, twenty times. And then there's me, surly-faced too and standing a couple steps back from Glo. I wanted that dress and all the white frill that went with it. Two years later when it was my turn to wear the dress, it didn't feel at all like I imagined. Just another hand-me-down from Glo. It even had hardened pink frosting from her cake caught between the layers of the poof. I remember tasting it—very stale. I didn't get a cake. Geno dropped it on his way home after a detour to the bar.

I wipe off the glass and set the frame on the table. Geno's dead-fish ankle makes yanking off his remaining boot diffi-cult. I tug harder, then stumble backward as his foot thunks to the floor. I cover my nose. His socks reek like rotten vinegar, random toes sticking out through ragged holes. I doubt he's changed them in weeks.

I drag the table within his reach. How did I miss the usual signs? He's been off the wagon for a while. I sit on the arm of the couch, raging that I feel any kind of sorry for him. People are dying right under our noses. Dancers at MDC—Nikki's father. And what about Glo and the never-ending war in her brain? Meanwhile, Geno's poisoning his liver, testing his sorry fate over and over again.

"This is on you, Geno." I shove his legs. "You hear me? On. You."

His lids flutter and I jump off the couch.

Like last time, there's no thinking involved. I snatch his keys from the floor and I'm out.

The River of Confession

I'm back in the Buick, idling in the lot and overanalyzing where I want to go. Then I glance at the empty passenger seat and I'm shifting into Drive and heading to Teener's.

Nikki's styling the display window when I pull up, a bald mannequin in a bikini made of rainbow feather boas. My regions tickle just looking at it.

I honk the horn.

He looks up, sees me waving, and jumps from the tiny stage.

When he comes out and leans in my open window, I forget every intention I had in coming here other than letting his deep browns swallow me whole.

"'Sup, Strawberry." He kisses my sweaty forehead.

The car rolls forward and I slam on the brakes.

I shift to Park. "Umm, you wanna go for a ride?"

Nikki glances back at Teener's and then down the street. Hennepin is pretty quiet today. The calm before the clubs open up for the Three-for-Thursday storm.

"Where to?" His glittered nails grip the top of my door.

I spoke too soon. Sirens wail in the distance, becoming louder.

"I need some peace. Sound good?"

Nikki rocks back on his Doc heels, biting his glossy bottom lip. When he leaves the car, I think that's it. But then he knocks on the window at Teener's, waving at Oz at the counter. I wave too, and Oz blows me a kiss.

In the car with Nikki, I feel underdressed for the occasion in my short overalls next to him in his full makeup and jean skirt. But he's here, and I'm barely stressing about what I'm driving away from.

"Where does a girl go to find peace around here?" he asks, checking out his face in the visor mirror.

"The radio." I turn it on and crank the volume, A Flock of Seagulls, "Space Age Love Song."

The wind swirls inside the car. Nikki grooves in his seat while I drum the wheel.

We cross the Mississippi River, to Saint Paul, the high bridge tingling my toes. I stick my arm out the window, letting my hand glide over the hot current. Nikki must be game for a ride because he flies his hand too, never asking where we're going.

I could just drive us all the way to Wisconsin, totally forget about Geno, Kat's secrets, and Glo's painting. And Nikki can forget about the magazines outside Sun's, flying beer bottles, and why he had to wipe the makeup from his face before he saw G-ma.

We cruise down Summit Avenue, the mansions as impressive as the cathedrals anchoring the neighborhood. Neither of us says anything, way too absorbed in gawking at one gigantic Victorian after another. There's no peeling paint on Summit Avenue. No chain-link fences. No coffee cans filled with cigarette butts.

The Buick homes in on the formidable Cathedral of Saint Paul. I drive into the parking lot and shut down.

"Come on." I get out and shove my hands into the deep pockets of my overalls. I tip my face toward the sun, sweat running from my scalp, trickling behind my ears.

We're high on a hill, but the air is static, the only sound coming from two squirrels spiraling up a tree.

Nikki's still in the car. "Church? You serious?"

"It's nice and cool in there." I saunter toward Nikki and lean into the car. "Nico Madera, are you afraid of a little holy water?"

"It's just regular water, you know?"

"Come on. I followed you into a creepy basement at Sun's."

His eyes dance. "So, we're here to drop some guilt about that? 'Cause I have none." He plays with my stray curls and my face fires up.

I step away and Nikki pushes the door open. He takes my hand, squeezing it like hell as we climb the looming steps.

We slip inside and Nikki crams himself against the holy-water font, his eyes bugged like he's just been beamed up the Enterprise. I reach behind him and dip my fingers in the bowl, crossing myself.

"Man, everyone always looks on the verge of tragic," he says, peering inside at the paintings.

"That's half of the Bible. The rest is filled with sex, miracles, and a bunch of rules. You'd hate that last part."

"I do." He sits on a bench in the foyer.

Shit.

"Hey, I didn't mean anything by that."

"I was seven the last time I went to church," he says, picking at the hem of his skirt. "For, like, the First Communion thing, you know?"

"Believe me, I do. Did you at least get cake? Because I didn't."

He shakes his head, staring at the ground. "I wore a dress. Made it with Mom's sewing machine and changed behind a tree before we went in. She was mad as hell, trying to shove me back in the car to switch into my pants and button-up . . . but I was like, nah. The priest saw us and came over. I think she was crying by then. I don't know."

I sit next to Nikki. His legs are shaking. I scoot closer.

"The man said, *Nico Madera, you can be a good son, or you can be a boy who wears a dress. You can't be both.*"

Fuck.

Nikki's sharp, dark eyes find mine. They gleam, two deep spirals of Glo's glossy acrylic paint. "It was a kickin' dress, Strawberry. I mean, it was a steamin' mess, seams all crooked and the sleeves uneven, but it was mine. Green and purple stripes with a yellow sash. You know, the kind that ties in the back."

I nod, my heart so filled with Nikki I can't move.

"I know the kind," I say.

We stare at each other, the way people do when they want to crawl inside the other's head and see all the secrets. I tug at his arm. "Let's go. We don't have to be here."

Nikki stands. "Nah, I didn't change then. I'm doing my best not to now."

The church is deserted, except for two random prayers in one of the Sacred Heart chapels. Nikki shuffles along glued to my side, gaping at the sky-high ceiling, stained glass, and murals. The air in the cathedral is like the basement at Sun's— cool, damp, and smelling of candle wax and incense. It even has its own version of famous-people posters, like the painting of John the Baptist, *with* his head attached.

"They're empty right now." I point at the confessional booths.

Nikki's eyes go all dreamy. "Damn, girl."

Punching his arm seems about right in church. "I mean, we can go in and sit . . . and think. That's what I do."

"Think about what?"

"Whatever pops into your head."

I open the first confessional. "Sit." I point to a bench on one side.

Nikki surprises me by actually doing it. I shut the door and pretend to lock it.

"Rosa . . ."

I enter from the priest's side. "I'm here," I whisper through the tight latticed screen.

He jumps back. "*Whoa*. You're all witchy woman behind that screen."

"Close your eyes," I say, resting the back of my head against the wall.

There's something tranquil about holing up in the sin detox box: the dim light, the mixture of old-lady perfume and wood polish. There's no weight of those who've come before— rather, a buoyancy promising to float me the hell out of here with some answers. Like, what am I going to do about my mess of a life?

"Now what?" Nikki asks.

I pull in my knees and scrape at the dried blood on my Ked. "We think. Or talk, if you want."

"Why Prince?" he asks. "At Sun's you were a girl all in."

Why the hell not? I'm back in the packed Met Center arena with floor-to-ceiling fans of the Revolution, but in my exploding head Prince is playing just for me. The driving base of "Controversy" reverberates through the floor, pulsating through my feet and burrowing deep into my bones. A silhouette rises up from somewhere beneath, a vision in a purple trench. Prince and his guitar—the *1999* Tour. Four months ago, when Kat and I screamed ourselves dizzy. When she was still telling me everything.

"Getting lost in the moves . . . and the music," I sigh. "I guess that's it."

"Nah, there's gotta be more, Strawberry."

What I'll call *the Aroma of Nikki* fills the confessional, and

I Hail Mary ahead of time because I wish I was on the other side of the screen.

"There's always more." I prop my feet on the opposite wall, giving up on losing myself in my own head. "There's this thing called legacy."

"The apprenticeship thing?"

"Yeah, which leads to principal ballet dancer. At least, for me it's supposed to. In two days. This Saturday."

Nikki scoots closer to the latticed screen. "And you're not down for that, I'm guessing."

"The dancing part? Always. I've never wanted to be anything else. The pointes and the pink tights, no. At MDC, the rules are stiffer than the tutus. Classical ballet isn't ready for a girl like me."

Nikki laughs and I wonder if this booth has ever seen a smile like Nikki's.

"You look ready for the world to me. Why not a girl like you?" he asks.

"Because I'm a girl who likes to eat Pop-Tarts—the brown sugar kind. I'm a girl who's pissed half of the time and wants to work it out on the dance floor with a thrashing head roll. There's more than one way to tell a story." I ball my fists. "And I'm gonna do it, on that First Avenue stage, my own thing. Like you do."

Nikki sinks into his bench and leans into the partition. "Yeah . . . I do my thing, all right."

I'm leaning into the screen too, my head touching his through the tiny diamond-shaped openings.

I ask what I've wanted to since our first joyride. "Why'd you jet from G-ma's house so fast?"

"I got places to be."

"And you took your makeup off before you went inside because . . ."

Silence seals up the confessional and I think we're done. Then he breaks it. "G-ma is my mom's mother."

"Yeah?"

"Mom . . . she caught me dancing in a pair of pointes. I dug them from the trash behind a ballet studio. She kicked me out. Said I was a faggot like my dad. That I was gonna die, just like him, and that Miami was no longer my place."

"Christ, Nikki." I press my hand against his head.

"It's not like I . . . what I mean is . . . I like who I like, and I'm always careful." His fingers seep through the screen and touch mine. "When Dad got sick, he got himself up here, thinking . . . I don't know, that he'd find help, that he'd find better medicine. We have relations here that go way back. Most of them came up when my g-pa did, to work the railroad—lay the tracks, you know?"

I don't, but nod anyway. I've never thought about who built the tracks I cursed on the way to G-ma's.

"Dad's plan was a no-go. Medicine wasn't here either. No one'll care about finding a cure for what those bus-stop posters say is the *gay plague* until straight people start catching it."

My stomach hurts from tensing. I want to stop Nikki from saying anything more. Then maybe I can pretend his story has a happy ending.

"Anyway," he says, "I bummed around, here and there, and then came to Minneapolis because I wanted to be with Dad when he died. Which, like I said at Sun's, happened about six months ago."

I'm sorry is what I ache to say, but Nikki's made it clear this is not what he needs.

"He was a kickin' tapper," he says. "Taught me everything I know. I tap sometimes to . . . I don't know, feel like he's still here or something."

"He taught you well," I say. "And . . . pointe shoes, huh?"

"Yeah, I guess classical ballet isn't ready for someone like *me* either."

I press my forehead against the screen, taking it all in. I thought coming here would clear my head. Now it's bursting at the seams. There's more shit in this world than my own problems. Kat tried to remind me of this and I wouldn't listen.

"So, you're scared your g-ma will do the same as your mother?" I ask. "Is that why you're living in the stockroom at Teener's and not with her?"

Nikki takes forever to answer. I'm pretty sure I've gone too far. Then he says, "I can take being chased away by strangers. It's a whole lot different when it's family."

"You shouldn't have to take either," I say. "And don't you think G-ma knows about . . . about the lipstick and jean skirts? She didn't look like she cared about anything but you."

"She's half-blind."

"That dress you made when you were seven, you *owned* it.

You didn't change. G-ma sees the real you, Nikki. She doesn't need eyes for that."

He settles back against the wall. "You've got it all figured, huh? Maybe if I believed in God too, things would be easier. Having someone to talk to, I mean."

"Who said I believe?" I rub my cross.

"We're here, aren't we?"

"It's all I've ever known, so it feels . . . comfortable. Safe, I guess. A guy in the sky has nothing to do with it. And we're talking now, aren't we?"

Nikki taps out a slow beat on the bench. "Your pops, he gives you a hard time, right?"

"The worst."

"So, with the ballet you just keep on going on? For the sake of the funk on the First Ave stage?"

"I want First Ave, more than anything. But really"—my lungs fill to the brim, and then empty—"I go on because one of these days, he might care again."

"About what?"

"About me, without all the expectations and ultimatums. And if Geno can still care about me, after everything I've done, then there's a chance for us. For Mom and my sister. Then maybe he'll give a shit enough about himself to stay sober."

"Ah, that's a rough roll, Strawberry. But what'd you do that's so bad? Forget to tuck your pointe ribbons again?"

No amount of wishing that was true will change things. It'll just drain my heart dry until I feel nothing.

"I didn't mean for anything to happen," I say. "Not really. I just wanted her to stay."

"Who?"

"Gloria. My older sister. I didn't know she'd run after it."

Nikki scoots closer to the screen. "Run after what?"

"Everyone calls it an accident. Even me."

Nikki goes quiet, as if he's holding his breath.

I stare at the grain patterns on the walls, fixing on a swirl that resembles one of Glo's paintings. And before my feet can drag me away from here, before I can stop myself—I am talking about January 5.

Gloria Estrella
Dominguez Corredor

"I wanted to tell Gloria about something that happened in school. I can't even remember what it was now. Probably something stupid. It always was. I was fourteen. And Glo was the age I am now. It's weird to think about that."

The confessional disintegrates and I'm back in our kitchen, a year and a half ago.

"It's winter. And Geno is relentless about her training. Summer-program auditions for American Ballet Theatre are the next day. And we all know Glo will be perfect. She'll make it to New York. Which, for me, means an entire July as Geno's sole focus, because Mom will go with her.

"Glo tries to make me feel better, saying things like *I'll totally write you every day*. Or, *I'll smuggle back some real New York pizza*. But I know those things are impossible. She'll get off that plane and forget all about me."

A break in my voice brings me back to the now. For the first time, I'm not making up a bunch of shit to pacify some priest. I stare at the cross hanging in the corner, my heart thumping against the one around my neck.

I'm gone again, to winter 1982.

"Mom scolds me when I come home because I slam the door for the thousandth time. My sister, she doesn't even look up, so engrossed in tricking out her shoes for the audition. She's at the kitchen table, burning the ends of her pointe shoe ribbons, Mom peering over her shoulder to make sure she does it just right. Glo's wearing jean overalls. Funny how I can't remember why I needed to talk to her just then, but those stupid overalls are so clear—the iron-on flower patch on the bib, the left strap fastened with a giant safety pin.

"Glo's callused feet are bare, toenails painted with chipped black polish. Mom's hair up in a fuzzy bun. No plastic tubing and nutrition bags on the counter, just a pitcher of strawberry Kool-Aid and a box of graham crackers.

"I'm, like, waiting by the edge of the table for Glo to notice me. When she doesn't, I shake the snow off my jacket, which she totally ignores too. So, I start pacing, because I'm pissed. I want her to see me, hear me—maybe feel sorry enough to blow off the audition. I poke at her back and she spins around, barking at me like I'm five, *Patient pants, Rosa!*

"But I'm done being ignored. I snatch her pointe shoe and race out the door. Glo chases after me, bare feet and all. She laughs at first. I can hear her behind me. But then she realizes I'm not joking and starts yelling, *Don't even, Rosa! Grow up!*"

I press my thumbs into my temples, Nikki's breathing heavy from the other side.

"It happened so fast. Seconds maybe, because I can't see it anymore. Not really. Not the way I want to. . . .

"A truck drives down our street, and I see my opportunity.

I want Glo to pay for leaving, for acting like she doesn't give a shit, when I know she does."

My fingers hurt from squeezing them, but I don't stop. "I want her to forget about New York. I don't want to dance in our basement alone. So . . . I throw her brand-new three-quartered pointe into the street."

Nikki inhales with a squeak.

I squeeze my eyes shut and the world goes white, like hard-packed salty snow. And then I see Glo, leaping from the frozen curb—her overall strap whipping behind her like a broken tether as she races to reverse my mistake.

"She doesn't see the truck, or maybe doesn't understand how fast it's going. All she sees is her audition about to be ruined because of my childishness. I realize what I've done the second she jumps from the curb. But my screams don't stop her.

"The day before, everything is slush. The day after, too. But January fifth, it's icy. The truck tries to stop, but it's like a rink. It hits her and everything flashes, like I've gone blind for a second. But the scariest part is the silence. There's just . . . nothing. No Glo cursing at me for wrecking her pointe. No Glo screaming at me because I'm being such a baby. And for a second, I think, maybe I've imagined it all.

"But then I smell burning rubber. And when I drop to Glo's side, the street salt digs into my knees. That's when I know it's real. The driver says something to me, or maybe my Mom does, because someone's clawing at my shoulder.

"And then, I see her. Her eyes are open, but she's not my sister. It's like she's under a spell or something. I—I'm afraid to touch her, but I do it anyway. I fix her overall strap. Get her hair out of her mouth. I keep saying *You're gonna be okay, Glo . . . You're gonna be fine.* And I totally believe it, you know? Even though there's blood gushing from the side of her head. Even though her body looks crooked, and it's wrong in the middle, and something is coming from somewhere in her back and it's all over the road."

Nikki's sniffling constricts my throat.

"Glo made it to her shoe." I hug myself. "There wasn't a scratch on that Freed castle. I thought about taking it. Hiding it. Making up some other reason for what happened. What kind of person does that make me?"

Nikki doesn't answer.

I wipe the hot tears from my face, my knees aching when I stand.

"Afterward, when they tell us Glo will never walk again, that her brain won't work like it used to—that she'll never dance again, Mom takes me home. We're in the elevator at the hospital. And I'm crying. I can't stop. Haven't stopped since the street. Mom is yelling at me. "Just stop it, Rosa!" She sounds vicious, not like my mom anymore. If I could quit crying, I'd say I'm sorry. But instead, after everything that's happened, it's all about me."

My feet pace a circle in the confessional, the tang of oil soap on wood smelling an awful lot like Glo's paints. I press my forehead against the wall.

"I ask my mom if she still loves me."

Nikki's restlessness quiets. "What did she say?"

"She said, *Not today, I don't. I'll let you know when I do.* That was a year and a half ago. And I haven't been inside an elevator since."

I barely notice when Nikki appears on my side of the partition, don't know how long he's been staring at me with red puffy eyes.

"Let's go," he says.

He follows me out. Only, this time there's no leaning into my side in awe of the stained glass. He trails behind, his steps so light I check to make sure he hasn't bolted out one of the side doors.

Christ, why'd I spill my guts? It didn't change anything. I'm sure as shit not floating out of here with any answers. I am, however, certain I've left behind an aura of hell-bound misery for the next sorry soul to deal with.

We get in the Buick and I drive back to Minneapolis. I'm so exhausted even my bones have given in. It's a chore just pressing the gas pedal. No one's flying their arms out the windows when we cross the bridge, but my longing to keep driving is still here. I wonder if Nikki would stop me if I did?

Neither of us speaks the entire way. No music. Just thick dead air between us. I'm sure the Purple Funk *nothing* is happening tomorrow.

I park behind Moby's, leaving the keys on top of the back tire. Geno will figure it out . . . maybe. We get out, keeping the hood between us.

"Tomorrow, Rosa . . . ," he says, and I brace for the letdown. "Nine, at Teener's."

223

My shoulders thaw. "Teener's. Nine."

An ambulance and fire truck fly past. Nikki backs away from the car, checking the lot like he's ready for another ambush. He taps his chest over his heart, then blows me a quick kiss that'll carry me into tomorrow.

I watch him go until his quiet strut merges with the hustle of Hennepin.

Old Friends for Sale

Friday morning, and I've barely slept, the aftermath of the day before invading my icy dreams like a dead-of-winter virus. I even try Abuela's rosary, imagining her next to me. Like when I used to fall asleep to her hypnotic Hail Marys, her fluid Spanish coming from somewhere deep inside her chest.

I wind the rosary beads around my fingers and stare at the Prince posters on my ceiling, the twinkling lights in the Vault still going from Kat's visit. Reds and greens reflect off Prince's glossiness like he's groovin' in a disco. I roll over. The empty furnace room is more like a lonely grotto than a dance floor. I watch the purple goo inside my Lava Lamp swell and stretch like an alien stalactite. My eyes close for a second.

Mom talking to the nurse upstairs brings me back. They're suctioning Glo's trach, which always makes my sister do this raspy old-man cough. The bubbly sound of mucus being sucked out always makes me gag, and I sympathy-cough. I should go up, talk to her about the pointe shoe painting. But I'm scared of the *then what* part. Besides, my clock claims it's late afternoon.

Into my bag go a bunch of random clothes, my makeup

bag, and some hair spray. I scrawl a quick note to Mom, telling her I'll probably stay at the Johansens' for the night. Kat never minds, and I think we're okay enough for a sleepover. Besides, I'll have a lot to talk about. The Purple Funk anything-could-happen is happening tonight.

I chase down the bus as it makes its turn. I'm stressed to the max and totally annoyed when I see some stranger taking up space in my usual seat. I sit behind him and read the banners running down the length of the bus—the free clinic and AIDS testing sandwiched between Virginia Slims and ginger ale. I'm seeing stuff about AIDS everywhere since Nikki told me about his father.

We creep away from the stop before Kat's and approach the next block. She's not there. So, here I am, getting off the bus and headed to her beige-and-brown Tudor instead of MDC.

Kat's block is the best in the neighborhood. Sometimes I walk around it a few times before going to her door. It's not about the *Better Homes and Gardens* lawns, or the huge houses with peaked roofs and picture windows the size of movie screens. It's about what's going on inside them. I'm sure Minnehaha Parkway family dinners are the polar opposite of mine.

I skip circling her block when I don't see Blondie. Kat's car lives underneath a fancy tarp in the driveway. Her grandfather gave her the Camaro, and then died a few months later. That car is special to her, whether it moves or not. And it's gone.

I march up to the front door and ring the bell.

Martina answers, sees that it's me, and furrows her brow

behind her wire glasses. Her eyes look puffy. "Miss Katherine's not here."

"Hi, Martina."

I hate that we both look over her shoulder like we're not supposed to be talking or something. Just like we do when she brings sandwiches to Kat's room for us.

"Do you know where she is?" I ask. "And her car?"

She shakes her head, but I know something big is up. Kat's mom is pacing in the living room in a giant ratty sweater. And I've never seen her in anything that wasn't pressed to high heaven.

"Dr. Johansen," I yell past Martina.

Kat's mom won't look at me. And Martina is closing the door in my face.

I stop it with my hand. "Can you at least tell Kat I stopped by? Por favor."

Martina nods, then leans closer and whispers, "You tell her I'm here, if she needs anything . . . if you see her."

"If I see her? What's that—"

The door closes.

I pound on it, but Martina doesn't come back.

What the hell just happened? Where is Kat? And Blondie? Everyone's in the wind. We're all revolving around the same sun—that's about it.

I trudge back to the bus stop. The afternoon is shifting to early evening, but the heat is still like lasers through the canopy of trees. After a few minutes, the next bus shows. I get on and flash my pass. I wipe my sweaty upper lip and find a seat anywhere. My Walkman's ready but, *man,* I don't feel like pressing Play.

The bus barrels down the straights and I give in to the blur. Two-stories by Lake Hiawatha transition to smaller stuccos. Then it's all maples and elms, cars, more buses, and taller buildings filled with suits and shoulder-padded secretaries heading home. One big smeary city.

By the time I'm in the stairwell at MDC, my head is so cloudy I almost run past the fifth floor. I skipped stopping by Geno's office too, that part totally intentional. I'm trying not to think about how drunk he got from the coin he took from me. The last one I snuck into Glo's room and hid. So, it's safe to say, he'll never find it. I hop down the extra steps and push through the heavy door.

"Hey." Jeffery moves aside. "Skipping warm-up too, huh?" He has these eyes that look happy all the time. I don't know how he does it. Even when I'm being a snot to him, he's cheery.

I sigh. "Which sicko decided that a Friday night class was a good idea?"

Jeffery nods in agreement. "I think they're deluded that it'll keep us from going out and getting into trouble."

"Fail," I say.

He high-fives me.

"You and the Master too cool for us this week?" he asks as we make our way down the hall.

No. Too drunk.

"Where've you been?" he asks.

My shoulders go all hunchy. I don't have to care about my posture when Geno's not here. He's probably gone full tilt now. Which means I could find him anywhere—or not at all. I run my cross back and forth on its chain. Tomorrow's the audition. If Geno's a no-show, what does that mean for me and First Avenue?

"I haven't been feeling well," I tell Jeffery, wringing my hands. "Master Geno too. Probably just a bug."

"Well, you picked the perfect day to show." He scrunches his lips and opens the door for me. "Sylvia's teaching . . . and Chia Pet's here too."

I consider fleeing while I have the chance. And then I see Stacy in the corner, pounding out turns so fast she'll give herself a neck injury. Chia bounds up to me. I shove past the Great Dane of epic proportion and drop my bag. Geno or no Geno, I'll be front and center at the audition. And going in cold after several days off won't do my triple pirouettes any favors.

"Junk off, people," Sylvia shouts. "Elastics are to be worn today, ladies.

Chia barks in agreement.

Junk is heaven in a Hefty bag. So there's a lot of groaning when the stripping starts. Plastic pants, leg warmers, and sweater unitards mean more pounds raining on the hardwood. Plus, it's just comfy, and I don't have to hold in my stomach so much.

I pull on the elastic Sylvia demands we wear to mark our hip alignment. Really, I don't get it. Anyone with two eyes can tell if their hips are too anterior or posterior, or if one is jacked up higher than the other. But at MDC it's form. Form. And more form. Stacy is fucking giddy.

I'm doing what I can with the new pointes I haven't bothered to trick. I bend them into a C, then pound them on the floor while I stretch in my center split.

The doors swing open and Kat breezes in, her hair half up, her leo strap falling from her shoulder.

She tosses her bag next to mine. "Hi," she says, as if nothing's up.

I wait for something more. When she goes to the barre and starts warming up without another word, I'm pissed. I cram on my shoes and march over. She doesn't turn around, even when I'm literally breathing down her back.

"What the hell, Kat?"

"What?" She swings her leg like a pendulum.

"What nothing. I stopped by your house. Where were you? Martina was being all weird. Your mom too. And where's Blondie?" I'm spewing stuff as fast as I can, as if she'll bail before I finish. I scan her body for more bruises, which makes her fidget. The purple on her arm has faded to a sick yellow.

She adjusts her elastic over her sharp hips. "Everything's cool. I'm driving Blondie now. That's all."

My eyes widen. "Okay . . . and this new revelation is stressing your mom to tears?"

She stiffens. "Lay off, Rosa, okay?"

Stacy puts herself between us like we might ruin class by pulling hair. "Ladies."

230

Kat looks as if she might cry, which is totally not her.

Sylvia whistles. "Let's go! I don't care if it's Friday. A late start means a late finish."

Chia tears to her side, giant paws thundering across the floor like a summer storm.

I breeze past Stacy, taking my usual place at the barre, right behind Kat. I can tell by the angle of her bunhead she doesn't want to talk.

I poke her backside with my toe anyway.

She barely bothers with a nod. She brushes me off the rest of class. She doesn't even stick her tongue out at me during center, or press a *this sucks* into my palm when Sylvia keeps us until every last dancer demonstrates a perfect chain of tight chaîné turns—Kat's nemesis.

Eight-thirty. Sylvia's finally through with us when the sun drags its blazing nails down the auburn horizon. I gather my stuff, my nerves back on cue. I have half an hour until I meet Nikki. And from the looks of it, Kat won't be sticking around to sift through the clothes I brought. She's stuffing her bag with such fury I look around for the fire.

She slips back into her wrap sweater.

"Whatcha got going tonight, Rosa?" Jeffery probes.

Stacy inches closer to our conversation.

"Nothing much," I say. "Just meeting a friend."

"A boyfriend?" Mr. Nosy asks, and now everyone's interested.

"*Not* a boyfriend."

"Do we know who it is?" Stacy says, all excited. I'm sure she's stoked for Jeffery to hear I might be off the market.

I catch a look from Kat. She's the only one I want to tell, so I leave it at that.

Stacy tugs on Jeffery's sleeve.

"Don't do anything I wouldn't do, Dominguez." He drapes an arm around her, which she eats up. "Until next time, ladies." He snaps a photo of Stacy before leaving, and I'm pretty sure she's gone straight to heaven. They're actually kinda cute together.

Kat leaves too, but she's waiting for me at the turn on the fourth floor. "So, who is he?"

"Who?"

She gives me "the look."

"What's it to you?" I shove past her, trying to sound easy-breezy, but it comes out gravelly and pathetic.

Kat stays on my heels. "Okay, I deserve that."

I spin around. "Yes. You do."

"I'm sorry, Rosa. I really am."

"Sorry for what?"

Kat squirms, swinging her bag around to her front. There's something clipped to the strap and it's not a Prince button.

"What's that?" I point at the black box, knowing full well what it is.

Kat covers it with her hand. "This? Oh, it's a pager."

"What the hell for?"

"Uh, my dad. Just an easy way to get ahold of me. He carries one. My mom too. You know doctors."

Kat's trying to come off all bubbly, but my best-friend radar hasn't quit yet. She's totally lying.

"Are you in trouble? I want it straight. Because you're my boulder, the one stable person in my life. And . . . and if you're falling apart, then I'm truly fucked." I push around a balled-up gum wrapper at my feet.

She picks up the piece of foil and drops it in her bag. "I'm fine. Well, I will be."

"What the Christ does that mean? I'm your best friend. When did we stop telling each other everything? The other day, you said you needed time, and I've given it to you."

"We'll talk soon. I promise."

"Why not now?" I press.

"Because . . ."

"You have to go. Yeah, I get it. You know, it really sucks that you're avoiding me. It would be so much easier if you'd just tell me we're done being friends." I take off before I scream at her. She doesn't follow me like I hoped she would.

Inside the dressing room, I collapse where Glo used to change.

The room is empty, everyone already bolted for Friday night. I'm sitting in something tacky, probably years of rosin pressed into the gross carpet. I glance at the corner, the "silo," as everyone calls it. The building's corners are rounded, like windowed turrets. Beginning-level dancers pine for a spot in the coveted upper-level corner. And now that my rose leo gives me the right to take up space there, I still use a grungy bathroom stall.

Usually I crouch on the toilet and eavesdrop on the chatter about weekend plans. I don't know why I do this. It's totally depressing. I usually have nowhere to be but here. Even Kat dedicates only one weekend day to me. The other her parents monopolize with things like tennis tournaments and boating on Lake Minnetonka—stuff you have to wear white for. I've never been invited. And I try to tell myself it's not because my skin is too dark. I mean, even my white undies aren't white anymore.

I'm alone, so I skip the stall and move to the mirrors. Plopping onto the floor, I should get to it, but the thought of slapping on eye shadow and doing something with my hair feels like the closing night of a marathon run of *The Nutcracker*. If I hear one more "Sugar Plum Fairy," I'm going to hurl.

I never spaz over things like fashion and makeup. I look how I look and if people don't like it, they can jump off a bridge. But now I'm freaking out major. Nikki still wants to hang. And I want his eyes to pop out of his head when he sees me. I want him to forget about what I said in the confessional.

I unravel my bun, then close my eyes and revisit kissing Nikki.

"Must be a juicy daydream."

I open my eyes. "God, you're like a fucking deer."

Stacy's looming over me all red and sweaty. "Thank you." She checks out her backside in the mirror. "Just running some stairs."

"Why?" I ask. "The ten thousand calories we burn every day not enough?"

"There's always room for improvement." She flicks her eyes at my chest, and I stick my boobs out more.

"Hey. No amount of running will get rid of these. There are many generations of DNA packed into these C-cups. Just like you probably inherited your flat chest from your—"

"I don't know who my mother is, so it's anyone's guess where my flat chest came from."

"Sorry. I didn't know."

"Weren't you listening the other day? I told you I was adopted. I practically shouted it for the entire universe to hear."

"Being adopted is nothing to be ashamed of."

"Who said I was ashamed?"

"All I'm saying is, some biological parents are way worse than the stand-ins. I mean, most people who adopt really want kids, right? Why else would someone—"

"Why else would someone take another person's rejects? That's what you were thinking, right?"

"Umm, totally not what I was thinking. Jesus, you're a pro at putting words in people's mouths." I peel myself from the carpet. "Well, I've got to get ready, so . . ."

Stacy doesn't leave, watching me like a mother hen as I procrastinate the undressing part.

I pull out a red tiered skirt, smoothing out the ruffles.

"Yup. You're totally going out on a date."

"That's so hard to believe?"

"With that hair, it is."

I glance at my curly mop, which resembles a rabid-lion's mane. I smush it down on the sides.

"Here." Stacy spins me by the shoulders, snatching my brush. "Sit."

I don't know why, but I obey.

"Hair is everything," she says. "It's no different than a lopsided bun. A bad bun means you'll have a terrible performance. You've got to have good hair on a date, or he'll be a horrible kisser."

I blush. Not. Possible.

She pulls my hair back on the sides. "You have such thick hair."

"It's annoying. I want to cut it short. But Geno. Well, you know."

"It's kind of . . . pretty."

"Thanks. Kind of."

Stacy rats my bangs. "Where were you yesterday? You missed Madame Rebecca."

I catch a flash of a daydream, driving with Nikki across the river. "Saint Paul. I had something to do."

"I've never been on the other side of the Mississippi."

"You're kidding."

"My father never lets me go anywhere."

"You're kidding." My sarcasm is lost on her.

"He sees too much bad stuff, I guess. Maybe a little overprotective." Stacy suddenly looks so much younger than eighteen, a timid little girl who lives in a very small world.

She fluffs the ends of my curls.

"Why are you helping me?" I ask.

"I know the Master's drunk in his office," Stacy spits out.

"He's not drunk, just tired." Well, at least I know where he is now.

"*Duh.* I could smell him from the hall. Everyone knows about him—about him sneaking off to that gross bar. And it's *totally* not a secret that he carries a flask in his leather jacket."

It is to me. Why am I so clueless? Does Kat know too?

I spin around, suddenly protective of Geno. Gossip about me, I can deal. But the rest of my family? Off-limits. "Everybody needs to mind their own fucking business."

Stacy's hands fall to her sides. "That day in studio 6B."

"What of it?"

"That's why I'm helping you. I know what it's like, not being good enough. To have a parent wish you were someone else." She grinds her toes into the carpet. "My adoptive mom left us when I was little."

Shit.

"Why?" I ask, as if the reason will make a difference in how much it sucks.

"I don't know. Maybe when her badge-wife friends started having blond Gerber babies, she was embarrassed . . . by me."

Jesus. I stretch my legs out in a center split, my calves on the verge of cramping. Wishing we were someone else. Everyone's doing it, I guess.

Stacy holds my gaze in the mirror. "Odette's solo terrifies me."

I say nothing. I don't want to talk about Odette.

"Your dancing," she goes on. "It's not technically stellar, but when you perform, it's like you become someone else. And when you did the lift with the Master, everyone wanted to be you—or with you. I saw the look on Jeffery's face. I—I can't do that, totally obvious when you found me in 6B. And no amount of Sylvia's elastics and corrections will make a difference. That solo, well, you know."

Wow. Baby-Pink Eye Shadow is sort of giving me a compliment. And I sense there isn't a slam waiting in the wings.

"Anyone who wants to be me should have their head checked."

Stacy plops down next to me. "That day you and Kat saw me in the stairwell. I wasn't going to 6A. I just wanted you to think I was because I know how obsessed you are about Prince."

I grin. It's like I'm back in the confessional. "I figured."

"What gave it away?"

"Probably the Madonna lace glove, the sparkly MJ glove, the beauty mark, and the kitchen sink you were wearing."

"*Hmpf.* I don't like you. You know that, right?"

"I figured that too." I smooth out the flyaways from the arch of my bangs.

"Do you want to know why?" she asks.

Do I? Once I start to care, it'll hurt. And I'm so done with pain.

"I don't like you because you don't care. You have every opportunity to be a principal, and you act like none of it matters. Meanwhile, the rest of us are killing ourselves to prove we deserve it. I'd give anything to be in your position, and you're going to throw it away." Stacy slumps against the wall. "I really hate you for that, Rosa."

There it is, like Kat said. But I can't change how I feel

about becoming a principal. Not even with the knowledge of how much easier everything would be if I just fell in line.

"I dance at MDC on a scholarship," Stacy whispers, as if the toilets will hear.

Scholarship? I had no idea MDC offered those.

"Now that I'm eighteen, if I don't get the apprenticeship, I'm out. I won't be able to afford all the classes. And then what? I'll be nothing."

Nothing? Mother Mary, it's too late for me, but save this girl.

"I don't think you'll have to worry," I say. "Your classical technique is on point, and that's what MDC wants from their dancers. Besides, if you crash and burn, the dance world is much bigger than Minnesota Dance Company. I'm sure there's more to you than flawless brisés."

"You think my brisés are flawless?"

I shrug.

She leans away, cringing. "I cut the crotches out of your leotards . . . all three times."

"I put a bunch of tardy marks by your name in Lou's attendance book."

Stacy gasps and I cover my mouth so I won't cackle.

"I really liked your sister," she blurts.

Everything shrinks, the dressing room becoming hot and stuffy. "She's still alive, so you can still like her."

"Of course. I'm sorry."

No one ever talks about Glo. Well, except for Kat. It's like my sister ceased to exist after the accident.

"She was—*is* so nice," Stacy continues. "She used to help me after class, with my fouettés. Hers were so sharp—seamless. That day in 6B . . . you kind of reminded me of her, when you were helping me."

Me. Like Glo? I swear, my entire body is glowing from within.

"Everyone admired her," Stacy adds.

I know this. I just choose to forget I'm surrounded by people who miss Glo too. She had tons of friends before the accident. And to say they ditched her really isn't fair. Some of them tried to stay in touch. But Mom wouldn't allow any visitors. So I guess they just gave up. I swallow, my throat stinging.

Stacy bows her head. "Everyone leaves. When my dad goes to work, I never know if he'll come back. And friends, whatever. Earlier this week one of the twins asked me to go shopping and then blew me off for someone else."

There's a memory in there somewhere of Stacy on the verge of tears when her dad picked her up in his cop car.

"And Glo," Stacy says. "She left too. Right when we were becoming friends."

I don't look at her. If I do, I'll cry until my eyes seal shut.

"She's not gone," I say. "You can come and visit her. Anytime."

"Yeah?" She lights up. "I'd really like that."

"So would Glo," I say, without a doubt.

Stacy scoots to her knees, studies her work, then rats my bangs some more, finishing them off by smoothing over the top layer.

"May I?" She eyes the Aqua Net peeking from my bag.

"Knock yourself out." I squeeze my eyes closed and hold my breath.

She sprays my entire head, enough to choke Mötley Crüe. "It'll do."

It will. My hair never looked so awesome. Stacy's a genius. But I'll keep that little gem to myself. She works her magic with my makeup too. Then I get changed—right in front of her, without any weirdness or anything.

I wriggle into a tight tank top, then pull on a mesh top over that.

Stacy yanks the wide neck off my shoulder. "There. Showing a little skin always works."

"Thanks for this." I swirl my hand in front of my face. I meet her eyes in the mirror again. "Jeffery likes comic books. Those *Archie* ones he always reads between classes? They sell them at Shinders."

She blushes.

"Why are we so awful to each other?" I ask.

Stacy shrugs. "I'm awful to you because you're terrible to me . . . and I guess I can be a little guarded and . . ."

"Defensive, insensitive, and mean," I add.

She crosses her arms.

"I meant, me," I say.

She drags her bag over and pulls something out. "You'll need shoes."

I grab my chest. My Docs—pink rhinestones glued in place of the purple ones that had fallen off. I can't do anything but gawk at them. It's like a part of Abuela has come back to me.

"I meant to give them right back. . . . I would wear pumps." Stacy shoves the shoes at me, her eyes all watery. "But you're not me."

I take the Docs, the uppers polished, the soles scrubbed clean of Hennepin's filth.

"I shouldn't have taken them," she says. "I'm sorry."

"Stacy . . ."

"Purple rhinestones are hard to come by, so . . ."

"I can deal." I sit and pull on a pair of black over-the-knee socks. Then the Docs, my eyes welling too.

"Oh, and this." She fishes out the shirt I was wearing that day, Glo's neon MTV. "I don't know where everything else went. Sorry."

I take the folded shirt. "This is Glo's." I hand it back. "Why don't you bring it to her yourself?"

Stacy smiles. "Okay." Back into her bag it goes, and then she helps me up. "Let's see."

I yank down my skirt. I wish Kat was here to give me her runway critique. But she's doing her own thing now. I guess it's time I do mine. "This really okay? The length feels a little short."

"Yeah, but it works."

Kat's crisp voice spins me around. My eyes flick to Stacy like I've been caught cheating. She must feel the same, because she's already gathering up her stuff.

"I thought you had someplace to be," I say. I so want to be

mad at her. But inside I'm amped like we're back at the Met Center, about to witness Prince sing his tight ass off.

"I'm where I need to be," Kat says, doing an awful job of hiding how much the scene hurts her feelings.

Stacy shoulders her bag and gives me a timid wave. "Have fun tonight, Rosa."

The urge to hug Stacy is there. But I don't. I tap my chest over my heart like Nikki, and I hope she gets it.

"There's no way I won't," I say, clicking the heels of my Docs together.

The Gay 90's

Kat follows me down Hennepin. I've been waiting for her to start guilt-tripping me about Stacy, or explain herself, but the clack of her Dr. Scholl's on the pavement is the only thing coming out of her. Somehow, somewhere, we lost our ability to speak to each other.

Like always, I slow up at Moby's to take a peek inside. "It's Nikki," I finally say, because the silence is fucking excruciating. "From Teener's the other day." *When you were still telling me stuff.*

"I guessed as much." She kicks a can down the sidewalk, then picks it up and tosses it into an overflowing trash can. "So, you and Stacy are friends now?"

"I don't know . . . maybe."

Kat kicks another can, this time into the gutter.

"I told my mom I was staying at your place tonight," I say.

"You can't. Not tonight."

"Why?"

The quilted pleather door to the XXX opens and we both pretend we're not dying of curiosity. Bill Withers's "Use Me" booms from inside. Kat cranes her neck over my shoulder. The door shuts, moving us on without her answer.

"Why, Kat?" I push.

"You just can't, okay?"

"Not okay." I stop us, glancing at her pager.

Kat catches my meaning. "These things aren't just for drug dealers and prostitutes, Rosa." She walks again, slowing up at Teener's. "Let's be done with it, for now. You're here, and . . ." She shifts the neck of my T-shirt. "You're positively glowing. Hennepin won't need streetlights tonight." Her soft smile reminds me that we're still best friends, no matter what's messing with our lives.

Teener's is closing up. Oz is stacking a shelf of glittered top hats in the window next to Nikki's feather boa creation.

I check my reflection in the glass, like I've done in every storefront for the last few blocks. I lift my foot to make sure my Docs are really on my feet. My skirt is a little more mini than it was last year, but it still covers my ass. I don't know about glowing, but maybe I should run stairs with Stacy. I turn around, scrutinizing my backside. *Nah.*

"My girls!" Oz pounds the window, the giant belled sleeve of his kimono swaying.

Kat waves back. "I'm really happy for you, Rosa. You deserve good things."

"So do you." I grab her hands.

"I want you to have some fun, sexy dancer."

I tighten my grip as she pulls away. "We aren't finished.

You said you knew what you had to do, whatever that means. But tomorrow. After the audition. I'll call you, and we'll talk."

"Yes. Talk then," she says, her words quick and sharp.

She opens the door for me.

I hesitate and then step inside. I turn around, a ball of schoolgirl nerves. "Any advice?"

"Yeah. You and Nikki tonight. Don't think about anything else." She looks away.

I watch her go, my gut seizing like it does when she leaves me at her stop.

"I felt your frown before it got here," Oz says.

I cover my mouth. "I'm frowning?"

He breaks into song, balancing a sequined hat on his head like he's Liza Minnelli at the Kit Kat Club. I wish I'd known him back in the day when he was on Broadway.

"Don't stop," I say when he does, because now I'm totally smiling.

"What are you seeking today?" he croons.

"Umm. Nikki?"

"Ah. Of course. Everyone's always looking for Nikki."

"Like, who?" I ask. I'm curious. Who trolls for Nikki at Teener's? What girls, or boys—or both?

"Eh." Oz waves his hand. "He's in the back. Just follow the Concerto in D Minor."

"Thanks." I elbow through a narrow aisle of wigs, to the rear of the store.

It'll be my first time in the bowels of Teener's. I've imagined it an endless secret garden of vintage props, costumes, and glitter makeup. I pass through a curtain of glassy beads, and it's like a portal to a sparkling galaxy.

A maze of shimmery colors and textures meanders in all directions, which makes me think of Glo's pointe painting, so I guess I'm already failing at taking Kat's advice because now I'm dwelling on the both of them.

The waxy scent of clay mixed with plastic beckons me deeper. I follow the echo of strings, running my hand along a rack of fake fur as I track the violins through the maze—Concerto in D Minor, playing off the prism lights of the disco ball overhead.

I come upon Nikki without being noticed. Watching him in secret is becoming a habit. One I don't intend to break because my insides are flashing over. He's heavy into something on a table, brushing and patting away.

Heat spreads from my numb toes to the top of my head as I check out his space—the cot in the corner, his nightstand littered with packs of gum, expensive hair products and makeup. Closest to me is a dressing-room station that looks like it was relocated from an old theater. Clear bulbs frame the mirror, a sea of jars filled with makeup brushes on the tabletop.

I sneak closer. A photo is taped to the mirror, the edges curled and worn. It's a picture of a man who looks a lot like Nikki. He's wearing shorts, a T-shirt, and tap shoes. His dad. It has to be. I pat my chest like Abuela used to.

My reflection in the full-length mirror doesn't catch his attention. I squint to see what he's focused on. A pair of pointe shoes, maybe? And he's doing something to them with a makeup sponge.

"What's up?" I ask.

"Jesus!" He yanks a towel over the stuff on the table. "Girl, you can't sneak up on people like that. You'll make them dead." He faces me.

"What're you doing?" I crane my neck.

"Nothing . . . art, I guess." He wipes something brownish from his hands. "For a friend," he adds.

"Really? My sister's an artist." It comes out before I can stop myself.

He clutches the edge of the table behind his back. "That's cool."

Nikki has a strut, and he uses every inch of it getting to me. God, my daydreaming did a suck job of remembering how gorgeous he is.

Tonight I'm the only one in a short skirt. Nikki's in acid-washed jeans and a red skintight fishnet tank. And with his rad high-heeled boots—he looks like he just moonwalked out of the TV from *Friday Night Videos*.

By the time we're face to face, I don't care what's on that table. He smells like mint and expensive hair gel. His Jheri curls are slicked back into a low bun, making his face even more dramatic. I won't tell Stacy his makeup is way better than mine.

His eyes tour my legs. "Look at my girl. All cleaned up and ready for the Funk Factory. Dig the shoes. And just when I thought you couldn't get any finer."

I'm totally smiling because he is. Can't help it. "I was afraid, after the confessional . . ."

He takes my hand. "Hey. We all got stuff, am I right?"

"Well, my stuff and your stuff could fill one of those giant blue dumpsters outside."

If air could be awkward, we're suddenly surrounded by it. So there's no point in avoiding the question I've wanted to ask since Sun's. "Why'd you ask me out?"

"For real?" Nikki caresses my hand.

"You're not, like, one of those bun chasers, are you?" I'm kidding, but not really.

"Nah. It's not like that."

"Okay. Then why me?"

"Because I like you."

"Why? I'm asking because . . . not very many people do." I pull back. Saying this aloud hurts a little more than I expected.

Nikki sits on his cot, the heels of his boots swallowed up by a white bearskin rug on the floor.

"I like you because you're real, Rosa. I mean, *damn, girl,* with all the questions. But at least you're not afraid to ask. Most people don't bother. They assume. Or just make up shit. I get it. I know I'm not everyone's bag, with the makeup and all. What sucks is when people say they're cool, when they're really not. Shinders, when you saw me checkin' the *Drag* mag . . . it was easy being myself that day. You made it safe. *I* felt safe. It's not always like that."

The beer bottle incident. I get it, but then again, will I ever really? I go to Nikki and sit beside him. "The company in the magazine, that Trockadero ballet. I know those are pointe shoes underneath that towel. You say they're for a friend." I rest my hand on his knee. "Does that friend have time for ballet?"

Nikki picks at his iridescent blue nail polish. "You saw. My days aren't always an easy afternoon in Shinders." A shower of goose bumps spreads across his arms.

"And still you're, like, the most confident person I've ever met."

He swishes his feet around the fluffy rug. "Confidence and fear don't look all that different on the outside, Strawberry."

I lean into his side, leaving things there.

He jumps up, wiping his eyes. "All right, let's see the twirl."

I spring from the bed, smashing down my skirt before spinning around, the draft from the vent douching my ass with cold air.

"Oh yeah." Nikki's dark eyes glimmer beneath the rotating disco light. "Definitely funk ready."

"About that. Exactly where're we going?" Not that it matters. I'd go about anywhere with Nikki.

"Come on." He takes my hand, his skin so soft I doubt he's done a lick of actual work for Oz.

"Wait. My leotard? You said it'd be in today."

"You never take a day off, do you?" Nikki slips my bag from my shoulder, hanging it on a hook next to the vampire capes.

"Hey! I'll need that tomorrow."

"You need a cape for the audition?"

I sigh.

He dots his lips with some gloss. "You'll get it back later, along with your leotard on the front counter."

I snatch his tin of gloss, using it too. "My audition's at eight a.m. sharp. Doors locked after that, according to Master Geno."

My body is suddenly part of Nikki's, his hand firm against my back. "Then it's a good thing I got you."

He kisses me so deeply, anything else I wanted to say dissolves on his minty tongue.

I don't have to go far to find out where the Purple Funk Factory is—sort of. We start by leaving Teener's through a back entrance. Nikki even shows me where he keeps the hidden key inside a rusty can filled with nails.

"What if I come back here and steal all the feather boas?" I ask.

"I trust you," he says, and I tell him with my fluttery eyes I might love him.

We backtrack, going one block past MDC. Nikki holds my hand the entire way, which tingles every inch of me.

There's a whole lot of commotion ahead, spilling off the sidewalk and into the street in front of the Gay 90's. The club is the pinnacle of the drag scene—Nikki's scene, by the way his face animates as we get closer. Colorful marquee lights pulse off the crowd. It takes us a sec to clue into the fight happening in the center of the masses. It's not a fair match. A much smaller guy is on his back, getting the crap kicked out of him.

Nikki lets go of me and shoves his way through, right behind a bouncer made of head-to-toe muscle.

I shout after Nikki but doubt he hears. He's already in the thick of it, pushing back on some dude coming at the bouncer from behind.

"Enzo!" Nikki yells.

The bouncer spins around, zeroing in on Nikki with sharp panther eyes.

"Get outta here, Nic!" he shouts.

"Nah!" he yells back, holding off the guy who's, like, twice his size.

Enzo grabs the guy who is pitching kicks by the collar and peels him off the other man.

I'm suddenly in a mess of sharp elbows jabbing me from all directions. I can't tell whose side I'm supposed to be on, so I slam my shoulder against anyone coming up too close. I focus on glimpses of Nikki through the crowd. He's still standing.

"Rosa!" I hear Nikki shout, but I've lost sight of him. My heart thrashes against my ribs. I'm grabbing at random T-shirts to stay upright, and pretty sure my skirt is jacked around my waist by now. Thank God I've got my Docs, or my toes would be pancakes. Something I hope isn't warm spit hits my cheek. I wipe it away with the back of my hand.

Sirens blare in the distance and everyone scatters. A handful of guys pile into a car. They swerve up onto the sidewalk, a beer bottle sailing toward Nikki and Enzo.

"Smear the queer!" the asshole hollers from the window as they peel away.

The bottle hits Enzo, blood trickling from his forehead. I think I let loose a scream.

Nikki jumps to it like he's going to give chase, until Enzo stops him.

Nikki rips off the bandanna tied around his leg. "Hold this here, Enz." He presses the cloth against the cut, eyes darting from one end of Hennepin to the other. "Man! Why'd someone call the cops?"

"Shouldn't they?" I huff.

Anyone still standing snaps in my direction. I straighten the hem of my skirt.

Enzo shakes his head.

"Girl, you wanna make things worse, go right ahead. Call them every time." A bouncer in drag emerges from inside. She's a Greek statue, at least seven feet tall, I swear. I'm sure my mouth is gaping.

"Nic, get outta here before they show," Enzo says. "And take her with you, huh?"

I hug myself and shrink into the shadows. I've heard some of the MDC dancers talk of the 90's. Straight girls aren't exactly a favorite at the club. And neither are Nikki's "dates," which is confirmed by the sour look Enzo is giving me.

A cop car skids to a stop, followed by another, earsplitting sirens and blinding lights blaring. The guy from the fight circle is limping, holding a yellow scarf to his puffy eye.

Nikki pats him on the back. "You okay?"

He nods, and then it's all blue and badges.

Enzo points down the street and, kind of half-assed, says, "They went that way."

The first cop takes in the scene, his gaze pausing on me, then resting on Enzo. "You fighting again?"

"Defending," Enzo says, waving Nikki away.

The cop saunters around Enzo and yellow-scarf guy. "I've got a carload of men down the block who say otherwise."

"Liars," Nikki spits.

I grab his arm and try to drag him away, but he's like a fucking elm tree.

The cops are unclipping their cuffs from their belts. "Anyone bleeding, you know the drill," one of them says. "Don't make it uglier than it already is." He flicks his nasty gaze toward the Greek goddess.

This is bullshit. We all know it. But Enzo turns around like getting cuffed for something he didn't do is old news. Yellow-scarf guy is already being stuffed into the back of a cruiser.

"Wait!" I shout, everything on fire—my eyes, ears, all of it.

Enzo taps his chest. "Go, Nic. I'll catch you later."

"But you didn't do anything!" I'm yelling at everyone now. Why the hell am I the only one? "Why aren't you arresting those guys in the car?"

Nikki's got a good grip on my arm now. He kisses Enzo on the cheek. His lips linger there, the side-eye he's giving the cops testing the waters.

"See you on the flip side," Enzo says. "The club will bail me out." The statuesque bouncer places a red vase on the stool at the front door, a sign taped to it, BAIL MONEY.

Nikki nods, and then he's pulling me away.

He moves me alongside the street traffic, cars idling bumper-to-bumper, waiting for the light. His sweaty arm is wound tightly around my waist like I might dash back to the scene.

"That was so wrong, Nikki. What the—"

"It's just easier, Rosa," he snaps. "Don't question something you know nothing about."

I'm trying not to feel stupid, but it's impossible.

We stop at an inconspicuous door in the alley. My head is crammed with rage. I want to talk about it, and don't just the same, because I'll scream. What does one say to someone who gets assaulted for who they are and then arrested for defending it?

Nikki covers my hand with his. He's shaking, his face beaded with sweat.

I touch the small scratch across his nose. "Some of the dancers have talked about nights like this. Guys getting harassed, the awful things that've happened to people who come here."

"You mean people like me." It's subtle, but the quick glimpse of Nikki's shame compels me to gather him up in my arms—or fucking punch someone.

"The people at the 90's," he says. "They're my real family.

They were for dad too, when it really mattered. Every hour inside those walls is another I can dress the way I want, be the way I want, without all the shit, you know?"

I press my palm against his chest, feeling his heart thumping hard and fast. "I'm sorry for what those assholes did."

"Don't be sorry." Nikki's eyes home in on mine. "Be angry."

The gloom of the alley consumes us. He yanks me against him and I grip his shirt until my knuckles turn white. I kiss him. Pissed off, angry at the universe, kiss him. And he kisses me back, soft open lips smashing against mine. I tug at his tank top, wanting to tear something apart because I swear it's the only way to calm the tornado under my skin.

Nikki breaks away, chest heaving. "Mad kissing, Strawberry. You got that down."

I pull him toward me again, but the mood is shifting like his fidgeting feet. He doesn't want to dwell, and I must try to understand this. His enduring show of confidence makes all sorts of sense now.

"You have arrived." He opens the door. It closes behind us and we're alone in a dim, empty hallway.

"Arrived where, exactly?" I wrap my arms around myself, still shaking from the last several minutes.

Nikki must feel it, because he takes my hand, drawing tiny circles in my palm. My stomach turns circles too as we descend a creepy flight of stairs. The air transitions from humid summer night to cold and cryptlike. But the last time I went to a basement with Nikki, things didn't turn out horribly. So I follow.

At the bottom, his shadow stops. "Shhh. Do you hear it?"

I strain to listen through my shivering. "The sound of hindsight and utter regret?"

He laughs. "If you don't want to go further, say the word and I won't push it."

"Ha! If every girl had a pounded-out nickel for every time she heard that."

"Smooth, right?"

In the distance—a faint bass pulses in the darkness. "What is that?" I grasp Nikki's arm.

His lips brush my ear. "That, girlfriend, is the Funk."

The Purple Funk Factory

A tunnel. And we're in it. A very old one. Probably part of the secret system of underground passageways everyone thinks is just an urban legend. I back against a spider-webbed shelf holding a row of flashlights. Nikki chooses one, clicks it on, and we navigate the tunnel. The bass pounds louder, like when I rest my ear against Glo's chest to hear her strong heart.

"We're under the city." I run my hand along the cold, dewy rock wall. "Railroad tracks are probably right above us now." I've heard about the tunnels. How workers once used them to move lumber and, later, drug runners smuggled everything from people to cocaine through them. The mob has supposedly killed lots of people down here too. Nikki catches me crossing myself.

"It's not haunted. Some people say it is, but no way. I don't get any juju vibes."

"And you normally do?"

The corridor pulsates, a throbbing boom mixed with the energy of a riotous crowd as we take a right at the fork. Nikki snaps his finger to the beat, all slick and sashaying along with it.

He shines the light on another set of stairs, leading up. I

trail on his heels to a door at the top, so amped I can barely stand the wait.

"*X* marks the spot." He aims the light.

There's actually an *X*. A silver mark on a black door. Music plays from the other side. We have arrived.

I bounce in my Docs, squeezing my gold cross. "Open it! Open it!"

Nikki whirls me around, holding the ghostly beam below my chin. "Rosalia Lorena Dominguez Corredor—Strawberry Girl."

"Yes?" I squeal.

"Tell me something."

"Anything."

"Were you born to dance?"

"Huh?"

Nikki moves so close our chests brush. "When you wake up in the morning and step into those superfly Docs of yours, do you know from the deepest parts of your soul, all the way to the top of your foxy little head, you were born to dance?"

Touching Nikki makes my answer difficult to gather. Born to dance? Is it really all about genetics and nothing else? Was the choice ever mine? I'm overthinking Nikki's question to death, but what would my world look like if I couldn't dance? My mind is all Glo, but I'm not lamenting the fluttery brisés she used to do. It's her art. And how, when I watch her paint, I'm totally mesmerized by her movements—her hands sweeping down the canvas like fluid Sylvia chaîné turns. Glo and I, we were born forever-dancers.

My chest is on fire. *"Yes,"* I say. It's the only possible reply. "I was born to dance. Raised to dance. I would die without it." I lick my lips.

"Then, my Strawberry Girl, tonight you're immortal." Nikki knocks on the door, two quick taps, followed by three long ones.

The door swings open and we're swallowed up by the rhythmic bass, the same that haunts me at MDC. I hold my breath.

"Welcome to the Purple Funk Factory." Nikki leads me inside.

If Teener's is heaven, then the Funk Factory is the rapture in a huge warehouse. I turn a circle with my mouth hanging open like a dorky tourist. I'm beyond caring about how I look. Onstage at the far end of the undulating space, backlit by a purple glow, are the musicians, some of whom I recognize as part of the Revolution.

"Holy—" I clutch Nikki's hard chest. "Is that—"

"The one and onlys."

"Is he here?" I shriek, so uncool.

"The word is, not tonight. But you never know. Sometimes he shows up and jams for a few."

"Are you kidding me?"

"My uncle sits in when he's in town. He's laid some tracks with the man."

"No. Way."

"You're cute. Drink?" Nikki asks.

"Uh-huh," I mumble, unable to tear my eyes away from

two women gyrating their hips against each other on the dance floor. Everyone is breaking the barrier of fineness, dressed in the latest everything and moving in a way I'm never allowed. A wiry chick slides across the floor in pinstriped vest and trousers, her short hair slicked back like Bowie's. A guy in a leather corset and purple tulle skirt twirls past. The freedom of the 90's is undeniably here at the Funk.

I glance at my own hodgepodge outfit. I am way out of my league.

We make our way to the bar, which is really a table set up in the corner with a bunch of bottles crowding the top.

"What's your poison?" Nikki asks. "There's pop, water . . ."

I point to a bottle of bubbly stuff. "Champagne, please."

Nikki crinkles his nose, sticking it in the air. "Oh. Pardon me. The lady drinks champagne."

Actually, I've never tasted champagne in my life. But it seems miles away from whiskey and I don't want to be sixteen tonight.

Nikki pours me a glass, the foam spilling over the top so I have to suck it up fast, which he totally loves.

"I think I like champagne too," he says, mischief in his razor eyes.

Really, it tastes like nasty sour vinegar, but I take a delicate sip anyway, my pinky in the air for whatever reason. I'm so nervous, I end up gulping the entire thing. I hold out my glass for more, the fizz erupting in my nose making me cough.

Nikki's smile falters.

"I thought you liked champagne too." I push my empty

glass against his abs, ignoring that I skipped hydrating after class.

"You have an audition tomorrow."

"Oh, now you're all business?" I grab the bottle and fill my own glass. I drink it down, Geno and the audition tucked away.

"Watch it, girl." Nikki snags the bottle back. "That stuff'll sneak up on you."

I drape a lazy arm around Nikki, telling myself I can't possibly be tipsy already, just high on wild purple energy.

He takes my glass, setting it aside. "You and me. Out there." He points to the dance floor. "Next song. Whatever they play."

"You're on."

"I'm dying to see your famous moves."

"I never said I was famous," I squeak.

"I take six classes a week," Nikki teases. *"Only the best of the best will make the apprenticeship."*

I'm about to sock him in his bulging delt when a beauty from the dance floor sidles up and drapes her arm around him. "Finally! Where've you been? No one's worthy of me out there tonight."

"Hi," I say.

She totally blows me off. I mean, doesn't even look at me.

Nikki unwinds himself from her grasp, a stack of gold bracelets jingling from her wrist. "Jade, this is Rosa."

Now she checks me out. "Tasting the entire rainbow, huh, Nik?"

My skin prickles. Tonight is mine and Nikki's. And no one,

262

not even a girl with flowing red Godiva hair and legs that start at my rib cage will ruin it.

"That's some wicked wit," I shout over the music. "Jade and Rosa. Both colors. But I think pink is above green on the rainbow. So, the only one worthy of *me* tonight is Nikki." I tug him onto the dance floor. He doesn't look back at Jade, which gives me hope I'll live up to my big mouth.

"Damn, Strawberry," Nikki gasps. "No one burns Jade like that. She's, like, a top-tier Funk Angel."

"Whatever that means."

"Just a tag for the girls who can really move." Nikki's hands go to my hips and I let him shake them, swishing my skirt.

A Funk Angel. I'd sell my soul.

"I made up that rainbow stuff," I say. "I have no idea what I'm talking about."

"Sounded good to me. Just don't go to the bathroom solo, is all I'm saying."

I grasp his hands. "You and me, *solo* tonight. Okay?"

He spins me out, and back around to face him. I want to kiss him again, but if I do, I'll never stop.

A killer alto is belting out Chaka Khan's "Sweet Thing" like her life depends on it. Nikki and I stay on the fringes of the pulsating crowd. He grips my hips again, and it's clear I have no idea what to do. My dancing-with-a-boy experience is limited to a pas de deux en pointe. I've never danced with anyone the way Nikki obviously wants. He pulls me close, and my legs shift into instinctual mode, tensing as if preparing for a lift.

Nikki's pelvis sways with the music and my hands find the

back of his neck. The rest of me remains as stiff as a tutu. My partner doesn't seem to care, as long as there's no air between us. His slick, smooth arms glisten beneath the spotlights. I move my hips with his and it's clear how turned on he is. Everything below my waist fires up.

He sings against my cheek, things like wanting to satisfy me—love me.

Bless you, Chaka Khan.

I nuzzle against him and there's no one else in the room but Nikki. I kiss his neck. He groans, and I feel my skirt lift a little.

The band segues into another song, the infectious beat of Prince's "D.M.S.R." My head snaps to the stage.

Is he here? Good Lord Baby Jesus, let tonight be the night.

But Prince doesn't appear, so I find my bearings on the overcrowded floor. It's happening now. Nikki's jammin' to the music, feet barely touching the floor between spins. For a few beats, I just stand there, ogling him like I did in secret behind the rack of clown shoes.

"C'mon. Show me whatcha got, Strawberry." He claps, then backs up. We catch the attention of a few next to us and they give me some room. I want to dive under the nearest table but I'm frozen, the moves I've bragged about tangled up in my damned self-consciousness.

Jade smells my fear, swooping in like a witch in black fishnets.

"Never hesitate, girl." She kicks her leg so high she almost beans me in the forehead.

Oh, it's on. I spin like Nikki, following it up with a head roll that whips my hair like a Whitesnake video diva. It takes a second for my eyes to catch up, the champagne swirling my brain.

"Yeeeaass!" Nikki hollers, answering my steps with a few of his own.

I jump into another revolution, churning my hips in a full circle.

Nikki's bright eyes follow every inch of my body. "You've got badass rhythm, down with the D.M.," he shouts. "Now show me your S.R.!"

"What?" I yell back.

Jade's suddenly in my ear with her annoying Love's Baby Soft perfume. "You've got no Sex, little girl. No Romance." She touches Nikki's nipple ring poking through his mesh shirt. "Where'd you find this one, Nik? Ballet class?"

"Cut it, Jade." Nikki steals me away before I tell her to kiss my classically trained ass.

But I catch her meaning.

"I'm not the first bunhead you've brought here, am I?"

"My one and only. For real." His hand brushes my stomach, and I'm all flutters again. Tonight what Nikki does outside the Funk doesn't matter.

The crowd spins around us. There are some ace moves on the floor. Dance, Music, Sex, Romance. It's all here.

Nikki squeezes my shoulders. "You wanna take a break?"

The band switches out a few players, taking it down a notch with a sexy, smooth instrumental.

I drape my arms around his neck and arch back into a deep bend.

"I guess not."

His hands are confident and steady at the small of my back, supporting my weight, but not so much that I can ignore my abs.

Ballet, love it or not—Geno's meticulous corrections have given me an awareness of every inch of my body. It's about committing to the moves and feeling the rhythm. It's about looking with my whole body, coaxing the audience to follow my focus, which is what everyone around me is doing now.

Nikki's hands press into my flesh, urging me to come back to him. His fingers trace a line from my hip, to my navel, all the way up to my chin as I uncurl. I extend my arms like wings, fingers fanned, pinkies flared as if they're the tips of my flight feathers.

All my years spent onstage, an illusion in pointe shoes. One night, a flower. The next, a snow queen. The magic never lasts, because underneath the satin and tulle, I'm still me. Rosa, the girl who's afraid to be herself.

Something different is happening under the whirling lights of the Purple Funk Factory. I come in for a landing and begin to move like never before. Even in the Vault, the fear of getting caught lingered, stunting my extensions—weighing down my leaps. There's nothing but the dance floor here. I don't care what I look like. There's no skinny mirror to fight over. No Master Geno. No photos of Mom and Glo scrutinizing my turnout. The crowd is singing, chanting—chewing gum with their hair down in a sea of purple eye shadow. And they're waiting to see what I brought.

The rhythm builds inside my chest. I dare to peel off my Docs, then turn a quick soutenu, following up with a développé that would shatter another teacup test. Nikki gives me space and we lock eyes. My pointed foot hovers above my head with flawless Stacy McGee form. I sweep my leg down and across like a pendulum, the momentum drawing my body across the floor. I windmill my arms, arching back into a deep port de bras derrière until my fingers graze the floor.

"Get it, girl!" Nikki taunts, groovin' around me in a slow circle.

I pop up and get back to it with an ear-smashing battement. Lights pulse. The beat vibrates the floor, a mellow rhythm, moving us as if we have no say in the matter. I'm peeling open, heavy layers shedding onto the floor.

I have no idea how long we dance, how many counts of eight I swish my skirt above my ass. Only that by the time we stop, the floor is completely ours. My face is drenched with sweat, and I'm pretty sure I've flashed the total of the room my black satin undies a hundred times.

Nikki twirls me one last time and escorts me away to a massive ovation of cheers. I think I might explode. My heart is sprinting a staccato rhythm in my ears. I can't wait to tell Glo where I've been. How I danced, in front of everyone at the Purple Funk Factory with my elbows wherever I fucking wanted.

We stop on the fringes of the dance floor, Nikki holding me close. I think I'm speechless. He raises his perfectly tweezed eyebrows. "Damn!"

"So, you think I'm good?" We're panting all over each other, but neither of us seems to care.

"Uh, I brought you here thinking I'd teach you a thing or two about the groove." He kisses me, his upper lip as wet and salty as mine. "I stand corrected."

My body zings with so much energy I could dance all night. And maybe we will. I watch Nikki's biceps flex while he pours us some water. Or . . . maybe we'll do something else. I'm so ready to graduate beyond making out on a washing machine. My world blew up tonight. Stacy says she's never been to the other side of the Mississippi. I just flew to another dimension.

"You're trying too hard. It's desperate." Jade's suddenly at my side again.

"I didn't see you trying at all." I prance away, my Docs clutched in my hands like weapons.

I snatch an abandoned glass of champagne from a table and pound it, swallowing an erupting cough before anything sprays from my nose again.

Nikki joins me, and I snatch another glass.

"You might wanna pace your bad self."

I grip his shirt, yanking him against me. "Is this too fast?" My voice has a foreign smokiness. Rosa Dominguez, the good girl, has left the building and I don't want her back.

Nikki kisses my forehead. "Find a place in that brain to remember you have an audition in the a.m."

My grasp tightens. "Secret. I'm only auditioning so I can dance at First Ave. I don't really want the apprenticeship. I mean, I'm sure I'll get it. Because of who my . . . who Geno is. But I'm over cramming my feet into pointes, you know?" My words are all slurry and blasé, but Nikki appears to have understood. There's a hint of change in his face that looks an awful lot like Geno's disappointment.

"So," he says, "if I'm following, you've got this cool opportunity, and you're gonna dump it? Nah, Rosa."

He's against the wall now, instead of me.

A couple approaches, carrying two shot glasses filled with something green.

The woman hands me a glass. "Those were some badass moves, honey."

"Can't say I've ever heard that kind of a review after *Swan Lake*." I look straight at Nikki and take the shot.

He shakes his head.

My body sways. "Here's an idea. Why don't you audition tomorrow, with me?"

"Serious? You'd be cool with that?" Nikki's back to sparkling.

"Promise! We'll be ready for excellence together." I fall into his chest and seal the deal with a kiss.

He holds me at arm's length, the music changing up again. His impossible brown eyes lock with mine, and he says, "You sure you're down for that?"

I cling to his shoulders, steadying myself. "How long did you carry around that magazine in your pocket? The one with the dancer on the front?" I tease.

"I . . . I'm psyched you're cool, Strawberry. I don't know what else to say." Nikki backs me into a shadowy corner, smashing me against the wall. We're all over each other in a hot minute, our hands exploring way more of each other than is legal in public. When I come up for air, my mesh shirt is half off.

The warehouse ripples with steamy, sweaty bodies. My bare feet beckon me back to the dance floor. I sashay through the crowd, my partner on my heels.

Nikki grasps my hips from behind, nuzzling my neck.

I spin around, my champagne head whirling. We kiss so long, I barely remember how we end up back at Teener's tangled up in each other—ever so completely forgetting about the rest of the world, and the promise that I made for tomorrow.

The Most Dumbest Girl
in the World

I'm turning without spotting, everything a blurry fun house. Something's soft against my back. Fur? I grasp it to stop the spinning, but this only makes the momentum more obvious. My face is hot, the rest of me, freezing. I touch my legs. They're bare and cold.

Where am I?

My eyes won't work right, burning and swollen as if someone replaced my eyeballs with . . . much bigger eyeballs. There's a glass of something on the bedside table. I claw at it, hoping to God it's water. I knock everything next to it on the floor, then sit up way too fast. The room swivels. I sniff inside the glass. Water! The entire thing goes into my desert of a mouth, then I fall back into bed and drift off. . . .

Someone honks at me. I flip them off and continue my high cancan kicks in strappy jazz shoes in front of the White Castle on Lake Street. Geno's here, clapping out my count, yelling *"Higher! Higher!"*

I kick so high, my heel strap catches on my dangly earring.

Ouch! I sit up with a jolt, clutching my earlobe. The fog clears. Fur beneath me . . . empty glass on the table.

Teener's. Nikki's bed. Half-naked. The Funk Factory. *Yes!*

The jumbled events crawl back to me. I left the Funk Factory with Nikki, the two of us kissing and tearing at each other for the few blocks it took to stumble to Teener's.

It feels like morning, although there are no windows to confirm this. My sore body screams at me for sleeping in the same position for too long. Or should I say, passing out. The fuzz underneath me is the white bearskin rug, and by the way my stomach's protesting the liquid green garbage I consumed last night, I'm shocked I haven't ralphed all over it.

"Nikki?" I call, adjusting my twisted shirt. I did barf. Just not on the bearskin. A wastebasket splattered with a greenish slurry turns my face the same color and I wipe the slime from my upper lip.

My skirt is crumpled on the floor next to my bra, and my brain won't tell me how it got there. I feel between my legs, shifting my hips around. Have I become one of those girls who gets so wasted she doesn't remember her first time? Somewhere in the web of my memory is my answer. Me, hurling in the trash can, Nikki holding my hair back. No. There's no way he touched me after that.

I crawl out of bed and scoop up the rest of my clothes. A half-open jar of sienna-toned makeup is on the table. The pointes are gone. As I get dressed and shout for Nikki, I realize he's gone too. There's a note scrawled in red crayon taped to the bedside table: *Merde. See you soon.* With a heart around the message.

That's a good sign. Nikki wrote "Merde," the French swear

word that doubles as "good luck" for dancers. *And* he wants to see me after the audition—even after all the hurling.

I step into my skirt, catch my foot on the waist, and about topple over.

Water. Need more water—and a bathroom. Anything to sober me up before eight a.m.

There's no need to kick myself for drinking too much. My entire body aches like I rumbled with a bag of hammers. Just putting one foot in front of the other is work. I shuffle down the center costume aisle—Victorian gowns, gorilla suits . . . scary clowns.

I find the bathroom, a tiny closet with a sink and a rusty toilet. More of Nikki's makeup and hair stuff is stacked on every surface. I reluctantly look in the mirror.

Jesus Christ. I'm ready for a Teener's vampire cape. Black eyeliner and mascara smear my pale cheeks. What's left of my eye shadow is giving me a shiner. I belong at the morning-shift table at SNY.

I sit on the toilet and pee for a straight minute, leaving the door open and everything. If Nikki sees me, whatever. He watched me do a lot worse last night. I don't even remember when I stopped slamming drinks.

"¡Buenos días!"

I jump. Oz.

I slam the door, hoping Nikki won't get in trouble for our little sleepover. A quick splash of cold water on my face and a few swipes with the towel erases most of my makeup.

Oz knocks on the bathroom door. "You still here?"

"It's me, Rosa." I crack the door.

He doesn't appear shocked to see me. "Ah, Rosa. I've just opened up. A little late, but I won't tell if you won't."

"Where's Nikki?"

"Don't know, flower. He left me a note. I'm supposed to give you this." He holds up a dusty-rose leotard in plastic. "But like I said—"

"Uh, yes." I take the package. "Thank you so much. *Wait.* Did you say *just opened up?*"

"*I know. I know.* I'm usually in by seven. And here I am, two hours later." Oz fluffs a row of hoopskirts and petticoats. "Friday nights are my weakness."

I can't feel my legs anymore. "It's nine o'clock?" I screech.

"Si, cariño."

"Oh my God! Oh. My. God. No. No. No. *No!*" Everything hazes over except for the apprenticeship audition that's been happening for an entire hour without me. I scramble for my shoes. "This is not happening. This is *not* happening." I choke on my breath.

"Honey, what's wrong?"

"My other shoe. I need my other shoe!"

Oz tries to help, but things are way beyond anything he can do. I find one Doc and drop to my knees to search under the bed for the other. "I have to go." Tears run down my burning cheeks, my stomach in a full-on cramp. One look at the trash can and that's it. I puke again.

I get to my feet. Screw the shoes. "Which way is out?"

"Darling, I don't think you're in any shape to go anywhere."

274

"Tell me how to get outta here, Oz!"

He points past the costumes. "Straight and to the left."

I gulp down a second round of sickness. I snatch my bag, still hanging by the vampire capes, and bust through the beaded curtain. Where is Nikki? He knew I had an audition, and he ditched me.

A customer comes in and I'm pretty sure I hiss at him when he asks for help. I dash outside and sprint down the block.

Running. I fucking hate running, but this is worse than the building on fire. My skirt flies up around my waist, bare feet sticking to the tacky sidewalk. I reach MDC and double over the garbage can inside the door, my stomach screaming like I've done a thousand crunches with Stacy.

Stairs—two at a time and then, cold and clammy, I reach the fourth floor.

"You're too late," Lou has the balls to inform me.

"Shut up," I shout as I dump myself into the dressing room.

I tear off my stale clothes. Tights go on backward, bunched at one hip and stretched out at the other. Leo out of the plastic, I pull it on. My hands are shaking so bad, tying the ribbons of my pointe shoes is impossible. All I want is a bed and a gallon of water.

But the audition. I fucked up royally. And I have to fix it.

I try with the shoes again, this time getting myself together enough to make a couple of messy knots. Gathering my hair in a ponytail, I hit the stairs again, shouldering through the door to floor five. From the studio—a piano waltz.

Shit. Barre is done. They've moved on to center.

The music stops.

"Next line, from the top," Geno orders.

My heart is beating way too fast, and the floor must be sucking my feet into the carpet because I can't get there soon enough.

"And the next person who doesn't give me a clean double can consider themselves cut," Geno threatens.

Jesus. My eyes are already seeing double. I dab my face with the front of my leo, cross myself, and push on the door. Locked. Geno wasn't bullshitting. He's locked the door. I relevé en pointe and peer through the small square of glass.

"Places!" he barks.

Half the room scrambles, Stacy sticking herself in my spot, front and center.

Hair combed and wearing a clean T-shirt, Geno got his shit together enough for the audition. Which is more than I can say for myself. I knock, and his steely eyes flick to the door. They glaze over. I press my hand against the window.

For a second, I think he'll let me in—give me a chance. But it's my blurry eyes playing a trick.

He points at the pianist. "Let's go."

She begins another waltz. I pound on the door. No one comes to my rescue. Stacy hits her double perfectly—the way I would have, sober, and in the damn studio. Two dancers fall off pointe, one stupid mistake taking down their audition in flames.

The lines switch up and the ousted hopefuls head for the door. I shove past them as they leave.

"Stop!" Geno shouts.

Everyone freezes except me.

Stacy, Jeffery, the panel up front—every eye in the room watches me toss my bag aside and shoulder a spot for myself at the front. The studio is more stifling than usual. I'm off-gassing a liquor store and looking like I've been shot out of a cannon in a room full of dancers who got up at the crack of dawn to do their performance hair and makeup.

Director Joyce clears her throat, smoothing her long white hair. I haven't seen her all summer. How impressive I must look.

"You." Geno jabs his finger at me. "Out. Now."

I flatten my curls, getting a whiff of the spew-crusted ends. "No," I say.

He glances at Joyce, humiliation clouding his face.

"Excuse me?" Geno says with a fiery glare. *No.* In the Dominguez domain, that two-letter word is worse than the four. And I've never braved such a thing in my life. Not when he demands crazy teacup challenges—not when every inch of me wants to scream until I lose my voice like Glo.

"No," I say again. And it doesn't feel nearly as triumphant as the first time. "I'm here to audition," I mumble.

"Sober, and on time. Bare-minimum requirements." He sniffs me. "Both of which you have ignored."

"Just like you, right?"

The studio shrinks. Geno opens his mouth, but nothing comes out. He's scared. I've become just like him.

I find Stacy, and she is no Kat. One nod from my best

friend would've given me a smidgen of strength. Stacy's eyes well with pity. I shrink on the spot.

Geno bears down on me, nostrils steaming like a bull ready to gore a matador. "Rosa, you are done here. *We* are done here."

"No, I'm not."

"Yes. You. Are." His ropy neck pulsates.

"*No.* I can't be. Just give me another chance. *Please.*"

Christ, help me stop crying. I'm back in the hospital elevator with Mom. I feel her dark marbled eyes on me. Glo's too. I glance at their photos on the wall behind Geno, my entire family watching me burn.

Blistering tears stream down my face—tears that taste like the ocean I've never seen because MDC has been my entire planet. Mom's water broke in this studio. Annoying little me—showing up a week early. I've been a screwup from the very beginning.

Joyce vacates her chair, tapping her cane on the floor as she comes to my side. She gives Geno a stiff nod. "The Master's right, Rosa. You need to go." She rests a wrinkled hand on my shoulder.

I shrug it off and stay where I am, surrounded by a company of hopefuls, while my own dreams die a slow death on the very spot where I came into the world. The dance world. Because there's never been another for me.

Geno grips the edge of the piano as if he wants to throw it at the mirrors. I expect whispers at my back, wish for it, actually. Then I won't hear my soul spilling from my body like hot sand. But no one says a word.

I go for my bag and for the first time in ages, my feet don't hurt. Maybe because the rest of me is rotting from the inside out. I want to see Kat more than anything, collapse into her arms and hear her voice. But she's not here. This isn't her future. It's not mine anymore either. I wanted to leave MDC, but not like this. *So* not like this.

And . . . Nikki.

He's standing right in front of me, with an audition number pinned to his shirt.

I poke his chest.

He's here, in the studio. Rock-solid Nikki. Wearing black tights, a white T-shirt, and—sienna-stained pointe shoes.

"Rosa . . ."

My gut spasms. Nikki's at my audition. In pointe shoes. "I don't understand." I stare at his pointes, all tricked out like a professional dancer or some shit.

"I . . . I left a note for you. I called Teener's, like, ten times when you didn't show."

I back away, so totally confused it's impossible to piece together what he's babbling about.

"You were sleeping," Nikki says, wiping his sweaty forehead. "I set an alarm for seven. I had a backup plan and everything. Oz was supposed to wake you up. What happened?"

"You—you lied to me. That's what happened."

He glances around the studio, panic widening his eyes. "No. I would never—"

"It's pretty clear that, *yes,* you would." The other dancers retreat to the far edges, as if I'll explode any second.

"Remember"—Nikki reaches for my hand—"at the Funk? You invited me."

No. I don't remember, like most everything else after I crossed over into the super-drunk range of things.

Geno claps. "Let's move on. Nico, is it?"

Nikki walks in a circle like he's not sure which direction to go. "I had to get here early because I'm a walk-in."

"In those?" I jab a finger at his pointes. "I see it now. You're trying to steal *my* spot."

"Nah, Rosa. It's not like that."

"Anyone not in preparation in three seconds is cut," Geno threatens.

Nikki looks at Geno, then back to me. I'd like to say he's falling to pieces like I am, but I can't see his face anymore. He spews more lame apologies, fading into the background of the audition murk.

"Piano!" Geno shouts, and the playing starts.

I fumble for a way out, seeing nothing clearly until there's a bus ride, a freeway, and five cigarettes between me and the Minnesota Dance Company.

A Tangerine for
the Tears in Your Eyes

Nikki crashed my audition?

Nikki crashed my audition.

Nikki is a ballet dancer, and he crashed my audition.

I say it over and over, first in my pounding head, and then loud enough to get a dirty look from the bus driver. I want to tear my hair out. Nikki said I invited him, but my pickled brain won't show me if it's a lie. And does it really matter? He left me.

I rub my arms to settle my trembles.

The guy behind me rings the bell and I follow him off. I don't care where I am. It could be Beirut and I still wouldn't give a shit.

My dance bag—dumped in the lost and found at MDC. But not before flipping through the attendance book and ripping out any and every page that had my name on it—right in front of Lou and his broom. At least, I've given him something to do. I spared my soft ballet shoes, only because I needed them for the bus. My Docs are gone again, this time for good. I'm never going back to Teener's.

I'm on the other side of the city, in Dinkytown, sandwiched

between the University of Minnesota campus and Northrup Auditorium, where MDC performs *The Nutcracker.* Everything looks bigger, a whole lot of open space blanketed with U of M maroon and gold. People walk past me with places to be, and I don't belong anywhere. Tomorrow will be more of the same, the days ahead a kaleidoscope of question marks.

A couple veers around me, when it becomes clear I'm not about to move. All I can do is stay on my course to nowhere, because when I turn my head, the rest of the world takes a second to catch up. The couple ducks inside a bar advertising dollar-fifty pitchers of beer. *Bleh.*

Wandering without my dance bag feels strange, so much air between my empty arm and the rest of me. I don't have my Walkman anymore either. It stayed with my bag. I only wish I could turn off the Prince in my head. The ghost of his rich baritone drags my feet deeper into the scorching concrete like quicksand.

I catch myself in a storefront window, hair exploding from my ponytail, humidity frizzing the ends. The red ruffled mini Nikki drooled over last night has traded its hotness for just—hot. I'm a walking JUST SAY NO poster.

How does Geno make it through the hangover part? How does he emerge on the other side psyched to do it all over again? He must feel dead inside twenty-four seven.

I roll my cross between my fingers, the prospect of air-conditioning pulling me inside the building.

A gallery. I've wandered into a cavernous space, high brick walls on one side, paintings on the other. Tiny figurines carved from what looks like butter are on display in the center. I touch the fox.

"*Oh*. No touching, please," a woman says from a glass table stacked with papers. "They're quite lovely, aren't they?"

Lovely isn't the word I'd choose. But they are something— weird.

The woman joins me. "The artist uses Land O' Lakes butter. Then she sprays the figures with something to keep them from melting."

She's wearing one of those fancy colorful tunics, the kind that's embroidered somewhere across the world and then shipped over here and sold for ten times more. She smells like oranges and I hope my own sourness isn't wafting up her nose.

"Honestly," she goes on, "I'm forever in awe of the creative process. I'm always in search of new stories to tell." She looks right at me. "Do you have one for me?"

I feel pressed to tell her something super cool. But all I have are things that'll make her want to dry up in a dark hole from bawling.

"No. I don't have anything."

If my answer disappoints her, I can't tell. She hands me a tangerine. "I'm Val. Look around. You never know when you'll be inspired."

Great. She takes me for a street rat. But the lady is being nice. No risk of *her* keeping massive secrets from me. I thank her for the tangerine and dig my nail into the skin by the navel, peeling from the top like Mom used to do.

I like it in the gallery. The space is so quiet. Clean. No

stench from hundreds of sweaty bodies. No medical supplies piled in every corner. I stop at a painting of a country landscape.

"You have a good eye." Val comes back to me. "What do you like about it?"

I shrug. "What do *you* like about it?"

"I asked you first."

"Umm, the colors are pretty. And the hills . . . I like those, I guess. I don't really know anything about art, so whatever."

"Okay, tell me what you *don't* like about it."

I'm afraid to slam the painting. She obviously thinks it's good, or it wouldn't be hanging on her wall. All I can compare it to are Glo's paintings, which have so much depth. Layers upon layers of a story unique to only her.

"I guess I've seen others that make me feel—more," I say.

Val hands me a tissue from her pocket. "Well, I'd love to see what moves you to tears someday."

I wipe my eyes, totally embarrassed. "Thanks for the orange."

"Come back anytime," she calls as I rush back out into the heat.

I plop down on a bench in a bus shelter, which is like being an ant under a magnifying glass. I stay until the sun scorches my back, the crowd shifting from daytimers to nightlife seekers. When about the hundredth bus stops, I pull my pass from my waistband and get on.

"Where do you go?" I ask the driver.

"South Minneapolis, Hiawatha Avenue, and such."

I nod and sit somewhere in the middle as if Kat's with me. She's cruising in her car to somewhere I'm not allowed to know. Our friendship has never felt so far away. I hold my cross, wishing hard for some Abuela wisdom. I can almost smell her mothball housedress, and it brings me down lower in my seat.

We reach the part of Hiawatha where the railroad tracks cross in front of the dog food plant.

I exit the bus.

A pair of mangy huskies gnash their teeth behind a chain-link fence on the corner as I run past. The sky is streaked with purple and pink, like the beautiful dusky scrim in *Romeo and Juliet*. Grain elevators in the distance, G-ma's yellow-and-white house is like a sunny-side egg among the dilapidated single-stories.

When I get to the door, I do nothing. This is a stupid idea. I hike back to the gate, and then turn around.

I knock, before I change my mind.

Somebody's Nobody

"Ah, Rosa, is it?" G-ma says after a sec, wiping her hands on a stained towel. She peers over my shoulder, probably searching the last bits of twilight for Nikki. I'm shocked she can see me at all through her cloudy eyes, as if a strong wind could scatter her pale gray irises like a fuzzy dandelion.

"It's just me," I say. "I'm sorry . . . I'm not sure why I'm here."

And even less sure where to look because G-ma's gaze is searching for a place to land. I'm pushing the limits of presentable.

She motions me inside. It takes me a bit to decide if this is a good idea. Then I squeeze in past her, because whatever she had for dinner lingers in the air. My empty stomach growls as she closes the door, then turns a fortress of locks before setting the chain.

"Just being cautious," she explains.

"You should just get a couple of werewolves like the ones on the corner. No one will come within a mile of this place."

"*Eh,* no one does anyway." G-ma takes hold of the handrail running the perimeter of the house, following it to the kitchen. "Just Nico."

Her hands seem to know where everything is. She must be a mind reader, because she takes a spatula from a drawer, then pulls the foil from what looks like a casserole. My mouth waters. I could scarf down an entire Tater Tot hot dish right now. I feel like I should help her, but she's shooing me into the living room.

"Go, sit."

I back into the super-clean room, no garage-sale clutter or overflowing laundry baskets doubling as furniture. I collapse onto the plastic-covered tweed couch, slipping my worn ballet shoes off before propping my feet up on the color-coordinated ottoman covered with the shower cap. My eyes beg to close. I sniff my fingers, the tangerine lingering. Other than that, I really stink.

G-ma comes out from the kitchen, wringing her hands like Abuela used to. She said it warded off her pains. I wonder if G-ma wants me to leave?

"Shower, Rosa?" she asks, adjusting a pin in her hair.

My head is stuffy from too much sun and not enough water. I pull in my knees. "I don't have any other clothes."

She stares at me a little too long. Maybe I'm leaving a bouquet of stench on her couch.

"Down the hall and to the left," she says. "I'll lay something out for you."

I do as she says because, well, I can't go home. Not yet. Not like this. I swipe away my hair, which is up on one side and exploding out the other half. When I stand, my joints are suddenly eighty years old. I rub my aching back, meeting G-ma's dull gaze.

She's just going with it—no questions asked.

The aroma of cumin and garlic softens my shoulders. Coffee's percolating, the ashy scent mingling with the heat of the spices. I must be delirious. Or maybe not. My entire world is upside-down and I can still crave coffee and a hot dish. So there is that.

After the shower I was expecting to exchange my leo for a drapey flowered housedress like G-ma's. Instead, on the toilet is a faded North Stars hockey jersey and a pair of blue sweats that smell like dryer sheets. Though I spent the entire day in the heat, the cozy fleece feels like paradise.

I shuffle into the kitchen. G-ma's set a plate for me at the table, a large square of some sort of lasagna waiting.

"Agua?" she asks.

"A gallon."

She gives me a full glass and takes the seat across from me, and I hope she can't see the details of me stuffing my face like a cavewoman.

"This is amazing," I say with my mouth full of what tastes like plantains, around a spicy ground-beef filling. I sniff a forkful—cumin and garlic, cilantro, and a few other flavors I can't place.

"Pastelón. Nico's favorite." She messes with a bowl of fake fruit in the center of the table.

I stop chewing. "Is he coming here?"

G-ma's face falls. "*Nah.* He only comes once a week. And that already happened. You were here."

I don't want to talk about Nikki, so I look around the sterile kitchen. "Your house is so clean. You could eat off of any surface in here."

"I think you should keep your home as if the president will stop by at any moment."

I picture Reagan and his motorcade bouncing over the railroad tracks, past the dog food plant, to come to G-ma's yellow house. Today's been outer-realm. I guess it could happen. I swipe away some crumbs that strayed from my plate.

"Nico did call earlier, though," she says.

I stop eating.

"He was chosen for something. For his dancing."

Nikki made it. I don't know why my heart is thumping so fast. He is dead to me. But it almost feels like I'm happy for him.

"Nikki's a really good dancer." I push away my plate. "But you already knew that, didn't you?"

G-ma gets up and pours two cups of coffee. She hands me one and gestures toward the living room. I try to help her, but she shrugs me off.

Finally, we are sitting on the couch. I take a sip of my

coffee. It's so strong my teeth tingle. I place my cup on the plastic-covered ottoman. G-ma gives me a look, and I move the mug to an end table.

"The jersey suits you," she says. "It was my husband's. The pants too. I would have given them to Nico, but they're not really his style." She takes a long slurp of her coffee.

I'm totally about to be rude. "How well do you see?" I ask.

"Well enough," she says. "I saw the makeup Nico didn't completely rub away the other day, if that's what you're asking."

I'm about to defend Nikki, but then I sink against a velour pillow shaped like a turtle.

"He thinks I won't understand." She takes a gulp from her cup. "Because of his mother. But . . ." G-ma does this low humming thing, like Abuela used to when she didn't want to let out a cry. "Nico's mother was hurt. His father . . . and his death. She wanted him to be someone he wasn't. Someone he never was."

"And Nikki . . ."

"He is a reminder of everything she has to lose again."

I grab the turtle pillow from behind my back and hug it. "And now he's gone from her life anyway. Smart woman."

"Families aren't always as strong as this coffee, no?"

Nothing's as strong as G-ma's coffee. I don't think I'll sleep for a week.

"I messed up an audition today," I tell her. "The same one Nikki called you about." I squeeze the pillow harder. I'd actually managed to forget about the First Avenue benefit. This isn't about Prince anymore.

G-ma nods like she's already in the know.

My head starts to hurt, tiny pulses at my temples. I scrunch my toes under until they cramp. "You should tell him—Nikki."

"Tell him what?"

"That what you see is really okay."

G-ma fluffs the bolster while she hums softly. "You can sleep here. If you call your mother, or whoever keeps track of you." With some effort, she gets up. "My Nico . . ." She takes an embroidered handkerchief from her pocket and wipes her mouth. "He is beautiful. That is what I see."

Dammit, he is. But I won't let myself go there again. Not after today.

G-ma shoos me from the couch and pulls off the plastic. She takes our cups and leaves me alone in the dark with a mothbally blanket. I curl up in it and don't call anyone. The street sweeper comes by. I stare at the shadowy ceiling, losing myself in its swishy rhythm. Eventually I fall asleep, awakening to the sound of running water. For a second I'm home, listening to Mom prepare Glo's breakfast.

I sit up, and a living room that's not mine seeps through my crusty eyes. G-ma's in the kitchen making coffee. On the table, three glasses of orange juice next to flowery place settings.

I fold the blanket, then pull on my filthy ballet shoes. My soles feel bruised as I shuffle toward the kitchen and wait at the threshold, watching G-ma stir hot cereal in a worn metal pot.

"He'll be here in a minute," she says without looking up.

I hug myself. "And I won't be. I can't."

She nods. "He's a dancer. You're a dancer. One audition doesn't change anything."

At that, I almost stay. But she's wrong. That audition changed everything.

"Thank you, G-ma. For the food." I pull at the hockey jersey. "And the clothes."

She waves her hot pad and I go to the front door, unlocking the fortress. I slip outside, no longer an MDC dancer, or someone's special Strawberry Girl. I am Rosa. A regular girl—the nobody my father feared I'd become.

Just

I bus it home in the jersey and sweats. My skirt and mesh top went in G-ma's trash. I never want to see that outfit again.

When I'm finally home, I sneak in the back door, going straight to the basement. Mom's angry stomps will grace the stairs any minute and I want to at least run a brush through my hair. *Trouble* is an understatement. I've been gone two whole nights without a single call. I ditch the sweats, get into my own, and then I wait.

Glo's breathing machine is right above me.

Inhale . . . exhale.

My heart aches to see her, tell her what happened. But I've failed so massively. No apprenticeship. No Prince. Where would I possibly start? And her pointe shoe painting—she's probably done with me anyway.

I sit on my waterbed and ride the waves. Maybe they'll take me all the way to Abuela in heaven. Five minutes turns into fifteen, and then thirty. Mom's not coming. I wonder if she even noticed I was gone? Geno was probably too smashed to tell her about my train wreck of an audition. I guess I should be relieved.

I flop onto my back, the sloshing drowning out Glo's vent. From my ceiling, a dozen Prince eyes watch me as I pull my Pooh bear from the built-in shelf on the headboard. I curl around him, which is how I stay until I can't feel my insides raging anymore.

The basement door opens.

Light footsteps pad halfway down. "Rosa?"

I squeeze Pooh. Mom's footsteps creak down a bit more.

"I was worried," she says, almost at the bottom.

I turn away, my hair pasted to my ear.

"It was so late, and no call," she says, her voice way calmer than I expected. It's totally freaking me out.

She sighs. "When I called Katherine last night, she told me what happened."

Awesome. Everyone's squealing. And Kat knows about how I blew it, which bugs me to the max. If I can't know anything about my best friend's life, why should she get any info about mine? I pull myself in tighter.

"She said you were too upset to come to the phone, and that you were staying another night, which is the only reason I knew you were okay. And that is *not* okay."

Wow. Quick-thinking Kat covered for me. I don't even care why.

Mom sits on the frame of my waterbed, and I tense up like crazy. "You always call, Rosa. Do not do that again."

She sounds like she's at a yoga retreat, her words all soft and tranquil.

"And a boy came by. I think his name was Nikki?"

I bury my head in my knees.

"Rosa . . . I . . . Can we talk?"

Can we talk? Now? After all this time?

"No," I grumble.

"I really think we need to . . . *I* need to—"

"I said *no*. Leave me alone. And if you talk to Kat and Nikki again, you can tell them to leave me alone too." My voice is so dry and hoarse it hurts.

She stays for a second, then finally leaves. The door opens, and something clinks on the landing before it closes.

The phone rings a few times, but I ignore it like everything else in this house. Every now and then, the door at the top of the stairs opens and closes. I don't move, becoming one with my bed. Glo's vent is the only reason air goes into my lungs. I listen to the machine through the ceiling, inhaling when it does the same for her. Even then, sometimes it's so much work to breathe. I've seen Glo this way too, when her chest barely rises and falls. Then her ventilator alarms her back into the world, and her lungs fill again.

I let out a long exhale and take nothing back in, my eyes straining like they're going to pop. I have no alarm. Not until my angry chest forces me to cough.

It's strange, how doing nothing is so exhausting. I have no energy for anything other than cigarettes, my body beginning to resemble a hungry homeless person's in my stale sweats. Isolation becomes my best friend. It oils my skin and fuzzes my teeth.

Fuck basic hygiene.

I get dizzy when I stand, so I stop doing that too. The only time I get up is to pee in the toilet, surrounded by a shower curtain in the corner, and to crawl up the stairs to retrieve another plate of peanut butter toast and half a banana Mom's been leaving on the landing. I set down the newest plate on the pile of untouched others, and fall back against my pillow.

My back stiffens from being in bed for so long, the spidery window well shifting from dark to light for the umpteenth time. The benefit rehearsals come and go. Days of them. I torture myself, imagining the choreography I'd learned in 6B with Stacy. I wonder how they all look performing it—Kat, Stacy, and Nikki. I've lost count of how many sundowns have passed, but I think it's Friday. Which means First Avenue is tomorrow night.

I reach for Prince on my ceiling, as if he'll pull me out of this dark hole. It's always worked before. Now he's just a two-dimensional version of himself with thumbtacks in his feet.

Glo shakes her bed rails. She's been summoning me. Every day and all day, and I've ignored her. I haven't seen her in . . . Has it been a week since I saw her pointe shoe painting? The shrill of an electric guitar resonates through the ceiling—Scorpions. She's fuming. There will be a whole lot of muddy blotches on the canvas today.

Mom's yelling at her.

"No One Like You" amps up.

Glo's really testing her limits now, the Scorps bass making Abuela's rosary shimmy across my table.

I slap my mattress, making waves to drown out the noise.

"Leave me alone, Glo!" I yell, as if she'll hear me.

Mom's muffled shouts carry down the hall above. God help her if she cuts Glo's music.

And then there she goes. The guitar and drums stop. There's an earthquake of pounding, followed by Glo's raspy voice stretching to its limits as she cries, "Okay! Fine!"

"I said, that's enough!" Mom shouts back. "I'm going out of my mind, Glo! You too, Rosa!" Mom stomps the floor.

I snatch the broom next to my bed, the one I use to Morse-code with Glo. But I have no dots and dashes, only more hammering. I jab at the ceiling, right in the middle of Prince's forehead.

His fierce bedroom eyes bear down on me, like he's saying *Get your ass upstairs*. I glare back through my crusties. Just looking at him makes me feel raw. My skin stings as if it's been grated off, and then I lift my sleeves to see that I've scratched my arms to hell.

The one that started it all—the *Dirty Mind* poster of Prince in a trench coat and black bikini briefs—is tacked directly over my bed. I grab a piece of petrified toast and chuck it at him. It hits his washboard abs, leaving behind a splotch of peanut butter.

A thumbtack pops out from the upper corner, landing on my stomach. I roll over onto my hands and knees, crawling

to the edge of the bed. Mom and Glo are in the thick of it—
I can't even tell what they're screaming about anymore.

I stand, balancing on my bed frame. Grabbing the loose
corner of the poster, I rip it off the ceiling. I stumble and hit
the bed, but Holy Mother Mary, that felt good.

Don't be sorry. Be angry, Nikki said.

And I am there.

My stupid Prince obsession. Where'd it get me?

"Shut up!" I scramble to my feet again, pounding on the
ceiling. "Just, shut up!" I turn to the rest of the posters, tearing down every last Prince—a couple of Michael Jacksons are
collateral damage.

My legs buckle and I collapse, breathless. It's quiet upstairs
too. For a second, I'm panicked about Glo. Then I hear Mom's
soothing voice, and my sister panting, "Okay . . . fine."

I stare at the aftermath, regret seeping through my cool
skin. My paper-cut hands frantically wade through the shreds
of purple poster paper, searching for something whole. I pick
up a remnant—a lone smoky Prince eye. I fall back against the
headboard, blood racing through my bluish veins.

I'm sucking in air way too fast, all of my pent-up anxi-
eties rushing me at once. There's so much blank space, like the
basement should have an echo. I feel the absence of my dance
bag too—the maroon LeSportsac duffel no longer on my chair
in the corner because it's buried in MDC's lost and found.

My crime-scene leo was in that bag, the one Nikki washed
clean at Sun's. That leotard was Glo's first dusty-rose, the tiny
holes from the safety pin she used to make it a V-neck still

marring the material. Now it's gone, like so many other things I thought would be here forever. When did it start to feel normal, leaving Geno out of the equation? Glo would probably know. But when things get hard, I become our father and leave. Because I can. For the first time, I truly understand how fucked up this is.

There's a knock to my left, Kat's feet in the window well.

I get up, my head spinning in protest.

I open the slide. "What?" I snap.

"Geez, Rosa. What's the deal?" Kat takes in my trashed room. "I got to the door, and all I heard was screaming. I knocked, rang the bell, no one came. What the hell is happening?" Kat's talking at warp speed and pawing at the screen. Her long legs are folded in weird directions as she crouches in the well. "And your mom seems to think you spent two nights with me last weekend. I panicked and just went with it. Where were you? I know you weren't with Nikki the whole time. He told me what happened." Kat presses her hand against the screen. "I'm so sorry, sweetie."

I sit on my bed and she lowers herself into the dirt littered with my cigarette butts, her knees all smashed up in her chin.

"You're scaring me, Rosa."

"Right back at you."

Kat sighs. "Are you okay? You look thin."

"So do you."

She wrinkles her nose. "I called, came by every day. Let me in, will ya?"

I shrug. "The audition. Nikki. In pointes and everything."

"I know."

Kat glances overhead. "Glo is really pissed about something, huh?"

"Mm-hmm."

We stare at each other, all the things we refuse to say hovering in the thick, humid air. Kat's shorts and sleeveless oxford are way too wrinkled for her mother's approval. But I don't press her for any answers this time. This is the new us, I guess.

"You should go," I say. "I've got stuff to do." I'm not fooling Kat, in my dumpy sweats. But she unfolds anyway.

She ducks her head down. "Meet me today? I've got something to show you."

I shrug again.

"Thirty-Sixth Avenue and Fifty-Fourth. Look for Blondie."

"Why should I?"

Kat's eyes flick over my shoulder toward the twinkle lights. "You shared the Vault with me. Now it's my turn. Should've been a long time ago."

Hell yeah, it should've. And now I don't know if I want to see anything from Kat.

"Please," she says. "Five o'clock."

I fall back onto the bed. "What time is it now?"

"Three."

"What day is it?"

"Friday," she says.

I roll away.

"I'll see you there." Kat's Dr. Scholl's clack down the sidewalk.

Upstairs, there's music again—Prince, "How Come U Don't Call Me Anymore?" Glo must have coaxed Mom to break out her record player and put on the B side of "1999." I am powerless to ignore it, and my sister knows this. I close my eyes, giving in to Prince's falsetto and piano. They shower my room like rejuvenating rain. I stretch across my bed, end-to-end, my muscles taking their first real breath since the audition.

Abuela's rosary is on my nightstand, half of it coiled into a small pile of beads, the other dangling over the edge. I move to grab it, and the beads cascade to the ground. It's like her ghost just beaned me with her white patent leather purse. I clutch my cross, a quiet warmth spreading from my core to my frigid edges.

I'm up, sifting through a laundry basket for something that resembles clean. I strip off the sweats and throw on a sundress, my skin breaking out in goose bumps.

My reflection in my full-length holds me still for a sec. I barely recognize myself. And it's not because I've dropped some poundage, or haven't brushed my hair in a week.

I am Rosa Dominguez. That's it. No more "the ballet dancer" tacked onto the end.

I pull my hair into a ponytail. There are tons of reasons to leave it alone, bitter disappointment being one. But as I tuck the smoky Prince eye into my Ked, I'm certain Abuela's telling me I have to try. I blame everything on the accident, say that it tore my family apart, ruined our lives. And hell yeah, it did. But January 5 was only the widening of a fissure that began way before that winter.

Glo rattles her bed. I grab the broom and give her three soft taps back. She answers with a patient four raps of her own. I will face my sister and her painting. There's something I've gotta do first. Yeah, I'll swallow my stubbornness and meet up with Kat. But it's three o'clock. If Geno's upright, he's prepping for his evening master class.

Climbing the stairs is way more exhausting than it should be. When I reach the top, it smells like incoming rain, the kind that gushes from the sky in warm sheets and washes away the humid stink. I jot a quick note to Mom and Glo, leaving it on the counter. Slipping outside, I skip taking a jacket and close the screen door with a gentle push.

Love Without Trust

Hennepin Avenue. Same punks bumming cigarettes from strangers, same doughy aroma wafting across the street from SNY. Other people's lives go on like always, no matter what kind of shit's happening in mine.

Every working girl tricks my eyes, like they're all Kat. My acidy stomach churns. She said she'd never, but at five o'clock I hope to God she's not showing me her very own street corner.

It's midafternoon, and already there are police cars and an ambulance outside the McDonald's next to Moby's. The pull of the Funk Factory beckons me the opposite way. Even Nikki's lame-ass betrayal can't ruin the memory of how I tore up the dance floor, how it felt to be completely free.

The wail of sirens pricks my ears and I turn back around, heading for my last place on earth.

MDC is deserted, no students hanging out in corners, stretching, taping—or gossiping about me. Even Lou's gone for the break.

There's a sign taped to the counter: COSTUME APPROVAL FOR FIRST AVENUE—6TH FLOOR.

My throat tightens. I'm pretty sure it'll hurt forever.

I left the house braver than I am now, so I hover in the hall outside Geno's office. My dress is sucked to my sweaty back, my legs quivering from doing nothing for days. Geno will sense my atrophy coming a mile away.

My stomach is one gigantic knot. Do I have some grand speech prepared? No. Only that if this is the way the Dominguez family goes down, I need him to see me one last time. Regular girl or not, I want him to see I am not broken.

I knock.

I pound.

I try the door. It opens, his office empty. His leather jacket is crumpled on his tattered chair next to a full cup of coffee. He's here—somewhere. Maybe the fifth floor.

Waltzy piano keys greet me as I emerge from the stairwell. I've only been exiled a handful of days, and already the smell of sweat and rosin feels distant. Unlike the unmistakable crack of Geno's clapping. I walk the rest of the corridor with quivering sewing-machine legs.

The hazy air reeks of him, smoke lingering outside the far studio. The door is propped open and I peek around the threshold.

My heart seizes. Geno—and Nikki. In the middle of a private lesson. I slide down the wall outside the studio. Nikki knocks out a lovely attitude pirouette en pointe.

God, why can't he suck? Although . . . he is putting too much weight on his back leg during the plié.

"Center your carriage all the way, from plié to attitude,"

Geno instructs. "And most of your weight should be on your front leg during preparation." He smacks Nikki's stomach and I flinch.

Nikki stays solid. "Got it." He wipes his brow with a towel, his dewy chest glistening between the ripped V in his white T-shirt.

They move on to jumps and leaps. Nikki sails through Geno's difficult combinations, his cabriole so airborne he must be tethered to the sky. I want to hate what I see. Instead, I hold my breath, longing to be in that space with him again.

He's wearing the pointes from the audition. They're stained deep brown to match his skin. His quads pop as he relevés en pointe. Don't even get me started on his calves.

Nikki's lids are shaded with glittery purple eye shadow, and Geno doesn't say a word about how distracting it is. My eyes burn. And in Geno's shines a light that's been absent since Glo's accident.

I don't know how many combinations pass before I stand again, only that when I do, I'm face to face with Nikki.

"Rosa," he gasps. Even in the shadowed hallway, his dark skin gleams like it did at the Funk Factory. "Hey." He touches my arm.

I shrink away. "Don't."

"Where'd you go . . . after the audition? I looked everywhere. I called your house a bunch. Stopped by too. Your mom said you were sick."

"I am. In the head for trusting you. Got yourself a two for one, huh? Bagged me, then the audition."

"No. We didn't . . ." He peeks inside the studio, then turns back to me. "We didn't have sex."

So, there's my confirmation. If I believe him about anything.

I dodge his touch again.

Nikki takes a moment. Then he says, all slow and careful like I won't understand, "I set an alarm for you that morning. I had to jet, and figured you could use the extra minutes of sleep. The clock. I think you knocked it off the table. When I went back to Teener's, it was on the floor. And like I said—"

"You left Oz a note to wake me. How thoughtful."

That morning is totally distorted. I can't grasp any of the details.

Nikki paces a circle, gripping his bun. His ears and neck are naked. No hoops or gold chains. Just the way the Master demands. "This is all wrong," he says.

"You got that right."

"No, I mean, at Teener's, when we first met. You told me who you were, and who your father was." Nikki flexes and points his foot, his high arch perfect for pointe work. "You were going on about the apprenticeship. And . . . yeah, I was kinda jealous. I wanted to tell you I was thinking about auditioning too. I hadn't made up my mind about it, but it was there, you know?" He pats over his heart. "And then at the Funk you said we should go together. The two of us kickin' it side by side. I thought we'd rule it, you know?"

I can't steer my brain back to that conversation—whatever

Nikki thinks I said was totally dissolved in all the alcohol I slammed.

He goes for my arm again and I back away. "I'm here to talk to Geno. Family stuff. Go find your own." I glare so hard I can't see the ugliness brewing inside me.

"I don't want yours, Strawberry Girl."

"Don't call me that."

I can tell by the way Nikki's biting his lip he's getting frustrated with me. "Minneapolis, ballet, your father, he's a hometown legend."

I cringe, maybe even roll my eyes.

"Master Geno's helping me. I'm auditioning for the Trocks in the spring—like on the cover of *Drag* mag. I'm really going for it—because of you. I mean, nothing keeps you down, girl. So, I'll say what I should've before." He takes a deep breath. "I want to be a ballet dancer. En pointe, onstage, under the lights in front of a full house with all the tutus, makeup, and flowery shit. Like you, Rosa." Nikki exhales as if he's been guarding those words his entire life.

I lean my head against the wall and gaze inside the studio. Geno's wrapped up in walking through some choreography for Nikki. He'll get his prima ballerina after all. "Now that I've missed the audition, none of this is part of me. So, you're not like me at all, are you?"

Nikki squeezes his ears. "You didn't want the apprenticeship in the first place."

"Do you really think that's the point?" I cross my arms.

"I'm here for a chance to do what I've always wanted. A chance you were gonna toss after First Ave. But if you tell me right now you want to be in that studio more than me, then . . . then I'll step aside." Nikki paces again. He's probably afraid of what my answer might be.

I creep toward the threshold of 4A. My feet tense up as I watch Geno sweep his arms, the last bits of Rosa and Gloria, principals in the making, slipping through his graceful fingers like ghosts.

I've been clinging to my pointes, terrified of what I'd be without them—so scared my screwups would push Geno off the wagon. When, really, my biggest fear has been waiting in the wings all along. It's all around me. The studio, the dancers, the smell of earthy rosin, Mom's starry presence, and Glo's corner in the dressing room—they're all I have left of my sister and how things were before the accident. Losing the apprenticeship and MDC is January 5 all over again.

My vacant spot at the barre waits for another dancer to claim it. Nikki. He's standing next to me in the very place he clutched a box of fake flowers and watched me pass the teacup test. Now he's the one in pointes. He's the one dancing his heart out for Geno. No. I don't want the apprenticeship. I want Geno to look at me the way he looks at Nikki, with or without ballet. That is all.

"Rosa." I've forgotten Nikki's right in front of me. "This ain't over for you. Dancing makes your world go round. That fire in you . . . I saw your truth at the Funk. The way you moved."

I stare at my stained Keds. "Well, I'm not dancing, and the earth is still turning. So . . ."

Nikki jams his toe box into the floor. "You know I get it. How messed up family can be. I didn't tell you I wanted to audition because I was freaked you'd be like my mom. Which is so weak because you're cool, Rosa. You always have been."

Jesus Christ.

My anger toward Nikki softens. I almost tell him about G-ma, that I went to her and what she said. Maybe he already knows and can't let himself believe it. I fight the urge to hug him, another messed-up person like me cowering behind perfected confidence.

Nikki undulates his fingers. "Master Geno says my grand adage is fluid like . . . like your sister's."

"Wait . . ." Something inside my head snaps. "Geno's comparing you to Glo now?"

"Hold on, hold on." Nikki waves his hands. "It's not like that."

I ball my fists—livid, and scared for Nikki all at once. "Has he burned your elbow yet?"

Nikki rubs his sweaty forehead. "What?"

"I'm sure he and his red lighter will take you to new heights."

"Rosa." Geno's rasp at my back drains my blood.

I take my time turning around. "Master . . ."

Geno's gaze flicks from my frizzy unkempt hair to my spindly arms. I grip the hem of my sundress. His expression is blank and grayish, like one of Glo's empty canvases. But he's clear of the whiskey stench too. His clothes even look clean. If I wasn't seething inside, I'd be relieved.

"No more *Master Geno*," he barks. "You're no longer a student here. And classes are not open for observation." He snaps his fingers at Nikki, which means break time and I are done. "Although," he adds, "if you stay, you might learn something about hard work and dedication."

My entire body's shaking. I wish Nikki would leave. But he's standing by my side like he's my rock or something.

"I came here to talk to you," I manage to utter.

"We have nothing to say to each other." He taps out a cigarette, Nikki's eyes following the lighter until it's pocketed.

"I think we do. I do, at least."

"No, we don't. You're not my student anymore."

"I don't want to talk to you as a student."

Geno waves me away like an annoying mosquito and traipses inside the studio.

"Dad!" I start after him.

"Master," Nikki interjects. "Just listen to her."

Only then does Geno turn around, which trips me into overload. Of course he'll listen to Nikki.

"Shut up!" I shout.

Nikki flinches.

I'm so fucking angry I shove him, which barely makes him stumble. "I don't need your help. This is a family thing, and you aren't part of it. Go home, Nikki. Go back to Puerto Rico." I wipe my runny nose, seeing nothing but devil-red. Then, tangled in the midst of everything terrible I've ever done, I find an even lower level. "Oh yeah, that's right. You can't." All the air leaves my lungs the second I say it. I swear I don't mean a word of it. Not even a little. But the tears rolling down Nikki's cheeks choke my apology.

I back away from his burnt-sienna pointes. I don't deserve to breathe the same air.

He nods at the scuffed tiles. "All right, Rosa. . . . All right."

"Nikki—"

He holds up a hand, meeting my welling eyes.

I run away before my body gives out, barely making it to the stairs. I stumble and slide down the steps as if I've turned to liquid, a river of deadly lava flowing over everything in my path.

Burning. Suffocating. Silencing.

Soul Sirens

When I crash through MDC's doors and stumble onto the street, Hennepin Avenue is lazy and hot, for once not a single siren breaking the sound barrier.

A man bumps into me and I don't even give a crap when his hand brushes my ass. I catch the hungry look in his eyes as he passes, and thoughts of Kat taking money for sex drags me deeper. I almost scream her name. And then I realize I *am* screaming it.

"Kat!" I shout again.

Is it her—across the street, leaving SNY? The volume of the avenue winds up with me when a couple of cop cars race past.

"Kat Johansen!"

She disappears around the corner.

I sprint across the street, narrowly missing a guy on his bike. He curses me out, but it doesn't slow me down.

By the time I reach the corner, she's an entire block ahead, her damned giraffe legs way faster than mine. I inhale saliva and choke on it. Cigarettes and I are done.

Thank God, she stops at a bus shelter. I make my legs move again, reaching the corner just in time to see it's totally not her.

I collapse onto the sticky metal bench and fan my face. When I can breathe again, I check out the schedule posted on the shelter. Across the street, the number eight should take me to Thirty-Sixth Avenue and whatever Kat's been hiding. I've become a pro at pushing everyone away. If I keep it up, I truly am dust.

The bus ride gives me dangerous time to think about what I've done to Nikki. *Oh God,* his face when I said those unforgivable things. The tears come in waves, saturating my already sweaty neck and chest. Even Prince can't help me now.

My head is silent.

The beat has abandoned me.

I ring the bell and exit the bus.

I'm not far from my house, just the other side of the baseball diamonds and the wading pool Glo and I played in when we were kids. Thirty-Sixth and Fifty-Fourth is up the next block. When I get there, I'm alone and across the road from a fire station. The clock on the brick wall of the building tells me I'm early, for once. I look for Blondie, like Kat said. Not seeing her, I sit on the boulevard grass and wait. Mother Mary in heaven, we really are meeting on a street corner.

After a while, a huge red fire engine roars up the road and backs into the station. At five on the nose, I get up and cross the street. Then I see her. Blondie's yellow bumper, around the corner in the fire department's parking lot. When I get closer, I see that it's jammed with stuff—Kat's stuff, taking up every space but the driver's seat. Christ, is she living in her car?

I turn and, no shit, Kat's rounding the corner in a fire department uniform. My mouth hangs open.

"You showed," she says, eyes flicking to Blondie.

"Yeah." I cross my arms, wanting to be mad. But she looks so fucking impressive—professional—grown-up. She's wearing dark blue pants and a light blue collared shirt with a badge pinned on her left chest, a JOHANSEN nameplate on the other side. Kat exudes radness. Then again, she's never needed a uniform to convince me she was ready to save the world.

"You work here?" I say. "That's the big secret?"

"Volunteer, for now. Hopefully, someday, it'll be my job."

"But, doesn't that include driving big red trucks and stuff? You hate driving." I glance at Blondie again. "Or at least you used to."

"It's so much more than driving. A firefighter-EMT. That's what I want to be." Kat's eyes widen, her indigo-blues sparkling like sunlight on the Mississippi. "As far as money goes, they make nothing compared to a plastic surgeon. But it's unreal, Rosa, helping someone on the worst day of their life. When that alarm goes off . . ." She points to a speaker mounted on the corner of the building. "This is what I'm meant to do. Not nose jobs and fake boobs."

"How long have you been doing this?"

She kicks at a pebble on the ground. "A month."

"*A month?* Why didn't you tell me?" I'm spinning up again. "Why keep it a secret? It's not as if you're trolling Hennepin like I thought."

"I should've told you. I tried. But . . . there's still so much you don't know. Please say everything's A-OK with us." Some of the bruises on her arms have faded to a pale yellow.

"No, we're not *A-OK*. I don't know anything because we're barely talking."

"You were the one who wouldn't let me in earlier."

I grip my dress. "I was convinced you were a prostitute? The pager you're wearing. That weird day at SNY. Those bruises on your arms and knees like the other girls. I lost days of sleep over it. I called you. I went to your house. I called you again. Hell yeah, you should've told me, way before squishing yourself into my window well."

Kat crosses her clunky boots. "The woman at SNY, she was our patient the night before. I couldn't say anything because her pimp was there, and she didn't want him to know she'd called 911 after . . . you know."

Jesus, Kat's heartstrings could stretch to Australia.

"Where'd you get the bruises, then? Do they thrash you here if you forget to polish the fire pole?"

"*No*. From the fire academy. We're on our knees a lot, crawling, bumping into things and stuff." She crosses her arms too, eyes spearing mine. "You've been crying. You okay? Is it Glo?"

"She's fine . . . I'm fine." Not even close. But I guess we've both become good at the lying thing.

Kat leans against Blondie. "You say I have everything, that my world is one big opportunity. Well, there's only one choice for a Johansen like me. And according to my parents, it's not here." She points at the station. "I know you think I don't understand you sometimes, and all the things your family's been through. But you don't get mine either."

The speaker above crackles, followed by a series of ear-splitting tones that steal at least ten years from my life.

Kat freezes.

A monotone voice comes up: *"Engine seven, dumpster fire. Fifty-Sixth and Twenty-Fifth."*

Kat unwinds. "That's for the fire crew. I'm on the ambulance today." She tugs at my arm. "Come on."

I follow her inside as the engine pulls out of the station, red lights rotating. She motions me toward another room, flicking on the lights—a classroom. Or a morgue. Pale rubbery mannequins are arranged in rows on the floor, the infant ones on the tables.

My insides curdle. "Umm, creepy."

She pulls over two chairs and we sit. "We're having a CPR class tonight. Meet Rescue Annie."

We study each other like we're kids meeting for the first time. Checking out the new girl is exactly how it feels after days circling around the truths of Kat.

I smooth my crazy hair. Her bottom lip gives me the pity pout.

"Why the packed car, Kat?" I flip over the icky CPR baby next to me.

She picks at a stray thread on her pants. "My parents are cutting me off. They won't pay for anything unless I plan to go to med school. And I've declined my acceptance at the University of Minnesota."

I don't have to dig deep to envision how that conversation went between Kat and her parents. They froze her out for weeks when she got a B in civics.

"They must be really pissed," I say. "I get how that feels."

"Yeah. *Pissed* is a nice word for what they are."

"What're you gonna do?"

"I don't know." Kat bursts into tears. "I need money to pay for the EMT class I'm taking this fall."

I've only seen my best friend cry three times. Once when her cat got run over. Once when she broke her arm. And then the day she found me cowering in my bedroom—after Glo's accident.

Fuck being mad at her—I squeeze her hands.

"My parents kicked me out. I'm living in Blondie."

Assholes.

She leans in. "No one here knows."

I shake my head. "Kat, it can't stay that way. You know that, right?"

"I know, but what can I do? I've never been on my own, you know? *Never.* I mean, my parents aren't home a lot, but everything's always taken care of. Food's in the fridge, house cleaners come and go, gardeners . . . and Martina." She glances away at this. Someday we'll figure out a way to talk about why we're both staring at the floor. "I'm eighteen years old and I don't know how to do anything for myself, Rosa."

"You make good Jiffy Pop."

This doesn't help.

"I'm always the one double-dog-daring. Look at me now.

I'm a total fraud. I'm not you. I'm not . . . capable. I didn't tell you because I'm so embarrassed. And I'm scared. No, I'm stupid because I'm scared. And the longer I waited to tell you, the harder it got to admit how useless I am." Kat winds the thread around her finger until the tip's so red it looks like it'll pop.

"Well, I doubt you'll be in the market for a house cleaner or a gardener anytime soon. So, you can stop worrying about that."

She laughs and sobs at the same time.

"Hey. If *capable* means standing and breathing, then yes, I guess I'm okay. But it's about figuring it out, every second of every day." I press an *okay* into her palms. "And fuck *incapable*. You're here. Wearing *that*." I point at her badge. "People depend on you for a reason. I wouldn't've made it through the last year and a half without you. If EMT school is what you want, then we'll find a way."

I have no idea where my words are coming from. I'm sounding like the bullshit positive-affirmation kitten posters hanging in my dentist's office. Difference is, I actually believe what I'm saying to Kat. I've been jealous of things she never really had. For the first time, she needs me. And I'll apologize to the sky for how good it feels being her shoulder.

Kat wipes her eyes with the back of her hand. I bring her the box of tissues from the front table.

She blows her nose. "I'm floating out to sea."

I hand her another tissue. "I'll be your life raft if you'll be mine." I touch her shiny collar brass. "This is brave as shit, Kat. I'm so proud of you."

She smiles, and the world tips a little toward okay again.

"The apprenticeship audition," she says. "And First Avenue. Again, I'm so sorry."

My head doesn't want to think about that awful day. But my heart hasn't forgotten about the smoky eye in my shoe. Prince has returned to me, like a loyal guard of what's left of my soul. I don't need a Walkman or sexy posters to feel the soothing rhythm of his guitar.

"I almost told you the truth, that night you went out with Nikki," she says. "It's why I came back. But then you looked so happy. I hadn't seen you smile like that since . . . well, I can't even remember. I didn't want to spoil it."

I nod. "How are they going?" I ask. "The rehearsals for the concert?" I don't know why I need to know. Maybe I already miss being a part of something.

"Umm, they're going well, I guess. The show's tomorrow."

"Well, merde."

"It's weird being there without you," Kat says, as if it'll dull the pain. "Especially with Baby-Pink Eye Shadow asking me how you're doing every second."

I bite my lip. "I think we're friends now."

"I can learn to live with that." Kat blots her nose. "But seriously, none of us should be dancing at First Ave if you're not. Your friend Nikki said as much. I think he really likes you."

My heart drops. "After today, I doubt he'll ever talk to me again. I said the most terrible thing to him just now." I slump into my chair.

"Don't keep the silence too long. You'll beat yourself up about it. I would know."

The emergency tones blast again and I about fall from my chair.

Kat jumps up, and I'm watching her transform into a superhero. No one will ever guess she just fell apart.

The intercom beeps and then, *"Engine six, medic seven, eighteen-year-old female, status seizure . . ."*

I barely hear the rest of the dispatch, my ears ringing like someone's shrieking. But I do catch the address—the numbers for a yellow house with a peeling wheelchair ramp.

Kat grabs my arms. "She's going to be fine."

I can't respond. The words are stuck in my throat. All the while, Glo is screaming inside my head.

The Arms of a Sister

Kat drags me into a huge garage. The ambulance fires up, my heart thumping so hard the crushing starts immediately.

She's talking to someone, but my hazy vision can only make out the shiny badge on his uniform.

"Captain," she's saying. "This is the patient's sister—and my best friend. Can she come with us? She knows the patient better than anyone."

The captain must've agreed, because I'm climbing into the back of an ambulance. Kat's next to me on a bench, her arm wrapped around my shoulder. We lean against each other as the ambulance leaves the station and turns onto the street.

The wail of the siren hurts my ears, the tangy odor of rubbing alcohol nauseating. Kat must sense my impending hurl and hands me a plastic basin. I cling to the pink bean-shaped dish, willing myself to keep it together.

Mom never calls 911 when Glo seizes. The doctors say they're just another part of Glo's new existence. If Mom called the ambulance, something really bad has happened. And I left without saying good-bye. No—I left her a week ago.

I recognize the left turn onto our street, and I suck in mouthfuls of air.

The ambulance slows, the driver honks, and then we speed up again. I have no feeling in my hands or feet. I drop the plastic kidney bean.

"Rosa. Slow down your breathing." Kat rubs my back. "Are your hands numb?"

I'm spacey, but manage a nod.

"It's because you're breathing too fast. We're almost there. It'll be okay. Glo's a strong one."

I press my fist into my chest. Yes. Glo's always been the strong one. But even I know there's only so much a damaged brain can take. And it feels like it's taking fucking forever to get to her.

We've stopped, the siren winding down. Kat helps me to my feet and opens the back doors. She jumps out and I stumble after her. The team pulls equipment bags from the ambulance.

I run.

Crashing through the front door, I'm immediately assaulted by alarms—Glo's breathing machine.

"In here!" Mom's terrified voice.

"Mom!" I race to Glo's bedroom. Rounding the corner, I grip the doorframe to keep from passing out. I'm splitting open. There's no limit to how many times your heart can break.

Mom's on the floor with Glo, my sister's frail convulsing body in a pool of beige vomit.

Glo's blank stare pierces the ceiling, her arms rigid and curled into her chest. Her skin doesn't look like it's supposed to—grayish-purple and shiny from sweat. The ventilator has fallen over, the tube disconnected and spewing air into nothing. Mom must've shoved Glo's wheelchair and bed out of the way because everything is smooshed into one corner.

Glo had been painting, her brush-mitts still on her hands. Black enraged strokes streak the front of her shirt.

Mom wipes her pale, wet lips. "Help me, Rosa! Please, help me." She has Glo on her side, holding her there. My sister's back contorts into an arch, a thing of my worst nightmares—like watching my beautiful Glo transform into a werewolf.

"She threw up," Mom cries. "I only left her alone for a minute. I promise."

I can't move, the room fuzzing at the edges. The ventilator alarms are overtaken by the screams inside my head. Glo hisses through ragged bubbly breaths. My sister is drowning on the floor of her bedroom.

There's a hand on my shoulder.

Kat.

Two responders shove past, dropping everything at Glo's side.

Mom falls back. The responders open their bags. They connect an oxygen tank to a mask and place it on Glo's face. Someone tries to suction her mouth, but her teeth are clenched together. They move on to suction her trach, the frothy sound making my stomach reel.

"How long has she been seizing?" a medic asks.

Mom doesn't answer. She's lost, staring right through the horrible scene.

Kat leaves my side to put something together that looks like an IV bag. She hands it over to one of the responders.

The medic tries again. "Anyone? How long?"

"Mom!" I shout, finding my footing.

She's looking my direction, but I don't think she sees me. "I don't know . . . I think I fell asleep." She sobs again. "We were fighting earlier. Is that why this is happening?"

I help her from the floor amidst the controlled chaos. She collapses against me and I hold her upright, grasping her scrawny waist. She feels like she'll break into a million pieces, tentacles of thin, ropy veins tenting the papery skin of her wilted arms.

"Rosa, how long does she usually seize?" Kat asks calmly.

Glo's breathing sputters, her legs twitching violently—the most they've moved since the accident. Suction's happening again. I squeeze my eyes shut. "Umm. Maybe two or three minutes. I don't know. It always feels like forever, you know?"

"Do you give her Valium for her seizures?" a responder asks.

Valium . . . I open my mouth, but nothing comes out.

"Please make it stop!" Mom cries, her body rigid. "Give her whatever you want! Whatever the hell will work! Just make it stop!"

Mom falling apart turns my insides. I can't think. We lock eyes. Hers are dark and sunken, like tiny tunnels with no light at the end.

I clutch her tighter because I feel her muscles go so soft. My fingers smash into her thin skin, her gaze totally vacant.

Mom's breathing too fast, her lips ghostly white, skin waxy like a Rescue Annie.

Jesus Mother Mary, what is happening?

"Slow it down, Mom. Look at me." I turn her face toward mine. "It'll be okay. In for five . . . and out for five." She follows my breathing.

I lower her onto the corner of Glo's bed and dash to the ventilator, switching it off, for once finding the right button. I spin around, tripping over a responder's bag. Equipment is strewn everywhere. Someone shoves a needle into Glo's arm, and a clear fluid runs into her vein. Another responder is talking on some kind of portable phone.

"Five milligrams," I blurt out of nowhere. "I think that's how much Valium she gets when she seizes."

I step over another bag, heading back to Mom.

Everything shifts.

It's quiet.

My sister's seizure has stopped.

"Glo?" I drop next to her, my knees stinging as if I'm kneeling in sharp, crystallized snow. She doesn't open her eyes. Air rushes from the mask covering her face and it sounds like her soul deflating. We're back in the street, the rumble of a truck engine at my back—Glo clutching her pointe shoe.

The responders work around me. I rest a gentle hand on Glo's chest, willing her to wake up so we can crawl into bed and watch metal videos, *The Facts of Life*—anything she wants.

The medic peels open her eyelids and shines a light. "She's in what we call a postictal state," he says.

I know. The forever amount of time we wait for Glo to wake up.

The dam breaks, and everything I've filed away from watching Mom take care of Glo spills out of me. "Umm, sometimes she vomits after she wakes up, so if you have to suction, it's best to start from the right side of her mouth. She has less feeling there. And . . . save her trach for last. Then she won't choke on her cough." I stroke her chest, my hands shaking so badly. "Suctioning her trach always makes her cough."

Kat kneels next to me. "She might take a while to wake up. And because she seized for so long, she needs to go to the hospital."

The hospital. Glo hates it there. I swipe away the slimy hair stuck to her forehead, not caring at all that her vomit is wetting my hands. My knees are saturated with it, the sour smell wafting from the carpet, and still my stomach remains calm.

A stretcher is rolled in and Kat offers her hand to help me up. But this means leaving Glo. I stay right where I am.

"Talk to her," she says. "Even though she's unconscious, I believe she can hear you."

I remove the brush-mitts and squeeze Glo's limp hands, a thousand flashes of the two of us coming at me all at once. I can't think of a single thing to say. Nothing sounds right in my head, so I massage her cold fingers.

Kat taps my back.

"It's time to go," she says. "You and your mom can ride with us if you want."

I glance at Mom, tear-streaked and hugging her knees by the door. She looks half her age, and twice as much. They wheel Glo out on the stretcher. I hang on to her hand until I have to let go in our narrow hallway. Then I go back for Mom.

Glo's easel is tipped over. I right it and pick up the painting next to it, flipping it over. My breath seizes. Her splintering-Freed work, the one I had such heartache over. The paint is still tacky, smeared at the edges from falling facedown on the floor. But I get the meaning. And it's nothing like I'd thought.

Glo wasn't finished. Because now there's a shadow of a girl emerging from the remains. Me, with my crazy abstract curls and chunky Docs. The beauty of it hits me hard. I barely get the painting back on the easel, my vision smudgy like the Rosa in the center of the canvas.

Mom's still parked on the edge of Glo's bed. I help her up and she shuffles from the room as I guide her toward the ambulance. One heavy step after another, she climbs into the back and sits on a bench as instructed. She doesn't seem to notice when they roll in Glo next to her and click the stretcher into place.

"You'll ride up front," Kat says, opening the door for me.

I climb in. Doors slam in the back. I turn around, way too

far away from Glo. Mom's out of reach too, an apparition of her broken self under the stark white lights.

Kat and I lock eyes through a square opening dividing the front from the back. As we pull away from the house, she gives me a reassuring nod. I can practically feel her thumb pressing into my palm.

I feel the Prince eye too—inside my shoe, balled up beneath my big toe. But I can't hear the funk anymore. It's buried beneath the wail of sirens.

Still Silent Sadness

The ride to the hospital is a confusing mess of scary sounds, words I've never heard, and sharp corners. We idle underneath a cement canopy outside the emergency room. The medics roll Glo out of the ambulance on the stretcher. Mom and I follow Kat inside a set of glass double doors and reluctantly part ways with Glo to fill out a stack of paperwork. A nurse fires questions at me when Mom stays silent, and somehow my brain tells my mouth what to say. I'm shocked I know most of the answers.

What medications does your sister take on a daily basis?

How often does she have seizures?

Is she allergic to anything?

There are some questions I can't answer.

When was the last time she ate or drank anything?

Is she depressed?

And the worst of all: *Has she ever tried to harm herself?*

I glare at the nurse. "Of course not. What kind of question is that?" I hope my hesitation isn't obvious. I would know if Glo was depressed . . . wouldn't I?

Kat brings me some vending-machine mud and Mom

some water. The coffee scorches my throat and tastes like ass, but I gulp it down anyway.

"She's going to be all right, isn't she?" I ask.

The nurse gathers up my paperwork. "Have a seat. We'll call you back when she's been stabilized."

My family hasn't been stable for years. Why would one trip to the ER make any difference?

Kat and I claim a corner surrounded by coughs, sneezes, slimy crying babies, and a guy who's talking to himself. Mom hovers in the hall, stalking the double door leading to the back.

"You should call your dad," Kat says, then waves at her crew leaving the ER.

"Don't you have to go?"

"No. They'll be back when they get another call. I'll connect with them then."

Kat's not bothered at all by the cesspool of sick we're floating in. She moves a box of tissues closer to the guy hacking up a lung across from us.

"You seem comfortable here," I point out.

"Yeah. Weird, huh?"

I rest my hand on her knee. "It suits you. The uniform too. Only you can make blue polyester look sexy."

"Shhh. I'm supposed to be one of the guys. No sexiness allowed. And no way can anyone know my parents are doctors. The expectations would suck. I don't want that kind of pressure."

"That doesn't seem fair. You can't hide who you are or where you come from."

"How right you are. So, why don't you call your dad?"

I sigh. "What if he doesn't care? What then? I won't know what to do with that."

"Call him. He'll care. He's not Master Geno anymore. He's your dad. And right now I don't think your mom's gonna be much help."

I watch Mom lean against the wall, her legs so thin I'm surprised she's still standing. How had I missed how emaciated she's become?

A sniffling little girl totters into the waiting room. A man who must be her father gently supports her arm, telling the nurse she might have broken it falling off her bike.

"Is there a pay phone around here?" I give in.

Kat tugs at my dress. "Come on. You can use the phone in the EMS break room."

The EMS room is quiet and empty. I plop into a rolling chair and stare at the phone.

Kat picks up the receiver, handing it over. I take it, dialing the only place I want to call—Geno's office at MDC. The other possibility, I'll leave alone.

I give him several rings, then hang up. "He's not there."

Someone pops their head in, a doctor type. "Any Dominguez family in here?"

"Yes." I jump up, my hands shaking immediately. "I'm Gloria's sister. And my mom . . . I'll go get her."

I duck into the hall. She hasn't moved.

"Mom. The doctor's here."

"Okay," she says absently, and shuffles into the break room.

The white-coat shakes our hands and motions for us to sit. "I'm Dr. Bolton. I've been taking care of Gloria."

Kat drags her chair closer to mine. Is she expecting bad news? What does she sense that I don't? There's suddenly too much air-conditioning. I rub my goose-bumped arms.

"Before you see her, I'd like to talk about a few things."

We've gone back in time, when the doctors told us Glo would never walk again—when they told us her brain would never be the same. I'm sitting on the same side of Mom that I was then, still terrified to hold her hand. I grip Kat's arm, my fingers cold and purple like a cadaver's.

"Gloria is awake."

I shift forward. "That's good, right?"

"Have her seizures become more frequent?" he asks. "Are they lasting longer than they used to?"

"For a couple of months now. But her doctor said they're just a part of her life, because of her . . ." I glance at Mom. I can't tell if she's hearing any of this. "Because of her brain damage. They said there's nothing we can do about it."

Dr. Bolton crosses his legs, looking right at Mom.

My heart's thumping so hard I feel it in my temples. "There's something wrong with my sister, isn't there?" I ask.

Kat presses her thumb into my palm. She's scared too.

"We did a scan of her brain," he continues. "We compared it to the one she had last year. Gloria's brain has a considerable amount of scar tissue that wasn't there before. And there is a small amount of bleeding and swelling, probably from seizing for so long before EMS was called. Does your sister fall a lot? Has she had any recent trauma to her head?"

"You mean, other than getting hit by a truck?" I say.

Kat pats my lap. "He means, has Glo fallen? Maybe out of her chair or bed?"

Mom doesn't answer, and I shake my head. But in truth, I have no idea.

I should have a million questions. But really, there's only one I need answered. "Is she going to die?" I utter. And I have no clue how I'll leave this chair if he says yes.

"I feel comfortable saying not today. She's a tough one— very stable. We expect the swelling in her brain to decrease on its own, without our intervention. The scar tissue could be due to a series of small strokes that went undetected. Which is understandable, given your sister's deficits."

"Deficits?"

"Her limited abilities."

I straighten up, on the defense. "But . . . I would've known if something was wrong. She'd tell me."

If I'd given her the chance. If I hadn't avoided her for days.

"No one is placing blame," Dr. Bolton reassures. But he doesn't know why we're here in the first place. "I need the family to be aware of the likelihood of her condition progressing. Meaning, she will probably have more episodes like today. I've spoken to her neurologist."

Neurologist? I should know who that is, but again, I don't.

"She plans to increase Gloria's medications in an attempt to decrease the frequency of the seizures. But Gloria could possibly lose more abilities if her brain continues to scar—if she has more strokes. We just don't know for sure."

Have I missed the signs? Did Glo try to tell me something was wrong, and I blabbed on about Prince and how sucky my life is because I'm too chicken to ride a damned elevator? I look at Mom for something more. She must be holding her breath, because her chest is barely moving.

"I am sorry to give you this news," Dr. Bolton says. And he appears to really mean it. But his compassion does nothing to loosen the fist around my selfish heart.

My shoes are crusted with Glo, fluids from who knows where. She's on my knees too, and my hands. I fold them over my chest, Geno on my mind. I imagine his arms around me, stronger together than we are alone—like the arabesque lift. He should be here with us, hearing this terrible news about Glo. Mom is next to me, but I'm on my own, plummeting through blackness.

I lock eyes with Dr. Bolton. "How long? How many years can her brain take?" I ask, before I can't.

He tips his head toward Kat. She wraps her arm around my shoulder.

"It's difficult to say. But looking at the trajectory of the scar tissue over the last twelve months . . . a year—maybe two."

Mom's breath hitches.

A year—maybe two.

Unfathomable.

Finite.

A year—maybe two.

"Does my sister know?"

"Yes."

I close my eyes. The protective part of me doesn't want Glo to know. But that isn't fair to her. She's not a kid anymore. And after today, my childhood is a tiny speck in the distance.

Kat's crying and I scoot my chair away from her as if she's contagious. I have to see Gloria. And she won't find me broken, though inside I'm filled with splinters.

"I'll take you to her now." Dr. Bolton opens the door. "We've moved her upstairs."

For a second, I think Mom won't get up. She's dry as a bone, not a single tear, her jaw set like she's holding off a brewing storm.

Kat doesn't move either. "I'll wait here. Okay?" she says.

Mom leaves the room, and I give Kat a hug. I follow the doctor, my footsteps quiet like the world has gone.

Analisa Corredor Ramos

Glo's in a double room by herself, the other bed empty. I hover in the doorway.

"Mom," I utter, my feet cemented to the floor.

She squeezes her eyes closed, as if hoping I'll go away.

Glo's arms bounce on her lap when she sees me. The relief is like breaching the surface after riding beneath a forever wave.

"Hey." I rush to her, determined not to cry one single tear. "You look all awake and—okay." I suck in a sob, my chin quivering like crazy. It's such a small change, maybe something only I would notice, but her right eye doesn't look the same as her left, the corner drooping slightly in an unfamiliar way.

"Okay . . . Fine," Glo says, her mouth crusted at the corners.

She has a purple valve on the end of her trach, like the one at home, her speech made easier. No oxygen. No ventilator. I rest my head against her chest, needing to hear her beating heart. It's there, strong and true. For a year—maybe two.

She swirls her fingers around my hair—fingers that will eventually lose their way to the canvas. "Okay . . . Okay . . . Okay." She begins to cry. There's no communication board here. We don't need one to interpret the sorrow in the room.

I sit on the bed and slide my arms under her upper back, pulling her weighty body against mine. She presses her forehead into the crook of my shoulder, her arms trembling as she wraps them around me. We hold each other, blubbering all over her bleachy hospital gown. So much for the not crying.

I hear Mom's soft feet behind me. I turn around and she's lowered herself onto the other bed. She's so pale and brittle. Her head sinks heavily into the pillow, her greasy hair spreading out like stringy tentacles.

The institution-green walls make everything worse. I try not to look at anything too closely, the clear canisters mounted behind the beds, rubber tubes protruding for who knows what. Dark green oxygen bottles are strapped to the bed rails, the fluorescent lights casting a sickly hue on our realities. No wonder Glo hates hospitals. This space won't heal anything.

She rakes her hands through my tangles, and my scalp tingles beneath her soothing touch.

God, I promise to remember what this feels like forever.

I ease her back to her pillow and take her hands, pressing an *I'm sorry* into her palms.

Glo's eyebrows pinch together.

Before I choke on my words, I say what I've been afraid to for so long. "I'd do everything different, Glo." I curl my toes around the crumpled Prince eye in my Ked. "I'd let you go to New York. I wouldn't be happy about it, but I'd find a way to cope. I'd pay attention to your dreams, like you've always been here for mine."

She taps her knuckles together, and I swear she's telling me she's okay. But how could she be? We're here, in a hospital bed.

I brush her damp hair from her forehead.

"I am so sorry." Mom's voice is barely there, but it slices through the room.

Glo's arms go limp.

"I should've stopped it," Mom says, her gaze fixed on the ceiling. "Your fight. I should've stepped in before . . ."

I take Glo's hands back, my puffy eyes stinging when I blink. Mom is talking about the accident. She blurs into a faint outline across the room.

"I should have been there for you too, Rosa. You were hurting," she mutters. "Look at what I've done to us, to our family."

Glo grips my arm, breathing faster.

"Leaving you that summer, Rosa, it wasn't the right thing to do," Mom continues. "And, Gloria, pushing you into something I knew you didn't want wasn't fair either." Mom chokes on something I can't understand. Is she apologizing to both of us?

I face Glo. "You didn't want to go to the audition in New York?"

"Okay . . . Fine." She nods her head—her way of saying *no*—then grates her fist across the dried paint caked on her arm.

"You wanted to paint?" I wipe my eyes.

"Your father and I, we're to blame." Mom hugs her plastic pillow. "The fight between you two that day, I did nothing to stop it. You're my girls. I'm supposed to protect you." She looks at me for the first time since the house. "*Both* of you."

I can't let her go on. "I'm the one who threw the pointe."

"Rosa, please let yourself believe for a moment that you can be freed from this guilt."

I shake my head. Did she not hear the doctor just now?

"Let me help you," she says.

I'm not even close to this being a possibility. Glo starts to shiver, and I pull her covers up. Regret whirls around the sterile room, threatening to reduce us to a pile of dust.

"Gloria," Mom says. "I think you are a beautiful artist."

I brush the hair from Glo's cheek, and her face relaxes like I've injected her IV with a tranquilizer. She seems different than only a moment ago.

"I see you both," Mom says. "For who you were before, and who you are now."

I catch Mom's gaze, wondering if she really can. If she really means it.

Her eyes close, and her breathing becomes slow and heavy. She's exhausted herself into a restless sleep.

"Okay . . . Fine," Glo urges, and I do what I think she means.

I inch across the room. Mom is snoring, which is new for her. Her grayish twiglike arms are splayed out over the white sheet, her skin so dry she looks like a peeling birch tree. How pitiful, and yet ever more graceful. She embodies the tragic swan, Odette, performing her mournful solo in a cold metal hospital bed. But she's still Mom. And like the tingling I feel when Glo runs her fingers through my hair, the closer I get to Mom, the stronger I feel our connection.

I touch her clammy arm. My fingertips zing. Strange—confusing—faint familiarity.

She opens her eyes. "Don't be scared," she whispers. "My lovely girls, don't be scared." Her gaze is soft and tender, how it used to be.

"I don't want to be sad anymore," I whisper back.

"Then let's not." She wipes my cheek with her cold bluish fingers.

"I don't know how."

"We'll figure it out. As a family."

"I'm not sure I believe you." It's the truth.

She doesn't have an answer for me. Mom's right in front of me, but she still feels miles away. We've been avoiding each other for so long, it's all we know.

Glo rustles around. "Okay . . . Fine."

She's far away too. I rush to her side of the room and tug on the footboard of the hospital bed. It won't budge.

Glo's arm shakes in the direction below my knees. The brake.

I kick it, and she's free. I shove the bed over to Mom, sliding the guardrails down between them. Glo loves this idea, reaching out to Mom as the two beds become one. I reengage the brake so they won't separate.

Mom pats the trench between them. I hesitate, then crawl into the middle and collapse onto the crisp pillows, half of my head on Mom's, the other on Glo's. All that's missing is a Dr. Seuss book and a sober Geno.

Mom reads my thoughts. "Did you talk to your father?"

"Not yet. I tried. He didn't answer."

Glo nuzzles up under my chin, her head tremoring a bit before settling down.

"I'll find him," I say. "I have an idea where he is."

Mom doesn't probe for details. She knows the coins are gone from the windowsill. She says we'll figure things out as a family. Maybe this means we'll fall apart together this time? I move my arm until I feel Glo's strong heart against my side. Maybe we'll only fall apart a little.

I massage away a splotch of dried purple paint from Glo's arm. "The pointe shoe painting," I say.

"Okay . . . Fine." Glo pulls my hand to my chest, like she did the day I told her about the deal I made with Geno.

"I get it now. It's about following my heart." I hold her palm against my chest. "Can you feel the rhythm?"

Glo shakes her head. "Okay, okay, okay."

We stay this way until she falls into a peaceful sleep. Mom reaches over and strokes her cheek, then starts to disconnect the purple valve at the end of her trach.

"I got it," I say. "She never sleeps with it. I know."

Mom hesitates.

"I want to help." My gaze settles on her thin fingers. "And maybe it wouldn't be so bad to let the nurse come more than once a week too."

She grips my hand. "I am the one who is supposed to take care of you. I failed you before. That won't happen again."

"You just said we'd figure things out as a family. And that means together, right?"

Mom's eyes are one blink away from wherever Glo has gone. "Yes. I did say that, didn't I?"

Her body mellows, and she lets me go. I pop off the valve, my hands a little shaky. Glo's breathing softens, and I relax too.

When Mom drifts off, I study her face, her thin straight nose like Glo's—same lips and cheekbones. I'm part of her too, minus the hair. Mine has never seen a straight glossy day in its life. Rather, it has a mind of its own like Geno's—thick and coarse with waves and curls springing in every direction.

Glo makes a snorty noise through her trach. I reach for the call button, realizing there's no ventilator in the room. Glo bats my hand away. She wasn't sleeping, *the faker*. Just giving me the chance to prove myself capable to Mom.

I kiss her temple. "Thank you."

Glo folds her hands, her wrists twitching as her fingers curl inside her palms.

"All right," I say to my sister. "If you get tired, wake me up. Or press the call button, because—"

"Okay," she interrupts, her voice a raspy, airy whisper without the valve.

I fight my own exhaustion, the insides of my eyelids burning. I blink once . . . twice.

"I love you girls," Mom slurs.

My body goes rigid. I feel exposed, stretched out on top of the covers between Mom and Glo. I don't say anything back.

"I can wait," she says. "I can wait for as long as you need." Mom intertwines her fingers with mine, our special way.

I rest my head in the crook of her arm, the rest of my body molding itself around the curve of her sharp hip.

Glo's steady breath reassures my own.

I blink my stinging eyes again . . . and then again. The third time, they don't burn anymore.

A Whale of a Drink

I wake up to darkened windows, rain pelting the glass. Mom and Glo are sleeping, a whispery ventilator attached to my sister's trach. Someone covered me with a hospital blanket, the culprit revealed when I see the note sitting on my legs.

Hey, Rosarita. I have to go back to the station. I didn't want to wake you. Besides, I could barely get through all the love in the room. Hugs to you, Kat.

PS I left you my jacket. Crazy weather. In my pockets, my bus pass and some change. You'll probably need it for where you're going.

Kat, my hero forever.

Untangling my fingers from Mom's, I kiss Glo's cheek before sliding out from between them and sneaking out the door.

Lightning strobes in the stark corridor. It'll be a wet bus ride to where Kat knows I'm headed. I pull on her jacket, MINNEAPOLIS FIRE DEPARTMENT embroidered on the left chest. I sniff the collar—Kat's Prell shampoo mixed with something that smells clinical. My upper half looks so official. The lower—short flowery dress and Keds—not so much. But I'm not stressing it. I doubt that Martin, my bouncer friend at Moby's, will give a shit.

I didn't bother calling MDC again before I left the hospital. By this time, Geno must be in his other office.

I step off the bus, the rain immediately soaking me. Thunder greets me with a crack, and I scurry under the marquee at the XXX. The change in my pocket jingles and I think about Nikki's nickel-quarters. My legs go soft. I'm pretty sure we would've checked a few *X*'s in the back of this theater. Fat chance of that now.

Hazy drunken memories from the night of the Purple Funk Factory find their way back to me. There's an alarm clock in there somewhere, and Nikki's soft, gravelly voice telling me he'll set it for the early morning. MDC, the apprenticeship, and First Avenue were my entire world then. Tonight all I want is for Geno to know about Glo.

And my Prince won't let me go it alone. "Free" fades into my thoughts like a security blanket, the rain's tinny sound bringing track seven with me as I jaywalk around a few crawling cars.

Hennepin Avenue is as empty as I've ever seen it, anyone left on the streets huddling underneath alcoves and awnings. I run from my cover, my grand jeté off the curb splashing my legs with warm gutter water.

I swear the blue whale logo grins wider as I approach—A WHALE OF A DRINK. But the cartoonish sign doesn't match what's inside. Everyone knows there's more bloodshed at Moby's than at a North Stars hockey game.

Pulsing neon illuminates the rain, silver bullets assaulting the sidewalk, a halo of misty gloom on the fringes. I shiver, Kat's jacket totally drenched and sucked to my arms. Her bus pass is crumpled in my hand. It should be easier to turn around and leave.

A random drunk stumbles out, same leather jacket, same jeans—not him. I tuck the pass underneath my bra strap and glare at Martin.

Even in shitty weather, Moby's door is propped open. Martin has his stool just inside the threshold. He drags on a cigarette, eyeing me like I've got nothing on underneath Kat's jacket. I zip up, rain spilling over my head like a cracked egg.

His smoky gaze fixes on the fire department insignia on my left chest. "Someone need CPR?"

I sneeze on him. "Funny. I'm going in."

He sticks a bulbous forearm in my way. "He's not here."

"Liar. Come on, Martin."

We stare each other down. And then he actually moves. "See for yourself."

I slip past Martin and inside Geno's lair.

Cigarette air and pungent beer overtake my nose. The secondhand smoke tickles my lungs as I move through the crowd, the wood floor sticking to my wet soles. My temperature spikes from the soupy atmosphere, my face slippery with rain and sweat.

I'm here for Geno, but I have to check out Moby's. I want to know what the big deal is—what's more important than coming home for the family game nights we never have any-more?

Swiping my dripping hair from my face, I try to act like I belong—whatever that means. There's every kind in Moby's—working girls, working class, slumming upper class, and no class. The back corners are darker than the alleys outside. A packed bar barricades the man behind it, dewy bodies steam-ing up the blacked-out windows. A couple of college students in U of M sweatshirts order shots, trying to outdo a group of guys in greasy coveralls.

Every pool table is taken, foosball too. Four men are in the middle of a heated argument over a tabletop hockey game—a power play gone bad. Blue-T-shirt guy shoves plaid-shirt guy, and the tattoo-covered bartender becomes the referee. "Drop the puck in the center and replay, or get the fuck out!" he shouts.

The puck drops and I worm my way back, searching the crowd for Geno.

The bartender rubs his fingers my direction. "I'm gonna need some ID from you, little lamb. I'm not as easy as Mar-tin." He adjusts his faded VIETNAM VET baseball hat, the word *BOOM* tattooed across both forearms.

I'm back to shivering. "I—"

A Blue Öyster Cult cowbell clangs from the jukebox.

"I'm looking for Geno." My left foot sticks in something tacky, like chewing tobacco.

"Oh yeah?" The guy checks me out.

"Yeah. Is he here?"

A dude a few stools away slides his beer mug down the bar, shouting, "Set me up, Boom!"

Boom flips a dirty towel over his shoulder, tipping his chin at me. "What d'you want with Geno?" He fills the mug from the tap and slides it back down.

"To tell him his daughter's in the hospital."

Boom grasps the edge of the bar. "Then you must be Rosa."

There's no way to hide how shocked I am. "Uh, yeah?"

"He went home."

Some greasy guy elbows past me and sits in the nearest stool. I elbow him back. "Are we talking about the same Geno?"

"Tall as you, feathered rock-star hair, leather jacket?"

I nod.

"He got a phone call. Then took off. Said he was goin' home."

"*Home* home?" I ask.

"Don't know, kid."

Geno went home? It doesn't make sense. Who called him? *Here.*

"Anything else?" Boom asks, then shoves a glass of something on ice down the bar.

The wall of medallions is behind the bar. I came here for Geno. I'm leaving with at least a part of him.

"I want Geno's AA coins back."

Boom finds this funny. "Honey, I don't keep track of the specifics. Gotta be hundreds up there."

"One month and six months. That's all I need."

His eyes flick to the other bartender, then back to me.

"Please." I lean into the bar, my hair dripping on the stack of wrinkled cocktail napkins.

Boom sighs and turns around. He pulls two coins from the wall and hands them over.

They feel heavy in my hand. I drop them in my jacket pocket. "Thanks."

"Yeah. Now, ID up—or out."

I shove my way through the crowd. I don't gawk at everything on the way out like I did on the way in.

"Tonight was your one and only, sweetheart," Martin grumbles as I leave. "Don't ask again."

"Once was enough," I say. "I won't be back."

I cross the street, and living up to Mom's given name, I run the rest of the way to the bus stop.

The Sun, the Moon, and Eugenio Dominguez Ortiz

When I step onto our boulevard, the Buick is in the driveway. The house is dark, the front door unlocked. I go inside and make my way to the kitchen. I flick on the lights.

"Joseph fucking Mother Mary!" I gasp.

"Jesus Christ, Rosa. *Language!*" Geno barks from his old spot at the kitchen table.

"Why are you sitting in the dark?"

He glances around the kitchen like he's never seen it before, a stranger to this house. The smokiness that used to cling to everything has been gone for so long, which is why his presence now is so palpable. His ashy scent drifts around the kitchen like a stinky ghost.

I try not to stare at his cowboy boots, the ones that brought him here days ago to take back his AA coins.

Geno's eyes dart to the empty windowsill over the sink. I squeeze the coins in my pocket. He wrings his tremoring hands and gets up—won't dare look at me.

Glo's feeding supplies are stacked on a drying rack. He picks up a bottle-shaped container marked for measurement.

"Mom mixes Glo's supplements in that. She can take some

of them at the same time, so it's easier to measure out the milli-liters, shake them up, and then infuse.

Listen to me. *Infuse*. Like I'm the expert. "They have to be really clean, so you should put that back."

Geno shoots me an *I'm still your dad* look.

But we're in *my* studio now. Mine, Mom's, and Glo's.

He puts the bottle down and instead of making a break for the front door, he heads down the hall. "I'll order some pizza. That sound good?"

I want to say no. But it sounds like heaven on a stick.

"Glo's in the hospital," I say before he disappears again.

He hesitates at the threshold of Mom's bedroom. "I know. Your mom called Moby's."

My back finds the counter.

"So, you know, then? Everything?"

"Yeah." He closes himself inside like it's his office at MDC.

I peel off Kat's jacket and pad down the hall. My dress could use some time in the dryer, my shoes so soaked they squish when I walk. I don't feel the Prince eye anymore. It must be mud.

A stray plastic wrapper sticks to the bottom of my foot, probably something from the medics. I turn on Glo's light, breathless at the sight of her room. It's trashed like the kid's bedroom in *Poltergeist*. Glo's bed is still shoved against the wall, wheelchair crammed in the corner with her ventilator. Torn medical-supply packaging litters the floor. And some of her paints are knocked over, pools of black and purple staining the shag carpet.

I hang Kat's jacket on the doorknob and drop to my knees, poking my finger at the hardened paint.

Mom will freak. This'll never come out. A forever reminder of Glo's worst seizure yet.

Everything aches. I sit back and draw my legs in.

Breathe in . . . breathe out. I pick up a piece of trash.

Again, in and out. I eventually stand and roll her bed to where it belongs.

Glo's easel.

The painting.

I sit on the edge of her bed.

She's added more depth with violet-purple strokes, her ability to transform flat canvas into an infinite universe of color and shadow mesmerizing. I touch the shards of the pointe. It has movement, as if the pieces will shoot right off the edges. And there I am, in the middle. My cheeks fire up. I am strong. I am beautiful.

I quickly arrange Glo's paints as if she'll come through the door at any moment, laying out her brush-mitts the way she likes them. When I'm done, I chill out enough to open her window and change her dirty sheets.

The doorbell rings, followed by Geno's cowboy boots shuffling down the hallway.

"Pizza's here." He has two plates, a slice of pepperoni on each. He holds one out to me from the doorway.

"You can come in, you know."

He eyes the paint on the floor. "Your mother's not going to like that."

I pull the clothes hamper over the stain. Geno almost smiles.

Taking the plate, I bite into the lukewarm slice. My face must give away my review.

"It's not Slice of New York, that's for sure," Geno admits.

I gulp down the soggy dough. "Nope." But I take another bite, because I'm starving, and Geno doesn't even smirk at my chewing with my mouth open. He doesn't reek like a liquor cabinet either. And going by the way his hands are shaking, I doubt he's had a drink today.

"I was born with flat feet," he says.

I swallow. "What?"

"I said, I was born with crappy feet."

"Yeah, right. Kat always says she could drive a truck under your arches."

He sniffles. "When I was ten years old, my father broke my feet so I'd have higher arches. I never would've made it in ballet with the flat boards God gave me."

I set down my plate. "Are you serious?"

"I wish I wasn't."

"But that must've . . . really hurt. Why would he do something like that?"

"I just told you." His jaw tenses.

"And Abuela? She just went with it?"

"Fear. It rules us more than love."

Now I'm thinking about Nikki.

Geno sits on the other side of Glo's bed. "He died, your grandfather, when we were crossing the border. A heart attack,

I think. His lips, I remember them cracked and caked with sand. And my father, flat on his back, choking on the dusty air." Geno squeezes the greasy edge of his pizza. "I did nothing. I waited, sipping the warm ginger ale my mother had given me—the one my father didn't want me to have. I watched him struggle to breathe until . . . well, until he wasn't anymore."

My hands are numb. And Geno's barely holding his plate now. I manage to take it, setting it aside with mine.

"The ravens." He traces a spiral on the knee of his jeans. "Circling with impatience. That's what I remember most. I hear their cries in my dreams. My mother, she didn't cry. Instead, she prayed by his side—always by his side. And I became a crow. I drank every last drop of my ginger ale, waiting impatiently for my father to die."

I clutch Glo's warm pillow. Yes, the cracks in this family happened long before I would've dared to imagine.

Geno looks at me, his brown eyes so much like my own—tired and sad. Always tired and sad. "Would you do the same? If it were me?" he asks, and I wish he wouldn't have. Because after Nikki, I never want to hurt anyone with my words again.

My fingers go to my necklace.

"I guess I deserve that," he says, then takes his pizza back.

I rub my cross and think of Abuela, and how she used to pray for Glo and me to find the courage to be ourselves—because she lost her chance with Geno. I don't know. It's messed up, but maybe this is what haunts him. Maybe with us, he saw a chance to fulfill what his father never got to see in him.

Setting the pillow aside, I adjust Glo's leg bolster and tuck in the sheets. "They need you," I tell him. "Mom and Gloria."

"Your mother was always the strong one."

"That's what I say about Glo."

He nods, but he's somewhere far away now. "Ana stayed."

Geno hasn't called Mom by her name in ages. I've forgotten how nice it sounds, like she means something to him again.

"No matter how impossible I made things," he continues. "Even when she had a way out, she stayed."

The check from my grandparents. The one Mom threw in the trash.

Geno's eyes sag at the corners. She gave up more than money when she watched her parents drive away, and he knows it.

Glo's pillows can't get fluffed enough. I smack them. "You're such a coward."

"Maybe I am. What does it matter, Rosa?"

"It matters because you're my dad. Glo's too. You're supposed to—"

"Protect you? *Eh.*" He clicks the heels of his boots, pulls a cigarette from his pack, and then stuffs it right back. "You don't need me."

"That's a total cop-out, a lame excuse to totally book."

He clears his throat, his scruffy cheeks twitching beneath his welling eyes.

I get up and move Glo's wheelchair away from her ventilator. I fight to drag the machine across the carpet.

Geno hands over his plate. "Where does she keep it?"

"To the left of her bed."

He rolls the vent and resets the brake. His hands quake as he presses down some of the peeling heart stickers on the vent. There isn't a cure for that here. Mom tossed those bottles a long time ago.

His finger hovers over a toggle.

"That one's the power switch." I point to a dial. "And . . . I think this is where you adjust the amount of air she gets. Adagio versus allegro, I've heard Mom say."

Geno appears to be listening. So I go on. "And this guy." I jab my finger at the bottom right button. "This one's your best friend. It silences the alarm. Glo doesn't like the alarm because it goes off at the tiniest thing, like when she coughs, or overbreathes the machine. That kind of stuff."

"All right." Geno sits on Glo's bed, studying her painting. "You've been good to her. Your sister's lucky to have you."

Gloria—lucky? Because of me? I'm not ready to believe this.

I take a bite of my crust. "This is the grodiest pizza I've ever had," I say with my mouth full.

"Agreed." He shoves our plates away from Glo's paints.

We lose ourselves in her work. Late-night cars whiz past outside. It's a new sound for her room. The windows haven't been opened since we shared the space. Maybe Mom's worried the crunching of tires on asphalt will scare Glo. But a rainbow of life goes on outside of our faded yellow house. There's no sense in pretending it doesn't. Because there's still plenty of it left in here.

"She's really good," Geno says, brushing his finger over the thumbprint stamp in the bottom corner, Glo's signature.

I gaze at the purple pointe, thinking about Val at the gallery and her question: *What* don't *you like about it?* There's simply no answer. Gloria's painting is perfection.

"She's saying she wants me to follow my heart." I brush my finger over a streak of violet.

"And where would that take you?" Geno asks.

I sigh. "I don't know anymore. Prince. Maybe choreographing rock-star videos." I've leaned into Geno's shoulder without realizing. I shift away. "I'm pretty good, you know?"

He traces the shreds of the painted ribbons with his finger. "Maybe . . . maybe she wouldn't've been this good if it weren't for the accident."

I gasp. "Don't ever say what happened to her is a good thing."

"I only meant she wouldn't have become . . ." He waves an elegant hand over Glo's paints. "*This.* I wouldn't've allowed it."

"Truth."

Geno's head hangs, his hollow cheeks sucking against his teeth. "Glo ran after her own shoe, Rosa. Do not carry that blame forever. Believe me, it will ruin you."

Nothing moves inside me, like all my blood has stopped.

I rub my cold arms. "You should take them some clothes."

"Me?"

"Yes, you."

He wrings his leathery hands. "They don't want to see me. You should do it."

"No." The last time I said the two-letter word to him, he was Master Geno, ordering me to leave the studio and never come back. I tighten my center.

Geno never breaks posture, I'm sure not even on his barstool. But now he's sitting next to me all slouchy. I'm sort of panicked, seeing this submissive side to him. He's always been the pillar of tyrannical strength. I have no idea how to exist with the other kind of Geno.

He tips his chin at me. "Is your hand okay?"

I make a fist, glancing at Kat's jacket, the coins weighing down the pocket. "Fine."

"Before I came here," he says, "I was sitting at Moby's, talking myself out of a drink."

I'm pissed, and kind of proud of him too. "Why's it so hard? The not drinking? You could lose everything, and you do it anyway."

Geno brushes off his lap.

"Like, where's your ring?" I ask.

He squeezes his fingers together, knuckles whitening. "Do you have any memories of me not drinking?"

There's no need to stretch my brain cells to come up with an answer. "Not really."

"Yeah, well, I don't either. I started drinking when I was a kid, younger than you are now. It was a way for me to forget. I liked the way it made me feel nothing. My father was not a good man. To me, or Abuela." Geno presses his hands against the back of his leathery neck. "When I'm not drinking, I miss it. That's the truth. So, I have a whiskey, thinking it'll just be the one. And . . ."

I'm sitting so close to him now, I almost sink into his side again.

"I don't know how to live sober, darling. Sometimes, I don't want to. Because I have no idea who I am without a drink."

I kinda get it. I feel the same way about ballet. I stare at Glo's Zeppelin poster.

"You call me Gloria when you're drunk. So, you're pretty clueless about the people around you too."

Geno's head hangs.

"Dancing is my life," I say. "Maybe not in pointes. But moving to the music? *Hell yeah*." I curl my fingers against my stomach. "You've kinda failed at the dad thing. But you've made me a better dancer. Sometimes I really hate you for that."

Geno looks away.

"I'm glad Nikki got my apprenticeship spot," I say. "It means more to him than it does to me."

"Your friend Nikki. He's quite the talent."

I bite my lip so I won't cry. "I don't think we're friends anymore."

"Unfortunately, he's not very smart."

I lean away. "What does that have to do with anything?"

"He's been arrested."

"Wait!" I spring from Glo's bed. "Nikki's in jail?" I shudder, envisioning him locked inside a dark, damp cell with a gang of horrible, violent people—which Nikki is not.

"What the hell? *Why?*"

"Right after you left, he grabbed his stuff and walked out. That kid wasted my time." Geno jabs his finger at the air all tough, but I can tell he's upset. "He left in a huff, without a word, and got himself into a fight at the 90's. Anyway, his apprenticeship is over. Another kid, throwing it all away."

I squeeze the sides of my head. "Nikki got into a fight at the 90's? Probably defending someone from a bigoted asshole. It's the only possible explanation. We have to help him," I cry. "He only left MDC because I said something unforgivable." My chest has the weight of a thousand elephants on it. Guilt is a bitch I'll never be rid of.

"I called Oz. No answer. Called the jail too. They won't let me talk to him. And I can't go there, Rosa. You know that."

I do. The police department and Geno. Just . . . no.

"Then I'll go," I say, already stomping down the hall to the kitchen.

"With what, darling? A couple of quarters?" Geno calls after me.

I've already found the number to the station when Geno joins me. It helps that it was dog-eared in the phone book. I dial, then wait, only to be told Nico Madera has already been released.

I hang up. "He's out. Someone from the 90's posted bail."

Geno sits. "I'm keeping this to myself. I won't tell Joyce. But I have my doubts he'll show tomorrow."

I'd forgotten all about First Ave tomorrow. I pinch the phone cord between my fingers.

"You should do it," Geno says. "At least, be ready to go on if Nikki isn't there."

My body responds to his offer, but not like it would've a few days ago, before I saw what could happen outside places like the 90's. I lean into the counter.

"No," I say, and it isn't even hard. "I won't do it. Not like this." I trudge back to Glo's room and collapse into her wheelchair.

Nikki left MDC and got arrested. I squeeze the vinyl arms of the chair, wishing I could see him this second. Wondering if he's hurt. And if G-ma knows.

My feet find their way to the metal rests connected to the bottom of the chair, and before I implode, I make myself go quiet, insides and all. I touch my collarbone where Nikki drew the paisley the day we met, our fiery auras intersecting. I have to believe he'll be okay. An aura ardiente will always find a way, Abuela would say.

Glo's favorite Van Halen shirt is folded on top of her dresser. I get up and pair it with a wrap skirt that's easy for her to get into, then go back to the kitchen.

"Here." I drop the clothes in his lap. "Gloria likes these. Her sandals are in the front closet. And Mom has a bunch of sundresses in the laundry basket in the living room."

He might bolt, and I'm prepared for this. But then he stands up with the clothes. "Sandals in the front closet. Sundresses in the laundry basket in the . . ."

"Living room." We're close enough to hug, but things like this aren't part of us. "You're really gonna go?"

"Yeah."

"Promise?"

He tucks the clothes under his arm. "My wedding ring . . . I'll get it back."

I want this to be true, but I know better.

Geno's tired eyes look over Glo's medical supplies on the drying rack. "Rosa darling."

"Yeah?"

"I want to tell you that . . . that I'm sorry."

"For what?" There are so many reasons.

He sighs, the overhead light illuminating his weathered face. "I, uh, I don't know where to start."

"Maybe there." I nod at the clothes under his arm.

Geno moves in.

"You should go." I back away. "Before it's too late." And we're both aware how sad this sounds.

He takes a final glance at the windowsill, and then he's gone.

I wait to hear the car start, then go to Glo's room and fish his coins from Kat's pocket. I hide them in the back of Glo's top dresser drawer, then collapse onto her bed. Her pillow smells like Mom's lotion. I press it against my chest.

Geno has never given us the sun. Or even the moon. But if miracles are possible and he finds his way back to us, maybe those medallions will mean more to him than free drinks someday.

Free

A horn blares inside my head. I groan. The noise becomes louder and faster, annoying enough to force my body to roll over and open one eye. I'm in Glo's room, having fallen asleep on her bed. I reconsider my idea to leave the windows open.

The day feels different—like, next-day different. Birds are singing their lunchtime songs.

Car doors open, then slam shut, girly chatter reaching me from outside. I pop up, my head stuffy and spinning.

The front screen door creaks open, followed by the main.

I jump from the bed. *Glo and Mom are home!*

Rounding the corner, I slam into Kat just outside Glo's room.

"Jesus Christ on a cross!" I gasp. "Between you and Geno, I'll have no lives left."

She looks me over. "Nope. You're still this side of the dirt."

Within my sleepy fog, I remember calling Teener's in the middle of the night, like ten times. No answer. And then bugging Kat at the fire station to bawl on her shoulder about Nikki.

Kat tugs at my gnarled hair. "Although, you could use a run around the drops in the shower."

"This fire thing's rubbing off on you," I say.

"Yes, it is," a familiar voice chimes in from behind Kat. "And it's not becoming of a lady who wants to snag a Prince Charming someday."

Kat moves aside.

Stacy's in my house—with Kat.

Kat's bug-eyes urge me to go with it. And hell yeah, I will. Gone are Kat's preppy Izods. Her hair is crimped to the max. It's bigger than mine. She's all decked out in tight black shorts and a green tank, a wide white belt swirling around her hips.

"Prince Charming can kiss my ass," Kat says, her gigantic neon hoop earrings bouncing against her shoulders. "The only Prince I'm after is the one playing at First Avenue in"—she checks her watch—"about six hours. So, we'd better get down to business." She tugs at my arm.

I'm being herded across the hall. "Down to business for what?"

"A change of clothes would be a start." Stacy eyes my wrinkly dress, smoothing the pleats on her own.

"Come on." Kat hauls me toward the bathroom. "You only have a few hours to learn the choreography."

I grip the doorframe. "Wait."

"And, Stacy"—Kat commands in ready-action mode—"Rosa's room is downstairs. Go find her something to wear."

"On it." She's already down the hall.

Firefighter Johansen has several inches on me, so she easily shoves me inside the bathroom and locks us both inside. "I'm sorry Stacy's here," she whispers while turning on the water. "I bumped into her earlier this morning while running around Lake Nokomis, and she insisted on coming. I didn't mention anything about Nikki. I thought I'd leave that up to you."

"Kat, *no*. This isn't how I wanted any of this to be."

"But this is the way it is. We're all sorry about what happened to Nikki. But you can't change it, Rosa. You know this. Now"—she yanks my dress off over my head, giving me instant chicken skin—"we are short a dancer, and you're the best understudy I know."

That last part doesn't sting like it used to. In fact, it'd be an honor to be Nikki's understudy.

She grasps my shoulders and hits me with her laser-beam blues. "Plan Indiana Jones is a *go*. Get it together." She herds me into the shower. When the hot water hits me, I'm fully awake. She pulls the curtain closed.

I rip it back open. "Is this really happening?"

"Damn right." Kat squeezes a dollop of shampoo into her hand.

She starts scrubbing my head like mad, the shampoo running into my eyes. It burns like hell, but I barely care. There's a race happening inside my veins.

Kat tips my head back for a rinse. "Stacy offered to help. And let's face it—hair, makeup, and Geno's choreography. We need her. Who knew, right?"

After our Friday night in the dressing room, I knew.

"Oh, and I talked to your dad."

The bottle of conditioner almost slips from my hand.

"I saw him at the hospital last night."

"Glo?" I blurt. "And Mom?" I hand her the bottle. She squirts some onto my head and massages.

"Your mom slept all night in your sister's room. Geno said he didn't want to wake her, so he crashed in a chair in the hall. And Glo's doing well. She should be discharged soon."

My shoulders melt into the cascading water, my tears washed away with the conditioner. Something good is happening, which isn't how stuff goes in my world. My life is never a happy-ending after-school special. It is more like the one where the girl gets gonorrhea from her boyfriend.

Kat turns off the water and shoves a towel at me. I wrap myself in it while she dries my hair with another. I can't talk. There's just this thing called breathing—and getting to Nikki. Let Kat believe what she wants, but I'm not doing this without him.

"Hey! I've got the clothes." Stacy pounds on the door.

Kat gives me a look.

"Yeah, let her in."

She opens the door to Stacy holding up two different outfits.

"First of all," Stacy starts in, "what happened to your room? Do you have demons or something?"

"Something like that," I say, remembering how I left my bedroom in tatters—literally.

"Okay, then, I did my best with what I had to work with. We have a choice between *The Last American Virgin*"—she hangs a lavender peasant mini on the door hook, followed by a sheer white, flowy tank top—"or *Solid Gold* dancer." The other ensemble is a pair of metallic satin hot pants I wore as a Halloween costume and a spandex tube top. It really does look like she tore it off of one of the dancers from the TV show.

I feel the delicate lace around the hem of the white tank. "This is my mother's top."

Stacy sits on the toilet. "She has good taste."

"She does."

"It's perfect. Sexy and demure at the same time. And the skirt has good twirl."

Stacy glances at Glo's room across the hall.

"Hey." I poke her shoulder. "I meant what I said. You can come and visit her anytime."

She clears her throat. "And I meant what I said. I'd really like that." She wipes down my bathroom sink. "Oh, and thanks for the *Archie* tip, for Jeffery. I went to Shinders like you said. But I got him *Wonder Woman* comics instead. Her hair's so much better than Veronica and Betty's. He liked them." She's blushing now. *"A lot."*

Way to go, Stacy.

After seeing the choreography at company rehearsal, I already know most of it. But thanks to Baby-Pink Perfectionist, two hours later I'm still in my living room. I turn out of a parallel pirouette and hit my end pose, right on the mark as "D.M.S.R." fades from the boom box.

"Hell yes!" I shout, arms overhead.

Stacy jams her hands into her hips, not looking the slightest bit out of breath. "Hell no. You're still missing the count at the beginning of the chorus."

I groan, adjusting my soft ballet shoes. My out-of-shape body is on serious strike. But no way will I be the clod onstage. A performance can have twenty of the most brilliant dancers, but one sickled foot will distract the audience from the rest of the perfect ones. I run through the beginning of the chorus again.

My forehead is sticky from sweat and hair spray. I wipe it and cough into my towel for the hundredth time.

I clap my hands like the Master. "Let's go again." And it feels like a triumph.

Another hour of Stacy's corrections, and I'm ready.

Kat pats her glistening cheeks. "You're going to need touch-up, Rosa. You look like someone dumped a bucket of water over your head."

"Who made the call to do my hair and makeup before the rehearsal? My hair is paste, and I'm sure my makeup is all smeary."

She laughs. "I forgot how much you sweat. Just fluff it." She produces a pick and does her best with more spray and gel. "And, you know what? Never mind with the makeup. You have a glow, totally not smeary."

"We are dancing to a song about sex." My cheeks redden even more. "What're we wearing?"

"What you have on. The company wanted to show off our individuality."

Mom's sheer top with my black bra underneath. It's totally perfect.

Kat tosses me a pair of black trunks from her bag. "Here. You might want to wear these under that skirt. Your Gar-animals underwear is showing when you pirouette." A pair of worn jazz shoes shoot across the floor. "Dug those out of the lost and found at MDC. They're your size."

I take them, wondering if my dance bag's still there.

"I'm so nervous." I grasp the back of the couch, over-whelmed by everything that had to happen to get me here.

Stacy scoops up her bag. "Well, work it out before we get there. You're front and center."

I pat my chest. We hadn't gone over placement yet. "Nikki is center stage?" I ask, but not at all surprised.

"Yeah," Kat says. "His turns are insane."

Before I plummet too far, I'm rushed through the front door like I'm being spit out of a makeover machine. My hair is teased to heaven and gelled to hell, so much Aqua Net, and even with what's left of my makeup, I barely recognize myself.

My brain is a Tilt-a-Whirl. Even more so when I see Blondie in my driveway—emptied of Kat's things.

"She's really not that scary," she says. "Not after driving an ambulance."

"You drove an ambulance?" Stacy blurts, fixing her mauve-on-white lipstick.

I run my hand along Blondie's smooth paint job. "So, you're back home. That's awesome, Kat."

"Not exactly home. I told my captain what's going on, and

he cleared it with the chief to let me stay in the dorms at the station until I figure something out. . . . So, can I live in your basement?"

Kat's question comes out like a joke. But my answer is dead serious.

"Hell yeah, you can." I throw myself at her, hugging her until she unwraps my arms from her neck.

"I'm confused." Stacy taps her jelly shoe on the sidewalk. She's feeling left out.

"She's going to be an EMT." I'm swelling with pride. "She saves lives."

"Well, I'm *going* to save lives." Kat blushes.

"No." I open Blondie's passenger door. "I got it right the first time."

I crawl in the backseat, giving Stacy shotgun. Blondie roars to life, my heart running a sprint of its own. We race toward the Minneapolis skyline, a maizy-yellow haze fading into the pale blue backdrop.

Glo can create color like this. I wish she could be with me tonight. Mom too. Neither of them has seen me dance since Glo and I took class together. And I've been totally fine with that, because I never wanted to rub my abilities in my sister's face. I realize now, this was all on me. My own demons. Not hers.

And Nikki. He should be here too, touching up his makeup like Stacy.

Kat catches me frowning in the rearview. "You're thinking about Nikki, aren't you?"

Stacy turns around. "He didn't show for rehearsal yesterday.

Very unprofessional." She notices my eyes welling. "But everyone knows talented artists are always a bitch to work with."

Only Stacy has a way of giving a compliment without directly saying it.

"And then I heard he quit," she continues. "You're better off, Rosa." She's trying to make me feel better. It's not working.

I scooch forward. "Kat, stop at Teener's first."

"You sure?"

I squeeze her shoulder. "Yeah. I'm sure."

"Why? They'll totally be closed at this hour." Stacy digs through her bag. "I have, like, everything here. Did you forget something?"

Kat grins at me through the rearview. The girl does love an impossible challenge. "Yeah, she did. But we'll find him."

The sky slowly transforms from pale yellow to deep blue. I thought my life changed in an instant on January 5. When, really, it didn't. Mom's pain began with her parents. And she retired from MDC because of her own injury, not Glo's. Geno was a drinker long before that winter, his demons housed in his perfect feet and a dusty Mexican border. And Glo. I'm back in the Vault, watching her black-painted fingernails reveal her metal tee. She was a fierce rebel then as much as she is now.

Me? I'd like to think I would've found my way here eventually. In the backseat of Kat's car, cruising toward a night onstage with Prince.

"Roll down the windows," I command with a sweep of my hand.

"Umm, *hair*." Stacy smooths her gleaming hair, which is

like a beautiful still lake, not a wave in sight. I hope she never cuts it.

Kat winks at me and rolls her window down. Her bruises are gone. She looks positively radiant, and I realize I'm in the presence of her true element. She punches the gas and we lurch forward so fast my heart smashes against my spine. Stacy doesn't appear to notice, her gaze fixed eastward. Maybe she's somewhere across the Mississippi, dreaming about dancing on the other side of it someday.

Kat pushes a cassette into the player—Prince, "D.M.S.R." The beat strums my chest. My face heats up—the Funk. Nikki. And me, showing him my own D.M.S.R.

Stacy braves it and rolls down her window too. The wind is no competition for the cans of hair spray shellacking our hair. And with Prince urging us to let loose, sing along, and shake it like we don't care, I slide to the edge of my seat again.

I drape one arm over Kat's shoulder, and the other out the window. The girls follow my lead, piloting their hands on the warm sharp breeze. If I reach a little higher, I swear I'll touch the sky. We have sprouted wings inside Kat's yellow Camaro. But I'm not ready to fly off yet. Because for the first time in two winters and two summers, my feet are on solid ground.

The Evolution of the Lows

"Go around back," I tell Kat when we reach Teener's. The CLOSED sign hangs inside the glass door, the store dark and creepy with all the silhouetted mannequins on display.

Stacy rolls up her window. "Not a good idea. These alleys are trouble. My dad's told me things."

"What things?" Kat asks, pulling in behind Teener's.

"I don't want to know." I get out the second Kat stops and go straight for the rusty can of nails. They fall in behind as I fish out the key.

"Teener's has a secret key?" Kat gushes like we're Indiana finding the Ark of the Covenant.

"Not a secret anymore," Stacy says, huddling against me. "Hurry up, Rosa. It's getting dark. Whatever you forgot better be important. We're going to be late."

I'm not ready to tell Stacy about Nikki's arrest. To be honest, I'm not sure how she'll take it. I mean, she is a cop's daughter. I'm sure she's seen firsthand what happens at the 90's from her dad's police car.

I open the door and we all go inside. We're in the stockroom, a couple of bare bulbs swinging from their cords lighting our way.

"Whoa." Kat turns a circle, the same reaction I had the first time I saw the bowels of Teener's.

They follow along while I search for something familiar, a landmark in this fun house to guide me to Nikki's room. It's weird being here. I never thought I'd come to Teener's again. I spot the vampire capes and everything speeds up.

"This way." I glance over my shoulder to find Kat wearing a red sequined vest, and Stacy with a furry boa around her neck.

I sigh and head for the capes. "Nikki," I call. "It's Rosa. You here?"

"We're here for Nikki?" Stacy whispers. "Why would he be at Teener's so late?"

"Because he lives here," Kat says.

"He lives . . ."

We round the corner and I stop, Kat and Stacy bumping into my back.

Nikki's sitting on the edge of his bed, a packed duffel at his feet. He's all hunched over, like his shoulders weigh a thousand pounds. He's wearing a plain pair of jeans and a white tee, nothing flashy—no earrings, not a speck of glitter anywhere. Everything that made him Nikki . . . is gone.

"Hey," I say, like nothing horrible has happened.

"Hey," he answers without looking up.

His sienna pointes are in the trash—makeup, hair gels, jars of glitter, all of it piled in a cardboard box.

I step toward him, Kat and Stacy staying where they are. "You're leaving?"

"Yeah."

My throat tightens. "Where will you go?"

He rubs his hands over his legs.

I crouch down in front of him. "I heard what happened. Are you—"

Nikki tips his chin up.

"Oh my God! You're hurt."

The swelling around his left eye is so bad, I'm sure he can't see through it. His upper lip is puffy too, dried blood in the corners of his mouth. I grasp his hand and he flinches. His fingers are injured, dark bruises blooming from his knuckles.

"Kat," I say, but she's already beside me.

"Let me see." She looks him over, then gently bends his fingers one by one, Nikki letting her like he's not really here.

Hot tears roll down my cheeks.

Stacy comes closer. "Holy moly, that looks really bad."

I shoot her a look.

"Bathroom? Towel?" Kat asks.

I point at the little closet, and Kat doesn't hesitate.

"You shouldn't be here," Nikki sniffles. "There's a show in a few."

"Fuck the show," I say. "Geno told me you got arrested."

"Arrested?" Stacy chimes in. "For what?"

"Defending someone at the 90's," I say. "Am I right?"

Nikki turns away. "I guess you could say that."

I touch his cheek, and he lets me. I want so badly to pull

him into my arms, but I've probably lost that right. "How long have you been sitting here?"

"I don't know, hours maybe."

Kat comes back with a handful of stuff and starts cleaning Nikki's wounds, focused like a real EMT, but a caring friend just the same—the way I should've been that day at MDC. "Did they get the bigoted asshole? The one who did this to you?"

"Nah." Nikki's eyes water.

"Why not?" I practically shout, standing up.

He doesn't answer.

"Why, Nikki?" I squeeze his shoulder.

"Because a cop picked up where the other guys left off." We lock eyes, his rigid dark browns encircled by rings of defeat.

I forget how to breathe.

"What?" Stacy clutches her boa. "What do you mean? Like, your face . . . and your hand? *Why?*"

He gives her a sour glance. "You'd have to ask him. But I'm sure it had something to do with everything I was wearing in that box." He juts his chin at the pile of makeup.

"Seriously?" Kat says.

Nikki winces as she winds a strip of cloth around his hand. "A couple of guys came down to the club, started making noise, saying stuff to the line outside. And I just snapped. I got some hits in, they got some. Then the cops came and . . . next thing I knew I was facedown over the hood of a police car, my hand bending the wrong way. I tried to tell the cop what was going on, but he wasn't interested in my side of the story. Hard to listen when you can't hear past your own prejudices."

"No, no, no." Stacy squeezes her ears. "Oh my God, was it my dad?" she gasps.

Everyone needs to fucking stop. And Stacy, she's turning inside out right in front of us.

"He would never!" she shouts. "I mean, he's a good man. I've seen him in action and he's always fair. Always. He would *never*."

"McGee, right?" Nikki asks, and I'm not sure what I'll do if he says it was Stacy's dad.

Stacy pales. "Yeah?"

"Wasn't him. So, you can chill."

The entire room deflates, as if it being some other cop makes it better. It doesn't.

"What can we do?" Kat asks. "File a complaint or something?" She's looking at Stacy, who's sunk into the nearest folding chair.

Helplessness swallows the space. My heart goes cold while the rest of me boils.

I sit next to Nikki to keep from tearing apart the entire stockroom. "Please don't leave."

Kat passes out tissues from her bag, like she's glad to have something to do.

"We'll figure this out." I dot his lip with a tissue. "Just . . . please don't go."

He shrinks away. "Figure out how to kill centuries of hate? Nah, Rosa. It's a cool belief, but that ain't gonna happen."

I don't want him to be right. I want to be the optimistic friend for once. But I'm not the one with the beat-up face and swollen fingers.

I have no idea what to do next. I only know that Nikki can't leave. And he can't curl up in his bedroom by himself either. I've been there, and it only dragged me deeper.

"Come with us," I say.

Kat bumps my hip. I'm onto something she likes.

"Come to First Ave. Dance with us."

Nikki shifts around, his feet moving like they can't help it.

"Seriously, it's either that or I swear to God, I'm going to light something on fire."

Stacy looks up at the last part.

Nikki stands. I snatch his duffel bag.

"Rosa . . . Strawberry . . ." He's looking at me with those eyes, the ones I could live in forever. I never thought I'd be Strawberry again. Not after what I said, and I wonder if he's letting me off the hook because he's so used to making nice, conditioned by the ugliness out there to let it roll off. Like everyone did when Enzo got hit with the beer bottle.

A drop of blood sprouts from Nikki's lip. "I don't have it in me, Strawberry. Not anymore."

"But you do." I inch so close it hurts to see his wounds in such detail—the tiny reddish vessels popping to the surface of the purple bruises. "Remember what you said to me? Don't fear the downs, because they bring on the evolution. Because . . ." I gently grasp Nikki's waist, resisting the urge to shake the life back into him. "Because the love is here." My chin trembles. "It's in this room."

I know I'm expecting a lot. Probably too much. I've seen the same humiliation in Geno's eyes—the last time Mom bailed him out and he showed up with bruises he refused to talk about. Bruises I know he didn't get inside Moby's.

"I look pretty bad, huh?" Nikki asks, his mouth stretching in a way that might split his lip again.

Kat and I pick one of each, answering no and yes at the same time, both of us cringing.

"I'm not asking you to forget this." I let go of Nikki. "This shit isn't over. But right now there's an empty stage at First Ave, and I can't think of a better way to blow off some steam than to dance it out, front and center, to some insanely mad Prince guitar."

"I'm in." Kat raises her hand. "Stacy?"

Stacy's removed her fake fur. She's staring at the ground, chest caved in a way that's so un-Stacy-like.

"Hey," I say. "You okay?"

She looks up, biting her bottom lip. "Yeah. That's sounds good. He'll need hair and makeup. And something else to wear."

I focus on Nikki again. "Close your eye."

He does.

Carefully I take his hands. "Remember that day, tappin' to Van Halen?"

Nikki's toes pat the concrete.

"And there's that guy I grooved with at the Purple Funk Factory. You know, the place with the whirling violet lights, where we could be anyone we wanted to be."

He nods.

"And G-ma. I went back, you know?"

Nikki opens his eye.

"She sees you. And she thinks you're beautiful. Sparkly eye shadow and all."

Tears bead beneath his long lashes.

"Tell me, Nico Madera, were you born to dance?"

I hear Kat all weepy behind me, and I swear if I start again we'll all be done.

Nikki squeezes my hand. "Born, raised, would die without it."

"Then tonight you are immortal. And no one, *no one* can touch you."

He bends his knees, looking everywhere but straight at me. "My legs feel pretty good. Guess I could groove with y'all. Can't let that badge steal my moment, right?"

"Yes!" Kat shouts, already digging through the box of makeup.

I can tell Nikki's still uncertain, and lying about his legs a little. But he's not leaving. Not yet. And looking at him now rewinds the world to the first day we met, before some of the light went out in his eyes—my Flower Boy in a red kimono.

"Stacy, we need you," Kat says.

This perks her up a bit. Her ears flush red. "If . . . if it's okay with Nikki."

He hesitates, then nods. "Yeah. It's cool."

Stacy crosses the room and vetoes a few of Kat's eye-shadow choices. "This one's way better for his skin tone. And it'll cover the . . . the discoloration around his eye." Her face is fixed like stone. She's a second away from losing it again. It's like she finally crossed the Mississippi, only to find the other side is fucked up.

My hand finds hers and she even gives me a squeeze back.

Kat and Stacy start primping Nikki. I take his pointes from the trash, holding them out.

He shakes his head. "Not ready for that."

I set them on the table, hoping he will be someday. Nikki has a dream to finish. The dance world can't go on without seeing his sky-high saut de basque onstage with Les Ballets Trockadero de Monte Carlo.

My own pointes are in my dance bag in the lost and found at MDC. I won't need them tonight, maybe never again. But it doesn't feel right, hoping Nikki will leave his out of the garbage, when I've left mine in a smelly bin to rot.

I pull Kat aside. She's still wearing the sequined vest. She'll probably walk right out of here with it. "I need to run by MDC. I'll meet you at First Ave, okay?"

"Sure." Kat squints at me like she does when her brain wheels are turning.

"It's no big deal," I say. "I'll see you there."

"Okay." She tightens the backstrap on the vest. She's totally stealing it. "Back door of the club. That's where the dancers go in. I'll leave your name on the list."

"Got it."

I turn to leave and Kat catches my arm.

She whispers into my shoulder. "What about Joyce? You know, Nikki's arrest?"

We glance at the makeover happening. Nikki's debating with Stacy about eyeliner colors.

"Geno said he didn't tell her," I mutter.

"Damn, Geno." Kat sways back. "It's about time he did something right. But . . . if Nikki dances, that means you're out."

I grab her shoulders. "We are *all* dancing tonight. Whatever it takes."

This bugs her eyes. "Look at you. Going all Indiana."

My head cues up Prince—"All the Critics . . ."— bringing on flashes of the teacup test. "Time?"

Kat points to the clock beside Nikki's bed, the one I knocked over in a drunken stupor, ending my story at MDC. "We've got an hour."

Nikki and I catch each other's nods. He's moved on to doing his own makeup while Stacy digs through his boxes of packed clothes.

I give Kat a big squeeze. "See y'all under the purple sky."

Rosa, in the Rose-Colored Leotard

I open the doors to MDC, a whoosh of cool air and familiar smells smacking my face. Some are a comfort, some sting my elbow and cause my feet to ache.

I'm here for my dance bag, but after a quick climb up the stairs, I find myself one level above the lobby—in the empty 5B studio. Geno's black-and-white photos on the walls remind me of the Dinkytown gallery, each photo telling a story. I stop in front of Mom and Glo. My gaze traces the fluid lines of their arms to the angle of their long necks. Strong, lovely—enduring. I mirror their poses, my own arms looking much the same.

The accompanist replaced the teacup I broke, a plastic Snoopy mug there instead.

I face the mirror and take fifth position. I sweep my leg, a slow développé à la second, imagining the teacup perched on my toes.

If I can do this, I can do anything. My promise to myself that day.

I count to ten.

I let my leg down gently, and head for the stairs.

Lou's guarding his post in the fourth-floor lobby, and he hasn't forgiven me for trashing his attendance book. There's a new one on the counter, and he clutches it as I approach.

"I'm sorry about your book," I say. "That was lame."

"Totally lame." Lou sets down the book and snatches his broom as if he'll swat me away.

"I'll pay for the new one."

"Two dollars."

"Okay. Next time I see you."

But when will that be? I'm no longer a student at MDC. Lou and I have a history—at least ten years of banter between us. I will miss it.

"The studio's closed," I point out. "What're you doing here?"

Lou purses his lips. "There was a rehearsal happening, and *I* was asked to open up, special."

Can't stop the smile. As I walk away, I catch a whiff of cologne, which Lou never wears. He usually smells like Hubba Bubba bubble gum and Fritos.

"And, you just missed him," he sings under his breath.

I sigh and spin around, my stiff ratted hair rustling like hay. "Who?"

Lou's eyes narrow, all bedroomy. He put some thought into his outfit, totally bodacious in tight leather pants and a hot-pink T-shirt with the sleeves cut off.

He waves his gangly Grover arm, then bows. "Your highness, Prince," he purrs, rolling his *r*.

My heart plummets. *"Prince?* Right here?" I throw myself against the counter. "Why'd he come through the lobby?"

Lou starts sweeping, swaying his hips. "Heck if I know. Don't let your hair hit you on the way out."

"Louis!" He hates being called this.

He whips around. *"Rosehip."*

If my spidery lashes weren't sticking together, my eyes would be wider. "Lou . . ."

"It was weird. . . . The man himself opened the lost-and-found bin and then left. Took the elevator a second ago."

"The lost and found? Why?"

"I'm not the 411."

I run to the bin, drop to my knees, and open it.

There it is.

Sitting on top of my dance bag, surrounded by a jumbled pile of used, BO-saturated dancewear—is my pointe shoe. The one I dropped at Prince's feet. I'm barely able to steady my hands as I lift my Freed out of the bin like it's the Holy Grail itself. Only seconds ago, Prince held this very shoe. I smash it against my chest, everything on fire. Lou's rambling on, but all I hear are pops and buzzes.

This pointe is the second shoe to cause me regret when it left my hands. I hold it closer, as if I've reached through time and plucked Glo's Freed from the endless beyond. I turn it over, examining every inch. There's a tiny teardrop shape drawn on the toe with purple marker. A paisley, just like the one Nikki drew on my chest. I'd squeal, but I've exhaled all the air out of my lungs.

I pull my bag from the bin and dream-walk toward the elevator.

I press the Down button.

It's here.

I step inside.

The doors close.

The steel box hovers, waiting for me to tell it where to go. But I'm facing the back, spellbound by the empty corner. This is where it happened, the most embarrassing seconds of my life.

The essence of Prince lingers everywhere—sweet-and-sour sweat mixed with cedar. I close my eyes. His ghostly energy swirls around my bare ankles and up my legs. A deep bass beat pulsates beneath my ribs, my own heart. I had a strong one all along. I clutch my shoe tighter. I've returned to the Purple Funk Factory—where my fears didn't exist—where nothing could stop me.

I open my eyes and I'm back in the elevator. I glance at the paisley on my pointe, imagining Prince's fingers tracing the shape. The Purple One remembered me, Rosa, the girl in the rose-colored leotard.

Tears mingle with my muddy mascara. I have no idea why I'm crying. Maybe I've done so much of it my eyes don't know how to do anything else?

I press the "1." The elevator moves, and I don't flinch.

When the doors open, I'm not ready to leave. I touch the

railing, running my fingers along the dulled metal. Everything aches, for so many reasons—my body a deep, but healing, bruise. Happiness and sorrow can exist together. I am the proof.

The doors begin to close and I squeeze through at the last minute. I rush outside, drawing in a lungful of city air. A slow-rolling rust bucket catcalls me into Saturday night reality. Hennepin Avenue's alive and stoked for anything. And after the elevator, I'm right there with it.

I turn the corner, and my gut seizes. *So* many people. The crowd spills off the curb. I doubt most of the people outside the roped area have tickets. All of Minneapolis has stepped out for a glimpse of their Prince.

A line wraps around the block at First Avenue, snaking under the big white letters and funneling into the front doors. The curved black brick building is ready for its star—spotlights, red ropes, the Hollywood treatment. It's impossible to believe it was once a Greyhound bus station. From elevated speakers, "1999" is blaring, a spontaneous dance party happening in the middle of the street.

I cross without having to dodge cars, making my way to the alley leading to First Ave's back door, where dancers and some sexy VIP-looking girls are waiting to get in. It's a ready-to-party procession of toned legs, cropped tops, ratted hair, and thick black eyeliner. My chest thumps so hard my eyeballs quake.

My clammy hands squeeze my pointe as I shuffle along, anxious to be reunited with Kat, Stacy, and Nikki. Most in line are company dancers. They totally recognize me as the Master's daughter, eyeing my hair and makeup as if full of questions like *What the hell are you doing here?* But no one asks. I wouldn't know where to begin if they did.

I'm next. The dancer ahead of me goes inside and I step in front of the doorman.

My legs stiffen.

"Name?" The doorman flips to the beginning of the list.

"Rosa. Rosa Dominguez." I pop up on my tiptoes, peering at the list.

Mr. Doorman comes to the last page, then sighs. "Not on the list, honey."

Everything seizes, and I start to sweat like crazy. "I have to be. It's Rosa Dominguez," I shout, as if it'll make a difference.

The line behind me is getting squirrelly, someone yelling from the back, "Move on, sweetheart."

Mr. Doorman's shoulders fall as he gives me an exhausted look of death. He points to the curb. "Step aside, miss."

"Please." I about grab his damn clipboard. "Can you just check again? Maybe at the bottom, handwritten? Geno, I mean, my dad said he'd put my name down."

He grunts, like I'm totally putting him out. Mother Mary and the whole mess of them, does it really end here?

"Dominguez, is it?" More pages flip. He reaches the end, squinting at something on the bottom.

I peek over the top of the clipboard, catching handwriting on the bottom of the typed list. And it's Geno's writing, not Kat's. My heart fires up as I hold out my wrist for a stamp.

Mr. Doorman puts a check by my name. "Sorry, sweetie. Didn't see you the first time." He stamps my wrist.

I bob against the crowd, speechless among the excited chatter.

"Well, get on in there before the rest of them trample you," he says.

Though I feel like hugging this total stranger, I don't. I walk past Mr. Doorman, leave the dusk outside, and step into the midnight backstage.

Legacy Mine

I'm totally inside First Avenue. Like the exterior, the walls inside are swathed in black paint. I smash against the side of the narrow hallway, dodging stagehands scuttling around like carpenter ants. A server passes flutes of champagne to three steamy women in skimpy lace. They are definitely "with the band." He offers me one too.

Just looking at it turns my stomach. "Umm, no thanks," I say, and make my way toward what must be the dressing area. Posters hang on the walls, artists who've actually played here— R.E.M., New Order, Hüsker Dü, Run-DMC. I run my fingers along the scratches and divots in the walls, imagining the hundreds of instruments that have graced this corridor. Un. Real.

I walk faster, searching the crowd for Nikki. I'm in the core of a Minneapolis music mecca. It feels all kinds of wrong that he's not here with me.

"Rosa!" Kat shouts from the far end of the hall.

I exhale at the sight of someone familiar. We worm our way to each other and I crash into her.

"Come on," she huffs. "We've got a problem."

"Nikki?" I stop walking.

"No. Stacy."

My questions go unanswered as we ride the swell through the hall, until Kat yanks me into the first dressing room, a small rectangle with one wall of bulb-framed mirrors, a few chairs, and a rolling rack with Odette's costume hanging on it. Bedazzled with sequins and feathers, the tutu's exactly as I remember, every plume imprinted in my memories of Mom as Odette. I catch my reflection in the mirror. I'm young Rosa again, sitting on a stool, watching Mom transform into a beautiful swan.

When I see Stacy crying in the corner, I set down my bag and my pointe. "What's going on?"

"I can't do it, Rosa," she mutters.

"Do what?" I look around. "Where's Nikki?"

Kat hands Stacy a whole box of tissues. "He's giving her some space. Well, they both needed it."

Stacy blows her nose. "Odette's solo . . . I'm freaking out. This has never happened to me before. I'm so confused about everything. Seeing Nikki like that . . ." She blows again. "My dad . . . I know he's not the one who hurt him, but . . . can't you see?"

"See what?" I ask.

Her breath stutters. "Things have already shifted. I can feel it. You don't trust me because of who my dad is." She's yelling now, and with all the shit that's gone down between us, she's never raised her voice. "This isn't even about losing the only friends I've ever had. It's about Nikki. Don't you think I feel sick about it too? I'm more than just hair and makeup, you know."

I go to her, though I'm not sure what to say because, yeah, she's called me out pretty accurately.

"What happened to him is screwed up," Stacy mumbles.

My arm brushes against Odette's stiff tutu. "We're still friends. All of us. Why do you think it hurts so much? I mean, Kat and I are in constant pain." Kat laughs at this. It's sick and true. "And I should've given you more credit. I'm sorry."

"Me too." Kat's beside me, glancing at the clock on the wall. Curtain in twenty.

Stacy calms a bit, her red puffy eyes smeared with black streaks. "I'm still not doing it. Look at me. This is Odette." She points to the costume. "*This* is not." She swirls her hand in front of her tear-streaked face. "I can't perform the solo tonight. The last place I want to be is alone. Like Nikki said, I don't have it in me."

I take the tutu from the rack, rotating it so it sparkles. I had so much heartache over Stacy performing Mom's Odette, and now that all seems so shallow. Stacy needs to be on that stage. She earned it. She didn't run all those stairs for nothing.

A downy feather falls from the skirt. "What if . . . what if I performed it with you?"

Shit. Did I just say that out loud?

My head snaps to Kat. Her blue eyes reach inside my head and drag me into hers like a fierce undertow.

I swallow, my throat like the Sahara.

"You've seen the piece a thousand times," Kat reassures. "You could do the choreography in your sleep."

"Are you serious?" Stacy stands up. "Like a duet? You and me?"

Thank you, universe. For sucker punching me with Tchaikovsky.

"Umm, I guess we could call it that. But if this happens, I'm not wearing this. It was never meant for me." I hand her the tutu. "You should."

She clutches the white bodice. "You sure?"

"For real. Though I'll never do the lame-duck diagonal sequence justice—like my mother did."

"That is not the Rosa Dominguez I know."

Geno's commanding voice spins me around. I notice how clean his clothes are, no wrinkles from sleeping in them. His signature leather jacket is with him, but the seedy bar smell is still gone.

"Never do it justice?" He sidles up next to me, which makes me scratch at my arms. "That is not the daughter of a Master speaking."

"Yeah, well, you're not my Master anymore," I find the balls to say. Even so, like a well-trained dog I stand up straighter.

"No. No, I'm not. But I'm still your father. And . . ." He grinds the toe of his boot into the ground. "And my daughters are the strongest young ladies I know."

The room quiets. Stacy looks like she wants to leave. Kat, however, beams like the sun itself. I can practically hear her smile, it's so electric.

Geno rests a gentle hand on my shoulder. "Right now my

eldest is out there, in the audience with her mother, waiting to see her sister dance. Do you think she cares at all about a perfect set of piqués en dehors?"

My head takes a second to catch up.

Glo? Here? Have I died and come back a girl who deserves such a thing? If it's true, after tonight, I swear to God, I'll never wish for anything more.

The Dominguez sisters—two regular girls, cruising the city. How long have I waited? And Mom. She's left the house. Left our yard. Christ, left our neighborhood. I wonder what the air of freedom tastes like to her? For both of them. Not Tater Tot hot dish, or beige in a bag.

My toes tingle like they always do on opening nights. "Glo and Mom, they're really out there?" I gather my center. There's a storm brewing beneath my skin. Suddenly I can't remember a single eight-count of the choreography.

Kat's patting her fingers together just like it's Christmas morning.

Geno nods. "Katherine got her fancy fire department to bring them in an ambulance. Glo's wheelchair and all. They'll bring them home afterward. Both of them."

When I look at Geno in this moment, the little girl in me does remember him sober. I'm being tossed into the air and spared the ground at the very last moment.

"What if I screw it up?" I say. "It's a real possibility, you know?"

"You keep going." He touches my chin, and there it is,

something like pride in his eyes. For me—Rosa. "And the daughter becomes the master."

I let everything go. Just for now. I jump into his arms and my feet leave the ground, as if he'll lift me into an arabesque press again—both dancers pushing against each other's strength. A pas de deux of perfection.

"Dad," I mumble into his shoulder.

"Mi flor pequeña." He sets me down and pats my shoulders.

"A duet?" I ask. "And Joyce? This whole thing isn't going down the way MDC planned."

"Sounds like you and Miss McGee have it handled," he says. "Just remember, shoulders back. Strong . . . Never mind. You've got this. Merde, my darlings." He blows us a kiss and is gone.

"You and Miss McGee have it handled?" Stacy says. "What just happened?"

Kat drapes her arm around me. "Rosa just landed the role of a lifetime. That's what happened."

She's so right. I am my father's daughter, and that's a little bit okay.

There's, like, literally no time to spare, but I plop into the nearest chair anyway. Two pairs of vacant baby-bobcat eyes stare at me from the bottom of my bag. I pull out the *Ranger Rick*, thinking about Shinders, wishing the Nikki from that day back to life.

"So, a bunhead wants to dance for Prince?"

I whirl around, dropping the magazine.

If there are rock-star angels in heaven, they shimmer like Nico Madera—in white patent leather thigh-high boots, a shocking-red miniskirt, and a shredded muscle shirt. May we never stop meeting like this because, Holy Mother Mary of the heavens, Nikki is a space-age love song.

I can't talk. I'm too busy cursing the cop who scarred his beautiful face. And yet his makeup is a *Drag* mag masterpiece. I lick my lips, tasting cherry.

He leans on the doorframe and crosses his biceps, checking me out with one smoky eye, the other half swollen shut—a gorgeous brown James Dean after a rumble, with glitter eye shadow, fluttery lashes, and a bandaged hand.

"You think you got the stuff?" he asks.

Kat disappears, I think. Because I see only Nikki, his muscles twitching like little earthquakes beneath his skin.

I ache to go to him, but there's something I need to say. Instead of staring at my Keds like I do when shit gets hard, I meet Nikki eye to eye, like he deserves.

"I'm sorry, for everything. For what I said. I didn't mean a word of it. And I know that's the lamest, because it's already out there. I just . . . the arrest . . . You never would've left MDC if I hadn't been so awful. We're done after this. I know that. And, I get it. What I said was unforgivable. I broke the trust you had in me, and I'm sorry. I'm just so glad you're here, for whatever that's worth."

His boots clack toward me, and I forget how to do anything but gaze at his sparkly bare chest. "The 90's . . . it wasn't about you. It wasn't even about me. It's about those guys who stirred it up, and that cop. That's what I came up with, anyway, sitting on the edge of my bed. And then you showed up all ablaze."

I nod, though I'm aware I'll never really get what it's like to live in Nikki's boots.

"The audition," he says. "I should've run my ass back to Teener's. Dragged your pickled butt outta bed. That was my fault."

"No. Your thing doesn't cancel out mine. I'm not . . . I'm not like your mother."

"I'm not here to talk about my mother." He's so close to me now, I can smell his cherry lips.

My body lifts, weightless like Odette's feathers.

He smiles. Nothing compares to Nikki's smile, even with a fat lip.

He presses his forehead against mine.

I brush the back of my hand across his cheek, embracing the first time I saw him, holding a box of plastic flowers. I kiss him, as gently as I can, inhaling his breath as if it'll make us one person. I tell him how much of my heart is his—all over his tongue and fruity lips.

"Umm, *hello*," Stacy shouts over the erupting chaos in the hall. "Ten minutes to call."

So much for warming up. The hall is a freeway, the rush of curtain call speeding up my heart. I grab Nikki's narrow waist. "You ready to kick it 'D.M.S.R.' style?"

"You know it, girl." His eyes glimmer like Odette's jeweled bodice. "But, it's your fiery ass on that stage first. 'Cause when

I came up on you outside the door, I heard there's a duet about to happen."

Nikki nods at Stacy. "Merde, Stace."

"Merde back." She sucks at hiding her uneasiness. "And . . . I'm really glad you're here too."

Kat scuttles about the room. "Okay, merdes all around. Come on, people, Stacy's gotta be a swan in five."

Stacy fluffs the feathers on the tutu, then hangs it back on the rack. "This never fit me right anyway. If you're wearing street clothes, Rosa, so am I."

She looks slammin' hot in her white shorty romper with rainbows striping the sides. It'll totally do.

"My hair!" she says in a panic. "I've got to—"

"Leave it down," I say. "It looks beautiful."

"Ditto," Kat agrees.

Stacy blushes. "Oh . . . but we've got to be en pointe at least." She snatches my paisley shoe from the dressing table. "You've been holding this like a glass slipper. Where's the other one?"

Prince Charming and my Freed—our little secret.

I rifle through my bag, finding my other pointe.

"Three minutes!" comes a call from the outside.

My heart sprints and I reach for my life raft. "Kat, am I really doing this?"

She hands me a batt of lamb's wool, so I guess I am.

Stacy pulls me into the chair next to hers. "Hair." She points at my head.

Nikki comes at me with a pick and starts fluffing my hair.

Kat tapes my left toes. I do my right. Stacy's already half-done with hers.

Sweat's pooling at the small of my back. All I can think about is tying my ribbons. I can't believe I'm stuffing my feet back into fucking pointes.

"I made sure the club set up a ghost light last night and everything." Stacy tucks her ribbons, followed by mine. "No sense in testing the theater gods."

"Theater gods—satisfied." Nikki asphyxiates me with more hair spray.

I stand up, taking one last look at Odette's sequined costume. "That sure is a waste of satin and tulle. It's a shame no one'll be wearing it. Onstage. Under the lights. In front of a full house."

Nikki's good eye goes soft, his other closing completely. He's seriously angel-like with his silvery cheekbones.

I want to remember every single second of this night. But when I reach my mark offstage, it's all a blur. How did I get to the wings? I must've walked down the same poster-covered hallway I'd taken to the dressing room. Kat, Stacy, and Nikki must've been by my side, because their faces are the last things I see before Stacy and I take the stage.

Like a strange dream, the kind where I'm suddenly in front of a full house, I awake center stage, illuminated by an indigo follow spot. Stacy's with me, stage right, but this feels like the solo of my life.

My pointes bring me pain and comfort all at once, my

heart beating faster than ever before, and I have yet to dance a single eight-count—counts I still can't remember. The crowd is here for Prince, not me—not Stacy. Even so, they're attentive, motionless, eager to see what makes this random girl in a purple skirt and her mother's pretty lace top so special.

I sense Stacy's nervous energy, hear her ragged breathing. She's feeling it too, the hushed anticipation for the beautiful willowy girl in rainbows.

I search the audience for a familiar face, something I never do. But I do it now, because Glo's here, and it's impossible to begin without her. A sea of leopard print, high hair, and so much black eyeliner stares back. I point my paisley toe harder, holding my beginning pose and . . . there they are. Geno, waiting with his hands clasped together like he does in the wings. Mom and Glo, seated next to each other, my sister urging me to breathe in . . . okay. Breathe out . . . fine.

It snuck up on me, this moment. Though I've been dancing toward it my whole life, I never expected my epic performance would be Odette in big hair, street clothes, and a paisley pointe. Anything really is possible.

The damp perfume of a fog machine signals it's "curtain." I tighten my carriage. I am no longer just going through the motions. Tchaikovsky begins. I don't think about blanking on the choreography, lazy turnout, or heavy jumps. I just move.

This isn't a solo, or even a duet. My family is with me, their dancer spirits permeating my own version of Odette. I sweep my arms through the hazy blue light, a swan parting the water and emerging from the mist.

I travel the floor in two soaring grand jeté leaps, and I'm back at the Purple Funk Factory—my body teeming with fiery passion like it was there. I close my eyes and relevé en pointe, fingertips whirring with white-hot energy. My shoulders roll, then my head, and all I see is hair. My feet are dying to spin. I give them what they want, sticking a perfect triple on the heels of my pointes.

I turn out of it, my sultry hips swaying when I swish my skirt. My fingers snap a flamenco tempo that's totally working with the Tchaikovsky. If George Balanchine could see me now. There's no mask; no tulle, satin, or sequins to hide behind. Just me. And I belong to the audience—a dancer's gift. One I couldn't have given without all that came before.

And Stacy, I've forgotten she's with me, but now she's impossible to overlook. She is endless extensions. She is tearful grace. She is pure emotion. I've never seen her shine so bright, a moonflower in bloom. I almost stop right where I am to watch her.

Stage left calls to me. Geno, cheering me on like a regular dad. Sapphire light reflects off of Glo's wet face, and I cry my own lake of tears. I mirror the memory of Mom's fouettés, balancing on a pin. And Glo, she is the heart of my brisés—fluttery and sharp.

I rond de jambe en l'air, softly kicking my leg to the sky like a strawberry girl, the one who used to wear the dusty-rose leotard. I hold my swanlike arabesque so long there's a ten-second teacup teetering. I spin a feverish chain of lame-duck turns, before hitting one last grand arabesque—a master's daughter, a best friend, and a little sister who's finally begun to forgive herself.

Tchaikovsky strikes its final note, and so do I. A smoky haze settles over the house, the audience motionless, like shadowed black swans in the mist. No one claps. No one's booing either. All I hear are the clinks of glass and my own panting.

I glance at Stacy. She's statuesque under the lights, waiting—ready for anything.

Sweat runs off my chin, dripping onto my heaving chest, the only reason I'm certain the last few minutes were real. I hold my pose, catching a glimpse of Glo. She's silently smacking her knuckles together. Her version of a standing ovation.

I Wish You to the Heavens

The audience suddenly explodes, and for a panicked second I think Prince himself has taken the stage. I glance over my shoulder, adrenaline thrashing my heart. There's no one else. Just Stacy and me, alone in the twilight fog. They're raising the roof for us. I tap my chest a few times to settle my lungs. I know I'm supposed to do the ballet thing and curtsy, but I just performed *Swan Lake* at *fucking First Avenue*.

I punch my fist straight in the air. "Yeah!"

Stacy shoots me a look.

The people on the balcony, three-deep and ready to rock, pump their fists back. I find Glo again. Her doctors can suck it. I've never seen her smile so big. Geno blows me a kiss, looking at me in a way I thought had been lost forever. He's touching Mom's shoulder. I wave, and I'm back in time, five years old at my first ballet recital.

"Do something proper, for God's sake!" Stacy yells. "Curtsy!"

Stepping out with my paisley first, I give her what she wants and sink into a "proper" curtsy. She mirrors mine and I follow it up with another on the opposite side.

"Stacy!" I point at the roaring crowd. "We did that!" I yank her into a hug, her arms staying stick-straight at her sides. "You can hug me too," I mutter into her ear. "I won't tell anyone."

She pats my back. I'll take it.

The club goes full tilt when the stagehands appear. They work fast, setting up the band's instruments and adjusting the lights. A thunderous wave of boot stomps quakes the floor. An August tornado is bearing down on Block E. Minneapolis is hungry for Prince.

If Stacy wasn't dragging me off the stage, I would stay right where I am. She ushers me between the wings, where Kat and Nikki wait.

Kat picks me up and twirls. "You are the shit, Rosa! No doubt about it!" she shouts over the insane amount of noise happening.

She spins me out to Nikki, who gathers me close. "Unreal, Strawberry. Funk Angel number one."

I take hold of his bandaged hand, swearing I'll never let go.

The roof blows, the Revolution taking the stage. Bobby Z, Doctor Fink, Lisa, and a kick-ass new girl, strapping on a guitar. Still no Prince.

We hop on top of a giant speaker and scream our throats raw.

Then the man himself materializes onstage, sprays of heavenly light at his back.

Mother Mary, seeing straight is impossible.

Prince drapes his guitar strap over his head, and Lisa hits a funeral-like chord.

"Dearly beloved, we are gathered here today . . ." It's like Prince is giving a eulogy, the house a sea of hands raised in the smoky air.

We sit on the speaker, Kat and Stacy below us. Stacy looks up, and Nikki gives her the peace sign. She smiles back, and I hold tight to the moment.

Lisa plays a swift scale and I scream again. Prince is so close, his black-and-silver ensemble shimmering like a diamond in a deep purple sky—our North Star, no doubt.

Kat squeezes my foot.

I spot Jeffery across the stage and wave him over. He leaves the other dancers and worms his way to our side from behind the drums. He drops to one knee like Prince Charming and makes Stacy sit. He kisses her on the cheek. If that doesn't convert the girl into a hugger, nothing will.

A funky drum pattern begins, vibrating the speaker beneath me. I hold my chest, the beat reverberating against my palms.

Nikki pulls my face toward his. "This is movie magic, right here."

"It is." I throw my arms around him.

We watch the rest of the set from our perch, Prince giving his hometown the ultimate gift—songs we've never heard before. I lose myself in his quick feet, and the pirouettes I saw him master in studio 6A. I'm hypnotized by his voice—

deep and sexy one minute, a screaming falsetto the next. He electrifies the club, a swaying, jumping, groovin' house about to come down. And Glo's out there somewhere too, I'm sure losing her mind over his insane guitar solos.

Stacy tugs my leg. "It's 'places' after this next song." She's suddenly wearing a headset. Only Stacy McGee could turn a solo into a duet, then finish out the night as the stage boss.

We hop down as First Avenue decelerates. I back against the speaker. The energy has shifted, steamy air blanketing the entire house in a thick velvety haze. I feel it. I don't know what it is. But it's going to be fucking great.

The kick-ass new girl seizes the club with her rich melodic guitar. Chills shower my arms. For the first time since Prince took the stage, my gaze is on someone else. She moves closer to Prince, who's waiting center stage, prisms of light flickering off his iridescent jacket.

He takes the mic.

He sings about love, regrets, intentions—and purple rain.

The audience sways back and forth to the gospel-like melody. I lean against Kat.

She grabs my hand, and I look out into the masses. Everyone is spellbound. Tonight, under the violet lights of First Avenue, something special is happening. Prince soulfully singing about purple rain is like watching Nikki dance—utterly consuming.

There's no sense in trying to stop the tears. Kat's crying too, which only makes me lose it more.

Hands raise at Prince's command, Kat and I following.

We wave our hands over our heads, caught up in a moment I never want to end. I'm eons away from waiting impatiently for his "Little Red Corvette" video to play on MTV. Because he's right in front of me—the Purple One. I never would've survived the last year and a half without him. Maybe, someday, I'll get the chance to say thank you.

Prince winds down with a killer guitar riff. I wipe my face—total song hangover.

I come back to earth, and Nikki is nowhere.

"Dancers, take your places," Stacy commands like a pro.

"Wait. Where's Nikki?" My heart goes from zero to light speed.

Kat looks worried too. She begins searching the wings while I scramble for a way out. I expected too much. He wasn't ready.

I'm about to go for Geno when I feel something soft against the back of my ear. "You ready, Strawberry Girl?"

I whirl around, mostly because Kat's eyes are full-on bugged. Nikki's wearing Odette's costume, his narrow waist impeccably cinched into the sparkly bodice. He kept his white thigh-high patent boots on, the snowy feathered tutu only making his dark legs more stunning.

He's looking at me like he needs my approval, dreamy eyes tentative and unsure.

Stacy stomps up behind him. She takes hold of Nikki's scalloped corset, shifting it a bit. "At least *someone's* wearing it."

"Thanks for helping me get into it," he says, holding up his gauzy hand.

"Stacy . . ." I touch her shoulder.

She shrugs.

I take Nikki's arm, a faint quiver in my grasp. I thought I'd seen the extent of his beauty. I was wrong. He is positively glowing.

He raps his heels. "MDC wanted us to show our individuality, so . . ."

"You look absolutely, undeniably gorgeous. Like a kick-ass ballet apprentice." Saying this to Nikki unravels the last of my thready tether to MDC. I'm walking away from an old friend, and into the arms of a new one. I adjust his shoulder straps, swallowing down the rock in my throat. "G-ma would approve."

His tensed shoulders soften.

"Totally," Kat seconds. "I'd hug you, but your rad tutu is in the way."

"Get out there." Stacy rips off her headset. "We'll miss our cue."

I scramble for my mark, wherever the hell that is.

I'm still wearing my pointes. But there's nothing I can do about it now. Nor do I want to. I grin at my paisley toe, everything shaking so badly I can barely fix my crooked skirt.

"This is it, y'all!" Nikki shouts.

And it is. Everyone I've ever loved is here tonight. Nothing will ever compare. I swipe away my tears and flash my family a smile so big, I'm sure I look like a Muppet. Glo gives me a fist pump. The Vault has been breached.

The synthesizer riff of "D.M.S.R." triggers the entire club. It's time to groove.

My heart thumps to the rhythm of the funk. I pirouette en pointe, high on the intoxicating energy. Out on this stage, with Nikki, Kat, Stacy, and Prince, I don't know, but it feels like a turning point for all of us. The crux of our own stories.

I swear Prince glances at my paisley shoe. He hits a high-pitched yelp into the mic. Our eyes meet, my weepy browns fusing with his smoldering dark irises, and I pierce the roof with my grand battement. He seems to like this, sauntering toward me, dragging the mic stand with him. I'm not thinking about what comes next, because my body knows what to do.

I break away from the rest, encircling him with a sequence of sultry body rolls and sharp turns. Prince follows me with a piercing gaze, singing about taking deeper breaths, shakin' it, doin' what we want—the police, and how we don't have to run.

He belts out the chorus, nodding his head at my paisley. I pat my chest and turn it out—a triple. Prince thumps his fist over his heart.

I answer him by rolling my shoulders like a Funk Factory Angel, and relevé toward the heavens.

Snows in April

I take my mark, nervous I'll forget everything and mess up. It's opening night. All the hard work, all the sacrifice, boils down to this one single moment. The spotlight shines yellowish heat on my face, my heart even warmer as I look out into the crowd. My parents, Glo—and so many friends.

Kat waves, still in her fire department uniform. She'll be a full-fledged EMT in a month. And Nikki . . . I found several months ago what happens when I gaze too long into those spicy eyes. I blush, hoping no one catches on.

Timekeeper Stacy taps her watch, signaling "curtain." But I ignore her.

Glo's gaze is fixed on me—*Breathe in . . . okay. Breathe out . . . fine.*

I've never been so proud of my sister, and nothing I'm about to say will ever do her justice. The gallery in Dinkytown is packed. Glo sold out the house. This is her night.

Force of nervous habit brings my hand to smooth hair that's no longer there. It'll take some time to get used to my cropped cut. But like a copycat little sister, I love that mine looks just like Glo's.

She taps her chest, and I follow her lead. She's ready.

"Welcome everyone," I utter, gazing at my bedazzled Docs. "Welcome," I say again, a little louder.

The room hushes.

"Uh, hello. I am Rosa Dominguez, and I was asked to introduce the featured artist, so . . ." I take another deep breath and find Val, who gives me a reassuring smile. She once said she wanted to see what kind of art moved me to tears. Well, we are surrounded by it.

"Gloria was born to be a dancer. She was born to be an artist. And really, they're one and the same, right? There wasn't anyone who could touch her sharp fouettés, and that was when she was twelve."

I glance at Glo, and her eyes return my smile. I don't avoid talking about my sister's dancing anymore. None of us do. If we did, it's like none of it ever mattered, like her first sixteen years didn't count. And it's not about what she's lost. It's about everything she brings to the world now. I touch the painting on the easel between us, the shattering purple pointe shoe bursting from the canvas.

"And now Glo has traded in her pointes for paintbrushes, and once again she is beyond reach. The triumphs, the failures, and everything in between, Gloria's paintings reveal every single part of her. And tonight you are at the core of her truths."

Glo thumps her chest with a fist. The increase in her medications has made her puffy, her skin fragile and pale. She pushes her knuckles together, an attempt to make a heart.

I make one back. "Big sister, you are my idol—my holy

grail—my sassy headbanger, and the bravest person I know. Ladies and gentlemen, may I present the artist, Gloria Estrella Dominguez Corredor."

My parents are the first to cheer, and the loudest when the rest join in.

"Thank you for coming," I say, and turn the spotlight over to the evening's rising star.

The crowd breaks apart, half engulfing Glo, the others mingling around her work. Her nudes are here too, finally out from hiding. Mom didn't even cross herself or anything.

Nikki shoulders through the crowd, giving Glo a Wonder Twin's knuckle tap, and then he comes to me.

"Another stellar performance."

"Except I wasn't acting." I kiss his cheek so I don't smear his cherry gloss.

He's tailored up for the opening, probably trying to impress my mother. He looks awesomely dapper in his pinstripe pants. He's still classic Nikki, though, his nipple ring poking underneath his pink button-up oxford. Gold dangling earrings. And his boots. White patent leather with sky-high heels.

"Don't you have rehearsal in a few?" He tucks a wisp of purple hair behind my ear. I didn't go full-on punk. Just a few streaks in my bangs, which are longer than the back of my hair now. I couldn't get it into a bun to save my life.

I run my cross along its chain. "I'm sure they'll manage without 'girl-dancer number three' for one run-through. It's high school *Rocky Horror,* not a Prince video."

"Not a Prince vid yet, girl three." Nikki snaps his gum.

I'll never be a normal high school student, because I don't really get what that means. But if it includes being a joiner, then I guess I'm treading in the realm of the ordinary. I've even made a few friends who don't know a thing about ballet. I've asked Nikki to the prom. And he said yes! We're already arguing over our color scheme and who will wear the most sequins. I guess what I'm saying is, Roosevelt High isn't so bad.

Of course, I recognize this won't last. Dance already steals me away four afternoons a week. But it's different this time. This is *my* future. My choice. And right now I am a regular at Kidz on the Wood, a street-dance studio on the other side of Block E. I'm even choreographing a spicy piece for an up-and-coming spring street fest. I'm not the Master's daughter at Kidz, which is so liberating it's like running naked down the beach at Lake Nokomis. Maybe someday I'll run all the way to a soundstage for a Prince video shoot.

Geno joins us, patting Nikki on the shoulder. "High school musical or not, cualquier cosa menos que la excelencia es inaceptable, Rosa."

I sigh. Geno's *anything less than excellence* is programmed into his DNA. But he's chilled out a lot. We're even having normal conversations in Spanish, without all the yelling. It's such a confusing space we live in, how it only took one generation to snuff out where we came from, but the pain from the past seems like it'll linger forever. I have to believe we're moving forward, though, because Geno sits with me sometimes when I break out Abuela's flash cards. And when he does, I feel the empty parts of me filling up, one grain of Mexican sand at a time.

"That is true for you too, Nico," Geno says. "Pointe class tomorrow morning."

"I gotcha, Master."

The benefit at First Avenue was the last time I wore pointes. And also the last time I danced in MDC's studios. Most days, I'm okay with it. But there are moments that sneak up on me and I feel the loss. Sometimes I ride the nineteen with George to wash it away. Other times, I distract myself with the juicy rumors about Prince's movie coming out in July. And how recordings from the MDC benefit concert will be on his new album.

"Without the gum." Geno tips his head at Nikki.

He's found a new muse in Nikki. And they're scary good together. What'll we do with ourselves when he leaves next month? Nikki's the newest Trock—a ballet dancer, en pointe, onstage, under the lights in front of a full house, with all the satin, tutus, and makeup—everything he's ever dreamed of. He says dancing at First Ave in Odette's tutu gave him the courage to go for it. The audition came and went so fast, exactly how he'll come and go from my world. I almost lose it if I dwell too long. But then I think about all he's sacrificed to get here, and I'm okay until the next freak-out. Will his mother ever understand what she's lost?

We all went down to the police station with Nikki—Kat, Stacy, and me. Filed a report about the night he got arrested.

The complaint department was seriously a closet with a desk crammed inside, a stack of blank forms, and an empty plastic soda bottle cut in half and filled with pens. That was it—with the exception of a metal bin screwed into the wall. Nikki filled out the form and dropped it into the bin with a stack of others. He hasn't heard anything since. But he's still a regular at the 90's. They didn't break him all the way.

"'Sup, G." Kat punches Geno in the shoulder.

I'll never get used to her calling him that.

"Katherine." He nods and returns to Mom's side.

Mom hands him a soda water. He takes it and inches closer, which she allows tonight. They're working on it. Being in the same room without fighting or slipping into excruciating silence is a start. And Geno's sleeping at the house now. On the couch, but at least he's home.

Mom takes off her cardigan, Geno offering to help. Yoga instructing's been good for her. She's getting her strength back. The curtains are open in our house, windows too. Kat hooked us up with something called home health care, which gives us a nurse three days a week to help with Glo. We're all in this together. And most days, even Geno.

He's been sober for eight months. Maybe he's finally figuring out who he is without drinking. I still don't trust him enough to give back the coins. Hope is all any of us can do—hope that he'll like who he sees in the mirror enough to stay this way. He never did get his wedding ring back. Instead, I dared him to get Mom's name tattooed around his finger, which he did without too much protest. My sister wheeled away with one on her shoulder—our names entwined around a paintbrush. Me? Maybe someday when I have her nerve.

I watch Glo work the room, maneuvering her electric wheelchair around like a gallery debut is something she's done a thousand times. I still think about what's hidden beneath her clothes, the tubes and collection bags her body needs. I don't try to ignore them like I used to, because pretending they don't exist means she doesn't either. My sister may have lost her ability to speak and walk, but I've never known anyone more present. She is out in the world, on her own. And I have to let go.

She stops to pose for a photo with Stacy. Three years later, when she is gone, this is how I will remember her. Surrounded by admirers. Poised, lovely—independent.

"You know, she's already sold three pieces?" Kat says. "And the gallery is matching the prices with donations to the Minnesota AIDS Project and AA. Just like you wanted."

Pride floods my heart. "You mean, like she wanted."

"Are we crying again?" Stacy whines as she approaches. Tears make her so uncomfortable. Too bad she likes hanging with such a bawler like me.

"Nope," Kat answers. "Only happy little clouds here. Which reminds me, they say it might snow tonight. It'll get ugly if it does. So, I have to get back to the station."

I groan. "Snow shouldn't be allowed in April. I vote you to drive us to the Funk Factory tomorrow night."

Nikki raises his hand in agreement. Prince is rumored to show, and we are totally there. If I'm lucky, it'll be this Funk Angel's third time onstage with the man. My gratitude is in every roll of my hips—the thank-you I promised to give him at First Avenue.

"But it's my turn to drive," Stacy interjects.

Asking Kat to drive is strictly about survival. Stacy behind the wheel is scary as hell—on dry roads. The girl's a total pole-position racer. Who knew?

The sound of tires crunching over frozen ice still messes with me. I'm pretty sure it always will. Geno once said Glo wouldn't have become the artist she is without the accident. It's a strange way to look at things, an uncomfortable one. But I wouldn't be taking classes at Kidz without that terrible day in January either. I'd still be at MDC, probably dancing on an apprenticeship and wishing upon a faraway star that my life was different. I'm not saying I wouldn't change things if I could. It's more like, if I were to wish for anything now, it would be to never lose the courage to chase down my own dreams—like everyone surrounding me in this gallery has.

"Stacy." Kat has a plan. I see it in her sparkly eyes. "I'll pick you up early. Then we can go to that makeup place first, get what you need for the spring show?"

And there's the Kat I love. The finder and fixer. Her parents are missing out on the daughter of a lifetime. And mine have gained another. Kat is welcome to live in our basement as long as she needs.

Stacy lights up. "*Sweet.* This queen needs her pink eye shadow." She fluffs the giant Madonna bow in her hair—although she's embraced the idea there's more to her than hair, makeup, and flawless brisés. She's been relentless about Nikki's arrest, and finally convinced her dad to help secure an audience with the police union to talk about the injustices with a few other activists. We're all psyched to be her entourage, witness yet again what the girl can do when she puts her mind to it.

"Okay, beautiful ones. Bring it in." Nikki gathers us close. "What happens at the Funk?" he asks.

"Love. Soul. Groove," we answer in unison.

"And wherever you go, whatever you do," I continue, "remember what the Funk discovered in you."

"Amen," our circle chants.

"Hey!" Stacy points at the window. "It started."

Downy snowflakes fall from the sky, so light they blow in every direction. We'll be that way someday, the four of us—Mom, Dad, and Glo too. All of us going our own way. It's difficult to imagine—impossible really. But as I squeeze an *Okay, fine* into Kat's and Nikki's hands, I hold on to my belief that we'll meet again. Tattered in pointe shoes, protected by steel-toed boots, paralyzed by tragedy, and broken by a father's obsession, our feet will bring us back to each other. On the seedy streets of Hennepin Avenue. At the ballet in New York City, or maybe on a stage in a park full of paisleys. Always in spirit, under the purple haze, groovin' to that unmistakable Minneapolis sound—forever the Purple Funk Factory.

ACKNOWLEDGMENTS

Crafting a book is an ever-consuming labor of love, one that begins long before a single word makes it to the page. It starts with a spark of an idea and picks up speed, like my heart when I know I'm onto something good. That spark is born from memories, chance encounters, both the everyday and the extraordinary—always a story brewing. As with most writers, my head is balancing between two worlds—heck, sometimes three or four. I'd like to take a moment to thank the people in all of mine.

I'll start by gushing gratitude for my husband and daughter, Jeff and Evie. Many days and nights were dedicated to these pages, and the hundreds that came before the final draft of *The Turning Pointe*. Jeffrito, thank you for supplying me with endless support, pep talks, shoulder rubs, and snacks for the weary. Evie, during this difficult homeschooling pandemic, you wore your patient pants every time I asked, and even when I didn't. The pride in your eyes kept me going during those exhausting long days and close deadlines. I love you both with every beat of my heart.

To my mom and dad, Michael and Yvonne Torres, I am the person I am today because of you. You never discouraged, but rather watched me take buckets of risks, fail, succeed, and find my own way. I'm sorry about all the rock climbing, skiing, diving, firefighting, bungee jumping, working in helicopters, and that thing that happened in Budapest. But you know I wouldn't change a second of it, and that's what makes our family ready-for-anything Torres-Strong.

My sister Valerie Torres-Comvalius and my bro-in-law Pascal Comvalius. Valerie, thank you for reading my shitty first draft, and for being my ballet consultant and '80s fashion expert. I would have had way too many shoulder pads and scrunchies without you. To Pascal, my all-things-Prince guru. I know the Purple One is out there somewhere, remembering you shaking your booty in your SPAM T-shirt—his Dutchie number one fan.

My sister Andrea Torres. You are my go-to person when I need to offload the "can't do's." Because you are a rock star—seriously, the strongest person I know. I am so lucky to be your *slightly* older sister.

To my agent extraordinaire, Louise Fury. Really, there is not enough space on this page to express how much I love being on your team. And I'll cry if I dwell, so I'll just say this: You deserve a bejeweled sword, because you are my champion. We did it! I can't wait to see what's next for us.

The Bent Agency and Jenny Bent. I am so honored to be one of your authors. The debut experience is one wrapped up in excitement, unknowns, and, yes, a bit of stress. Through it all, the agency has had my back—like family. I wouldn't want it any other way.

To my editor, Karen Smith, and the entire team at Penguin Random House/Knopf. Thank you for taking a chance on me.

Thank you for loving this book as much as I do. Thank you for bringing out the best in my writing. Thank you for getting Rosa and her crew in the hands of readers. This wild ride has been more than I could have ever imagined, and you helped make that happen.

I am so grateful for my copy editors. Artie Bennett, Alison Kolani. My grammar and punctuation mistakes owe you a raging party. And Iris Broudy. Your attention to detail kept this book in 1983 Minneapolis. It was hella radical working with you. And thank you to Jake Eldred in Managing Editorial, for herding the cats and keeping us all on schedule.

My cover artist, Jonathan Bartlett, and designer, Regina Flath. The first time I saw your beautiful version of Rosa, I cried. From out of my brain to the page to the cover, you made her into something even more real. I love it so much. Many thanks!

This book wouldn't be what it is without the eternal support of my trusty critique partners. Dante Medema, my agent sister. You were the first to read *The Turning Pointe,* and your love for this book is the reason I'm here. I will forever be in awe of your plotting superpower, and your never-ending ability to see the forks in the road and choose the wrong way (because that's what makes a great story, right?). And to Lindsay Pierce, for teaching me how to squeeze every last drop of emotion from a scene. Absolutely no one does it better than you. *sniff-sniff.* I love you both. May we create many more beautiful stories together.

To the readers who have been with me from the beginning,

the ones who suffered through the first drafts and still hung in there.

Anja Hendrikse Liu, I hope you know how grateful I am for your commitment to this book. Because I am, to the moon and back.

To Jessica Lee, your read-through was invaluable. Thank you, all the way to the stars. A Seattle celebration will be had.

Jennifer Larsen Fortner, our days at the Minnesota Dance Theatre were so long ago, but I swear it's like you were there just yesterday. Thank you for reminding me of all the quirky Hennepin Avenue, dance-world things I'd forgotten about. This book would've been missing so much without its Lous and elastic waistbands.

And to Mizz Honey Bucket, from one TAB lover to another, like, thank you, I'm sure.

To the early-day, old-school members of the Olympia Writers Group—Alan Shue, Kiki Powers, Tiffany Grassman, Chris Murray, Sid Doyle, Donnie Whetstone, Peter Dodds, Johanna Flynn, Marlee LaMontagne, Leslie Romer, and Christina Wiley. I was a rookie writer when I showed up with a handful of wrinkled pages all those years ago. I had no idea what I was doing. I only knew I wanted to write a book. You all listened to my fumbling words and taught me how to make something out of them. The pages of *The Turning Pointe* have a little bit of Oly in them because of you. Bless you all!

I wrote the entire first draft of this book surrounded by people in a busy café. Olympia Coffee Roasting, you have my absolute appreciation for letting me camp out at the corner table to get the words out from my head. Thank you for keeping my caffeine at a manageable level. And to the baristas who asked me every day about my progress, you were the cheerleaders I so desperately needed during the dreaded second act. Cheers!

To my best friend, Debbie Brenna Minarik. We survived the '80s together. So much hair spray and blue eye shadow! You are one of the few constants in my life. You are my Kat Johansen. I don't know what I'd do without you.

To my fellow Las Musas authors. You've given me a place that is authentic, comfortable—like home. Musas are brave, inspiring, and proud, exactly how it feels to be part of you. Gracias mis amores.

Kevin Herbert Ottosen, thank you for making sure I didn't show up for my author photos with a scrunchie in my hair and clown makeup. XOXO

Young Lee, thank you for bringing out the best in me. Having my photo taken by anyone other than myself kind of freaks me out, and you made me feel so comfortable. We had an awesome day!

To my brothers and sisters at my fire department. You drive me nuts. You make me laugh until I can't move. After twenty years with you, we are a family in every sense of the word. You are a magnificent example of strength and courage, all of which I needed to write this book.

All of my love to my sweet goddaughter, Lorena Dominguez, Rosa's namesake.

To the Mouseketeers—Lisa Hayes Clark, Peggy Seipp-Roy,

and Tara Cullen Bickerstaff. We were navy-blue leo-wearing first levels when Prince was rehearsing for *Purple Rain* upstairs at MDT. But we had the guts to sneak away and get a peek at the legend in the making. Those times, and there were many I must admit, were the spark for *The Turning Pointe*. Thank you for the memories, ladies!

Many moments from my time as a young dancer at the Minnesota Dance Theatre made it to these pages. The teachers who taught me how to hold my center and to project to the very last row—they are all here. And to the person who is no longer with us, the founder of MDT, Loyce Houlton. Dancing for you was my very first glimpse of sweat, tears, cheers, and hard work, all wrapped into one incredible experience, one that remains with me today. I can still hear you chanting our counts of eight.

All the Block E businesses no longer standing. Sun's, Shinders, Teener's, A Slice of New York, and Moby Dick's, to name a few. You were the heartbeat of this funky town. And to The Gay 90's, may you withstand whatever the future brings. You've proven unstoppable so far, which warms my heart.

If you're reading this, it means you took a chance on me. Thank you to everyone who followed Rosa's story. I would not be here without you.

Finally, to Prince Rogers Nelson. I came of age on Block E, a young dancer exploring the street culture, a club called First Avenue, pining for a glimpse of you, our very own Minnesota North Star. I'm totally not sorry for all those times I stalked the MDT elevators, just so I could ride down with you and

Big Chick. Thank you for picking up the ballet shoe I dropped on purpose. Like Rosa, I may have peed my leotard. Because my insides were racing, kind of like they are now as I listen to "D.M.S.R." I hope you're out there somewhere in the universe. I hope you like what I wrote about you. I hope you hear me saying right now, U will 4ever be my inspiration. U will 4ever be my Purple Funk Factory.